The Divine Secrets of the Whoopie Pie Sisters
The Complete Trilogy

By Sarah Price &
Whoopie Pie Pam Jarrell

D1590819

Other Books by Sarah Price

The Amish of Lancaster Series
#1: Fields of Corn
#2: Hills of Wheat
#3: Pastures of Faith
#4: Valley of Hope

The Amish of Ephrata Series
#1: The Tomato Patch
#2: The Quilting Bee
#3: The Hope Chest
#4: The Clothes Line

The Plain Fame Trilogy
Plain Fame
Plain Change
Plain Again

Other Amish Christian Romances
Amish Circle Letters
Amish Circle Letters II
A Gift of Faith: An Amish Christmas Story
An Amish Christmas Carol: Amish Christian Classic Series
A Christmas Gift for Rebecca: An Amish Christian Romance
Gettysburg's Chosen Sons

The Adventures of a Family Dog Series
#1: A Small Dog Named Peek-a-boo
#2: Peek-a-boo Runs Away
#3: Peek-a-boo's New Friends
#4: Peek-a-boo and Daisy Doodle (2013)

Other Books, Novellas and Short Stories
Gypsy in Black
Postcards from Abby (with Ella Stewart)
Meet Me in Heaven (with Ella Stewart)
The Prayer Chain Series (with Ella Stewart)

Other Books By Pam Jarrell

Whoopie Pie Pam's Kitchen Collection
Cookie Exchange Party
Home For The Holidays
Delicious Easter Memories
Sizzling Summer Fun
Tasty Touchdowns!

Table of Contents

Foreword

Writing about the wonderful culture and religion of the Amish people is something that I have been doing for over twenty-five years. As many of my readers may have noticed, my novels, novellas, and short stories present an authentic glimpse into the lives of the Amish, a glimpse that comes from my growing up Mennonite and having lived among the Amish since I was nineteen years old.

Most of my stories are love stories. Whether you are reading about Shana and Emanuel's struggle to balance the differences of their upbringing with their love for each other (Fields of Corn) or Amanda and Alejandro trying to find a way to survive the clash of their individual and very different cultures (The Plain Fame Trilogy), there is a degree of love written in the stories.

This trilogy, however, is a bit unusual. Whoopie Pie Pam and I embarked on this project to take a break from the love stories among man and woman in order to explore the other love, so prominent amongst the Amish: the love of family. In particular, these books explore the love among Amish sisters.

While many of us who admire the Amish see their culture and religion as idyllic, a step back in time to a place where stress and technology are foreign words, that image is actually quite far from the truth. The Amish are people just like you and I. They, too, struggle with relationships, disappointments, questions of faith, and even temptations, a fact that some Christians might not want to know but, nevertheless, does exist among the Plain people as well.

I know I speak for my dear friend, Pamela Jarrell, when I say that we hope that you'll enjoy this trilogy. But, notwithstanding your enjoyment, we feel that it is important to understand that these pages are meant to explore another side of the Amish, a path less travelled: the relationship among the siblings and how they deal with potential problems. I hope it makes you smile, laugh, frown, and perhaps even shed a tear or two. But, more than anything, I hope you continue to love the Amish as much as both Pam and I do.

Blessings,

Sarah Price

http://www.sarahpriceauthor.com

http://www.facebook.com/fansofsarahprice

A Note About Vocabulary

The Amish speak Pennsylvania Dutch (also called Amish German or Amish Dutch). This is a verbal language with variations in spelling among communities throughout the USA. In some regions, a grandfather is "grossdaadi" while in other regions he is known as "grossdawdi".

In addition, there are words such a "mayhaps" or the use of the word "then" at the end of sentences and, my favorite, "for sure and certain" which are not necessarily from the Pennsylvania Dutch language/dialect but are unique to the Amish.

The use of these words comes from my own experience living among the Amish in Lancaster County, Pennsylvania.

Book One

Part One

My soul and also my spirit
I commit into your hands.
Help me out of all tribulation.
O Lord, do not turn away from me,
Take away the great strength of my flesh,
That I might overcome,
And be victorious in you.

Ausbund, Song 39 Verse 9

I lift up my eyes to the hills.
From where does my help come?
My help comes from the LORD,
Who made heaven and earth.

Psalm 121:1-2

The Dock

Sitting on the dock, a sense of relaxation washed over Leah as she let her eyes wander nonchalantly over the water. It was crystal clear and completely calm, the serene glasslike surface barely marred by the occasional ripple caused by a dragon fly fluttering down to dip its legs into the water, from the edge of a water lily. The sun had already begun its nightly descent over the hill, right behind the Millers' family farm, its orange glow from the perfectly shaped orb casting glittering embers all across the pond. A bird flew overhead, heading toward the woods that bordered the large farm property. It disappeared into the sea of green leaves that clung to the branches, motionless in this breezeless late summer evening.

Leah sighed and returned her attention back to the pond, contemplating that it wouldn't be long before the surface would turn into a crystal sheet of ice. It was only late August and she knew that she shouldn't be already thinking about winter, but she so dreaded that season: cold, grey, dark. *No*, Leah thought to herself. Winter was not her favorite time of year, that was for sure and certain!

But, as her *grossmammi* had always pointed out, "You have to go through winter before you can get to spring!" *Wise advice from an even wiser woman*, Leah thought. If only *Grossmammi* Maggie was still around. Leah could sure use her advice and her wisdom right now.

Instead, Leah felt alone. Even more than alone; lonely. Whenever such feelings overcame her, feelings of worry and fear, she would escape the craziness of her home, even if only for a few moments, to sit on the dock, her bare feet dipped into the cool water as she reflected on the problems at hand. After all, this pond had always been her favorite spot; her place to find solace and to recapture her spirit. And of late, Leah Mast needed a lot of that.

As she watched two little sparrows play in the branches of

a nearby weeping willow, Leah found herself smiling. *That* was a peaceful moment, she reckoned, one that gave her a sense of tranquility after a long and stressful day. Oh, how Leah loved these sparrows, always thinking of the Bible verse that stated God even took care of the little sparrow! They were her favorite bird and observing them always made her realize that there was more to life than met the eye. Watching those little birds flit and flutter through the branches always made her wonder why life couldn't be that simple for humans. Their play was as innocent as that of a newborn baby.

Leah began to shiver. She wasn't sure if it were the cool northern wind that was now blowing an evening chill through her bones or the acknowledgement that her family's lives were a mess. From the day that they each entered the world, Leah had felt a responsibility for her siblings. And more so, two years ago, when their parents were killed in a car accident while on their way to a cousin's wedding in Pennsylvania. Leaving behind the family business, her parents had also left Leah with something else to tend to: their two youngest *kinner[1]*. Even today, that was not easy for a young woman of 34 years who already had her own growing family of seven children.

How can I hold it together? She asked herself again, more as a statement than an actual question. Indeed, it was the question that she asked herself every single time she escaped to the pond, just after shutting down the store and before preparing for evening chores. Yet, holding it together was the one thing that Leah was good at doing. After all, she had been given no choice. Her family *needed* her. Of that, she was constantly reminded. Not only was she the oldest, but she had always been considered the strong one: the one that everyone depended upon in a time of crisis; the one her mother had entrusted with her prize bakery: Whoopie Pie Place.

---

[1] Children

To Leah, this responsibility gave her a great secret. But that secret came with a weight. It gave her pride, something she would never admit among her peers or family. Pride was one thing that Amish people were supposed to avoid. But Leah knew that she was proud of the bakery and of its widespread reputation as *the only place* outside of Berlin, Ohio, where one could purchase authentic Whoopie Pies. People ordered them from all around the country, asking for shipments to arrive in time for birthdays, anniversaries, Christmas and Easter.

Yes, the continued success of the bakery gave Leah great pride. But, at times, it made her bone weary as well.

Indeed, she thought as she started to get to her feet, her eyes scanning the horizon. *How long can I hold all of this, the family, the business, and my sanity...together?*

Earlier That Day

Whoopie Pie Place

The hustle and bustle of Whoopie Pie Place, the most renowned bakery located just outside of Berlin, Ohio, right off of Route 62, was at an all-time high on that particular morning. It was the peak of the tourist season and that meant the busiest time of the year at Whoopie Pie Place. Indeed, tourists wanted two things when they came to Holmes County, Ohio: to meet authentic Amish people and to enjoy some authentic whoopie pies.

At Whoopie Pie Place, they were able to do both.

Tourists flocked to the bakery from every corner of the country. And that meant that summer time was the busiest time of the year. It was time to make Whoopie Pies and sell them by the dozens, day in and day out, five days a week, Tuesday through Saturday, from nine in the morning until four in the afternoon. But the baking had to start in the wee hours of the morning. They did close two hours earlier on Tuesdays and Wednesdays so that the sisters who ran the bakery could share time with family during the summer season.

It was usually Sadie who got up extra early to start the baking and the three married sisters took off one extra day a week each. It was a tiring schedule, with baking and frosting, packaging and displaying, selling and smiling; always the smiling! But, as the owners of the most popular whoopie pies in the entire county, all of them knew that smiling was part of the deal. After all, Leah always explained, it became a whole lot easier to smile when they remembered that whoopie pies kept some...*real food* on their own tables.

The bell hanging over the door tingled, announcing yet another visitor and Laverne, the local tour guide and owner of Amish Heartland Tours, escorted in a busload of people. With a warm smile, she waved at Leah and lifted one perfectly manicured hand as she held open the door to let her clients single-file into the store. Leah had been forewarned about this particular tour, a group of Amish-loving women that had met on Facebook, some strange *Englische* virtual world that none of the Miller sisters were too familiar with. Apparently, this virtual group had weekly book club meetings and had finally gathered in Berlin for an actual face-to-face book club reunion.

Leah smiled back at Laverne and immediately braced herself for the inevitable questions that would be asked by the tour patrons. Always the questions. If there was one thing that Leah could count on, it was the sun rising in the morning, setting in the evening, and the endless stream of questions from the *Englische* tourists. She could see it in their eyes as the tourists descended upon the bakery, their curiosity clearly at peak. One by one, they each took their turn to order whatever their hearts desired from the bakery case. Most came for the famous whoopie pies, others for the fresh homemade bread. But, without fail, they always came with those crazy, silly questions.

The questions were always the same from each tour group that entered the doors of Whoopie Pie Place. Leah could almost repeat them by heart:

What Amish order did they belong to?

Answer: Old Order Amish.

Did they really not use electricity in the bakery?

Answer: No.

Did they actually brush their teeth with ashes?

Answer: What?

Is there truly an Amish mafia?

Answer: Only on your silly television.

Can Amish people have their photos taken?

Answer: Not if you want any whoopie pies from this store!

And many more. There was never a day that the questions didn't continue to amaze Leah. Where on earth, she often wondered, did these people get their information from? But she knew the answer: the wrong places!

As the oldest sibling in the family, Leah was the front sister, the one who worked the counter and greeted the customers. She was the only one with the patience to respond without an edge to her voice, despite the intense desire to lean forward and smack the nearest tourist who waved a camera in her face.

The Miller family was known throughout the Amish community for their scrumptious whoopie pies: chocolate, vanilla, pumpkin, coconut. Anyone could request just about any flavor and, without doubt, one of the sisters could make it. The strangest flavor they had ever made? Pomegranate blueberry with chocolate raspberry filling.

This particular day, the featured whoopie pie was chocolate-strawberry shortcake. These were seasonal, produced during the time when strawberries were at their ripest. Picking the strawberries was the responsibility of the only Miller son living at home: Tobias. And today, he was running behind schedule. Glancing at the clock over the door, Leah was suddenly distracted from the women filing into the store as she began to worry about what might possibly be delaying him and if they would have enough strawberries today to finish up the orders that they had already received.

"Excuse me, Miss," a woman called out, waving her hand, which held a small piece of paper in the air. "I think you just called number fifty? That's me! Hello, Miss?"

Leah took a deep breath and turned around, forcing the forty-ninth smile of the day onto her face. Her first smile of the morning was always easy and never forced: it went to their first customer, Jenny Yoder. She was the older mother of the Yoder clan who lived down the lane and came almost every day to get ten whoopie pies. What she did with those pies Leah never asked. But any woman who raised eleven children, all of them having happily joined the church after eleven low-key and uneventful *rumschpringes*, was bound to get a genuine smile from every member of the *g'may*[2].

"Miss, I'd like a dozen of those whoopie pies," the woman demanded, her high-pitched voice tinted with a definite New York accent, cutting Leah back to reality. She let the piece of paper flutter from her hand and, for just a moment, Leah watched as it floated through the air and landed on the floor, just beside her, on the other side of the counter.

"Ja," Leah said, lifting her eyes to meet the tired baby blues that stared back at her from behind small red bifocals. "A dozen of those will be no problem." Quickly, she took a white box from behind the counter and began to carefully place the whoopie pies into the box, silently counting to make certain she had exactly twelve in the box. Once it was folded and the money collected, Leah slid the box across the counter and said her standard good-bye: "You will enjoy these. They were freshly made this morning."

Luckily, the weather had been tolerable in Holmes County over the last couple of days. A cold front was moving through the area and had cooled the temperatures by 10 degrees or so. It was a welcomed relief for the five Miller children who worked at Whoopie Pie Place. On hot and humid days, the bakery could become quite unbearable, reaching over 95 degrees inside the store and even more in the back kitchen baking area. Without electricity or air conditioning, it was enough to cause even the kindest of souls to snap.

Today, however, that wasn't the case.

Indeed, the end of summer had brought along some cool mornings and afternoons. Yet, even though the heat was at a minimum, sister Lydia had been feeling rather flustered lately. In fact, she was often huffing and puffing under her breath, quick to

---

[2] Church District

snap at her sisters, her rudeness taxing everyone's nerves. Even as Leah was helping the customers, she could hear the tension building up in the back kitchen where Susie and Lydia were working. It was all that she could do to keep herself from bursting through the swinging doors as the confrontation began to escalate!

Unfortunately, that was not an option. With so many people in the store, she had to focus on the customers, first and foremost. Laverne always brought her guided tours to Whoopie Pie Place and Leah was not one to look a gift-horse in the mouth. *Tours* meant *tourists* and that translated to *customers*. Customers were vital to their thriving business.

"Fifty-one?" she called out, a forced smile on her face as she waited for the next customer in line to step forward.

Back in the kitchen, the heart of the store, two Amish women were busy kneading bread and making whoopie pies. The room was a disaster, the counters filled with countless whoopie pie pans, some filled and waiting to be baked, others sitting on the cooling racks by the open window. The hardwood floor, faded and in good need of being refinished, was covered in patches of flour and crumbs that had been pushed off the counter during the course of the day. Luckily, there was a ceiling fan overhead and it spun rapidly, keeping a nice breeze flowing through the otherwise stiflingly hot room.

"Lydia," Susie asked, reaching out a hand covered in flour and chocolate, and wiggling her fingers in the air. "Might you hand me that bowl of cream so I can finish the rest of these pies?"

There was a moment's hesitation before the younger of the two sisters responded. Her voice was strained and sharp. "Why, I'm just as busy as you are, Susie!" Lydia sassed. None too happily, she handed the bowl to her sister.

Susie looked up, a scowl on her face as she stared at her younger sister with glowering dark brown eyes. "No need to be so sassy, then! I only asked for a small favor!" Susie snapped back.

She had never been one to keep her mouth shut, not once. Especially from her sister.

Lydia rolled her own brown eyes. "It's always a small favor with you, ain't so?"

"Apparently you need to go back to bed and start the day over again," Susie answered none too happy. "Get up on the right side, I reckon! If you have one!"

Lydia whirled around, her face creased with anger and eyes bulging from her head. A stray hair had slipped from beneath her prayer *kapp* and, for a moment, she looked like a mad woman. "*I* need to go back to bed?" she snapped, emphasizing the word "*I*". Pressing her lips tight, she glared at her sister. "I need to go back to bed?" she repeated yet again, this time with an exaggerated emphasis on the words. "Well, my dear sister, mayhaps you need to think about someone other than yourself. You forget that I have just as much work as you do!"

A stern look crossed Susie's face as she replied, "How do you have as much as me? You try working here all day then going home to three children and a husband to take care of. It's not as easy a burden as yours!"

At that comment, the color flushed from Lydia's face. How dare her sister bring up the fact that she had no children! Susie seemed to recognize her mistake and immediately wiped her hands on the black apron that was wrapped around her soiled green dress. She started to walk toward her sister but Lydia stopped her, pushing away her outstretched hands.

"I didn't mean that, Lydia," Susie started to apologize, compassion in her eyes. It was clear that she hadn't meant to hurt her sister's feelings. However, it was also clear that it was far too late for that. The damage was done.

"Nee," Lydia said, the tears starting to fill her eyes. Her lips trembled and she swiped at her eyes. "You did and that was right hurtful. I need to step outside for a spell. You can just finish up in here by yourself!" And with that, Lydia spun on her heels and darted out the back door.

"Lydia!" Susie called after her but, by the time she got to the doorway, Lydia was gone out of sight and, Susie suspected, would not be returning anytime soon. With a scowl on her face, Susie turned back to the kitchen, instantly aware that she was on her own for the rest of the day. Again, she wouldn't be getting home in time to clean the house before preparing supper for her family.

With a sigh, Susie returned to the counter and lifted the spatula off the bowl to spread the cream between the layers of whoopie pie cakes. Despite Lydia's hurt feelings and disappearance, someone had to keep supplying the store with the freshly baked goods. As usual, that responsibility fell upon Susie's shoulders. It was a responsibility that she did not take lightly for she knew that the reputation of Whoopie Pie Place depended on delivering the promise of quality-baked goods, served with a smile.

Leah

"I'll take three of those Chocolate-Strawberry things right there, two of those glazed ones over here and one of those chocolate covered things in that corner." The woman spoke her order as she pointed to the different baked goods in the display case. "No wait, I need to change that." Another hesitation. "Oh shoot, I just can't make up my mind. They all look so delicious, don't they?" The woman laughed, the noise sounding like a scratchy cackle.

Despite not being amused, Leah put on an understanding smile as she waited patiently for the woman's order.

"Let's change it to..." The woman seemed to hesitate, a finger in her mouth as she looked around. "No, just leave it at what I said before... I think."

On the outside, Leah's face was as pleasantly solemn as she could possibly make it appear, but on the inside, her thoughts toward the lady's indecisiveness weren't quite so pretty.

Throughout the day, the crowd continued to filter in and out of Whoopie Pie Place. At times, there was barely enough standing room for the customers. Customers would wait patiently on the porch, right outside the entrance door, sipping the cool meadow tea that sister Sadie sold them for a dollar a cup. No one ever hesitated to purchase a drink and many came back for seconds. Leah always wondered whether it was Sadie's refreshing meadow tea or her own big, genuine smile and sparkling blue eyes that appealed more to the customers and made the sales.

Unlike her two sisters who continually argued from the kitchen, sister Sadie had a gentle aura of peace about her. For a long moment, Leah stood in the doorway, watching as the last of Laverne's tour guests bought their final cup of meadow tea. *Ja*, Leah thought, Sadie certainly had a right *gut* way about her with the Englische.

Everyone indeed liked Sadie. She was fun and lively, with

sparkling blue eyes and a way of lighting up the room whenever she walked into it. Despite being only 20 years of age, while she carried herself with an unassuming presence, she never failed to be noticed by *Englische* and Amish alike. There was no pride in her character but there sure was an awful lot of *giving*. Sadie made the other two sisters look like naughty twins with quick tongues and fire in their eyes. No, Sadie was definitely different.

Whenever there was a sick member of the *g'may*, it was Sadie who immediately spent her evenings visiting with them at their homes. She'd wake up extra early to bake bread or muffins to bring to those people right after she was finished with work. Leah suspected that she was often bone weary, but not once did Sadie ever complain. Always, she smiled; and always, she did what had to be done without being asked and, more often than not, without asking for help.

"You have a fresh batch ready for the 2pm tour bus, then?" Leah asked as she walked out the door onto the porch.

Sadie looked up at her oldest sister, the sister who had practically raised her while their *mamm*, Miriam, was starting the business five years prior. Now, with their parents deceased, Leah had taken over the role of the family matriarch. "I sure do," Sadie replied. "Even have my batch ready for the 3:30 tour!"

As if I had to ask, Leah thought to herself with a feeling of pride toward her youngest sister. "*Wunderbaar!*"

Returning to the inside of the store, Leah looked around. She wandered the aisles, straightening up the rows of whoopie pies and other little knick-knacks that were sold in the store: jams, jellies, apple and pumpkin butter, potholders and little wooden toys. Once everything was in order and rearranged to her satisfaction, she ventured into the kitchen, catching her breath before she did so, as she never knew what awaited her on the other side of those two swinging doors.

"What was all that ruckus about earlier?" she asked as she

saw Susie working on a new batch of whoopie pies. Most days, Susie left around two o'clock to get home in time to tend to her own *kinner* and home. As of late, she had been staying later and later, just one more thing that caused Leah some worry.

Susie shook her head. "That Lydia," she started. "Ran off in tears again."

Ran off? Again? Leah sighed, leaning against the counter, careful to not get any loose flour on the black apron that covered her magenta dress. She hated when her dress looked soiled as she greeted the customers. "What did you do this time, Susie?"

"What didn't I do?" Susie clenched her fists and put them on her hips. "No matter what I say, it comes back to her and then she runs off," she replied, a look of frustration in her eyes. "And I know what this means. Once again, I'm here working alone and we both know what that does for my own duties at home."

A small figure appeared in the doorway. From the corner of her eye, Leah could see her youngest brother, Tobias, as he quietly snuck in and slid a full basket of strawberries on the floor, toward the counter. Without a word, he started to disappear. Leah turned around, watching him as he slowly walked away. This wasn't usual for Tobias. Normally, he would burst into the kitchen, dropping off the strawberries before sneaking over to the counter and helping himself to whatever sweet treat he desired.

Walking toward the door, Leah leaned against the frame and watched as Tobias headed toward the main house. His hands were in his pockets and his head was hung low. From the way that his straw hat was tipped back on his head, Leah knew exactly what was wrong with her brother: He wasn't feeling well again.

"Oh help!" she whispered.

Everyone had their problems, their own little world of concern that usually centered on themselves: Susie with her balancing act between home and Whoopie Pie Place, Lydia with her desire to have a *boppli*[3] and tend to her home instead of helping her sisters, and Tobias with an illness that kept him from enjoying life the way other fourteen year old boys did. As usual, it was up to Leah to hold them all together.

Although exhausted by the end of the day, there was never a moment when Leah didn't feel blessed to have inherited their mother's love for baking. Their mother had been the epitome of happiness; a smile always adorning her face. While she had been a wonderful cook, it had been her baking that excelled above all the rest. She could make a shredded apple pie that would tantalize anyone's taste buds before it ever hit their mouth. For as long as Leah could remember, in their father's lunch and theirs, their mother would always place one of her whoopie pies. At no other time did they have these delicious treats. Where their mother had hidden them out of their reach for all those years was never known to this day. But, during those lunches at school, they could count on one being there.

On the opening day of Whoopie Pie Place, just a little over five years ago, excitement was everywhere. Their mother Miriam had been the first to walk through the door. Although she was taught not to show pride, it had been very hard not to. She was venturing out into a world where she could do the one thing she sometimes admitted to herself that she loved even more than caring for the family: baking. All Amish girls were trained early that all joys in life lay in the happiness of their family; an immaculate home, clean clothing, beautiful flowers in their trimmed yards, well-behaved children and the respect of their husbands and community were what pleased them. A simple desire of life but yet a fulfilling challenge; a life's purpose. Miriam had taught her girls this very task. Little did she know that this way of life was not something that each one of her daughters wanted to learn, let alone abide by!

----

[3] Baby

Leah had recognized that conflict within her two married sisters and she knew that they both struggled with trying to do what they had been taught; while doing so, they were all too aware that life had a funny way of throwing a fast one at them. Leah constantly worried about her two sisters and prayed each night that they would find the peace within them, the same peace that their *mamm* had tried so hard to instill within her children.

Of course, she knew that she could only do so much for her sisters. She had her own hands full, balancing her home life with the bakery, while tending to the needs of her *kinner* and young Tobias. With a sigh, she walked back to the front of the store. No one had ever said that it was going to be right easy, Leah told herself.

Lydia

Lydia stretched out on the sofa, a cool wet washcloth on her forehead. With her eyes shut, she didn't notice that her husband had walked through the doorway and was now standing there, staring at her. Indeed, Lydia breathed deeply, trying to calm her beating heart.

How on earth could God do this to me, she wondered one more time, with more than her fair share of bitterness.

"Lydia?"

Opening her eyes, she glanced at the doorway. He was standing there, a bored look on his face as he watched her. His dark eyes seemed to bore a hole into her. His arms were crossed over his dirty white shirt and she noticed that one of his suspenders was torn at the shoulder.

Sitting up, she plucked the cloth from her forehead and looked at him. "You back so soon, Abe?"

He took a short, quick intake of breath, a look on his face that was either disapproving or concern. She never could quite tell. With his weathered skin from years working the fields, he often looked angry when, in reality, she knew he was not. "I might be asking you the same thing." He walked into the room and stared at her as she sat on the sofa. "You didn't finish out your day at the store again, then?"

Lydia shrugged. "A headache came over me."

Abe glanced at the ceiling as he reached a hand out to tug at his greying beard, a gesture that indicated that he was thinking. He shook his head and sighed. "What was it this time? Susie again, I reckon?"

She could tell from his reaction that he was bothered by her early presence at home. Again. Just once, she thought, she'd appreciate a touch of compassion from her husband instead of his too obvious disdain. Oh, she knew the reason why. She knew why he acted in such a distant manner. What Amish man wanted a barren wife? A wife that could not provide *kinner* to help the man on the farm?

"It's not my fault, Abe," she cried out, immediately hating the defensive tone of her voice. "She was poking fun at my situation."

"Your situation," he repeated sarcastically. "And what, may I ask, is that situation?" The word rolled off of his tongue with great sarcasm.

Lydia lowered her eyes, fighting the urge to cry. She was tired of tears, tired of crying, and tired of him not consoling her when she wanted his arms around her and words of comfort whispered into her ears. When was the last time, she wondered. A year ago? "You know I want a *boppli*," she whispered.

"Oh ja, you remind me all the time," he snapped.

She gasped. While there had been tension between them for a while now, a year...maybe two...he had never spoken so sharply to her. "It's not as if it's my fault!"

"Nee," he laughed but it was without any mirth. "Therefore, it must be mine."

She started to stand up but he stopped her by holding out his hand. Lydia felt the tears threatening to fall down her cheeks for the second time that day. "Abe, I never said it was your fault, either. It's God's will, I reckon."

"Lydia," Abe said, his voice low and even. "If you would just release the idea and relax, stop thinking about it, mayhaps the good Lord would send you a *boppli*. But you can't seem to do that right now, can you? You dwell on the negative and push us away!"

"Abe! I've never pushed you away!"

He frowned at her, that look that she could never quite figure out crossing his face again. "You need to relax, Lydia."

"I try," she whispered.

"Try harder," he snapped, his eyes sharp and fierce. "Now,

go take something for your headache and, since you are home early, come out and help me tend to the cows. No use sitting here feeling sorry for yourself. I sure could use more help with the chores." He didn't wait for her answer before he turned around and walked back toward the door.

She sat on the sofa in the kitchen, staring at him as he left. For a long moment, she kept watching the empty doorway, wishing that he would come back and take her into his arms, to talk to her the way that he had during their courtship. But that side of her husband had disappeared long ago. Disappeared when she had lost hope of ever having a baby of her own.

If only, she thought, as she stood up and reluctantly followed in the direction of her husband.

Susie

Susie hurried into her kitchen and, after pushing aside several dirty plates, she set her empty lunch basket on the counter. Quickly, she did an assessment of the kitchen and realized that, once again, her kitchen was a complete mess. The sink was filled with pans and glasses. The table still had dirty plates from the dinner meal. Someone had attempted to make bread and there was flour all over the counter by the stove.

She wondered when that had happened since the *kinner* were supposed to go to her mother-in-law's house after breakfast and morning chores. She was more than certain that she had only put two things on the list for the *kinner* to do: clean the kitchen and weed the garden. Baking bread had most definitely not been on that list.

With a sigh, Susie stepped over a pair of dirty socks on the linoleum and walked toward the sink to try to wash the dishes that had piled up on the counter. No sooner had she turned on the water, she heard the back door open. The hinges squeaking as it did.

She dreaded the heavy footsteps that she heard on the floorboards in the other room. There was a shuffling noise that caused goose bumps to crawl up her arms. Susie felt her shoulders hunch forward as she tried to shrink within herself. Quickly, she immersed herself into the task of cleaning the dishes, washing them as fast as she could in the hopes of getting them tended to before her husband would walk out of the mudroom and into the kitchen.

"Should've known," he snapped as he walked through the doorway. "Having my *mamm* watch your *kinner* while you work outside the house," Merv scoffed. "That's just great, Susie! Keep neglecting your family and your home."

She cowered from his booming, sarcastic voice. "I should be done here in just a few minutes, Merv. Then I can get started on supper."

"Likely that!" he said, a harsh tone to his voice. "I want you quitting that store, you hear me? A married woman with *kinner* working outside the home!" She didn't have to turn around to know that he was shaking his head, mocking her.

Susie kept her back to him, busying herself with the dishes. She wanted to point out that she was not the only married Amish woman who worked outside of the home. She knew plenty of women who worked at market or stores during the week while their *kinner* stayed with a grossmammi or aendi. It was just the way things were done.

But Susie knew that arguing would only raise his ire and that was something she didn't want to do, for sure and certain. His mocking words no longer cut through her. She felt immune to the complaints and to his constant criticism. His coldness went to his core and she knew that nothing she did or said could change him. Instead, at night, before he retired to their bedroom, she would get down on her knees and press her hands together to pray, pray that God would lighten his heart and help her through this rough patch.

Only the prayers had gone on for several years now and the rough patch was being stretched far too thin. No matter how hard she tried, he continued to push her away. If Merv's main complaint was that she wasn't home enough due to her job at Whoopie Pie Place, Susie was certain of one thing: working at Whoopie Pie Place was the only peace and joy that she could count on, even if sister Lydia was known for throwing tantrums and leaving early.

Sadie

Sadie stared out the kitchen window, watching her sister Leah walking down the hill, by the pond. She knew that her sister often went there to think after a long day at the store. Sometimes, Sadie contemplated joining her sister, hoping to tell her some of the things that were on her mind. But she knew that her sister needed her own time and space, just a few short minutes, in order to decompress and reflect.

Sadie sighed and turned away from the window, quickly looking around the room. Everything was tidy and the table was set, ready for supper. If nothing else, Sadie wanted to make the evenings a bit nicer for her oldest sister. Leah had taken on quite the responsibility and Sadie knew that it burdened her with too much worry. She could see the grey hair at her crown and the deep furrows that seemed to permanently mark Leah's forehead.

The screen door opened, the hinges squeaking, as Leah walked into the kitchen. She glanced around and a look of relief washed over her face. "My word, Sadie! That's just like a gift to my eyes, sweet sister! You are ever so thoughtful and kind!"

"No more so than anyone else," Sadie replied modestly. Like many Amish women, Sadie was not the one to take a compliment without a gentle reminder of the goodness in others.

Leah sank down into a chair at the table. "Have you seen Tobias? He was slinking about today. Worries me that," she added.

Sadie watched her sister as she rubbed the back of her neck. Workdays were long days for everyone but Sadie knew that Leah suffered the most. Her two oldest *kinner*, Aaron and Rebecca, usually helped their father while the twins and her two year old, Anna, stayed next door with Esther, brother Jacob's wife. Of course, always, Rebecca came to the store on Saturdays to help her *mamm*. Today, however, Leah's husband, Thomas, had taken the *kinner* to visit with his *mamm* and *daed*. Sadie hated to admit it but it sure was nice to come home to a quiet house, for a change.

"Haven't seen him much today," Sadie replied, turning slightly so that she could glance out the window. "In fact, only twice."

Leah sighed. "I sure hope his illness isn't back."

Leah had always despised the word "cancer". It was like poison. No, she thought. It *was* poison, both physically and spiritually. Leah simply couldn't even bring herself to name the specific kind: Leukemia. It was as if, by not saying the word, the disease might go away. Poof! Vanish on its own, leaving no trace of fatigue or bad headaches or aches and pains.

"I'll go check if he's upstairs," Sadie offered, not waiting for her sister to stop her.

As she suspected, Sadie found him lying down in his room, the shades drawn and his arm tossed over his head, his blond curls stuck to his forehead from sweat. Tiptoeing across the room, Sadie leaned over and pressed her hand against his cheek. The touch of her skin on his caused him to stir and he quickly sat up, blinking his eyes rapidly as he tried to focus on his sister.

"*Wie gehts?*" he asked, his voice thick with sleep.

"Supper time, Tobias," she answered, keeping her voice soft. "Unless you are feeling poorly?"

He shook his head and, slowly, swung his legs over the side of the bed. A big yawn and a quick shake of his head helped wake him from his slumber. "Nee," he mumbled, rubbing the sides of his face. "I'm fine."

Sadie watched as he walked down the stairs, his feet shuffling and shoulders slouched. He had always been a small child, the other children outgrowing him by leaps and bounds. Yet, he had always tried to keep a positive attitude. Today, Sadie could see that he was struggling just to go through the motion of joining his sisters at the supper table.

No, she reckoned. *He's far from fine.*

He almost stumbled across the kitchen floor and tossed himself down on the bench where Leah's *kinner* normally sat. He didn't seem to notice that no one else was there except his two sisters. Propping his head against his hand, he leaned on his elbow, eyes almost shut. There was no color to his face, at least none that reflected the fact that it was still summer. Instead, he was almost an ash grey.

Sadie's eyes flicked over to Leah, too aware that her older sister was watching their younger brother. Quickly, Sadie busied herself with bringing the prepared food over to the table: Cold cuts, fresh bread, applesauce, and chow-chow. When everything was set upon the table before Leah and Tobias, Sadie joined them.

They bowed their heads in silent prayer, waiting for Leah to lift her head before they, too, followed suit. For a few moments, the room was silent; no conversation, the only noise in the room coming from the clinking of plates and utensils. Outside, a buggy rolled down the road, the familiar clip-clop of the horse's hooves becoming louder as it neared the farm. It was a comforting noise and Sadie paused, just for a moment, to listen to it. Savvy as she was with the farm animals she could hear a faint secondary click in the horse's alternate beat as he was ambling over the even road adjacent to the farm. Must be one shoe becoming lose, she pondered; will need to be tacked back within a day or two, that's for certain.

"Tobias!"

Leah's sharp tone snapped Sadie's attention back to the table. Her sister was glaring fiercely at their younger brother. It only took Sadie but an instant to realize why. He had put barely anything on his plate and he was leaning again, against his hands, his eyes drooping with fatigue.

"What is wrong with you, child?" Leah asked, her tone not necessarily kind and compassionate. But Sadie knew that behind the harshness was concern. Leave it to Leah, the mother hen of the brood.

"Nothing," he mumbled, avoiding Leah's eyes.

"Sure don't look like nothing to me! Now you eat, you hear me? I want to see you with a full plate! You are but skin and bones and you need good food to stay well!"

Obediently, he reached for more applesauce and dished it onto his plate. Sadie knew that it would make Leah happy, for applesauce would boost his appetite and help put some meat on his bones.

And that was when it hit her. Sadie stared down at her own plate and realized that she, too, had no appetite. Furthermore, like Tobias, she was tired. It wasn't a tired from working hard all day. It was a bone weary tired, the kind of tired that made her ache. Then her head began to pound, a deep throbbing behind the temples that caused little white lights to flash before her eyes.

"Leah," she started, feeling as if the room was spinning. "You mind if I excuse myself?"

At this question, Leah looked up and, with concern in her face, stared at her sister. It was unlike Sadie to leave the table without eating. "You, too? Mayhaps there's a bug going around, *ja*?"

Sadie shook her head. "I don't know," she mumbled. "I'm just tired and achy."

Leah tilted her head as if assessing her youngest sister. Sadie could feel her eyes on her back as she stood up and, after quickly setting her plate on the counter, began to move toward the stairs.

"I'll check on you after supper," a concerned Leah said, still watching Sadie, a frown on her face as she did so.

Sadie started to wave her hand over her shoulder when she heard Tobias. He leaned over and began to vomit on the floor, the applesauce obviously not settling in his stomach. As she ascended the stairs, she heard Leah divert her attention back to young Tobias, fussing as she jumped from her seat and took the boy in her arms. Sadie glanced over her shoulder, aware that her own sudden wave of fatigue and the dizziness that she had experienced were forgotten as Leah began to comfort Tobias and take charge of the mess. For a moment, she contemplated helping her sister but she felt dizzy and weak. Leah had everything under control. It hadn't been the first time that this had happened. Not with Tobias.

With a sigh of relief, Sadie continued upstairs and retreated to her room. It would do no good to add to Leah's worry. Of that, she was sure and certain.

Part Two

So the pious will be tried
Here on earth,
That their faith be found
Pure, genuine, and purified.
But after this short time,
They will rejoice forever
With unspeakable joy.

Ausbund, Song 124 Verse 8

Trust in the LORD with all your heart,
And do not lean on your own understanding.
In all your ways acknowledge Him,
And He will make straight your paths.

Proverbs 3:5-6

The Porch

Leah sat on the swinging chair that Thomas had hung from the porch. How long ago had it been, she wondered. Three years? No, definitely less. He had hung the swing there shortly before they had moved onto the farm when her parents had been killed. It had been his gift to Leah, a place for her to watch the day fade into evening.

Besides the pond, the swing was her favorite place to sit and reflect. She loved the creaking sound of the wood as she swung back and forth, a cool breeze caressing her skin as she reflected on the day.

It had started out like any other day: the chaos in the morning, the tourists in the store, the bickering among Susie and Lydia. *Why should anything be different*, she had thought to herself, too aware of the sarcasm building up in her own mind. But then, she had taken that message from voice mail. That had changed everything.

How in the world would Whoopie Pie Place be able to fulfill those orders? She second-guessed herself, wondering if she, perhaps, had been too quick to say yes. Had it been pride?

Leah shut her eyes and leaned back as she pushed the swing backward. Ja, she thought. Pride indeed. And now she was in quite the pickle, wasn't she?

"Leah?"

She lifted her head and saw her husband standing by the screen door of the kitchen. He must have gone into the house through the side door for she had not heard him returning from the barn. With a tired smile, she patted the seat next to her on the swing.

"Come," she managed to say. "Let me tell you about my day. Something quite amazing happened."

The screen door squeaked as he opened it and Leah was not

surprised to see that he held two glasses of fresh meadow tea. Thomas was thoughtful like that. He was her rock, so full of understanding and support. Leah prayed her thanks to God daily for having put Thomas into her life. Just when she was down, just when she was worn out, there he was…this time with a cool drink and loving smile on his face. He handed her one and took his place beside her on the swing.

"Tell me," he said, his free hand gently taking hers and lifting it to his lips to brush a soft kiss against her skin. "Tell me about that amazing day of yours…"

Earlier That Day

Whoopie Pie Place

Most mornings, Leah was the first to arrive at the bakery. Throughout the tourist season, she preferred to be the one opening the bakery. She didn't mind since she was up early in the morning. She loved having the laundry already washed and hung before the sun peeked over the horizon. After making breakfast for her family, she would clean the kitchen before it was time to leave the house. And always, she left a note of to-do chores for the *kinner*.

The night before, a storm had blown through their little community but it appeared that there had been no damage to the bakery beyond a few tree limbs that had to be removed from the walkway. However, the storm had downed some trees on the family farm so Leah was sure that her brother Jacob would be out clearing them for the better part of the day.

As Leah passed the family farmhouse, which was located within a stone's throw from the bakery, she noticed that her sister-in-law Esther already had her laundry out. Leah raised an eyebrow, wondering whether it was actually clean laundry hanging on the line or just dirty sheets that her sister-in-law had put on the line. Leah was too aware of the unspoken contest among the women to see who could have their laundry out the earliest on Mondays. Some women were known to go so far as to put dirty bed sheets out until they had a load of clean clothes to hang, thus giving the perception that they had   finished their laundry before others. Laughing to herself, Leah suspected that Esther was certainly one who might try to pull that trick.

In the quiet of the morning, Leah would unlock the door to the store and walk inside, enjoying the lingering smells from yesterday's baked goods. Without a moment's delay, she would begin making the dough for the morning bread so that, by the time Lydia and Sadie arrived, it would have risen twice and be ready for shaping and baking.

Structure and order. That was the way their *mamm* had raised them. Indeed, most Amish women went to great strides to achieve perfection in the cleanliness of their homes, obedience of their children, and the beautiful colors that donned their gardens.

That was why, after punching down the dough for the last time and rolling it into small loaves to rise in the metal pans, she stood on the front porch of the store and wondered where Susie was.

Timeliness was another typical characteristic of the Amish. Being tardy was just as much wasteful as it was disrespectful. Unfortunately, as of late, Susie was never on time. She always seemed hurried and out of breath, running late and apologizing for it. Leah knew that her sister's home weighed heavily on her mind. There was much for Susie to do and not a lot of help, in fact, practically none, that came from her young *kinner* or husband's family.

While it was true that, at the beginning of her marriage, Susie had been the perfect Amish wife, something had changed after the birth of her third child. When excusing her own tardiness in the mornings, she often complained of having too much to do. This was something Leah couldn't understand, especially since most Amish women normally had more than six children and the same amount of time and responsibility as Susie. For that reason, the more Susie complained, the more her complaints fell on deaf and unsympathetic ears.

As for Lydia, she seemed to increasingly show up with a splitting headache, a stomach ache or some heart palpitations. There was never a day when Lydia did not have some kind of ailment or a reason to complain about working at the bakery. And it seemed to be getting worse with each new day. Indeed, Lydia's constant complaints were taxing on Leah's nerves, especially given how much she was giving up herself, without nary a complaint.

This morning was no different. Susie arrived late,

completely out of breath and sweaty. It was quickly apparent that she had not come by horse and buggy. Instead, she had used a bicycle to travel the three-mile distance from her farm to the bakery. Leah frowned but kept her mouth shut. She wanted to ask why Susie's husband hadn't let her use the horse and buggy or, at least, driven his wife to the bakery. But she kept that question to herself.

As was to be expected, Lydia arrived complaining that she felt feverish (she wasn't, though) and was shaking (no one else saw it). Leah acknowledged her sister's fantasy ailments and saved the rolling of her eyes for when she turned back to the display where she was arranging the goods prior to opening the store for the public.

Yes, this morning was no different than any other. At least not as far as Susie and Lydia were concerned...

What was different this morning, however, was Sadie.

Sadie was the one person in their home that always approached each morning with a refreshing burst of energy and a smile. She never complained, willing to give the tasks at hand all that she had no matter what the circumstance or how busy she was. She never missed work, often accompanying Leah to the bakery to help her start the day's baking and never left early.

This morning, however, was indeed, different. She complained that her side hurt and very sheepishly approached Leah to apologize and request the rest of the day in bed. This concerned Leah. This was not like Sadie at all. Leah made a mental note to go and check on her youngest sister during the first slow spell of the store.

At nine o'clock sharp, Leah flipped the sign on the front door, announcing that Whoopie Pie Place was now open for business. As usual, their first customer was Jenny Yoder. Whom else, Leah thought with a pleased smile. Jenny had come to their bakery several times a week for a dozen or so whoopie pies. The girls often wondered why she didn't bake them herself since she needed so many. Now, if anyone had a right to complain about having too much to do, it was Jenny. Although she never did say one word about her busy life and was always seen wearing a pleasant smile on her face, Jenny could not mask the fact that having eleven children had to be a challenge.

"*Gute mariye*, Jenny! How are you this fine day?" Leah asked, genuinely happy to see her neighbor entering the store.

"*Vell*," she began, leaning against the counter, her eyes roving through the display case as she looked over the fresh baked goods. "I have to confess that things have been a little hectic since David's *daed* passed away."

Leah cringed, kicking herself for having forgotten about the elder Yoder's passing just the previous month. She had attended the funeral with Thomas, but, since Jenny was in a different church district, despite how close they lived, she hadn't given much thought to the loss. "How is David's *mamm* doing?"

Everyone knew that death was always hardest for the surviving spouse. Especially when people were married for so many years; death brought an empty hole to their family lives and abundant turmoil to the surviving spouse's daily routine. However, Leah was immediately reminded of how difficult it had been on her and her siblings when the good Lord had called both of their parents' home two years ago.

"She's doing the best she can," Jenny continued, shaking her head sadly. "Which reminds me, may I place an extra order for Friday? I will need a couple of your delicious strawberry pies. I'd make them myself but just do not have time before then. We're having an auction, you know: a Children and Grandchildren Auction, so the family can get what they want from *Grossdaadi*'s belongings on Saturday."

Leah smiled. "Why, that's a right *gut* idea, Jenny! I bet they will all love that."

"*Ja,*" Jenny replied, a smile lighting up her face. "Shall be a right *gut* time. The *kinner* are most excited." She hesitated for just a brief moment, the creases at the corner of her eyes deepening as she leaned forward as if about to share with Leah a forbidden secret. "*Vell,* except for my daughter's little Noah. He informed his *mamm* that he didn't want to go to the Children and Grandchildren auction because he didn't want them to sell him." Jenny spoke with a smile.

"Oh help!" Leah joined her, loving how Jenny was always so full of mirth and joy. It was contagious, that was for sure and certain. "Those *kinner* sure do come up with the cutest notions!"

"That they do," Jenny replied, glancing over her shoulder at the tingling of the bell over the door. She smiled as another woman entered the bakery. "Now, about those pies, before you start getting crowded…"

After Jenny left and Leah assisted the next wave of customers, mostly local women who came early to avoid the rush of tourists, she remembered that she had yet to check the answering machine for messages. Most Amish church districts banned the use of phones in the homes. However, the church elders, bishops and pastors, knew very well that the Amish businesses could not survive without telephone communication.

Doing business strictly within the community was no longer an option; with the farmland disappearing, raw materials were becoming increasingly expensive, be they fruits and vegetables, seed and fertilizer to grow crops to feed the animals or even just wood to build their furniture. So most families who owned a store or a small manufacturing business had to rely more and more on the *Englische* customers to round up their income; and to do business with the *Englische* meant to be able to receive orders via the telephone. Not being able to do so would ultimately mean the demise of the business.

So the elders had decreed that any Amish family with a

business that needed to sell beyond the confines of the *g'may* was allowed to have a telephone, strictly for that very purpose or for dire emergencies. Although some of the younger Amish men, especially the young men entering their rumschpringe years, often stretched that rule a bit far by insisting that they now needed *cell* phones. While it was a necessity for the bakery to have a telephone with an answering machine, Leah knew that she neither wanted nor needed a cell phone. When she left the bakery, she anticipated her peace and quiet.

As Leah walked over to the register, she grabbed a piece of paper and a pencil before pressing the round button on the answering machine.

"Hello, this is Deborah from The Dalton Chamber of Commerce. I'd like to place an order with you. If you could call me at 555-9283 by noon on Monday, I would truly appreciate it." Leah wrote the name and number down and wondered what it was that Deborah needed. She looked at the clock. It was only 9am and Englischers were later to rise than the Amish so she would have to try and remember to call her after the noon rush.

The rocking chairs out front were always the spot of choice for those who, after receiving their baked goods, often liked to sit and enjoy some of what they had purchased. Leah's husband had made those rocking chairs and her oldest son had painted them white. Quickly, however, they had found out that the customers wanted to actually purchase them. Good quality chairs weren't hard to find in Berlin but Thomas' chairs seemed very popular. He'd even had an order for twenty chairs for a restaurant in North Carolina. Some were even custom ordered to fit from the smallest to the largest of tooshies.

After wiping off the evening dust that had settled on the porch chairs, watering the beautiful flowers that hung from the porch rafters and sweeping the floor from any debris, Leah sat down for a brief moment. There was a cool morning breeze and she took that moment to shut her eyes and simply enjoy *being*.

But it didn't last long.

Her mind suddenly wandered to Tobias. Last night, he had been so sick. It reminded her far too much of when he was younger and going through his first treatment. Still, she held hope that it was just a virus. After all, sister Sadie had looked a bit peaked herself, the previous evening.

But this morning, he had stated that he was feeling much better and even insisted on helping Thomas with the chores. He had struggled so before. Was it really only three years ago when he had first battled his sickness? Leah remembered the smile on her mother's face the day the doctor had declared that Tobias was fine.

"Oh, the Lord has seen fit to allow me to keep Tobias a little longer," her mother had declared. It was truly a right *gut* day in their family.

Bringing herself back to the moment, Leah arose to go inside to check on the kitchen and see if any help was needed. Upon entering the kitchen she could hear Susie and Lydia speaking. Thankfully it was a pleasant conversation and they had yet to start bickering. Hopefully, having to take over the slack of not having Sadie there would keep them both too busy to argue with each other. Leah began to take inventory and to refill the counter with the delicious baked goods. They didn't keep a large variety of treats but what they did keep were good ones.

As she heard the bell on the door ring, she went to attend to the customers. "Good morning Mary, how are you this lovely day?"

"Quite well, *danke!*" she said with a smile on her face. "I'm quite well and would like to place an order please."

Um hum, Leah thought, recognizing the gleam in Mary's eye all too well. *A wedding for sure and certain.* "It must be a special order since you are just beaming from the core!"

The young woman giggled, the color flooding to her cheeks. "Indeed! I need 300 of your delicious whoopie pies for two weeks from Thursday. I so hope that's not too short of a notice. We had anticipated making them ourselves but everything is just so time consuming and…well, we just love yours. Could you possibly be able to do that? It would mean a lot to me."

Leah had watched Mary grow into such a beautiful young woman and now, as her anticipated marriage to Wilmer Weaver was approaching, she believed she was even more radiant. "Now Mary," she began, a hand on her hip. "If you think I would miss making whoopie pies for your wedding, well, I have half a mind to chase you right out of this store!"

Mary laughed again, her eyes sparkling.

"Besides," Leah continued. "The season is ending and we have no other large orders. I'm right honored that you asked us, truth be told!"

"Wonderful! I'll let *mamm* know".

After Mary left, the expected steady stream of customers began arriving. Time suddenly seemed to shift into fast forward. For almost two hours, there was not one moment to even take a breath. Around eleven o'clock when the customers slowed down for a couple of hours, Leah remembered to call that Deborah woman who had left her a message. Dialing the number, Leah tried to remember if she knew this Deborah but couldn't quite place her.

"Hello?"

"This is Leah from Whoopie Pie Place returning your call. You left a message, I believe, last evening?" she said slowly into the receiver. She disliked talking on the phone. It felt strange to be speaking with someone so far away or, as was the case here, completely unknown. Leah much preferred speaking to people directly and in-person.

"Yes, I did call last evening. I would like to speak to you about an order. We have a convention being held at our local arena in Dalton. Apparently one of their vendors backed out without giving us enough notice, so the organizers have a last minute request."

Interesting, Leah thought. She had heard about the event center in Dalton and even attended an auction there once, many years ago, with Thomas. They had bought a dresser and kitchen table. She knew that it was a large building that had the capacity to hold almost a thousand people, maybe more. "I see," she heard herself say. "And what might that be, then?"

Deborah paused and Leah thought she heard some papers shuffling in the background. "It seems that they'd like to sell whoopie pies and fresh baked bread at one of the stands. They could be individually wrapped but would need to be freshly made for the event. Do you think you could fill this order?"

Sell whoopie pies? And fresh bread? That would be a bulk order, for sure and certain. Leah felt her palms begin to sweat in anticipation of the numbers. "What exactly do you have in mind?"

"Well, the Mennonite Community Convention is in four weeks and there will be almost two thousand pre-registered attendees. We usually count on double that for walk-ins." More papers shuffled in the background. "At least a thousand whoopie pies and four hundred loaves of bread. That's what we sold last year."

Leah caught her breath at the numbers. She wasn't sure what to say. Indeed, for the first time in a long time, she was speechless. Stunned. Two large orders in one day? Both needed within the next month? Quickly, she tried to calculate how many hands it would take to make that many whoopie pies and the bread. She'd have to outsource the bread; that was something she knew right away. As for the whoopie pies? She wouldn't trust anyone to do that but her own family.

"I'm sure it won't be a problem," Leah said, surprised by how natural she sounded. She wondered if God would count that as a lie. "May I look at my order book and get back with you by the end of the day?" asked Leah, her words crisp and clear, almost spoken in the song-like manner that was so typical of the Amish.

"Yes, but I would need to know as soon as possible and I would also need to know the cost."

After replacing the receiver and walking back into the kitchen of the bakery, Leah sat down in the closest chair. Her knees felt weak and she could only sit there, staring at the stainless steel pans hanging on the wall. Thirteen hundred whoopie pies? One thousand just for the convention! How on earth would they be able to make that many fresh whoopie pies? Part of her wanted to giggle with delight. That would be a five thousand dollar order, for certain! Oh, what they could all do with that money, she thought.

Her giddiness lasted but only a few short minutes as her thought process was interrupted by Susie and Lydia. The two sisters burst into the room, Susie trailing behind a furious Lydia, from the looks of it. Leah looked up, a frown instantly creasing her forehead.

"What do you mean that I don't make as good a filling as yours?" Susie had all but screamed.

Lydia spun around to face her sister. She crossed her arms over her chest and lifted her chin in the air. "It's true," she snapped. "On the days when I'm here alone, my whoopie pies fly off the shelf. Ask Leah! Wednesday is our busiest day of the week besides Saturday and *that* is the day that I'm here alone!"

"Oh hogwash!" Susie said, waving her hand at her sister. "That's because the store is closed on Sunday through Tuesday!"

Lydia made a sour face at her sister. "What is *that* supposed to mean?"

"*Vell*," Susie replied, her tone suddenly full of superiority. "After waiting three days, they'll eat just about anything as long as it remotely resembles a whoopie pie! Even a cow pie!"

Lydia caught her breath and was just about to retort when Leah stood up, slapping her hands against the tabletop.

"Girls!" she bellowed. "Stop the bickering! Please!"

Simultaneously, Lydia and Susie scowled at each other but, obediently, turned to face their oldest sister.

"We have to try harder to get along," Leah said, lowering her voice. "Tension in the kitchen will help no one. It won't sell pies either, I reckon. Both of you make wonderful whoopie pies. I wouldn't put one over the other and, to do so, shows an awful lot of pride on your parts." She paused for a minute, letting her words sink in. Both sisters lowered their eyes, knowing full well that pride was a sin and that they were both completely guilty of it.

"Now," Leah continued. "We need to work together. I have just received two very large orders for thirteen hundred whoopie pies!" She leveled her gaze at both sisters. "I don't think I need to tell you what that means for us, financially. But we can't do it in such a short period of time if you two are going to be bickering!"

More silence from Lydia and Susie. Leah knew from experience that silence from those two meant that she had definitely made her point.

"If you can agree to a cease fire, even if just for a few weeks, I will accept these jobs. They will be our last big orders until next spring so I'd sure hate to say no," Leah added. And with that, she knew that they had all silently agreed. They would take these two big orders and get along during the process. The bakery would not disappoint their customers, that was for sure and certain!

Sadie

In the heat of the late morning, Sadie was thankful for the small breeze that was blowing through the open window as she laid in her room. She hadn't gone back to the bakery this morning because she had felt poorly when she awoke. The best she could hope for was that she would feel better to take her ride with Manny that evening.

Manny Yoder.

She smiled at the thought of him with his mousy brown hair that curled over his ears and his big chocolate eyes that sparkled whenever the two of them were together. She had met him years before when they went to the same one-room schoolhouse. However, he was older and hadn't paid much attention to Sadie. She was, after all, just a quiet young girl when he was already sixteen and taking a turn at his *rumschpringe*.

Oh, she had heard wild stories about many a young Amish boy who took advantage of those years between their sixteenth birthday and when they finally took the kneeling vow to join the church. But not so with Manny. He always remained in good standing with the church and the community. After he turned 16, he continued helping the elderly, visiting the infirm, and donating his time to help the destitute. In 2007, he had even joined the Mennonite Central Committee team to embark on a trip to New Orleans to help with rebuilding the community, two years after that horrid hurricane.

It had been four years after he returned that he first asked her home from a singing. By then she had just turned eighteen, seven years his junior. Now that he was twenty-seven, Sadie knew that this wedding season would be the one when she was going to become Manny's Sadie for the rest of her life.

Every Church Sunday, Manny had attended, his lips moving in song but his eyes watching her. Every time he could, he would invite her to ride home in his buggy. She never thought twice about saying yes. After all, Manny Yoder was the most handsome, generous, and godly man in their *g'may*. With his gentle nature and quickness to laugh, it hadn't taken her anytime at all to fall in love with Manny all over again, as she secretly had been when she was a young girl. She had only hoped that he would, one day, fall in love with her too.

Then, he began to visit her in the evening during the week. He liked to show up after supper to invite her for a buggy ride. Almost like clockwork, he would show up on Thursday evenings during the weeks between church services. They would drive his beautiful black Standardbred horse and open top buggy down the road under the black skies, a blanket of stars and a shining moon for a roof.

Indeed, Sadie loved these moonlight times with Manny. She couldn't deny that they had become close. They held hands, shared dreams and secrets and parked the buggy in the empty school yard to stare up at the majestic sky above them. Indeed, they were very close. Perhaps closer, she often wondered with a blush, than a couple should, before their wedding day.

But, when Manny asked to kiss her, she just hadn't been able to say no.

Most Amish men that were around her own age were, oh, so immature! But not *her* Manny. His mother Jenny had taught him to respect others and he was ever so good with his nieces and nephews. He loved working the land with his father and Sadie knew that he would be not just a good provider for her and their future *kinner* but also the perfect husband.

But now, as she bent forward with a sharp pain in the upper left quadrant of her abdomen, she wondered what she could have eaten that had put her stomach in knots. She hadn't had much of an appetite recently so she wasn't eating much. Whatever was happening to her body? Something just wasn't right. Not only did her stomach hurt, but so did her left breast. Once, as a teen, her *maam* had explained to her that when her breasts would hurt it was probably just growing pains; becoming a grown woman, she had said. At twenty years of age, surely those growing pains should have been over, she thought.

And her energy level was just drained. She felt tired, exhausted, as if she had been run to the ground. No amount of sleep could wash away her crippling fatigue.

As pleasant as she tried to be, even someone looking at her seemed to upset her lately. Sadie just didn't know how to handle all of these changes. Worse, she couldn't figure them out. It triggered a frightening feeling in her.

Fearing that they would be in dire need of her help in the bakery, she forced herself to change into a different dress. As she was pulling her light pink dress over her head, she suddenly felt lightheaded and decided to lie back down for a few moments. *Something is wrong, wrong, wrong,* she kept repeating to herself, secretly hoping that the more she said it, the more likely it would prove wrong.

She tried to think back to any other time when she may have felt this way: tired, sick, with headaches and dizzy spells. Quickly she came to the conclusion that she never felt anything like that. Indeed, she had always been in perfect health, only catching a bad cold in winter, from time to time.

Sitting up, she took a few deep breaths and told herself that she'd keep an eye on her sickness but speak not one word of it to her sisters. No sense in worrying them, she reckoned as she stood once again, setting her hand on the nightstand to remain steady. She had to go to work, she knew that much. In fact, she had never taken a day off on account of not feeling well. To do so, she realized, would certainly cause a stir among her sisters. And *that* was something she wanted to avoid at all costs.

By the time she made her way into the bakery, the day was in full swing. For some reason, the tourists' traffic had increased this summer. Try as they might, none of the sisters could figure out why. It had been one of their *Englische* friends, Michelle, a lovely woman who often drove the Amish to run errands, who had laughed when she informed them about some strange reality shows on television about the Amish. Certainly *that* was what had spiked interest about their Amish community.

"A reality show?" Leah had repeated, incredulous at Michelle's story. "Heavens to Betsy! About what?"

Michelle had laughed at her reaction. "Well, there's one called Amish Mafia…"

Even Susie and Lydia had laughed at that. "Amish what?" Sadie asked.

"Mafia," Michelle repeated. "A criminal group that rules the Amish."

Leah had scoffed, a disgusted frown on her face as she waved her hand dismissively at Michelle's words. "We know what mafia means," she exclaimed, "but this is Poppycock! Complete rubbish!"

This time, it had been Sadie who chimed in, with "Rubbish or not, we sure are selling a lot of baked goods!"

The five women had then laughed, realizing the truth to Sadie's statement. From that day forth, it had been an insider joke among them that Leah headed up the Whoopie Pie Mafia and that the rest were her henchmen.

"There you are," Leah said, sweat on her brow as she finished serving the last person of Laverne's midday tour. "Can you go in the back to restock the shelves? I need to run and check on Tobias."

Sadie smiled, "No need. I just did and he's resting. I made him dinner before I came out."

The look of relief on Leah's face warmed Sadie's heart. She didn't need verbal thanks. The gratitude that Leah showed in her eyes was more than enough.

Together, they both walked into the kitchen. For once, Susie and Lydia were busy baking, rather than bickering. Sadie noticed that right away and, surprised at the peace in the kitchen, peeked over at her oldest sister, a questioning look upon her face.

"We have a big order coming up, *Ja*," Leah explained. "Mary Glick is to be married and wants three hundred whoopie pies."

"Three hundred?" Sadie could scarce believe her ears. "Oh my!"

It was Susie who spoke next, a gleam in her eyes. "*Oh my* is right, *schwester*[4]!" She glanced at Lydia. "We've already worked out a way to fulfill those orders, just the two of us. 300 pies, piece of cake!"

Leah and Sadie laughed at Susie's enthusiasm and at the expression she had inadvertently used.

"Well, cake or pie, let's focus today on the job at hand, *ja*?" Leah said, reaching for a box of wrapped whoopie pies, which she handed to Sadie to carry out to the front of the store. "How's that bread doing, actually?" Without waiting for an answer, Leah wandered over to the cooling racks. "Looks right *gut*, Susie. Going to be needing those wrapped for the afternoon tour, then!"

Sadie hurried to the front of the store and began to restock the shelves. Her mind was in a whirl, thinking about Mary Glick getting married. If they had announced it already, Mary and her beau, Wilmer, were destined to be married in late September instead of November. Since they had both taken their baptism back in the Spring, it made sense, she thought, for them to be married earlier in the Fall instead of during the November rush. If only, she thought…

"Sadie!"

---

[4] Sister

She jumped at the male voice that called her name and spun around. To her great surprise, Manny stood outside the screen door, his left hand on the doorframe and a broad smile on his face. "Manny!" She placed her hand on her chest, willing her beating heart to calm down, at least a little. "Whatever are you doing here so early, now?"

He gestured for her to join him outside on the porch. Glancing around to make certain Leah wasn't there to scowl at her, Sadie set the box of whoopie pies on the counter and scurried to the door. She wondered if something was wrong, for Manny rarely stopped by to see her during the day. He had a job to do, after all.

"Is everything alright then?" she asked, her voice raising just a touch in apprehension at the end of the question.

He reached for her hand and pulled her toward the edge of the porch, away from the doorway and prying eyes. "Aw, everything is right as rain, *my* Sadie!" He smiled as he emphasized the "my", staring down into her face. "I just didn't want to go one more day without seeing you."

His words made her heart flutter and she felt the color rise to her cheeks. "Oh Manny," she whispered, her eyes darting away from his intense stare. "You shouldn't say such things."

To her surprise, he laughed. "Why ever not, Sadie? You are my girl, ain't so?"

She nodded but felt awkward having such a conversation right at this minute. She certainly hoped he wasn't going to try to kiss her, in broad daylight, on the porch of Whoopie Pie Place. It was one thing for him to steal a kiss, protected from public view in the darkness of the night, and quite unnoticeable from inside his buggy, but here, during the day, in plain sight of potential customers and passers-by! Well, that was quite another thing!

He tugged at the white ribbon that hung over her left shoulder from her prayer *kapp*. "Mayhaps this is the year that you become more than my girl…" he teased, but there was a serious undertone to his voice. "I have been thinking about you, Sadie."

Now indeed, her heart was beating faster, as she wondered if this was the moment she had been waiting for, the moment when he was about to ask her to be his wife. But, as the thought crossed her mind, she heard the bell hanging over the store door as it whooshed open. Leah poked out her head, quickly assessing the situation.

"Need your help in here, Sadie!" she said; then, as if an afterthought, glancing at Manny. "How are you today, Manny? Your *mamm* was in here just this morning."

He took a step backward, releasing the ribbon from his fingers. Sadie watched as it fluttered through the air and rested against her shoulder. She couldn't fault Leah for interrupting them but, oh, how she wished that Leah had waited a few more minutes.

"What would a meal be without the famous bread and whoopie pies from the Miller sisters?" he teased, motioning to take his leave.

Reluctantly, Sadie started walking toward the door, which Leah held open. She glanced over her shoulder at Manny, wishing with all of her might that she had more time to spend with him. A matter of such importance should not be left unfinished, she thought. But mayhaps, Manny could have chosen a different setting to express himself, she pondered. As it was, she doubted she'd see him again until that next church Sunday and, even then, it wouldn't be until after the singing that they would have a moment to spend alone. *Please Lord,* she prayed, *let him pick up where he left off. I love him so.*

Lydia

"So, you made it through a whole day of work, I see," Abe said when she walked into the kitchen. He was sitting at the table, reading The Budget, his eyes watching her from behind his readers. "No one stepped on your tail today?"

She glanced at him, annoyed at his statement, but didn't respond. What was there to say, anyway? A scowl on her brow, Lydia hurried to the counter and set her basket next to the sink. She glanced over her shoulder, but saw that Abe had already returned his attention to his paper. Disappointed, she let out a sigh and began to busy herself with preparing the evening meal. He turned the page with ostentation, knowing that she was looking in his direction. The noise broke the silence in the room and added to the heavy feeling in her chest.

Silence. It could be an ugly word. When she had been growing up, silence was unknown in their house. There was always activity and noise from her siblings. Mealtime was often her favorite time, a time when people got together, prayed, laughed, talked, and loved. Even after the birth of Tobias, a surprise by any stretch of the imagination, there had remained a happy aura in her *mamm*'s kitchen, the heart of every Amish home. Of course, when Tobias had become ill, things had changed. But there was still noise and never silence.

When she had married Abe, things had been different. Different in a good sense. For the first few months, she had remained at home with her parents, like most newlyweds among the Amish. It took time for Abe to find a farm for them to live. But during the weekends, he would come stay at the Miller farm and they would visit with family. It was a happy time for both of them, that was for sure and certain.

The problems hadn't started until a year had gone by and there had been no sign of a boppli. Abe had said all of the right things, comforting her when she was disappointed and wiping away the tears when she cried. By the second year, Lydia knew that he was harboring concerns. How could he not? That was when the headaches and the muscle aches began. Abe had teased her that she was making it up, putting too much stress on herself. Lydia, however, knew that it was just a mask for more criticism.

How could it not be, she reasoned with herself. All Amish men wanted large families. And the only way to have those large families was with lots of babies and, well, it was the women who had babies. Only, in Lydia's case, that wasn't happening.

By the third year, she had begun to suspect that Abe blamed her for not bearing him children. It had to be her fault, she reasoned. That often caused her to feel drained and tired. She was prone to napping instead of helping him with the chores. He never complained and often tried to tend to her needs. But Lydia knew that deep down he resented her, even if he seemed pleasant enough.

And that was about the time that the silence began.

Now, she had become used to that silence, despite loathing it so. If only there could have been a child to break it. How she longed for squeals of laughter from a young child or two. But the good Lord had not seen fit to bless them with a child. It was a burden she carried on her shoulders every single day for certainly it was *her* fault that *she* could not conceive.

She glanced at him, wondering why he always seemed so angry with her.

"Did you have a good day, then?" she finally asked, leaning against the counter and staring at her husband.

His response was a single grunt.

She put her hand on her hip and glared at him. "It wouldn't hurt you to actually speak to me!"

He glanced up and, after a brief moment, he sighed before setting down the paper. "My day was just fine, Lydia," he said drily.

"As was mine, *danke* for asking," she snapped. "I don't see why I have to work at that store. I should be home here, taking care of my family."

At this, he laughed. "What family?"

"Abe!"

He stood up and started to walk toward her. "If you mean me, I can handle the chores right gut, Lydia. But beyond that, we don't have *kinner*, do we?"

She looked away, fighting the tears that crept into the corner of her eyes. "We could but you refuse to talk about adoption or fostering, ain't so?"

He waved his hand at her, dismissing her comment. "It's God's will that we don't have *kinner*."

Defiantly, she rolled her eyes up to look at him and lifted her chin. "God's will but my fault, ain't so?"

"Not that again!" he groaned.

"The doctor said I couldn't bear children. You were there, Abe. You heard him." She would never forget those words, could hear them in her head…cutting into her heart as if she had been stabbed. "It's me that can't bear the children yet it's you who can't bear me!"

He took a deep breath and shook his head. "Lydia, that ain't true. You are blowing things out of proportion."

"I bet you are downright sorry you married me!"

"*Nee*, Lydia," he said, something suddenly softening in his tone. "I am not sorry I married you." He paused. "I am, however, sorry about the attitudes that you continuously keep."

That stopped Lydia in her tracks. He had never gone so far as to say something so horrid to her. "My attitudes?" she repeated, stunned that he would speak so harshly to her.

"Always pouting, making faces," he continued. His dark eyes watched her reaction. "And always sick. If it's not a headache, it's a dizzy spell. I think half of the time you make that up for attention!"

She gasped. "Abe! I can't believe you think so poorly of me! It's certainly from the stress!"

"Ah," he said, raising an eyebrow and nodding his head, "The stress, *ja*. You have much to stress about, ain't so?"

She certainly didn't appreciate his sarcasm. Without intending to, her voice became shrill as she retorted, "You think I have some reason to be happy and smiling?"

He took a deep breath, his chest rising and falling slowly as he contemplated his response. She could see that he was thinking. His eyes softened, just enough to let her know that he still cared. That had never been in question. But they just didn't seem to be able to communicate these days, not without it leading to an argument about not being able to have *boppli*.

She watched as he stood up and approached her. Instinctively, she tried to move away but her back was already against the counter. Abe lifted his hands and placed them on her shoulders, staring down into her face with a look of genuine concern. "Lydia," he started. "If you would just calm down and stop worrying about it, maybe God would see fit for us to have a *boppli*." He caressed her shoulders and smiled, the first time he had smiled at her in days.

She knew that he didn't mean his words. How could he? No man could truly be so understanding! She pushed his hand away. "God isn't working this miracle for us, Abe!" she cried out, hating his feigned understanding.

Abe shook his head, still smiling. "Give God time, Lydia. We both know that God can work miracles, ain't so? Remember Sarah and Abraham."

The color drained from her face and the tears began to fall freely. Was he truly comparing their situation to old Abraham with his disbelieving wife, Sarah? Was this just one more douse of salt on the open wound in her heart? She wiggled her shoulders, freeing herself from his grasp and moved away.

"Oh Abe," she cried, wiping at the tears that fell from her eyes. "You just don't understand!"

Turning around, she ran to the door, her hands covering her mouth as if holding back the sob that threatened to escape.

Leah

It was coming close to the end of the day, and Leah knew that she should return the call to Deborah and inform her that Whoopie Pie Place would be able to deliver that large order for the convention. Of course, they needed to discuss pricing but Leah felt confident that Deborah would be fair. She had come to that conclusion after reviewing their bills. Regardless of whatever was in their pending order book, Leah knew that these two new orders were desperately needed. Although finances were fairly good, Leah always liked to make sure they had a reserve to get them through the winter months when the tourists weren't as plentiful. And, in the back of her mind, there was that nagging and recurring feeling that in the future, excess funds may be needed.

The sisters had spent a few minutes during a lag time between tour buses to discuss the logistics of how they would be able to fulfill such a large demand of their baked goods in such a short period of time. With the help of the *kinner* and some benevolent neighbors, they had figured out how to manage it. They all knew that it would be a rough few days around the delivery date, but deliver the goods they would!

After the other sisters had left, Leah had spent a few lone minutes scribbling notes on a pad of paper. She would have to put in an order for more ingredients to prepare for the onslaught of baking. The good news was that they could certainly shut down the store during the week preceding both events. Tourists rarely came through after Labor Day weekend. She just made a mental note to inform Laverne in advance.

Something else was troubling her. Setting down her pencil, she placed her chin into the palm of her hand and stared out the open door. Manny had surprised her, stopping at the store during the busy day to see Sadie. And when Leah had opened the door, it sure looked like an intimate moment had just passed, with his one hand pressed on the side of the store while his other played with the end of her ribbon. How many times had Leah told Sadie to tie those ribbons! It just wasn't proper, she thought as she scowled. But the look in his eye was what bothered her. She knew far too well how those young men were with the girls. And Manny sure hadn't asked Sadie for her hand yet. Leah hoped he wasn't trying to take advantage of her youngest sister by stealing kisses and holding her hand! She made a mental note to talk to her sister about that once again.

Upon closing up the bakery for the day, Leah felt genuinely exhausted. Although it had been a good day, one with little animosity other than some bickering between Susie and Lydia, for which she prayed a quick "Thank You" to God, she found that she didn't have the strength to face making supper or cleaning the house. She just wanted to sit and think, reflect on the day and shut her eyes. She had gotten up too early that morning and still needed to take the laundry down from the line, unless one of the *kinner* had thought to do so.

As Leah walked down the lane and approached the family farmhouse, her brother Jacob stopped her with a simple hand wave. He had been in the barn, shoveling some manure from the main aisle when he saw her. Setting down the shovel, he hurried toward her.

"Have you seen Tobias today?" he asked, a frown on his face. "He was to help me and I have not seen hide or hair of him."

A dark cloud passed over Leah. *What now?* She wondered. Leah frowned. "He hadn't felt well last evening. But he had promised to help Thomas with the chores." A wave of panic washed over her. "I sure hope he's not coming down with something again."

Jacob shook his head. "That boy ain't sick," he scoffed "What he needs is to learn some responsibility. When he makes a commitment, he needs to fulfill it."

Here we go again, Leah told herself, but held back her tongue. At thirty-one, Jacob was old enough to have six or more *kinner* of his own but he had married later in life and a much younger woman at that. His wife had been pregnant several times but miscarried twice. Their only child was a four-year-old girl who loved to play with Leah's boy, Henry, but certainly gave no relief to Jacob with chores.

To that end, Jacob tended to rely on Tobias, despite him helping out the sisters at the store and having his own chores to do. As a result, Jacob had his own fair share of complaints concerning their youngest brother. Leah found herself continually defending Tobias.

"*Ja*, Jacob," she replied carefully. "But you know he isn't the normal boy."

Jacob waved his hand at her, dismissing what she had just said. "By the Lord's stars, you sure do pamper him, Leah. He is over his sickness and, despite your coddling, Tobias *is* a normal boy."

There was no winning an argument against Jacob. If Leah took after her *mamm*, Jacob took after their *daed*. He was as godly an Amish man as they came and that meant that hard work and no excuses were the only two options. She sighed and said, "I will speak to him when I get home."

As she continued walking down the lane, she felt a sense of dread wash over her. *No*, she thought. *Tobias is not a normal boy.* Worse yet, she feared he wasn't feeling well. Why couldn't others see this? Why was she the only one who seemed to understand how fragile her brother's health was? Even more troubling, why didn't Jacob, of all people, seem to care?

Susie

In that one peaceful moment, Susie listened to the birds chirping outside of her kitchen window. Mourning doves. She could tell by the mournful *coo-ah, coo, coo, coo* of their calls. If she didn't know any better, they were just outside of her window, nesting in the big pine tree near the house. In the distance, she could hear the cows of the neighboring farm. It was peaceful to listen to the sounds of life outside of the home.

Susie sighed. How she wished that her nights were, indeed, more peaceful ones ! But as of late, she found herself lying awake for the greater part of the night, dreading the morning light when she would have to rise and face a long, tiring day; A day that would typically start off with harsh words and accusations that she did her best to ignore but knew she wouldn't be able to handle for much longer.

Earlier that particular morning, after a quick glance at the windup clock on the top of her dresser she had realized that in order to have time for all that she needed to get done before leaving for the bakery, she would have to move quickly; very quickly. Yet, something deep inside of her just couldn't do it. Something seemed to be preventing her from doing it. She had been too sluggish lately, completely lacking any sort of energy. Despite her long list of to-dos, she had wanted to simply blink her eyes and disappear from the house, magically reappearing at the bakery with her hands full of flour and sugar.

Now, in the quiet of the kitchen, after returning home from the bakery, while the *kinner* were outside tending to the evening chores, Susie suppressed a sigh. Soon, the *kinner* would come into the house, a precursor to Merv's own entrance. The evening would commence with loud, unruly noise from the *kinner* and no way for Susie to reprimand them. To do so would be an invitation for Merv to rebuke her. It seemed as if anything she did just irritated him further. The last thing she needed was a full-blown outburst on his part.

She remembered how, just that very morning, Merv had greeted the day. After he had stirred and stretched, he had rolled over and opened his eyes, blinking twice when he had realized she was still lying in bed next to him. Immediately, his eyes had narrowed and three deep wrinkles appeared on his forehead. "Aren't you up yet?" he had grumbled.

"*Nee*," she replied softly. "I am on my way."

His next words had cut through her like a knife. "You have become something of a lazy woman, Susie!" Inwardly, she had groaned at his words, knowing what was coming next. "Not completing your chores and always running off to that bakery." He had scowled when he added the all-too-familiar accusation that hurt worse than being physically abused: "You are neglecting your duties!"

Every evening, she held her breath and waited for what direction his mood would take him. She felt as though she walked on egg shells, hoping that the night would be a peaceful one, one without conflict and criticism.

It hadn't always been this way. She often tried to dig into her memory, fighting to identify when everything had changed. Surely Merv hadn't been this way during their courtship, she reminded herself. So what had occurred to make him so verbally abusive toward her and only her?

Susie had been fifteen when she had met Merv at a youth singing. She had noticed his sparkling eyes and broad shoulders immediately and whispered to one of her friends, inquiring as to who he was. She quickly had found out that Merv Stutzman was visiting his cousin Daniel for the summer.

Despite her initial interest, which he had been made aware of, Merv had not seemed interested in much more than hanging around with his friends. She noticed that he disappeared outside frequently and eventually left the gathering completely. If she had been disappointed, she hadn't let it show.

It had been the following week when the youth held a volleyball game on Saturday evening that she ran into Merv Stutzman a second time. Once again, he had acted rather standoffish, preferring the company of his friends to meeting new people. Susie had watched him, realizing that he was just shy. She had decided that the only thing to do was to approach him directly in order to get him to talk.

He hadn't seemed very interested in conversation when she had tried to start one with him. Yet, to her surprise, he had asked to take her home in a borrowed buggy. That had been the beginning of their courtship. For the rest of the summer, he always asked to take her home from gatherings. Yet, he remained quiet during those rides, rarely engaging in any discussion. Susie had decided to fill in the silence with her own chatter, hoping that he might lose his shyness and begin to open up to her.

It never happened.

When the harvesting time came to an end, so did Merv's visit. Without a word, he had returned to Kentucky where his family lived.

For a few weeks, Susie had written to Merv, hoping to find out if he intended to return to Ohio. But her letters had gone unanswered. Susie tried asking Daniel about his cousin, but Daniel would divert the questions. Susie had a sense that something was wrong. As the seasons changed and there was still no word from Merv, Susie became depressed. So much so that her mother took notice. Out of concern for her daughter, Miriam had approached Daniel's mother in the hopes of finding out more information about Merv. From the moment she did, Merv's name was rarely mentioned again in the Miller home   . Susie was encouraged to forget Merv.

It was the spring when Susie turned eighteen that Merv returned to his cousin's farm but nothing was ever mentioned by anyone as to either why he had returned or why he had left so abruptly. No one asked, including Susie. It took him six weeks to finally approach Susie and ask to take her home in his buggy. And when he did, Susie noticed that he was a changed person. She couldn't quite put her finger on it, but he was, indeed, different.

After only seeing Susie for a month, he had surprised her by requesting that she'd marry him that fall. Against the wishes of her father, for reasons he wouldn't mention, both Merv and Susie joined the church and were married at the Miller home that October.

For the first half of their marriage, Merv worked at a local carpentry shop. Within the first four years of their marriage, Susie gave birth to their three *kinner*: Gid, Sylvia and David. After the birth of David, there had been no more talk of having additional *kinner*. Not between Merv and Susie. That did not, however, stop the women in the *g'may* from talking and wondering. After all, the other women in the community knew that, at the age of twenty-eight, Susie was still in her prime childbearing years. There was plenty of speculation as to why they didn't have more children.

It didn't help matters that Merv began to have problems with his job. For the first few years of their marriage, he continued to work hard at the cabinetry shop. It was shortly after David's birth when he began to show up late. There were even days when he didn't show up at all. Susie had fretted about this, wondering why he slept late or even never left the house at all. The more she asked him what was wrong, the deeper Merv withdrew inside himself.

And then he had been fired.

That had been almost five years ago. Five long years of sullen attitudes and snappy remarks. It was almost as if Merv blamed Susie for his problems. He had managed to find some work outside of the Amish community with another carpenter but that, too, only last for a year. After that, he picked up odd jobs for himself, building things for *Englischers*. Yet it was sporadic work, certainly not a steady income.

So Susie had picked up the slack by helping Leah with the bakery when their *mamm* died in the accident.

Her thoughts were interrupted when the door to the kitchen opened. Susie jumped at the noise and braced herself. She had spent the past hour cleaning the kitchen, washing dishes and even scrubbing the floor so that Merv could have no complaints about the house.

"*Mamm*!" Sylvia said, a smile lighting up her face as she ran inside, carrying a basket full of eggs. "Those chickens sure were ornery this evening! Had to chase them back into the coop! But look what I have!" As she ran toward her mother, she stumbled and dropped the basket. Eggs tumbled out, some cracking and spilling onto the freshly washed floor.

Susie caught her breath and bit her lower lip, wanting to lash out at her *dochder* but knowing that it had been an accident.

The young girl knelt on the floor, the front of her burgundy dress dirty and wet from broken egg. She lifted her big brown eyes to meet her mother's and the tears began to fall. "Oh *Mamm*," she cried. "I'm so terribly sorry!"

Susie took a deep breath and stepped over eggshells and runny goo to help Sylvia stand. "Now, now," she said softly, trying to reassure her daughter. "An accident is just that: an accident. But let's have you hurry upstairs to change. I'll wash that in the morning, ja?"

As Sylvia scurried up the stairs, sniffling as she did so, Susie sighed and bent down to clean up the broken eggs. Twelve broken and ten cracked, she counted. Could have been worse.

"What is this mess?"

Susie cringed as she heard the words, deep and full of criticism. She looked up and saw Merv standing in the doorway. "Just some broken eggs, tis all," she mumbled, hating how meek her voice sounded.

"Can't do anything just right, can you?" he snapped.

Oh, how she wanted to toss one of those cracked eggs at him! She wanted to talk back to him, tell him that it was Sylvia's mess, not hers! But she knew that it would get her nowhere. So, instead of talking back, she said a silent prayer to God, asking Him for the strength to continue carrying this burden that had been placed on her shoulders, begging Him to help her find the root of Merv's problems and pleading with Him to continue loving her so that she could be as godly a woman as she wanted to be, free of evil thoughts toward her husband.

Part Three

As you well know, the flesh is weak,
And fears the smallest pain.
So fill us now with your Spirit,
This we ask you from the heart,
That we may remain steadfast unto the end,
And bravely meet the suffering,
Not being fearful of the pain.

Ausbund, Song 61 Verse 2

Therefore do not be anxious about tomorrow,
for tomorrow will be anxious for itself.
Sufficient for the day is its own trouble.

Matthew 6:34

The Garden

Leah sat on the grass by the garden, staring at the neatly planted rows of corn, beans, tomatoes, and squash. The *kinner* had been weeding a lot recently, so it was almost picture perfect. Each row was lined up with soft mounds of dirt at the root base. In between the rows, there were soft imprints of bare feet from where the girls had walked. A small sparrow landed by the tomatoes and, after quickly looking around, picked at the ground before flying away. The season was ending but her vegetable garden still harvested plenty of food for her family.

It warmed Leah's heart that she hadn't needed to remind Rebecca, Sarah, and Anna to weed the garden. They had taken it upon themselves to see that the garden was weed-free. Leah suspected that Rebecca had taken charge of her younger siblings. At twelve, Rebecca was almost a mini-mother to the other *kinner* and a true blessing to Leah. Aaron and Amos often helped their *daed* with chores around the barn and, during the summer, both sons worked with their *daed* on building those rockers that the tourists liked so much.

It was their younger two sons that worried her. Marcus was only six years old and Henry was only four. They spent most of their time with their *aendi* Esther so that Leah could work at the bakery. During the week, on the slower days, the boys might join her at the store before the dinner hour, but always in the afternoon, someone other than Leah tended them.

And, of course, there was her brother, Tobias. Light-headed and blue eyed, Tobias was the baby of the family, even though he was almost ready for rumschpringe. She was worried about him to no end. She knew that she would have to find the time to take him back to the doctors if his nausea and fatigue continued. Facts were facts, even if they were ugly ones. It was clear that Tobias was not well.

From behind her, she heard the kitchen door open and

footsteps pad across the porch. Leah glanced over her shoulder, wondering who was leaving the house. The younger children were playing in the field down by the stream while the boys were still helping their *daed*. Sarah had gone visiting with their friends at a neighboring farm, although she was due home at any time to help prepare supper. And Rebecca was walking down the path to the pond, her willowy figure just barely visible on the hill. She was growing so fast, Leah thought. And so tall! In just a few short years, Rebecca would begin her *rumschpringe*[5] and, without doubt, there would be many Amish boys who would ask her to ride back home with them in their buggies.

Everyone was busy doing their own thing.

So Leah was curious.

She was surprised to see Sadie, hurrying down the driveway toward the bakery. She kept looking around, as if searching for someone. But, when she slipped into the store, Leah realized that something was wrong. Terribly wrong. Why on earth would sister Sadie be returning to the bakery when it had been closed for almost an hour?

---

[5] Period of time before youths become baptized

Earlier that Day

Whoopie Pie Place

Quietly, Susie slid out from underneath the sheet and quickly began to dress. She picked a dark blue dress for it matched her mood: dark and dismal. She grabbed a handful of pins from the chipped china bowl on the dresser and her prayer *kapp* before hurrying out of the room. It did no good to awaken to listen to his grumbling, she told herself. The sooner she was up, the sooner she could leave. It was her day to open the bakery.

Downstairs, as she walked into the kitchen, she spotted the sink of dirty dishes and the mess she had left on the kitchen counter last night. What was wrong with her? She had spent so much time cleaning the kitchen the previous afternoon but Merv's outburst over the broken eggs had diminished any possible inclination that she might have had to clean up after supper. Instead, Susie had left the dishes on the counter and excused herself from the kitchen as soon as she could. She went to bed early, even though she had been anything but tired.

Now, she was faced with extra chores for surely she could not leave to go to work with a mess like this in the kitchen. What would Merv have to say about that? Susie sighed and began to quickly wash the supper plates, scolding herself for yet again, having put off finishing her chores before going to bed.

She would barely have enough time to prepare the family breakfast before they all came in from their morning chores and before she had to leave for the bakery. It seemed as though her life was spiraling out of control. After the death of her parents, it seemed that she no longer had a grasp on anything at all.

"You aren't going to *that* bakery this morning!"

She froze at the sound of his voice. *Why, oh why,* she thought. If she had only washed the dishes the previous evening, she would have been long gone before he would walk in. She would have been happily on her way. She would not have to turn around and face the start of the day with yet one more confrontation.

"Merv, it's my day to open…"

His brow knit together in a deep frown. His eyes fired at her as he waved his hand at her, dismissing her comment. "Nonsense. You know we're holding church service here next weekend! This house needs to shine, Susie. And that sure won't happen if you are at that bakery every day!"

"But Merv," she countered, trying as hard as she could to calm his temper. "They need me. Leah is tending to Tobias and Sadie hasn't been feeling well. And you know that Lydia. Why, getting her to show up on time and stay late will take an act of God to get her to do it willingly."

With gritted teeth, Merv glared at her. "How you going to clean this house?"

"I'll get it done," she responded, hating the way her words sounded so weak and whiny. "You'll see."

He made a noise in his throat, clearly indicating that he didn't believe his wife. But, instead of arguing, he moved over to the doorway. "I expect breakfast ready when I'm done with chores," he snapped before pushing the door open and disappearing outside.

It was almost two hours later that Susie fiddled with the key in the lock of the door to Whoopie Pie Place. As it opened and she slipped inside, she felt as though a weight was lifting from her shoulders. The sweet smell of yesterday's baking wiped away her worries and problems. For the next few hours, she was in the one place where she would find solace, comfort and joy.

Before she tucked the key back into her apron pocket, she leaned over and flipped the "OPEN" sign on the window so that it faced the outside. It was a habit of hers for they wouldn't be open for another two hours. But Susie knew that if she didn't flip it now, she'd forget later.

She hurried to the kitchen to begin making large batches of dough for the afternoon bread. There was enough bread from the previous afternoon's batch to hold over for the morning crowd. It was creeping up on the weekend and they would have to double their baking for the Saturday crowds. And then she still had to worry about next week when she would host the Sunday service.

"Bright and early, I see," Leah chirped as she swept into the store. "Ummm, smells *wunderbaar gut*! You already have bread baking, then? Good for you, Susie!" Smiling, she set her basket on the edge of the counter nearest the door in the kitchen. "You must have started extra early today!"

Susie smiled at the compliment, feeling better already. Leah had that magical way about her, a way of making people feel six feet tall with just one twinkle of her eye. Of course, she also could tear someone down with that same eye, but never without just cause.

"I heard Laverne say she was bringing in a special group of people today that came all the way from Nebraska!" Leah continued as she hurried to the large commercial oven to oversee how the bread was baking. "You put this in how long ago, Susie?"

"Twenty minutes," she replied. "Nebraska? You don't say."

Shutting the oven door, Leah rubbed her hands together. "*Ja*, Nebraska. That's way out west, I seem to reckon. Said we are to make a special fuss over the tour leader. A woman named Juanita, I think she said. I'm going to ask that you and Lydia come out to meet her."

"Sounds right nice," Susie replied while keeping her attention on the twenty-four small cake bottoms that were spread out before her. She was spooning fluffy white filling on them and had the tops ready to finish the whoopie pies. She glanced at the clock over the door. "This batch is almost finished."

As if on cue, the bell rang, indicating that someone had

entered the front of the store. It was too early for a customer. Leah frowned and glanced at Susie who merely shrugged her shoulders. "I'll go check that," Leah sighed, slightly annoyed at the inconvenience but also curious as to who was already at the store.

Jenny Yoder was waiting outside, her eyes bright and sparkling, as if she had a secret that she was itching to tell. Yet, despite her glow, she merely greeted Leah with a warm "*Gut mariye.*"

"So early, Jenny," Leah observed, a glance at the clock to insure that it was still before opening hours. "Is everything alright then?"

"Oh *ja, ja,*" the older lady replied, that glow still more than apparent in her eyes. "Have a lot of errands to do and saw your OPEN sign. Thought I'd pop in to get my bread and whoopie pies." She hesitated for a moment then leaned forward. "Need to visit some farms for extra orders of celery," she whispered.

Ah ha, Leah thought, her heart flip flopping in her throat. *The secret is no more, then.* Extra orders of celery always indicated an upcoming wedding in the family. Was Jenny suggesting that her son, Manny, was going to ask Sadie to become his wife?

"You don't say," Leah replied, cocking her head to one side and watching Jenny's expression for further indications. "Lots of weddings coming up, I reckon. Anyone in particular that you are getting celery for?"

At this question, Jenny's eyes darted away and she began fussing with her purse. "No, no," she said, although her tone said otherwise. "No one to speak of, so to say."

Leah held back her smile but knew what Jenny was really saying. She wasn't certain how she felt about Sadie getting married. In many ways, it would be a sad day. After all, Sadie was more than a younger sister. She was a dear friend, someone that Leah could always count on for extra help and a shoulder to cry on. "Well," she said, turning to hide the emotion that began to swell in her eyes. "Then I reckon we should get your goods, *ja?*"

The morning started off slowly. Being the tail end of summer, the volume of tourists was beginning to dwindle. Mothers were focused on back-to-school so the *Englische* visitors began to take on a different characteristic. Gone were the young children who eagerly touched everything in the displays, much to Leah's chagrin. Gone were the silly questions from middle aged men and women, people who Leah always had the distinct feeling were judging the Amish lifestyle as they compared it to their own. Instead, the visitors tended to be retired housewives who came with stars in their eyes and smiles on their faces.

It was the Miller sisters' favorite time of year.

"Lands sake!" Leah said when she saw the tour bus pull outside their door. She looked at the clock. Ten forty-five. "Laverne's early!" She looked over at Sadie who was straightening up the shelves near the entrance. Leah hurried to the kitchen door and poked her head through. "Get ready, girls. Laverne's early."

Lydia looked up, flour on her hands and apron. "What? She's never early." She shook her head and clicked her tongue disapprovingly. "Thought you talked to her about that."

Leah frowned but didn't reply. They had a staunch rule with Laverne to call ahead if her tour bus was going to come early. Leah always liked to be standing outside with Sadie on the porch, waving to greet the guests when they arrived. It was a small gesture of friendship that made a big difference, at least in the Miller sisters' mind.

"Oh help!" Susie hurried over to the oven. "I think I burned the bottom pans!"

Lydia huffed as she spun around. "That's the second time this week, Susie! I think you have flies rattling 'round your head! What's going on with you?"

"Girls! No bickering today!" Leah snapped and quickly shut the door. She hurried to the open screen door, pleased to see

Sadie outside, already greeting the guests with a warm smile and cups of cool meadow tea. With one hand, Leah opened the door and joined her younger sister. Meeting the guests from Laverne's tours was always the part of the day that Sadie seemed to love the most. It tickled Leah to watch her sister shake everyone's hand and say a kind word. She had a natural flair for warming up to strangers, something that the rest of the family struggled with on a daily basis. Oh, Leah knew that she masked it well, but she often wished that it came naturally to her.

"*Wilkum*," Leah said as the older women started to mingle about the porch, a few hesitating before approaching the steps. "Come in and browse, *ja*? We've been waiting for you." She forced a smile on her face, her eyes seeking out Laverne's blue eyes and bright grin. "*Gut mariye*, Laverne," she said. "Early today, I see?"

With an apologetic shrug, Laverne looked away, her eyes searching through the crowd of women. Her ginger hair caught the sun and, without realizing it, Leah had to smile at her *Englische* friend. She had been a godsend to Whoopie Pie Place and there was no way that Leah could stay upset with her for such a minor infraction.

"Leah," Laverne said as she placed her hand on the arm of one of the women. "I want you to meet Juanita. She arranged this tour all the way from Nebraska." Laverne beamed as she said the word Nebraska. "I don't think I've had any tours all the way from Nebraska!"

"Why, that's a whole world away!" Sadie exclaimed. "I bet it's right *wunderbaar* out there!"

The woman, Juanita, seemed to glow with delight at the attention from the Amish woman. It radiated from within and instantly became contagious. "It sure felt that way driving here," she said. Her voice was soft and sweet. Immediately, Leah knew that, had Juanita lived closer, they would definitely have become friends. "I don't fly, you see," Juanita added, leaning forward and whispering the words as if telling a secret.

"Me, neither!" Sadie added in her own whisper then laughed at her own little joke. The other three women joined in.

"Come in," Leah said, a real smile on her face. The tension had vanished from her shoulders. "I arranged a special something for you, Juanita. A box of specialty whoopie pies to take home. A gift from us to you."

It was times like these, Leah thought, that she thanked the good Lord that her *mamm* had started Whoopie Pie Place. Meeting good hearted Christians like Juanita and Laverne made it all worthwhile.

Lydia

"How on earth are we going to fulfill all these orders?"

It was early afternoon and the last tour bus was due in an hour. Susie and Lydia had taken a break to rethink their strategy for baking the orders that were due in the upcoming weeks. There was a cool breeze blowing in through the open back door and, despite the heat emanating from the oven, the kitchen was rather pleasant for a late summer.

"Lydia," Susie said, a slight edge to her voice. "If you would let me finish…"

Lydia tossed her hands in the air and shook her head. "You can explain it twenty ways to midnight and it still makes no sense! Even with the help of the *kinner*, we have no choice but to hire extra help from the *g'may*!"

Susie rolled her eyes, a gesture that, she knew, infuriated Lydia. "Then we won't make any profit, Lydia! We have to try!"

"I think your common sense just went the way of the cows after milking!" Lydia snapped. "Right out to pasture!" With a huff, she stood up from the table where she had been sitting and stormed out the back door.

She needed a moment, just a short one, to be alone and to think. Her head was beginning to hurt and she felt tired, a tired that came on her when she was upset. If only she could go home, escape the stress of dealing with her sisters at Whoopie Pie Place. Leah was always so bossy and in charge. Susie always acted as if Lydia didn't know a pea from a hill of beans. And Sadie…well, Lydia didn't have any complaints with Sadie. She stayed out of everyone's business and was quick to smile when the tour buses arrived.

"Hey Lydia," someone called from the shade of the barn.

She stopped walking and squinted in the sun. To her surprise, Tobias was sitting down, his legs outstretched and his straw hat resting on his legs. She noticed that he looked pale and thin, the realization that she hadn't really spent any time with her younger brother striking her as odd. Where had Tobias been these past few days, anyway?

"You supposed to be helping brother Jacob, ain't so? Thought he was doing haying this week."

Tobias lifted a finger to his lips and motioned for her to join him. Lydia frowned. Her bare feet crossed the dry ground as she walked toward the barn. When she approached him, she crouched down, annoyed to hear her knees crack…a reminder that she was getting older. "*Wie gehts*?" she asked.

He glanced around, his dark eyes large in his almost translucent face. He was a pretty boy, taking after their *mamm*'s side more so than their *daed's*. He had always been a favorite of their parents, being the youngest of their *kinner* and also the most sensitive. Now, as he lifted his eyes to look at Lydia, she saw sorrow written on his face.

"You won't tell sister Leah?"

Lydia frowned. She didn't want to make a promise she couldn't keep but she was certainly curious as to what Tobias had niggling at his mind. "I can't rightly promise that, Tobias," she admitted. "If something's wrong, I can't hide it from her."

"A secret? Please?"

The longing in his eyes tugged at her heart. Oh why had the good Lord not blessed her with her own *boppli*? She almost felt like crying, wishing with all of her might that she could wrap her arms around Tobias, her maternal urge was so great. Yet, such displays of affection were saved for small *kinner* and certainly not the custom among siblings. With a sigh, she nodded her head. "A secret, *ja*."

Once again, he glanced around to make sure no one was nearby. "I'm worried," he started, his words so soft that she could almost not hear him. "It's Sadie."

At this, Lydia blinked and frowned. Sadie?

Her face must have shown her surprise for Tobias nodded his head. "She's been sick. A lot," he whispered. "I think she has what I have. I heard her in the bathroom yesterday and this morning."

Leaning back on her heels, Lydia stared at the sky. A dozen different thoughts rattled through her mind but they kept coming back to just one. Sick? Mornings? Her first thought was complete dismay. How could Sadie have let something like this happen? Her reputation would be ruined. The entire family's reputation would be ruined! Then, as the realization sank in, Lydia felt anger. If this was true, she thought, how could God give Sadie what she, Lydia, prayed so hard to conceive! The color faded from her cheeks and Lydia stood up, too quickly for she suddenly felt dizzy. She lifted her hand to her head and felt the dampness of a cold sweat.

"I…I have to go, Tobias," she mumbled. "You tell Leah I'm feeling poorly. I need to get home and lie down."

Tobias scrambled to his feet, holding his hat in one hand as he reached out to grab his older sister's arm. "You won't say nothing, *ja*? It's a secret!"

Lydia nodded. *Oh*, she thought, *I won't be telling anyone that secret*. "A secret, *ja*," she agreed, then turned to hurry away, not even hearing Tobias as he called out to her. She had to get home, had to get away from Whoopie Pie Place. She needed to be alone in order to ponder this possibility. If only Abe would be understanding and offer a shoulder for her to cry on, she thought. Instead, she knew that she could tell no one for this secret was far too great a burden to place on anyone. In fact, she was sorry that Tobias had shared it with her in the first place.

Susie

It was nearly twenty minutes later when Tobias poked his head into the kitchen, his abrupt appearance startling Susie and causing her to knock over a container of flour. With white particles floating through the air, she gasped and clutched at her chest.

"Tobias!"

He laughed, a curl of his blond hair covering one of his eyes. He scurried into the kitchen to help her clean up the mess. "Sorry, Susie. Didn't mean to scare you so!"

"Well you sure did a great job of that!" she snapped, but her tone was only partially angry.

As he was scooping the small mound of flour back into the container, he glanced at her. "Lydia went home. Told me to tell you she's sick."

His words cut through Susie and she immediately froze, her hand in midair as she stared at her younger brother. "She's what?"

He nodded his head, oblivious to the scowl that crossed his sister's face. "*Ja*," he said, wiping his hands on his black work pants. White smears of flour were left behind. "Said she needed to lie down a spell."

Pressing her lips together, Susie breathed in heavily. How often could Lydia be sick? If it weren't a headache or extra fatigue, it would be heart palpitations or stomach pains. Everyone knew that her real problem was in her head. If only she would stop fretting so about having a *boppli,* the good Lord would surely show Lydia the way. He always provided. Didn't Matthew 6:26 say it best? *Look at the birds of the air, that they do not sow, nor reap nor gather into barns, and yet your heavenly Father feeds them. Are you not worth much more than they?*

"That's it!"

Tobias jumped at Susie's exclamation. He backed away as Susie stormed out of the kitchen and into the storefront. She could feel his presence, following behind her, his curiosity surely piqued.

"Leah!"

Her older sister had been checking voice messages and held up one finger to silence Susie as she jotted down notes on a scrap piece of paper. When she finished, she pressed a button on the machine and turned to face Susie, a look of concern on her face. "Ja?"

"I've had it with sister Lydia! I can't do all this by myself!"

Susie watched as Leah took a deep breath and braced herself for the news. "Now what?" Leah asked.

"She's left again!" Susie tossed her hands into the air. "Just like that! Stormed off, went home, doesn't feel well. You know the story. I can't have this. It's too much stress put on my shoulders and it's just not fair."

"No," Leah admitted. "No it's not."

"And I have church service next week," Susie admitted, her shoulders hunching forward. She felt heaviness on her chest and emotion in her throat. She glanced over her shoulder at Tobias and frowned. Out of the corner of her eye, she saw Leah motion him to return to the kitchen, to leave them in peace.

"We will help you, Susie," Leah said as she walked forward. "Mayhaps we ought to close the store for a few days. It seems we all could be using a break."

Blinking her eyes to hold back the tears, Susie shook her head. "*Nee*," she replied, feeling her own pulse quicken. While something had to be done about Lydia, they had too much on the line with those two big orders in the upcoming weeks. They needed every willing hand to make sure that they were able to deliver what they promised. Closing wasn't an option. "That's not fair to the tourists. Not fair to Laverne."

"Oh hogwash!" Leah scoffed. "Laverne is understanding. If we give her enough notice…"

And then the floodgates opened. Susie felt the tears sliding down her cheeks and, despite her embarrassment at openly crying, she didn't try to stop them. "It's not that," she cried. "I can't stay home. I just can't."

Leah frowned, clearly not understanding what her sister was saying.

"It's Merv," Susie admitted, her eyes on the floor. "He's so upset with me. All the time." With a finger covered in flour, she wiped at her eyes. "Constantly criticizing. Constantly putting me down."

Leah placed her hand on Susie's arm and forced her to look up. "What are you saying, Susie?"

"Oh, I pray at night," she said, a heartsick smile on her lips. "I get down on my knees and pray that Merv will change. I loved him so much at one point in time, of that I'm sure." The words sounded horrid to her ears and she suddenly felt regrets at having spoken them out loud. "*Mayhaps* I could love him once again," she whispered. "If only he'd let go of his anger."

Her sister caught her breath and lifted her chin, staring at Susie with fierce eyes. "You need to speak to the bishop."

The words had barely slipped through Leah's lips before Susie grabbed at her hand. "*Nee!*" She held Leah's hand tightly. "You must promise to never tell anyone."

"But..."

"Promise!"

Leah frowned. Susie knew exactly what her sister was thinking. How could she not? It wasn't often that such things were heard of, although one would have to assume that it was merely because marital problems were kept private and not shared; not even with extended family. Only once in her life time had she heard of a bishop getting involved with a couple who seemed to be having issues. But those issues involved something worse than just harsh words and anger. Alcohol had been involved. If Susie recalled properly, the husband worked among the *Englische* at a construction company and was too often tempted by the non-Amish workers who would drink at a bar after their day's work. The guilt of breaking the *Ordnung* must have weighed heavily on the husband and he took it out on his wife. After strict counseling with the bishop and a change of employment for the husband, the problem seemed to have ultimately disappeared.

But alcohol was not involved in *their* problem, Susie told herself. It was Merv's horrible temper and hostile anger toward her. The root of his problem? She truly didn't know. But going to the bishop would surely create even more issues. Merv would be humiliated and embarrassed. She shuddered to think of how he would react should the bishop decide to take action and confront him.

"Why don't you go home early, then? Sadie can finish up the baking, *ja*?"

Susie shook her head. "*Nee*," she replied. "That's the last thing I want. Being here makes me right happy, even if Lydia is so unreliable."

Leah

The last tour bus had just left the parking lot, the sound of its noisy diesel engine fading the further away it went. Leah watched from the store's window, a strong wave of fatigue washing over her. It had been a long day and she was both physically and mentally drained. She needed to close up the shop and head over to the store to pick up some supplies for next week and to place a bulk order for the upcoming wedding and convention.

She had arranged for Michelle to pick her up at four-thirty and only had a few minutes to prepare. Quickly moving to the kitchen, she accidentally ran into Susie who was hurrying past the door, carrying a batch of fresh-made whoopie pies. With a gasp, Leah watched as the whoopie pies tumbled to the ground.

"Oh help!" Leah said, steadying Susie before she bent down to start picking them up. "Didn't see you there, Susie. Let me help you with those."

"*Ach vell*, all is *gut*," Susie replied, avoiding Leah's eyes as she crouched down beside her and helped. "At least these were wrapped." She stood back up and placed the whoopie pies on the counter. "It wouldn't be the first batch I have ruined today. *Mayhaps* Lydia is right," she sighed. "*Mayhaps* I have flies rattling 'round in my head."

Leah wished that she had some words of encouragement for her sister. But she knew not what to say. She could not begin to imagine the hardship of living with an angry man who never had a kind word to speak in her direction. "Never you mind, Lydia. You have no such flies in your head. But I am concerned for you. Why have you not left? The baking should have already been finished an hour ago. Sadie is gone, *ja*?" Leah asked, looking around the room.

"*Ja*, she left about thirty minutes ago. That child wears herself out sometimes. She is looking pale, *ja*?" replied Susie.

Leah didn't have time to answer for she heard the honking of the car horn. Grabbing her handbag, she headed toward the door. "Michelle is again right on time. I will see you in the morning Susie. Don't forget to lock up and we'll talk more about..." She hesitated, not quite certain of how to refer to the news that Susie had shared. "...your situation tomorrow, *ja*?"

Outside on the porch, Leah breathed in the fresh air, still smelling of fresh baked goods emanating from the store. She hurried down the porch steps and over to the vehicle, which Michelle had already turned around ,waiting for Leah. Opening the door and climbing into Michelle's mini-van, Leah let out a sigh. How good it felt to be inside a cool place! Despite her love of the Amish culture and religion, the only ones that she knew, she certainly wouldn't have minded the *Ordnung* permitting air conditioning during the hotter months, especially in a place where so much baking was involved!

"Hey there, I have the air on for you. I figured you would like something to cool you off after being in that hot bakery," Michelle said, a smile on her face and a twinkle in her eyes. "I have no clue as to how you and your sisters can work in such heat. Won't the Bishop allow you to have air conditioning in the bakery? It is a business, after all, and would be helpful to the customer's comfort."

"We tried that with the bishop. We were lucky enough to have permission for electricity to run the kitchen appliances!" Leah said, shaking her head. "I reckon that if the customers complained, that would be one thing. But we're too successful to argue that the hot air keeps them away."

Leah and Michelle's relationship was an odd one. Michelle was an *Englischer* and the driver for a lot of the local Amish community. From the time they had met as young girls, when Michelle would sometimes ride along with her father who drove for the Amish community to support his family, the two young girls shared a friendship of closeness. Neither understanding the other's way of living, they agreed to disagree on most things. But Leah knew that she could always count on Michelle. Not just to arrive on time, but to be a good and faithful friend.

Reaching behind her seat, Michelle swerved on the road. As she did, Leah grabbed the handle to hold on and glanced at Michelle. The *Englischer* seemed oblivious to the momentary panic that her companion had felt as she handed a folder to Leah.

"This is the information you asked me about when you requested a ride. I did a quick search on Google and came up with a few things. A lot of it is over my head in understanding. Why they can't just put things in simple language is beyond me."

As Michelle continued to rattle on about the Internet and all of its good and bad points, Leah opened the folder. Reading over the contents, she became engrossed in what she was reading and, without knowing it, ignored her friend.

"You haven't heard a word I have said, Leah Mast! What's going on?" Michelle asked, placing a hand on her friend's arm to get her attention. "Something is wrong and I can tell just by the look on your face. Something amiss with Tobias? Is he sick again?" She paused, a stern look on her face. "Leah, what are you not saying?"

Looking up from the paper in her hand, she looked at Michelle. Knowing that of all the people around her, Leah could trust her. "*Ach*, I think he is, Michelle. I've seen signs that do not please me," she admitted. "It gives me cause to believe that possibly his sickness has returned. I cannot thank you enough for getting this information to me. To find time to read these before anyone sees them will be a challenge, for sure and certain."

"You do carry the weight of your family on your heart and shoulders, Leah. What can I do to help? Does he need to see the doctor? Can I help you get him to one? I have a cousin in the Cincinnati area that works at the Cincinnati Children's hospital. Perhaps she can recommend a doctor there?"

"Yes, I do need your help. I need to take him to the doctor but I fear Cincinnati would be too far. Mayhaps a local one?" responded Leah.

Michelle pulled her mini-van into the parking lot of Walnut Creek Cheese, one of the local bulk stores in Holmes County. Frequented by all the locals, Amish and English, as well as the tourists, on some days, the parking lot at Walnut Creek was chock full of horse and buggies, tour buses and automobiles. Today was no exception. Getting out of the van, Leah noticed one of Laverne's tour buses. Leah guessed that Laverne had brought the Nebraska group to shop for some meats and cheeses, which were a specialty here.

Completing her shopping for the bakery and a few things for home as well, Leah unloaded her cart of goods into the back of Michelle's van. A woman, who was obviously a tourist, began taking pictures of Leah. Turning her head to prevent this, Leah noticed that the lady was getting closer. Covering her face, she asked nicely for the woman to stop taking her picture.

"I just want one good picture. What's wrong with that?" the lady spouted harshly at Leah. "You Amish make money off the tourists here but act like we are villains when we just want to take your picture."

Hearing the harsh words addressed at her friend, Michelle jumped out of the van, quickly helping Leah load her groceries into the van.

"Get in, I'll get these groceries." Michelle told Leah.

"No, I'll not. These are my groceries and I will continue," she whispered back. "But thank you anyway." She glanced over her shoulder. "She's leaving anyway."

Getting into the van when they were ready to leave, the two women just looked at each other. Not sure whether to laugh or cry, they began laughing.

"Some tourists sure do rub me the wrong way," Michelle

said, looking at Leah.

"*Ja*, me too, I reckon. At least some of the time, but there are so many nice people that come. We cannot let one bad apple spoil the whole bushel," Leah admitted. "I will say that I would have loved to have stuck my tongue out at her. That would give her a good picture of the Amish lady. *Ja*?"

Once back at the bakery, Michelle turned serious.

"Here, take this. It's the name of a local doctor. I want you to take Tobias there to see this doctor. I took my son to him once and I really like him. He comes highly recommended. I took the liberty of calling and making an appointment and I have cleared my schedule so that I can drive you. If that's not okay with you, I will call and cancel it. "

Studying the piece of paper Michelle had given to her, she saw that Michelle had done just that: made Tobias an appointment. A rush of emotion overcame Leah. Although she suspected Tobias wasn't feeling well, knowing she was taking him to the doctor made it more of a reality. Leah looked up at her friend, fighting the urge to cry. It wasn't proper to show such emotion. "Thank you, Michelle," she finally said, folding the paper and slipping it into her handbag. "This appointment date will be right *gut*."

Sadie

As the afternoon turned into evening, Sadie stared in the small mirror that hung on the wall of her bedroom. Her brown hair peeked out from beneath her prayer *kapp* and her large, gentle eyes stared back at her. She gave a big sigh as she glanced at the door, making certain that it was still shut tight. The last thing she wanted was anyone to walk into the room. Not now.

Standing in front of the small mirror, she raised her hands to feel her breasts. It took her a second to find the small, round spot, but when she did, she felt the sharp, shooting pain throughout her right breast and moving into her left one. Wincing, she quickly dropped her hands and squeezed her eyes shut, willing the pain to go away.

It had been ten days since she had first noticed the tenderness in that area. She had never felt such swollen, tender pain in her breasts, not even during her monthly cycle. She had hoped it would go away, hoped that it was normal. She was afraid to ask her sisters. No, she corrected herself. She was embarrassed. And now, it was so tender and painful that she could ignore it no longer.

Oh, she had tried. Tried to ignore the way that it bothered her. Tried to ignore how she was feeling inside, especially in the early evenings. And the mornings? They were just dreadful. But she had pushed herself, knowing that one glimpse into Manny's eyes would correct all that was wrong with this. He loved her. She knew that he did. And after his surprise visit? That had made her feel as if she walked on top of the clouds for the rest of the day.

But she also knew that she had waited long enough. Too much longer and there would be nothing else to do. At least she suspected as much. She didn't know a lot about these things but time was important when it came to certain medical issues. And this was one of them. Manny loved her enough that he would understand...would stand by her side, she reasoned. After all, hadn't he practically asked her about getting married?

Sadie glanced in the mirror one last time before she took a deep breath and hurried out of the room.

Once downstairs, she quickly crossed the kitchen floor and slipped out of the backdoor. She didn't want to bump into Leah for she was always so inquisitive about her comings' and goings'. The last thing that Sadie wanted was to have to voice her concerns for herself. Leah had too much to worry about, with running the business, raising their youngest brother, Tobias, and tending to her own family's needs.

The store had closed over an hour ago. It always closed at four. Sadie glanced around and thought that she saw her oldest sister wandering down the path to the pond that was just over the hill. Sadie knew that Leah frequently went to the pond to sit and think in the afternoons before evening chores. It was the perfect time for Sadie to steal into the store without fear of being disturbed.

She opened the door to the store and hurried to the front counter. With a quick glance over her shoulder to make certain no one had spied her, she slipped around the display case and walked over to the cash register. Her heart was pounding and she had to take a few long, deep breaths in order to calm herself.

It had been too long that she had been procrastinating. Too long that she had put off doing this. Yet, Sadie knew that she had no choice.

She reached out a shaking hand toward the register and then paused. For days, she had been mentally yelling at herself, convincing herself that she had to simply do it. Today, she knew that she no longer had time left to delay.

Shutting her eyes, she said a quick silent prayer before reaching down to pick up the receiver of the telephone on the far side of the register. It felt cold in her hand and she tried to steady her finger as she dialed the number that she knew by heart.

On the other end of the line, there was a brief silence before she heard the sound of ringing. Once, twice. And then a friendly female voice answered the phone with a cheerful "Good evening, Dr. Lohman's office."

Sadie had to force the words from her mouth. Yet, her lips were dry and she felt queasy. Swallowing, she tried to moisten her lips and speak. "I…I…"

The woman on the other end of the phone sounded as if she was used to this hesitation. With a smile in her voice, she said, "What is it, dear? You can speak to me."

"I need to see a doctor," Sadie blurted out, wiping the tear that threatened to fall from her eye. "And right away!"

Book Two

Part One

God said, "Learn from my Son
Meekness of heart,
Without which you will fail.
Through patience and reproach in all suffering,
Take up your cross, and follow after me."

The cross and yoke, My Lord,
I do not want to avoid,
But I beseech you exceedingly
For the strength of patience, because it is
Not with me to always stand fast.

Ausbund, Song 66 Verse 5-6

Blessed are the meek:
for they shall inherit the earth.

Matthew 5:5 KJV

The Kitchen

Leah sighed as she sank into her rocking chair and covered her eyes with her hands. For a few moments, she let her bare feet push the chair back and forth, the rhythmic motion immediately beginning to have a calming effect on her. It had been a long day, of *that* there was no doubt: long and tedious, chock-full of tension, problems, and heartache.

It had started with more quarreling at the bakery, which really shouldn't surprise her anymore, she pondered. It was just one short week until Mary's wedding and three weeks before the big convention. Stress levels were at an all time high, that was for sure and certain. Not to mention that Susie was hosting the *g'may's* church service at her home on Sunday.

Leah shook her head. It would take the help of all four sisters, and Esther as well, to scrub that house from top to bottom after work on Thursday and Friday. Leah rolled her eyes at the thought. Who was she kidding? Saturday, too! There would be no rest for the remainder of the week in order to help their sister have a clean house to welcome the rest of the church district to worship on Sunday.

And that also meant more baking! Fresh bread and pies were definitely most expected from their part, in order to feed the *g'may* after the service. Sadie had offered to make cup cheese, a favorite for many who loved to dip salted pretzels into the gooey cheese or spread it on bread. While that wasn't for Leah, she knew that it would be a welcomed treat during fellowship.

Despite the seriousness of all those problems, they paled in comparison to another one: Tobias.

"Mamm!"

Leah looked up and forced a smile at ten-year-old Sarah. The little girl had changed into her nightgown and was ready to say goodnight to her mamm, all without being asked. She suspected that Sadie had something to do with the kinner being especially quiet that evening. As always, Sadie seemed to read Leah's mind and do what needed to be done in order to help when things were stressful.

"You washed behind those ears, ja?" Leah asked as she put her hands on the little girl's shoulders, twisting and turning her teasingly as if inspecting her.

Sarah nodded her head, missing the teasing tone in her mamm's voice. "Oh *ja*," she said. "And Amos did, too! I saw him."

"Did not!" came the boisterous voice as Sarah's twin, came storming down the stairs. "Whatever she said, I didn't do it, Mamm"

Leah and Sarah blinked at his announcement, watching as he crossed the room and stood before them, hands on his hips and a fierce look on his face. Leah glanced at her daughter and, when their eyes met, they burst out laughing.

"What is it now?" Amos demanded.

"Mayhaps you'll think twice before barging in on a conversation," Leah scolded gently. "Your sister was telling me that you washed behind your ears already. But since you say you didn't, you best be going back upstairs and do it proper now!"

The stunned look on Amos' face almost caused Leah to laugh out loud again. He made a face and kicked at the linoleum, a sheepish expression making him appear humble and embarrassed. "Aw shucks," he mumbled and turned around, heading back upstairs to do as his mamm had said.

Small blessings, Leah thought. Wasn't it what that Englische woman, Lisa Ann, had said at the store earlier? *Count your small blessings for God always provides!*

Earlier that Day

Whoopie Pie Place

Papers were spread across the desk, the surface barely visible. Leah removed her glasses to rub her eyes. It was already eight in the morning and she felt as though there was not enough coffee in the world that could help her have the energy to get through the day.

For two hours, she had been trying to create a schedule for managing the production of the two big orders. The way she figured it, they would need to borrow several additional bread pans and baking sheets for the whoopie pies and the loaves of bread. She knew that the *g'may* would help them by lending whatever was needed but she sure didn't like borrowing from others.

She had created a baking schedule depending heavily upon the cooperation of Susie and Lydia, as well as the assistance of Leah's *kinner* and Tobias. It would require almost round-the-clock work to fulfill the orders and she wasn't certain how Susie's Merv would feel about that. In fact, she wasn't certain how Merv felt about anything anymore.

They hadn't talked about their conversation from the previous week, the one in which Susie had revealed her secret of having to live with Merv's constant anger and criticism toward her. Yet, all the time, Leah thought about what her *schwester* had shared with her. Oftentimes, she wondered how she would have handled a similar situation, had her own husband, Thomas, behaved in such a non-Christian way. Yet, Leah kept concluding that she did not have any answers. There was no way that she could begin to imagine her marriage in any other light than perfect. Oh, she knew that there were days she wanted to put her hand on her hip and give Thomas *that* look. But those days were rare…far and few between. There had never been a time with a cross word spoken from their lips. It just wasn't something that they did.

With a big sigh, she tried to focus, once again, on the

scattered papers and her lists. She didn't have a lot of time as she was taking Tobias to that doctor appointment in another hour. Glancing at the clock, she shook her head, that overwhelming feeling of stress building up inside of her chest. Doctors appointments, helping Susie clean her house for church Sunday, working at the store, tending to her own chores…it was too much to think about today!

"You all right, Leah?"

She turned her head and smiled at Sadie. "Just worried about Tobias," she admitted. Then, gesturing toward the desk, she added, "and all of this. I can barely figure out how we are going to fulfill these orders!"

Sadie walked around the counter and stood behind Leah, peering over her head. She placed her hand on Leah's shoulder to steady herself for a long, drawn out and silent moment. "Oh help," she finally muttered. "This all looks so complicated!"

Leah frowned. *That* didn't help her any. "Mayhaps I should call and tell the convention that we just can't do it," she said, taking off her glasses and pinching the bridge of her nose.

"*Nee, nee!*" Sadie quickly cried out. "We can do this, Leah. I know we can." She leaned over and pointed to one of the pieces of paper. "Look, it's not that hard. We already have twenty baking sheets. The oven holds eight pans at a time, ja? That means we can make seven batches an hour in this oven. We can use the house oven for another four and Esther's, too. That's fourteen batches an hour!"

A big sigh escaped Leah's lips. "That's 140 batches in a ten hour day, Sadie, with no interruptions or issues." She sighed and tapped her finger on the table as she craned her neck to look at her sister. "As if *that* would be possible on a regular day! We need 500 batches and the woman said they had to be fresh."

Sadie chewed on her fingernail, deep in thought for a few seconds. "Mayhaps the Mennonite Church might let us use their ovens for a few days," she offered as a solution. "That would double our numbers!"

A gasp escaped Leah's lips. Of course! The Mennonites! Their *g'may* was particularly close to one of the local churches. In fact, many former Amish joined the Mennonite church when they decided not to go through with the baptism. There was always some distant relative to be found at the nearby Mennonite Church.

But would it work? Furiously, Leah began to scribble on the paper and began to list names of family members that would have to help. With a team of three people at both locations, it could be done. "If Esther were to help..." she began. "That might work out..."

Sadie beamed at the realization that she might have presented a good solution to the logistics problem.

"*Ach*!" Leah groaned. "The bread. They wanted four hundred loaves of bread!"

Another dilemma.

"We normally bake twenty loaves during the week," she said, thinking out loud. "Fifty for weekends. I can't see how we could squeeze in that much bread."

The kitchen door opened and Susie walked out, her apron covered with smudges of flour and shortening. She stopped short when she saw her two sisters huddled over the desk. "*Wie gehts?*" Placing one hand on each of her sisters' shoulders, she leaned over and quickly assessed the information on the piece of paper. "Ah, the bread," she surmised. With a simple nod of her head, she quickly added, "Ask the women of the *g'may* to each make fifteen loaves and pay them for their efforts." She patted both sisters' shoulders, leaving white flour marks on their dresses, and walked away.

It took a moment for Leah and Sadie to think about what Susie had suggested. Then, they looked at each other and grinned.

"Brilliant," Leah whispered.

"Ask the *g'may* to help!" Sadie said, repeating Susie's suggestion with a look of wonder on her face. "That's a right *wunderbaar* idea!"

Leah shut her eyes and said a silent prayer of thanks to God for helping her see the solution. This would mean she would neither have to order extra dry goods for the bread nor hire extra workers to make it. If they lost a little profit, it was well worth it in order to fulfill the order and her obligations.

Standing up from behind her desk, she looked around at all the clutter and sighed. She disliked disorganization, both physical and mental. With her hands on her hips, she glanced over at Sadie. "*Vell*, I reckon I've done all I can with this mess for now!" She pushed her chair under the desk, the feet making a scratching sound against the wood floor. "Best go round up Tobias for this doctor appointment," she added, glancing at the clock. "Driver will be here soon."

Sadie leaned against the counter, watching her oldest sister with a quizzical look on her face. Leah could tell that she wanted to say or ask something but was contemplating just how to do so. Rather than question her outright, Leah began to hunt under the side counter for her purse. Her knees cracked when she bent down and she had to steady herself against the sides before she could reach into the darkness of the lower shelf for her bag.

Sadie took a deep breath. "Last I saw, Tobias was in the back field picking the last of the ground cherries with Jacob," she offered. "Didn't look none to happy about it either."

Setting her bag on the counter, Leah began to ruffle through it, making certain she had enough cash to pay the driver and the doctor. "Ja, I bet," she said, laughing. "Reckon he'll be right happy when we bake up those ground cherry pies, though!"

A smile crossed Sadie's face. She didn't need to speak for Leah to know what she was thinking: Ground cherry pies had been everyone's favorite in the Miller household. It was a tradition that

Leah and Jacob had passed down to their own *kinner.* She sure hoped that they had enough ground cherries from this year's harvest to make enough pies to appease the sweet tooth that ran rampant among the *kinner* in both families.

"I sure hope they picked a good selection of ground cherries," Sadie said, looking off into the distance. But it was clear that her mind was elsewhere.

Leah watched, wondering what she was really thinking. "As do our autumn customers," she said. Then, with a short laugh, she reached out and touched Sadie's arm. "Remember that one tourist last year? Oh, she was a funny one!" Her laughter rang deeper now as she remembered. "Why, the look on her face when she asked what a ground cherry was! That was priceless, for sure and certain!"

"Oh *ja!*" Even Sadie smiled at that memory. Englische tourists were always wondering in amazement at some of the things that the Amish did. "Why, she thought we had made it up!"

Leah gave a soft *tsk, tsk* with her tongue and shook her head. "Not knowing ground cherries! Can you ever imagine?"

"Guess the Englische don't realize that they don't know everything after all, ain't so?"

They both laughed at Sadie's teasing comment, although there was a lot of truth behind her statement. Despite their heavy reliance on technology for living, the Englische tourists often seemed to feel as if it were the Amish who were backward, not them! It was something that caused many Amish in their church district to shake their heads in wonder. Processed food? Daycare? Internet? All of those things took away from the family working together and creating a strong bond that would last generations. In fact, those types of things separated the family, isolating each member in their own world where the individual was at the center, not the collective community or family.

Nee, Leah thought. *That's not for me.*

With a sigh, Leah slung the purse over her arm and headed toward the door. "Best go collect Tobias. He so hates these Doctor appointments. And I don't want to be paying the driver for waiting for him." She glanced at Sadie, noticing the sad look on her face. "Reckon I hate these appointments, too, truth be told. I had so prayed we were done with them. But, God's will..."

She knew better than to question God's will. She had been raised to accept His decisions in her life. *Let us not pray for lighter burdens,* her mamm used to say. *But pray for stronger backs.*

Looking out the screen door on the back of the bakery, Leah wiped her brow and exclaimed, "My, it's going to be exceptionally hot today, *ja*? Indian summer."

Before Leah could walk out the door, Sadie cleared her throat. "Leah, I've need for a ride today. I called Michelle but she said she had to take you and Tobias to Millersburg this afternoon. Would you mind if I rode along with you?"

"You need a ride to where, Sadie?" Leah was startled by the request. It wasn't like Sadie to ask for such favors. "Is it a necessity? It's your day to be here in the bakery. Lord knows we can't leave Susie and Lydia alone for too long. They are likely to destroy the place, give all the whoopie pies away or worse yet, burn the place down trying to outdo each other on who can bake the best."

Looking sheepishly, Sadie responded, "Oh *ja*. It's a necessity. Need to meet someone at the hospital." Hoping that Leah wouldn't ask further, she left it at that. "Besides, it's a slow day, ain't so? Shelves are stocked and no buses scheduled until later this afternoon. We'll be back by then, *ja*? And they can handle the in-between, ain't so?"

Leah eyeballed her, wondering what was going on. However, she knew better than to pry. With a sigh, she acquiesced. "I reckon that's fine, then," she said. "But let Susie and Lydia know you will be gone." She had her hand on the door, pausing for a moment before she looked over her shoulder and added, "And you tell them after I leave, so I don't have to hear all their whining!"

Whatever was Sadie up to, of late? Her behavior had become most peculiar, Leah thought. Sick. Disappearing with her special friend. Locking herself in the bathroom. Sneaking into the store after hours. *Oh help*, she said to herself. *Sure don't need Sadie up to something.* After all, Sadie was the one in the family whom never really gave her much to worry about. But, something was definitely up with her youngest *schwester*. That much was evident in her chocolate brown eyes, no matter how innocent they usually appeared.

Walking toward the barn, Leah noticed Jacob and Tobias returning from the field. She smiled to herself, pleased that their return was just as she expected. That's one thing the Amish were known for, promptness for their meals. She watched as they walked, side-by-side, so similar in stature and appearance. They were the only blue-eyed Miller babies, something that their mamm had always pointed out to the rest of the family. But Jacob had been so much older than Tobias that their bond was not one of brotherly bonding but more authoritative on the part of Jacob.

"Tobias" Leah called, lifting her hand to shield her eyes from the sun. "It's time to wash up now. Our ride will be here shortly."

Even from a distance, she could see the expression on his face change from contentment to concern. "Where we going?" he said as he approached.

She pursed her lips and frowned. "You know we have a doctor's appointment today." She felt as though she was the messenger of bad news but they had discussed this just the previous evening.

"Appointment?" asked Jacob. "What appointment is that, Leah?"

"Tobias hasn't been feeling well of late and I've arranged for him to see that specialist at the hospital this afternoon." Leah responded. "Come on, now, Tobias. Go get cleaned up then."

With his head hanging down and his shoulders slumped forward, he slowly moved his feet in the direction of the house. If her heart broke for his disappointment and apprehension, she knew that she, too, felt the same. Only it was her job to put on a brave face and make certain that he attended that appointment, regardless of the dread they both felt. Over the years, doctors had not delivered a whole lot of good news to Tobias Miller, that was for sure and certain.

When he finally disappeared into the house, Leah turned back to her other brother, somewhat surprised that he had also been watching Tobias. There was a disapproving look on his face, his brow wrinkled in deep creases. She didn't have to be a mind reader to know what he was thinking. If Tobias was going to the hospital to see a specialist, the rest of those ground cherries would have to be picked without his help. That meant Jacob had a long afternoon ahead of him, at least until the older *kinner* returned from school. And that thought did not please him.

"Why, that boy's not that sick anyhow!" Jacob grumbled. "Don't know why you insist on making such a fuss over him. We've been working all morning and he ain't complained none to me." Jacob shook his head and walked away, obviously displeased to have lost a field hand.

Leah watched as Tobias kicked open the kitchen door and walked back across the driveway toward her. He looked less pale than the previous days. Maybe he wasn't as sick as she thought, but she had a feeling, in the pit of her stomach, that something just wasn't right. How she disliked those feelings because they were usually right!

At that moment, there was a rustling sound, the sound of tires on the gravel, on the driveway by the store. Glancing over her shoulder, Leah saw Michelle driving her car into the parking lot by Whoopie Pie Place. Always on time, she thought as she lifted her arm and waved. Michelle waved back and Leah started walking up the lane.

Michelle had a wide smile on her youthful face. Leah couldn't help but think that she was such a kind-hearted soul, a true blessing to the Amish community, but especially to her family. Wouldn't hurt a fly, Leah said to herself.

Or a turtle, she thought, hiding a snicker as she remembered the one time that Michelle's kind-heart almost lost her a world of business among the Amish.

It had been a few years back when Michelle had been driving Henry Swartzentruber, one of the elder Amish men in the community, to a horse sale they were having in Mt. Hope at the auction house. While going down County Rd 77, traffic heavy, and vehicles approaching in the opposite direction, Michelle ran off the road trying to avoid a snapping turtle that was crossing. Although no one was hurt and it was just off the road in a little grass, the sudden swerving of the vehicle had scared Henry.

Later that same evening, old Henry had taken it upon himself to call the chat line, the one used by the Amish, to expose the incident and report that she was a reckless driver. Almost immediately, Michelle stopped getting calls from the Amish that needed drivers. In distress, she came to visit Leah. Leah knew immediately what had happened and made it a point to call the chat line to help rectify the situation.

At the time of the incident, Leah hadn't explained to Michelle what had happened. It was too complicated. After all, she knew that Michelle, like most Englische, were unaware that the Amish used such a telephone number to call for news. They simply call the chat line and, after entering a code, all the recent news was played for them. Besides the spreading of gossip through visits with neighbors, the chat line was a major contributor to the "Amish

Grapevine". Later, when Leah had finally told Michelle, they both had shared a good laugh and the story had continued to be an inside joke between the two of them.

The honking of the van horn brought Leah back to reality. Time to go.

"You going to stand in the middle of the road all day or do you want me to take you somewhere?" Michelle yelled good-naturedly as she hung her head out the van window and waved toward her friend.

"*Ja*, I was just thinking that I hope no turtles cross our path on the road today," Leah retorted teasingly before she turned and gestured for Tobias to hurry along, for he was dawdling so. *What is it with him*, she wondered. As she got into the front passenger seat of the van, Leah greeted her friend with a smile. "We are taking Sadie with us too."

Michelle nodded but didn't say anything.

Leah set her purse on the floor in-between her black sneakers. "She said she called you for a ride. She's going to see someone at the hospital. Sounds peculiar to me. Haven't heard of anyone at the hospital from our *g'may*." With a tilt of her head, Leah studied Michelle for a moment. "You know anything about it?"

Michelle made a simple shrug of her shoulders, neither responding to the question, nor really avoiding it. Instead, her eyes flickered through the window and toward the store. "We need to hurry or you're going to be late. I think I see Tobias coming, but where is Sadie?"

At that moment, Tobias opened the back door and tossed his shoes onto the floor before he sat. He gave Michelle a half-hearted grin as he scooted into the seat and shut the door. Only then did Leah realize that he was holding a sandwich in one hand and his shoes were on the floor.

"Tobias Miller!" she scolded. "Now I know that I clearly

instructed you to wash your feet and put on your shoes!"

"Mmmph," he mumbled, pausing to shove more of the sandwich into his mouth.

"Speak so I can understand you," Leah exclaimed, frustrated at his lollygagging.

Swallowing the food in his mouth, he looked at her, his blue eyes sparkling. "You said to wash up. No mention of my feet."

Michelle choked back a laugh and turned her head to look out the window, hiding her amusement at Tobias' response. Leah, however, gasped at his sassiness and gave him a look. "You knew exactly what I meant," she said disapprovingly.

"*Ja, ja,*" he retorted playfully. "If it makes you happy, I *did* wash my feet. I just didn't have time to put my shoes on 'cause I heard the horn honk and I needed a sandwich. Reckon you'd rather have my feet dirty than being late, *ja*?"

Shaking her head, Leah knew better than to question as to why Tobias washed his feet yet came out of the house barefooted. What was the use? And to see him eat anything these days was always a blessing. Looking at Sadie as she climbed into the van, Leah was thankful to have at least one sibling who didn't give her cause to worry. Or did she?

Leah

"I don't understand," Leah said as she sat in the doctor's office. "What do you mean you want to put him in the hospital and run more tests?"

The doctor sat across from her, his elbows on the desk as he peered at Leah from behind the thick glasses perched on the tip of his nose. He was a patient man, used to dealing with the Amish and their lack of knowledge regarding modern Englische medicine. "His blood cell counts are too low, Leah. We need to run more tests and, depending upon the results, we may be looking at needing a bone marrow transplant."

Leah repeated the words in her head: bone marrow transplant. She would have to ask Michelle to use that Google thing to find out more information about this. "What does that involve?"

The doctor took a deep breath and leaned back in his chair. "Well," he started, averting his eyes. "We like to have a haploid-identical match." He paused and quickly translated that word, which was foreign to Leah. "A parent."

"Oh." Her heart fell inside of her chest.

"If that is not possible, there are siblings but they are not always matches," the doctor continued.

"There are five siblings in the area," Leah offered enthusiastically. "One of them will be able to donate, *ja*?"

The doctor shrugged his shoulders, but not in an unkind way. "That truly depends, Leah. We have to test everyone to see if they would be a genetic match."

"But this is only if his leukemia had worsened?," she said hopefully.

There was a long pause. The doctor removed his glasses and rubbed the bridge of his nose. He seemed hesitant to respond to Leah's question but, after taking a deep breath, he cleared his throat. "I think you need to be prepared for that possibility, Leah."

She knew what *that* look meant. It had been a look that she had seen many times in the past, both before and after her *mamm* and *daed* had passed. She could translate his words without needing to know how the Englische often circumvented the obvious by adding *I think* or *you should* to the facts. Vagueness was an Englische trait that Leah had learned to interpret many years ago.

"I understand," she said stiffly, collecting her purse onto her lap. The grey pleather exterior contrasted with her black apron and purple dress. "When will we need to run these tests and when would the results come in?"

The doctor seemed to change modes, from empathetic bearer of bad news to medical expert with a plan. It was clear that he was more comfortable with the latter than the former. He began to talk swiftly and discuss the different tests that needed to be conducted and, depending on the results, when they would want the family members to come in for testing to see if they could be a donor.

By the end of the meeting, Leah's head was spinning and she wished that she had brought Sadie with her, knowing that her sister could have taken notes and helped organize what the doctor said. As it was now, Leah could barely think straight, never mind remember what the doctor said.

"I'll have my nurse, Jamie, call over to the hospital to make all the arrangements for Tobias. They'll be waiting on him when you get there." Coming around his desk, he lightly patted his hand on Leah's slumped shoulder. "He's going to be in good hands, Leah. You did the right thing by bringing him here as soon as you did."

"We have to go now? We have to take him to the hospital now? No going home first?" Leah spoke quietly as she tilted her head to look up at the doctor. She hated the quiver in her voice, knowing that it exposed her panic. If there was one thing she had learned to dread, it was leaving Tobias overnight in the hospital. Hadn't her own mamm often spent the nights alongside his bed? But that had been years ago and her other kinner had been grown. Leah couldn't possibly do the same, not with her little ones at home waiting for her.

"Leah, I'm sorry. But time could be of the essence in his treatment," he replied. "By the time you get there, we will have it all set up. My nurse, Jamie, will be right in with all the information you need."

Hearing the doctor leave the room, it took every fiber of Leah's being to not fall apart.

Gathering her wits about her when the nurse entered the room, Leah listened, as she explained where to take Tobias at the hospital. Handing Leah the necessary papers, she left the room leaving her alone again. How was she ever going to explain this to Tobias? She needed to gather her thoughts before going in search of him. *Just breathe, Leah. Just breathe* she told herself. *God's will. Remember, God's will.*

As Leah walked towards the door, a sign on the wall of the office caught her attention. It read:

Be still and know that I am God.
Psalms 46:10.

How that spoke to her heart at that precise moment! Leah shut her eyes and said a silent prayer. God would take care of this. She had faith and knew that by letting go and trusting God's will, she was casting away her worries onto His benevolent presence. That sign was more than just a verse from the Book of Psalms; it was a sign that she no longer had to bear the burden of worry alone.

Oh, how she loved the Book of Psalms. She could remember many nights as a child when her father would read from it to the family in the evening hours. They would sit on the floor or at the table, listening intently as he read from the Holy Bible. Sometimes *Daed* would ask questions of the *kinner*, wanting to know what they thought of the verses. Later in life, Leah often thought back to those lessons, realizing that her *mamm* and *daed* had always listened to the answers from their *kinner* with thoughtfulness and respect. Leah could not remember her parents ever reproaching her answers or correcting her. After all, her responses were her own interpretations. And, she had appreciated how her parents would respect that.

Oh mamm, Leah thought, *how I need you right now. Yet I am glad that you cannot see Tobias sick again.*

Opening the door, Leah found Tobias sitting in the waiting area, his focus on the television hanging from the ceiling. He was so interested on what was playing that Leah had to touch his head to get his attention.

"Leah!" exclaimed Tobias. "You scared me."

Laughing, Leah replied, "*Ja*, reckon I did." She tousled his hair and glanced up at the television. Sports. She smiled. "You were too busy watching that TV, *ja*? We need to leave now, Tobias."

Looking around outside, Leah spotted Michelle sitting on a bench fanning herself as though she were a mad woman. "Ach, it's a scorcher out here," Michelle said as Leah and Tobias approached.

"For sure and certain. Why are you not in the van with your air conditioning, Michelle?"

Stammering, she tried to think of words to tell Leah so she wouldn't give away that she was sitting there in hopes to keep contact with Sadie and her whereabouts. "I just thought I would see how you Amish live and see if I could stand the heat," she replied with a smile.

Shaking her head, Leah spoke, "You Englische people sure do have the most peculiar ways."

"Are you ready to leave now?" Michelle asked.

"*Nee*, we aren't ready to leave yet. Have you seen Sadie? It's important that she come now from seeing her friend."

"She was going to see a friend but she didn't tell me exactly where that friend was. I'm sure she will be along soon," Michelle said.

Irritated that Sadie was missing, Leah took a deep breath and counted to ten. She knew that her annoyance was not truly with her sister but at the situation that was facing her youngest *bruder*. With a pounding heart inside of her chest, she finally turned to Tobias and placed a hand on his shoulder. "Tobias," she began slowly. "It seems the doctor would like for you to stay in the hospital for a couple of days. He wants to run some tests on you to make sure you are all right."

"Again! I have to stay again!" The look on his face broke her heart and she had to take a deep breath to fight the tears that threatened to spill from her eyes. "Aw Leah, I don't want to stay. I stayed a long time, last time. Are they going to keep me long again?" asked Tobias, his voice whining but with good reason. Leah remembered far too well the other times when he had been in the hospital. Needles and IVs and medicine that made him feel drowsy and uncomfortable…that was all part of the package.

"*Nee*, just for a couple of days," she replied, not entirely certain that she spoke the truth.

"Will you stay with me, then?" he asked, a hopeful look on his face.

Swallowing, Leah averted her eyes for a moment. "I…I don't think I can stay with you this time, Tobias." Looking back at her youngest *bruder*, she noticed a cloud pass over his face, the same dark cloud that passed over her heart. "Not overnight, anyway."

He nodded his head slowly, knowing better than to argue with her. "*Nee* Leah, I understand you can't stay with me at night." He tried to force a smile. "And you best keep an eye on the bakery.

Lydia and Susie will have each other's hair pulled out if you aren't there to stop them during the day, ain't so?"

Putting her arm around his shoulders, Leah spoke, "*Ach*, that's probably true, Tobias. Of course, if they pull each other's hair out, their *kapps* will hide it. Now, let's get you over to the hospital and have you set up and tucked into your bed for the night, *ja*?" She glanced over his head and looked at Michelle. "I'll be certain to come visiting tomorrow morning and later in the afternoon, once the bakery settles down." As they headed toward the van, she only hoped that she had spoken the truth.

Susie

The house was such a mess! She noticed it the moment she walked through the kitchen door. Despite the silence in the house, it looked as though the kinner had arrived home and been left unattended during the afternoon hours. There were shoes on the floor, a stick by the kitchen table, and pieces of cut-up paper littered the tabletop. Yet, as she looked around, she saw no sign of activity.

She sighed, her chest feeling heavy. She hadn't counted on Leah taking so long with the doctor's visit in town. Nor had she counted on seeing Leah and Sadie return to the store, being dropped off by Michelle but missing one person: Tobias. The look on both women's faces said it all. Bad news had a way of inscribing itself in their expressions. No amount of positive thinking or faith in God could erase the heartache of bad news, especially when it centered on Tobias and his health issues.

Deciding to tackle the task at hand, Susie focused on cleaning. With church Sunday just a few days away, she had a lot to do at home. She knew that the house was a mess. Her *kinner* were too young to help clean. It was all she could do to keep them from being underfoot in the evenings. Luckily, Merv's family had volunteered to help clean, along with Leah's daughters, Rebecca and Sarah, on Saturday. Merv's *grossmammi* was even willing to help watch the *kinner*; thank the good Lord for providing such *wunderbaar gut* small blessings.

While she had managed to wash all of the dishes from breakfast before leaving that morning, she noticed that there were dirty plates, cups, and a pan on the counter. With Gid having been at school all day and Sylvia and David at Merv's mamm's, she couldn't imagine what had happened while she had been working.

"Hullo?" she called out.

No answer.

It was clear that the house was empty. Had the mess been

from the morning hours? If so, that meant that they had been unattended before being taken to school and Merv's mamm's house. Now, with no noise in the house, Merv must have gone to collect the *kinner*, leaving the messy room for her to clean. Again. She frowned and set her basket on the floor as she tried to determine what to attack first.

She had left early in the morning, leaving the *kinner* in Merv's care. She had warned Merv that she would be home late: Those big orders were looming in the not too distant future. Since his own income was iffy at best, they had no choice. She had to work and he would have to drop Gid at school. The smaller *kinner* were to go to his mamm's house and he would just have to manage to get them over to his *aendi's* farm where his mamm lived.

Despite his grumbles and complaints, he had reluctantly agreed but told her to take the bicycle instead of the buggy. Susie had sighed but didn't argue. At least Merv was willing to help out today, she had told herself that morning as she set her bag in the basket of the bicycle and began the fifteen-minute ride to the bakery.

Even though Merv was not the best at helping out around the house or with the *kinner*, at least they had his *mamm* to watch the two little ones. It had been shortly after Merv's *daed* had died in a buggy accident that, not having any family in Kentucky, Merv's *mamm* had to make a choice: join her other *bruder* in Jackson, Ohio, or move to Holmes County with her sister and her family. She felt God had led her to Holmes County. Susie had never understood why, exactly. However, she had been grateful for the help with the *kinner*. Yet she never understood why Merv's *mamm* had decided to stay with her *schwester* rather than move in the small apartment attached to their own home.

Now, however, Susie was facing another problem. From the looks of the house, things had gone awry in the morning. Clearly the *kinner* had been home for some, if not all, of the day. Too much was disorganized and astray. She imagined that Gid had been late for school...again...and that had delayed the younger ones from going to their *grossmammi*'s house on time. It was a long buggy ride, almost thirty minutes from the farm, which meant an hour round trip.

That was when she realized that something was wrong.

Lifting her eyes, she stared at the barnyard, trying to figure out what was not sitting right with her. Everything looked the same as usual. She couldn't put her finger on what seemed out of place. When she had leaned the bicycle against the barn wall, she had heard the horse neigh from inside the building. If the horse was still in his stall, that meant the buggy was not traveling down the road to collect her *kinner*. And if the buggy wasn't collecting her *kinner*, Merv would have to be home.

She felt a wave of apprehension overtaking her as she started walking through the kitchen and toward the master bedroom door. It was located next to the first floor bathroom and was shut, nothing unusual about that. However, she felt an odd feeling in her chest. Something was wrong. Very wrong.

With her hand shaking, she reached out for the doorknob and slowly turned it. She pushed the door open and peered inside, her heart in her throat. Her pulse raced through her veins, terrified that something bad had happened.

"Merv?" she called out in fear as her eyes fell upon the sleeping form, sprawled out atop the bed.

It took a short moment for her eyes to adjust to the dimness in the room, but when she did, she could barely believe what she saw: Merv was passed out on their bed, his one leg on the floor, an untied boot upon that foot. His white shirt wasn't buttoned properly, the two sides not lined up and the bottom un-tucked from the waist of his pants. His mouth was hanging open and a low, guttural snore filled the room. And in his hand...

"*Mein Gott,*" she whispered, lifting a hand to her mouth and fighting the urge to cry.

Without another word, she retreated from the bedroom, careful to shut the door behind her as quietly as she could. Her heart raced and her chest felt tight as she glanced at the clock. It was almost five and the cows needed milking, *kinner* needed to be picked up, and the kitchen cleaned. All the while, she needed to prepare supper and get a head start on cleaning the fellowship room for church service.

It was clear that Merv would not be bothering her this evening. With a heavy hearted sigh, Susie began to quickly clean what she could in the kitchen, spending no more than fifteen minutes before she hurried out the back door and headed to the barn in order to harness the horse to the buggy. She'd have to deal with her husband later. For now, she had to collect the *kinner* and continue with her regular routine. Already her mother-in-law had been inconvenienced enough and Susie certainly didn't want to answer any questions about why. As for Merv, there was simply no time to focus on him. She'd have to worry about that tomorrow.

With a heavy heart and a dozen questions floating through her head, she walked to the barn and quickly hitched the horse to the buggy. The task at hand kept her mind busy and, slowly, she was able to compartmentalize what she had discovered at home, shoving it into a far corner of her mind so that she eventually stopped thinking about it at all.

"Why Susie!" Dora exclaimed, her eyes travelling to the clock on the wall, the pendulum swinging back and forth with a gentle tick-tock noise that reverberated throughout the kitchen. "What a pleasant surprise. I was expecting Merv." Unspoken in her voice was the question of why the *kinner* were being picked up so late.

Susie resisted the urge to blurt out everything. After all, Dora Stutzman had always been kind to her. In fact, the first time that Susie had met her had been at their wedding. The Stutzman family had traveled all the way from Kentucky to attend the celebration that had been held at Susie's parents' farm. Dora was a quiet woman, small and frail but with a big heart and open arms for her grandchildren. Watching them was never an inconvenience and for that, Susie was thankful. However, Susie had never really come to know her mother-in-law until after Merv's *daed* passing. Once Dora had moved to Holmes County, her entire personality had seemed to flourish as if born again with her newfound independence.

The last thing Susie wanted to do was upset her.

"*Nee*, just me," Susie admitted, avoiding responding to the unspoken question in Dora's voice. "Have they been good for you today, then?"

Dora laughed and waved her hand at Susie. "Oh *ja*! They're always good for their *grossmammi*. Such well behaved *kinner*."

Susie wished she could say the same of her children at home. Her memory flickered to the mess that awaited her back in her own kitchen.

"Of course," Dora continued slowly. "I noticed that they tend to be a little more rambunctious when Merv is around." Lifting her eyes, Dora seemed to study Susie's face for a reaction.

Clenching her teeth, Susie said nothing in response.

"Mayhaps you'd like to sit for a spell and have some of my fresh meadow tea, Susie?" Dora didn't wait for an answer but hustled to the cabinet for a clean glass before opening the small refrigerator. "You look like you could use some. And mayhaps an ear to listen."

"*Nee*, but *danke*," responded Susie. "Best head back with the *kinner*, anyway. Need to fix supper, I reckon."

"Susie," Dora said as she placed a full glass of meadow tea on the table. "I already fed them and they are out back chasing the kittens that the old momma cat had last summer. Gid sure does like to take care of the little ones. So we have a little time." She gestured toward the table. "Sit a spell. Mayhaps we need to talk about something, *ja*?"

Seeing the seriousness in Dora's eyes, Susie sighed and pulled out the little wooden chair that was shoved under the table, adorned by a red plaid tablecloth, one of those simple vinyl coverings that could be wiped off easily. Looking around the room, Susie noticed how meticulously clean everything was. Despite having watched the *kinner* all day, Merv's *mamm* had managed to keep the kitchen tidy and orderly, something that Susie had never been able to do.

Dora took her own spot at the head of the small, square table. "I'll pull up a chair with you. My bones are aching today. Means the weather is going to change, I fear."

Susie felt her foot nervously shake against the floor. She wished she could leave, knowing that she had a full night of work at home. Still, she didn't want to appear rude or unappreciative of Dora's help, especially since she suspected that she would be needing her help again with watching the *kinner*.

"Not ready for changing weather, yet" she finally said. "Sure gets frightful cold out, especially in the mornings when Merv must tend to the barn chores before work."

Dora raised an eyebrow. "Been meaning to speak to you about that."

Inside of her chest, Susie felt her heart flip-flop. The last thing she wanted to talk about was anything that had to do with her husband. Not today. Not when she knew that he was lying on their bed, passed out cold from having drank alcohol. "About what, Mamm?"

"Been noticing some things," Dora offered slowly. "Hearing some things, too, from the *kinner*."

Susie tried to dismiss her mother-in-law's comments. "*Kinner* have fanciful imaginations, ain't so?"

A frown crossed Dora's face. It was clear to Susie that Dora was much more observant than she had given her credit for. "I saw

Merv, Susie," she began. "Oh *ja*, I have seen him when he comes to pick up the kinner. And I know that you are working much too hard at the bakery with no help at the home. I even heard that you sometimes do the barn chores because Merv doesn't even come home."

She was stunned by Dora's frankness. The color flooded to her face and she wanted to disappear under the table. "He's busy," she offered lamely, looking toward the floor instead of at Dora. "Working and all."

Reaching out, Dora placed her weathered hand atop Susie's. "I suspect I know what is really going on," she said softly. "I been suspecting it for a while, *dochder*. And, if I'm right, I know what you are going through."

Susie held her tongue, afraid to speak.

She didn't have to, for Dora began to talk in a soft, gentle voice. She spoke about how Merv's *daed*, John, had been an alcoholic. She talked about the life that she had endured while raising her *kinner* with a man who loved the bottle more than his own family. It was a sickness, Dora explained, that eventually led to his death. During the decline and before his death, John had hit bottom and became violent. That's when Dora had first sent Merv to stay in Holmes County with her sister for the summer.

"But Merv knew what his *daed* had become and, I'm afraid to admit it, he began to drink as well," Dora sighed. "My *schwester*, Malinda, finally had enough since Merv was trying to influence her own son, Daniel. Malinda had no choice but to send him back to Kentucky."

Susie's mouth fell open as she listened to Dora's story. All of those years, Susie had wondered what had happened when Merv simply up and left Holmes County after courting her. She had always wondered why he was so quiet and withdrawn. The truth was that he had been troubled about his *daed* and about having been sent away from home. And, as was so typical, trouble begets more trouble.

Now, she finally understood why he had disappeared.

"What happened that he returned?" Susie ventured to ask.

Dora took a deep breath. "His *daed* had gotten worse and the bishop stepped in, demanding that John stop this evil. I had prayed for so many nights, on my knees by the bedside, that John would get help and my husband would return to me."

"What happened?"

Dora shook his head. "He just got worse and so did his temper. I lived in fear of him and his tongue. Words hurt, ain't so?"

Susie found herself nodding, knowing exactly of what Dora spoke. Words did hurt and, for that very reason, Susie did what she could to avoid her own husband.

"Eventually, John was shunned. The bishop would have no more of that drinking business. That was when Merv up and ran back here. He promised Malinda he wouldn't drink, vowed that he was a changed man after seeing his *daed's* disgrace." She leveled her gaze at Susie, a compassionate look upon her face. "Yes, I can see the signs, child. Having lived with it for so many years, I can see that my son has broken his promise to me, to Malinda, to you..." She paused before adding, "To God."

"I...I don't know what to think," Susie admitted.

With a simple pat on her hand, Dora gave Susie a reassuring smile. "Ain't so much thinking, Susie," she said. "It's doing. And if Merv is following in his *daed's* footsteps, now is the time to do, not think. It might be the only way to save him."

Then, rising from the table, Dora headed toward the door. She paused to pull her black wool shawl down from the hook and wrapped it around her shoulders. Glancing over her shoulder, she watched Susie for a moment before saying, "I'll collect the kinner for you. I reckon you have a few things to think about so, take a few minutes while I do that, *ja*?"

Susie nodded her head, her mind reeling after Dora's confession. Secrets, she thought. Secrets were everywhere. *If only I had known,* Susie thought, *I might have been able to do something sooner.* But hindsight was twenty-twenty. Now, she had to focus on the future. If Dora's story told Susie anything at all, it was that she had to act quickly for ignoring the problem would not make it go away.

Act quickly, she told herself. What exactly was she to do? She wished that she could speak to her sisters but she knew that they would be appalled to learn of Merv's story. *Nee,* she thought. *I would be appalled to admit it to them.*

One thing at a time, she told herself. Focus on today and worry about tomorrow later. She would give herself a few days to pray on this situation and ask the Lord to guide her. Her faith would lead her to the right answer. Of that, she was sure and certain.

Lydia

She was sick again. This time, however, she knew that it was for real. All of those headaches must be something just downright awful. Brain tumor? Cancer? Impending aneurysm? Stroke? Whatever it was, it was just awful bad and certainly something fatal. She just knew that God was going to bring her home any day now. And no one seemed to really care.

With a damp washcloth slung over her forehead and eyes, she stretched across the sofa and moaned. The only one that Lydia could count on anymore was God. Everyone else had deserted her. In fact, not one of her sisters ever came over to check on her, not even the other day when she left a voice message on the machine at the bakery that she couldn't come to work because her head ached.

Today, she had another one of those pains in her neck and head. When she had returned home, there was no sign of Abe. Oh, she knew that her husband had left the house after breakfast. But she had seen neither hide nor hair of him since she had gotten home. He had known that she had a headache when she woke that morning and surely he knew she was home already. What she could understand was why he wasn't there to see how she was feeling!

Of course, all that anyone cared about at Whoopie Pie Place was Tobias. The child didn't look sick, that was for certain. She had caught him wandering in the field just the other day, instead of helping Jacob in the barn. In fact, when she had been resting outside in the shade, she heard Jacob calling for him, quite angry that Tobias was nowhere to be found. Lazy? *Ja*. Sick? No.

And what was this nonsense he had told her about Sadie being ill? Sick in the mornings? While Lydia had mulled that over for a few days, her own suspicions raised as to the actual cause, she felt no sympathy for her younger sister. Since Sadie hadn't told anyone, it wasn't much of Lydia's business. After all, it seemed that everyone had an illness or something to complain about, but no one seemed to care about *her.* With her headaches and aches and pains, Lydia knew what *real* sickness was all about, that was for sure and certain.

Of course, she had to listen to Leah fret over and over again about Tobias. Then, she had been an emotional disaster over having been forced to leave him overnight in the hospital. When she dropped the news that he may need a bone marrow transplant and everyone in the family had to get tested, Lydia thought that was just crossing the line. Who did Leah think she was, telling everyone what to do?

Naturally, no one else seemed to have a problem with that request. Before Lydia could argue, Susie had readily agreed. And clearly, Sadie was on board. Not wanting to be the odd sister out, Lydia had kept her complaints to herself. Well, Lydia thought to herself, at least then the doctors would soon enough be able to see the results from her own blood test and tell everyone that something was wrong with her. She'd have the proof she needed that she was dying.

The door opened and Abe walked in, pausing for an appreciable moment when he saw her laying on the sofa. He lifted an eyebrow and stared at her, the expression on his face saying it all. "Sick again?" His tone matched his expression.

"Oh Abe," she started, her eyes large and full of pain from the stress that she was feeling. "You knew I had a headache when I woke, but you have no idea what type of day I've endured!"

He grunted and walked to the sink to wash his hands. His back was turned toward her and she wasn't certain that he was listening. Still, she continued talking, hoping that she could drudge up some minute display of concern on the part of her husband.

"Leah and Sadie abandoned Susie and me at the bakery!" she continued. "Literally just left, the two of them. They were supposed to return before the afternoon tour bus but they didn't! It was pure chaos!"

No response. She took that as a sign that he was listening.

"Now Tobias is at the hospital and may need a bone marrow transplant!" She shook her head and sighed. "Leah is demanding that if he needs one, we all go to the doctors to be tested as possible matches for donating blood or something of that nature!"

Abe turned around and stared at her. "Tobias is at the hospital, then? Sounds serious."

Lydia fluttered her hand in the air, dismissing her husband's comment. "When hasn't he been in the hospital?" she asked, the sarcasm thick in her voice. "You'd think someone would be concerned about *my* health for a change."

She noticed him rolling his eyes but chose to ignore his reaction.

"And there I was, stuck at the store, listening to that... that Sister Susie boss me around all day long. I fail to see why *she* feels so inclined to be in charge whenever Leah leaves the building." Leaning her head back against the pillow on the sofa, Lydia sighed. "Just because she's older doesn't make her wiser."

"When will Leah find out if everyone needs to be tested?"

She glanced over at him, a scowl on her face. "Don't you even care that I'm feeling poorly?" she snapped.

He pressed his lips together and stared at her, a blank expression on his face. For a long moment, he said nothing, just stared. The longer he remained silent, the less inclined she was to comment. His muscles tensed along his jawlines and his eyes narrowed.

"Lydia," he said stiffly. "Your *bruder* is ill. He's in the hospital for a reason. He may need a bone marrow transplant in order to live." He took a step toward her, his upper body tense as though he was holding himself back. "You, however, are not sick.

You make up these illnesses for attention and I'm getting right tired of it."

She gasped at his words. "Abe!"

He held up his hand. "I can take no more, *fraa*[6]. First it was the issue with *boppli*. Now it is the headaches and fears of heart disease and brain tumors. And yet you are downplaying your *bruder*'s real illness! A true life-threatening illness!"

Her mouth fell open and she sat up, swinging her feet over the edge of the sofa. "What are you saying to me, Abe?"

"You need to see a doctor, Lydia, but I don't think it's a medical one that you need to be speaking to!"

It took a moment for his words to sink in. When she realized what he was saying, she quickly stood up and placed her hands on her hips. "Abe, I sure don't appreciate that type of comment. I don't need no head doctor!"

"It's either a head doctor or the bishop, Lydia! I can take no more of this nonsense!"

The expression on his face frightened her. In the past, he merely had ignored her or made a few small comments before leaving the room. This, however, was different. There was finality in his tone of voice. He had never confronted her nor had he ever raised his voice to her before today. In fact, during her entire childhood, she had never heard her *daed* or *mamm* say a cross word to each other. His response caught her totally off-guard and she let her hand fall from her hip.

He walked toward her, his eyes piercing as he stared into her face. He seemed to be studying her, searching her face for something and she couldn't help but wonder what it was that he sought. The answer soon became apparent when he stopped moving, standing a foot before her.

"Where *are* you, Lydia Miller? Where is the woman that I

---

[6] Wife

married? She is no longer before me, I fear," he said, his voice a bit softer.

"I…"

He held up his hand to stop her from talking. "*Nee*, Lydia," he commanded, his voice firmer than she had ever heard during their marriage. Stunned into silence, Lydia stared at him as he continued. "I don't want to hear more excuses from your lips. I'm tired of excuses. You have to get some help, you hear me? You find glory in others' misfortunes or flaws, yet, never once have you looked at yourself in the mirror. You hold yourself much higher than others, thinking you are above them in your needs and deeds."

"That ain't true!" she managed to say, her voice shaking.

"And your sicknesses!" He shook his head. "You make them up so rapidly, I can't even keep track of them! There is a name for that condition, Lydia. I have asked my Mennonite friends. They call it hypa…hypochondria or something like that. And now you are dwelling on your death? It's time, Lydia. Time for you to see someone."

"I am not making them up!"

He softened his gaze and placed his hands upon her shoulders. Holding her at arms length, he stared into her brown eyes, his knees slightly buckled so that they were on a leveled ground. "I want my Lydia back," he said softly. "She's been gone far too long."

She felt her heart pounding. Fear ran through her body. Did he really think that she was making up these illnesses? Did he truly believe that she found joy in others' misfortunes? Was it possible that her own husband thought she so yearned attention that she would feign fatal illnesses?

"I can't believe you would say such a thing," she whispered, her eyes wide and staring at him. "Do you love me so little?"

Abe shook his head. "*Nee*, Lydia," he responded. "It is

because I do care so much about you that I simply cannot tolerate this anymore. It's time to get some help and move beyond. Mayhaps releasing these…these fallacies will release some of the tension you feel and help you relax, relax enough to have that boppli at last."

Back to the boppli, she thought bitterly. *That's what this was all about!* Hiding her sudden shift in emotion, Lydia remained quiet. From the way Abe was acting, so self-righteous and bold, she knew better than to argue with him. Only now, his apparent lack of compassion and understanding caught left her speechless.

"Lydia?" he asked softly. "Will you agree to see someone about this?"

Had he been waiting for an answer? She narrowed her eyes and stared past his shoulder, her eyes trained on the window. She wished that she could ignore him, ignore his silly question and horrid demand. Still, she knew now that he thought she was crazy. *Seeing someone* meant a doctor but not the type of doctor that could cure her ailments. Instead, he wanted her to see a doctor that might prescribe her some medicine of a different nature. Medicine that the Englische were known to give to crazy people. And that was not something she wanted to do.

"Let me pray on it," she finally responded, shifting her eyes to look at him directly. She tried to appear honest, as if actually considering his offer. "God will tell me what to do, Abe. That's the best that I can offer."

He raised an eyebrow and removed his hands from her shoulders. With a shallow nod of his head, he watched her. She wasn't certain whether her response had made him happy or not but she certainly knew that it bought her time. If only she could convince her husband that she was truly ill, she knew that everything would change. It was just a matter of time, she told herself, as she quickly slipped away using the excuse that she had to make him supper. At least, that would buy her the evening and she'd have time to think hard on how to handle his proposition before next morning. Certainly, nothing could be done in the next few days, she thought, as she quietly began to open cabinets and pull out pots and pans in the hope that a good home cooked meal would assuage her husband's suspicions.

Sadie

It had been a long and exhausting day for Sadie. Her sides ached, her head pounded and she was tired. Bone tired. She had never felt so tired in her life, not even after the spring plowing and autumn harvest. Working in the fields made her muscles ache but there was always something pleasing about having worked outdoors with her *daed* and *bruders* in years past. She could still remember the smell of freshly tilled earth under her shoes or the feel of cornstalks in her dry hands.

This kind of *tired* was different. She could barely lift her arms from her sides or move her feet as she trudged up the stairs. Desperate for relief from the pain throbbing at her temples, she shut the door to her bedroom and stretched out across her bed. The coolness of the quilt was comforting and she took a deep breath, shutting her eyes as she tried to relax. Too many ideas were swirling around in her mind. She felt sorrow wash over her, like the water from the pond on the hill.

Sadie wished she could swim now and let herself sink into the edge of the pond. Would the water wash away her fears? She knew that she should put her trust in God and the knowledge that He had a plan for her, one that she should not dare question. She knew that she should not fear the road that was suddenly lying wide open before her.

Yet she did.

Fighting the urge to cry, for far too many reasons than she cared to think about at the present moment, she shut her eyes and sighed. The doctor's words rang in her ears and she knew that telling her sisters, especially Leah, would be hard. Very hard. She wasn't certain that she had the strength to do it. And what about Manny? She cringed at the thought of what his reaction would be. Would he accept her after he knew? Would he accept what she had to do?

Indeed, that was the big question: What on earth *was* she

going to do?

Her mind traveled back to the previous week. After working at Whoopie Pie Place all morning, she had managed to sneak a ride to the medical center with Michelle, telling Leah that she had an important errand to run. But Sadie hadn't expected to be tied up for so long and the news had not been what she had wanted to hear.

Standing before the doctor in that too short, blue hospital gown, Sadie had been horrified to see that the doctor was a man. With her eyes averted, Sadie had shared her symptoms, her voice soft and barely audible. But the doctor had smiled and held up his finger, stopping her in midsentence.

"I'll be right back," he had said. True to his word, less than a minute later, he returned with a woman, Dr. Conceicao. He had quickly explained that it might be more comfortable for Sadie to talk with a female doctor and, to her relief, he had left the two of them alone.

Indeed, as the woman stood before her, Sadie's words flowed easier and Dr. Conceicao nodded her head, listening with deep concentration and without any sign of emotion on her face. It wasn't that her expression displayed a lack of caring. No, it was something different. It was a look that said it all: *I've heard it all before. You can confide in me.*

Sadie had known immediately, just from looking at Dr. Conceicao's face, that something was wrong.

Oh, whom was she kidding, anyway? She had known it before she had gone to see Dr. Conceicao.

In hindsight, she knew that she should have no complaints about that exam. Dr. Conceicao had been very attentive to her situation and understanding of her discomfort while talking to her through the examination. Then, when she had finished examining Sadie, the doctor had invited her to come sit down and talk in the privacy of her office.

"Sadie," she had said, leaning forward in her chair. "I'm not going to tell you that I'm not concerned. That's a very large lump and the fact that it is so painful..." Dr. Conceicao's voice trailed off, leaving the rest of the sentence unsaid and lingering between them. "I want you to go to Pomerene Hospital. I have a colleague who will see you. He deals with other Amish women and will do a more thorough examination in the same appointment. He understands how hard it is for you to go back and forth. If he sees something, he'll arrange for you to have a biopsy on the spot."

Sadie had nodded her head despite the fact that she felt faint. Lump? Concerned? Biopsy?

"I took the liberty of asking them to have a pathologist ready to read the results, Sadie. It might still take a day or two but, from the size of that lump, I have to admit that it is most suspicious. I do not like it one bit."

Swallowing, Sadie had asked the question that was hanging over her head. "What happens if it turns out to be..." She had hesitated before she could say the word. It tasted like spoiled milk on her tongue. "Cancer?"

Dr. Conceicao had glanced at the floor, avoiding her eyes. And Sadie knew. The verdict was already in. The tests that the doctor wanted were just formalities. "You'd be scheduled for either a lumpectomy or a mastectomy as soon as possible and then, we'd have you meet with an oncologist for the follow-up treatment based on the results of examining the tumor."

There had been no "if" in that sentence. No reassurance that this might not be a possibility.

Sadie had been smart enough to schedule the second appointment to coincide with Leah and Tobias' appointment with Dr. Bodine. She didn't tell anyone, not wishing to raise unnecessary alarm among the family. Yet, if something was discovered, she knew she'd appreciate Leah's presence on the ride home.

When they had finally arrived at the medical center for Tobias' appointment earlier that day, Sadie had excused herself and made her way toward the hospital to locate the radiology center. The different floors and hallways confused her and she had to stop twice to ask for directions.

When she finally found it, the receptionist had handed her forms to fill out and asked for a credit card to pay the bill. When Sadie had stumbled over her explanation that she didn't have a credit card, the woman behind the desk had rolled her eyes. Fortunately, an older woman had walked by, a pile of folders in her hand, and spotted Sadie standing there with the clipboard and pen in her hand.

"Send her back, Janice," the other woman had directed the receptionist, a gentle and understanding tone in her voice. "I'll arrange a payment plan with her afterwards."

The digital mammogram and subsequent ultrasound had been awful enough. She had never had anyone look at her breasts, not like that. Even Dr. Conceicao had been more discreet, looking away when she had conducted the initial breast exam at the other medical center the prior week. Sadie had fought the urge to cry on the table when the doctor, a man at that, had spread the cold gel over his ultrasound probe and run the instrument all over her breasts for what seemed to be a very long time.

And then, she had glanced over, just in time to see his expression. He had paused the probe right over the spot where she knew the lump was located. When he pressed, just a little bit, a wave of pain shot through her chest and she cringed.

"That hurts?" he had asked, one eyebrow neatly raised over his left eye as he looked at her.

Her response had been a simple nod of her head while she squished her eyes shut, fighting back those dreaded tears.

"I want to arrange for a biopsy, Ms. Miller," he had announced, leaving no doubt in her mind as to what he saw on the screen in the fuzzy white and black images that looked like a big blob to her: cancer.

Within thirty minutes, she had been at a second office and whisked into another room where she had been asked to lie on a table. A doctor and a nurse came in, smiled pleasantly and explained what they were going to do. Their words went in one ear and out another. Needles? Aspiration? Pathologist? The entire procedure took less than ten minutes but the pain of the local anesthesia and the humiliation of having even more people looking and touching her one breast was more than she could bear. She cried.

Before Michelle had driven her back to the farm, Sadie had wanted to confide in Leah. But with everything that was happening with Tobias, she thought better of placing her burdens on her oldest sister's shoulders. Leah was already a nervous wreck for having left Tobias alone in the hospital. *I'll wait for the pathologist report*, Sadie had finally decided. *No sense alarming anyone on a what-if...*

During the drive home, it had been easy to shed tears for Tobias as Leah explained what had happened. From the back of the van, Sadie felt terribly alone and out of place without Tobias beside her. Leah sat up front, wringing her hands and repeating what the doctor had said, not once but twice. At one point, Leah almost broke down but, being the strong one in the family, she forced the emotions to stay deep within her and let others cry on her behalf. Sadie had been only too overwhelmed to oblige her oldest sister.

Now, as Sadie laid on the bed, feeling her heart palpitating inside of her chest, she knew that she had to get up and prepare for sharing supper with the family. There was no sense in hiding in her room and feeling sorry for herself. She had to put on a happy face, especially during this time of need. With Tobias' illness and hospitalization, Leah was an emotional wreck and that meant Sadie would need to step in to help with all that she could.

After checking on the *kinner*, Sadie went into the kitchen to see what food she could muster up for supper. She hadn't intended on being in her room as long as she did . What a day this had turned out to be. One she would not likely ever forget. But, as she had learned from her *mamm* and from Sister Leah, she must put her own emotions aside and help those around her. *Let this be God's will,* as she has heard the bishop, her mamm and Leah reference so often. But, it was hard, she thought, to accept the hardships and bad news as *God's will.*

When Thomas came in to wash up for the dinner meal, he looked at Sadie as he was drying his hands. His hair was a mess from having worked in the barn all day, his straw hat having left a ring of pressed hair around his head. Still, despite his own long day, he immediately expressed his concern for his wife's sister. "Sadie, you feeling all right?"

"*Ja*, I'm ok. Just trying to get some food on the table. I need to get the *kinner* all washed up. I'm sorry it's later than normal. I know you like a prompt meal."

"*Nee*, don't you fret none," he said, trying to sound cheerful. "Too much going on around here to add to the fretting, ain't so?"

She wanted to respond but found that there were no words that came out of her lips. Instead, she continued working.

Thomas leaned against the counter. "I sure do appreciate all that you do around here, Sadie. You are a right gut help. There is too much going on. Speaking of which, where's Leah?"

She gestured in the direction of the bakery. "Said she was going to the bakery to call the hospital and check on Tobias," she explained.

"Surprised she's not there with him and came home at all," he commented. "*Ja vell,* best be collecting the *kinner,* then" Thomas gave her an understanding smile and tipped his head as he walked through the doorway in search of the children.

After the evening meal, while Sadie and Rebecca were doing the dishes, Sadie couldn't help but overhear Thomas talking outside the open window in the front yard. With his deep voice, it was impossible not to hear, for it carried on the wind. Normally Sadie wouldn't have cared but this time, straining her neck, she tried to see who he was talking to and wasn't really surprised to see that Esther and Jacob were standing before him.

"*Ja*, it's awful," Thomas said with a solemn shake of his head. "Tobias has to stay in the hospital. You know how Leah gets. I'm surprised she left his side today, " Thomas went on.

"I'll watch the younger *kinner*, then." Esther offered. "That will help some. Anything else I can do?" She added.

"*Nee*, not that I can think of. We have Sadie. And Rebecca and Sarah offered to help, too. Will have to wait until school's out, mayhaps Saturday, I reckon. *Ja,* a true blessing to have them Leah and I are right grateful."

With that, Sadie felt sick to her stomach and a lump formed in her throat. How was she ever going to tell them about her not feeling well? They needed her right now. Good ole Sadie, always putting others' needs before her own. They would need her to help with the big order, help with the *kinner* and help with the house. Leah would want to spend time with Tobias at the hospital, of that Sadie was sure and certain. And it would be up to her to step into the role of caretaker. With so much going on, she couldn't tell them about her own secret and add to their burdens. They needed strength and solutions, not more problems. No, she couldn't tell them. Not now.

Part Two

Where love has entered in,
It does drive out fear.
For fear has torment, and also misery
Cannot abide with love,
For God's love has no torment.
Wherever it is
There is great joy, at all times
It turns sorrow into joy.

Ausbund, Song 87 Verse 15

Love is patient and kind;
love does not envy or boast;
it is not arrogant or rude.
It does not insist on its own way;
it is not irritable or resentful;
it does not rejoice at wrongdoing,
but rejoices with the truth.
Love bears all things, believes all things,
hopes all things, endures all things.
Love never ends.

1 Corinthians 13:4-7

The Bakery

It was quiet at the bakery. Leah stood at the front door, staring at the sign she had taped onto the glass pane so many hours ago: CLOSED FOR THE DAY. The shelves of baked goods were thin, the inventory not having been replenished from the prior day. She wondered how many customers had stopped by the store, surprised to see the sign in the window and wondering what could possibly have made Whoopie Pie Place shut down for the day.

It had been a long day at that. After morning chores, Leah had rounded up all of her siblings and herded them into Michelle's large van. Then, they had driven over to collect Susie and Lydia from their homes. Despite the grumbles of Jacob and Lydia, everyone had willingly participated in the day's excursion to the hospital in order to be tested as a possible donor for Tobias.

After the hospital appointments, Sadie had joined her to help *ready* up Susie's house for church Sunday. Lydia had begged off, claiming that her head felt feverish from the stress of having been tested at the hospital. All that medical poking and prodding had clearly unnerved her. At least that was what Lydia had claimed. With the store shut, it hadn't mattered that she went home. In Leah's tired mind, it had been one less bother to deal with at Susie's house. In hindsight, she was sure that the good Lord had been watching over them when Lydia pulled *that* stunt.

The door creaked and Leah looked over her shoulder. She wasn't surprised to see Sadie slip through the door, her face pale and her eyes cast down upon the floor. It had been a hard day for both of them and Leah wished she could wrap her arms around her youngest *schwester* and cry on her shoulder. It was too much to deal with: Tobias, Susie, Lydia, and that ever stressful order for the convention that was due in just another couple of weeks .

"You are well?" Sadie asked softly, avoiding Leah's eyes.

Leah laughed but it was mirthless. "Oh *ja*, well indeed!" she scoffed but with no ill-intent toward Sadie. "I just needed a few minutes alone to think before I went home, I reckon."

Sadie nodded but did not speak.

"I've prayed to the Lord for His guidance and support," Leah confessed. "I know *Mamm* would not want us to bemoan our situation but I must say that my shoulders are not strong enough to bear this burden."

Once again, Sadie nodded. "I agree that it is a lot." Both women knew that the events of the day at Susie's were best not spoken aloud for now.

With a sigh, Leah glanced at the clock; almost four-thirty. The *kinner* would be helping Jacob and Thomas with evening chores. It was time to return home and prepare the supper meal. Then, she would need to pray on what to tell Thomas. When he would ask how her day had been, what would she do, she wondered. Divulge the truth or continue to keep hoarding these secrets from her husband in order to protect him from the same stress that she was feeling?

"Best get going," she said as she reluctantly began to walk toward the door. "Chores await and bellies need to be fed, -?"

As she passed Sadie, she felt a soft touch on her arm. Surprised at the gesture, Leah turned around. No sooner had she done so than Sadie flung herself into her arms, resting her head on Leah's shoulder and sobbing softly into the soft burgundy fabric of her dress. Uncertain how to react at first, Leah merely patted her sister on the back, trying to soothe her with a gentle touch.

"Now, now," she comforted. "Everything will be all right. You'll see."

If only she could believe those words herself…

Earlier That Day

Whoopie Pie Place

Leah was a nervous wreck. She had never shut down Whoopie Pie Place during the week and hated having to write that sign. With a thick black marker on a sheet of white paper, she neatly wrote the words "CLOSED FOR THE DAY". She felt as though she should post an explanation, let people know what was happening in their family, but she knew better. Family issues were not meant to be aired to the public. The bishop would inform the *g'may* when the time was appropriate and, most likely, that would also be a time when donations would be raised to help pay for Tobias' medical bills.

She taped the sign to the door, the blank side facing in. With a big sigh, she stood back and looked at it. Closed. A very lonely word. She didn't like the sound of it and knew that many customers would come today, seeking their baked goods, only to turn away, disappointed. It just couldn't be helped.

Still, the guilt weighed heavy on her shoulders.

True, Thomas had offered to spend time at the store but Leah had declined, merely shaking her head as she thanked him for the offer. She knew that he needed to cut the hay in the backfield while Jacob was working the front pasture. The hay needed to dry while the sun was shining before they would bale it in a few days. Plus, the far field of tobacco was almost ready to be cut, the thick leaves stripped and hung in the upper rafters of the barn, the sideboards opened just slightly to let enough air circulate through and expedite the air-curing process. Autumn was a time of preparation for the winter and she knew better than to interfere with the schedule of a farmer.

Leah walked back into her office, a small quaint square room situated between the front lobby and the kitchen. She noticed the pile of papers she had left laying on her desk. "I'm sorry my little pile, you will have to wait till tomorrow to get any attention from me," Leah spoke as she sighed. Why did she take on those orders? Especially the large one for the convention center? It seemed like a good opportunity at the time. Now, she was no longer so sure.

In her defense, she had not known that Tobias was going to require medical attention. He had been fine for so long, except for a few late night vomiting spells and an occasional weakness. But that could happen to anyone. Even Sadie had been sick a bit recently. No, Leah knew that she could not blame herself for taking on that order just before Tobias was hospitalized. She just hadn't known.

Or did she?

It bothered her, the fact that she had missed so many important signs. She kept asking herself the same question, over and over again: *Did I know it in the pit of my stomach and turned a blind eye against it? Should I have spotted it earlier? Would it have mattered with his diagnosis?* There were so many self-incriminating questions swirling in Leah's mind. Oh how she wished there was a switch that she could turn off and on. She needed an escape from her thoughts, an escape from the knowledge that she couldn't turn back the hands of a clock and, especially, an escape from the guilt..

Closing the door to her office, she walked into the kitchen area. The absence of the normal hustle and bustle of the daily activities of her sisters in the kitchen and the tourists packed in the front store spoke in loud volumes to her this morning. Not since the death of her parents had they closed the bakery on a normal business day. Although that was only two years ago, it seemed much longer since that horrible day, a day that had changed the lives of their whole family. Their passing had left a hole at the center of her core being, a hole that Leah was constantly trying to fill. A senseless accident that took two of the most important people in her world.

Walking over to a pitcher of water sitting on a tray on the counter, she poured herself a drink. She looked at that crystal clear glass of water. For a moment, she couldn't help but ponder about how, in God's creation, everything was so perfect. *Whoever believes in me,* the scripture said, *streams of living water will flow from within him.*

"Lord, please send your flowing waters over me to give me strength," Leah whispered.

The past few days were difficult. She had spent far too much time talking with her siblings…two of them, anyway. Jacob and Lydia had been most resistant to Leah's pleas to get tested in order to see if either of them were a match for Tobias. Jacob didn't want to be bothered and truly tested Leah's patience with his constant grumbling about Tobias taking after Lydia, with her fake illnesses and constant yearning for attention. It had taken a few soft words from Esther to convince Jacob to give up part of his day in order to accompany the others to the medical center.

Lydia, however, had been far too adamant that she was ill and, even if she were a match, her blood was too sickly to be used for saving Tobias. Sadie had stepped into the conversation, begging Lydia to help their *bruder.* To Leah's surprise, Lydia had snapped at Sadie with a strange comment: "Doubt you'll be any better off than me for donating!"

But Leah didn't have the time to ponder what Lydia had meant by that statement. She did, however, notice the color drain from Sadie's face as she quickly excused herself from their presence, disappearing outside before anyone could apologize or ask questions.

It had taken the better part of half an hour for Lydia to finally agree. Yet, her words were half-hearted and Leah knew that, despite her promise to ride along to the medical center, Lydia's fight was not yet over. But fight Leah would! She had made a promise to her *mamm* and *daed* two years ago, when visiting the cemetery and she wasn't about to let grumpy Jacob and selfish Lydia get in her way of fulfilling it.

Setting her glass down, Leah went looking for her purse. "Might as well get this over with. Look out siblings, here I come," she mumbled as she closed the bakery door behind her and marched across the driveway, toward the house.

Leah

"Jacob!" Leah yelled from the fence, cupping her hands around her mouth.

Jacob was clearing some brush in the field adjacent to the barn, ignoring her arm waving and shouts in the air. He seemed to be too intent on the task at hand, one that included paying no mind to what she was yelling.

"It's time we go! The driver will be here shortly."

Short of climbing the fence and racing across the field, there wasn't much left for Leah to do. However, she needed to catch his attention. With a hefty sigh, she pulled herself over the fence, hoping that the top board wouldn't crack under her weight. She forced herself to walk across the field, angry that it had come to this, especially since she had talked to Jacob just this very morning.

"Jacob!" she yelled as she approached. "It's time!"

"Hmmph!" His displeasure was more than apparent and, for a moment, Leah wanted to grab him by the ear, the same way she used to reprimand him behind her *mamm*'s back when he was a child. "Is this really necessary?"

"Jacob!" His question tore through her and she glared at him. "This is Tobias we are talking about! It could save his life!" Taking a deep breath, she counted to ten quickly. When dealing with Jacob, a different approach had to be taken. "You know Dr. Bodine called yesterday and said it's necessary for all Tobias' *bruders* and *schwesters* to be tested. Please come and stop being a stubborn mule," Leah pleaded.

"Stubborn mule." Jacob scoffed under his breath as he strolled toward the barn alongside her. "Give me a few minutes," he mumbled. "I'll wash up and be right there."

"Hurry Jacob, the driver will be here at any moment. The test only takes a minute when we get there and then you can return to your chores."

He didn't seem to pay any attention to her as he disappeared into the barn. With a sigh, Leah thanked the good Lord for having given her enough patience. Without it, she was afraid she might have not one but two brothers in the hospital to visit.

When she heard the approaching vehicle, Leah turned and headed toward the house to find Sadie. She didn't have to go far for, as she neared it, the door opened and her youngest sister emerged.

"I should have known I didn't need to worry about you being prompt," Leah said to Sadie as her sister hurried down the porch steps to join Leah on the front yard.

"*Ja*, I heard Michelle coming up the driveway. I figured you could use at least one sister today who didn't give you any trouble!"

Sadie smiled as she said it, but there was a dim light in her eyes. Leah watched her youngest sister, concerned with the worry in her expression. Putting her arm around her as they walked to the van, Leah spoke."*Ja*, that would be ever so welcome, sweet Sadie. But hopefully you're wrong."

Ten minutes later, the van approached Lydia's home. Despite beeping the horn twice, Leah noticed that Lydia was nowhere in sight. Not like Susie who had been waiting on the porch of her house, prompt and willing without any fuss.

After waiting for five minutes, Leah shook her head and got out of the van. "I should have expected this from Lydia. Why does it not surprise me?"

Receiving no answer after knocking on the back door, Leah went inside. "Lydia? Lydia, it's Leah," she called as she walked into the house. The kitchen was empty and Leah felt her blood pressure begin to boil. She crossed the floor to the master bedroom that was on the first floor. Hesitating just a moment, she pushed the door open, cringing at the sound of the hinge squeaking in the silence and peeked inside. "Lydia, are you ready?"

Instead of finding Lydia fixing her hair or getting her handbag, Leah found her still lying upon the bed. With a gasp, Leah put her hands on her hips and stared down at her sister. "Lydia! You're not even out of bed yet?"

Pretending to be startled from the pretense of sleep, Lydia jumped at the sound of Leah's voice. "Leah! You didn't have to yell. Can't you see I am not well?"

When *are* you well, Leah thought and quickly found herself counting to ten for the second time that morning. Like Jacob, when Lydia was in one of these moods, a different type of approach was needed. Softening her voice, Leah walked toward the side of the bed. "Lydia, you know we have an appointment this morning."

Shutting her eyes, Lydia sank deeper into the pillow. "I'm not feeling well," she repeated. "I can't go this time. Maybe next time."

*Ten, nine, eight…*Leah took a deep breath. *Seven, six, five…* She sat on the edge of the bed. *Four, three, two…* "What's wrong now, Lydia?" The sympathetic approach always worked. It had become increasingly apparent to Leah that Lydia needed attention and, despite not wanting to cater to her childish thirst to be at the center of everything, she knew she had no time to play games today.

Obviously, the sympathy hadn't been thick enough. Lydia's eyes popped open and she frowned. "What's wrong *now*?" she snapped, emphasizing the word *now*. Leah cringed at the mistake that she had clearly made. Lydia's next words confirmed it. "What do you mean by that. You make it sound as though I am making it up!"

If Leah wanted to shout that everyone knew she was making up her illnesses and that everyone was tired of keeping track of which illness she claimed to have, she kept those thoughts to herself. Tobias was what was important today. And a confrontation right now would only make things worse. She could not risk being any later for their appointment than they already were going to be.

Once again, Leah softened her tone. "I'm sorry Lydia if that sounded wrong. I'm just worried about Tobias. I'm also sorry that you are ill. Can I help you get ready? Is there something I can get you that will help you feel better so you can go with us?"

This time, hearing the sympathy in Leah's voice, Lydia brightened a bit. She sat up and took a deep breath. "I do feel weak, Leah. But, I'll do this for Tobias, I reckon. Mayhaps you could help me dress? If you will watch over me this morning, I will go."

"*Ja*, I will help you, Lydia," Leah agreed, all the while wishing that what she could really do was smack her dear attention-seeking, self-centered sister right in the side of her head. Smack some of the nonsense and selfishness right out of her. *That will have to wait until after the test for Tobias,* she told herself with a private glean of delight at the image in her mind of actually doing what she wished.

After grabbing a drink of water, Lydia walked to the van, approaching it just as Leah was getting in the front seat.

"Leah, I really need to be up front this morning. I'm not well, you know. It would help me. Could you hold the door open please and help me in?"

Looking at Michelle, Leah saw her roll her eyes and shake her head at Lydia. Shrugging her shoulders, Leah helped Lydia into the front seat.

Climbing into the back, Leah told Michelle they were ready. "Can you step on it, Michelle? We're going to be late."

Jumping and turning in her seat, Lydia exclaimed, "I guess it's all my fault that we're going to be late?"

"*Nee*, Lydia. " Leah said. "Just 95% of it" she added under her breath.

During the drive to the hospital, Leah tried to focus on everything but the reason they were traveling to the hospital. She thought about the upcoming orders, the weather, even the laundry that was piling up at home. But she kept returning to the phone call from Dr. Bodine the previous day. He had informed Leah that Tobias was resting well but the test results showed that a bone marrow transplant was an imminent necessity. She hadn't liked the way he had mentioned sooner rather than later, expressing an urgency that had caused her a sleepless night. The minute that Leah had hung up the bakery phone, she knew that getting everyone to agree to be tested would not be an easy task. But it was definitely a necessary one.

"We have an appointment," Leah started to say to the woman who greeted her from behind a desk inside the testing facility. "The Miller family for Tobias Miller, *ja*?"

"Do you have your doctor's referral ?" the pleasantly plump lady asked from behind the glass window in the outer office of the testing center. She looked over the black rimmed glasses that sat upon her nose as she waited for Leah to respond.

"Referral?" Leah repeated, uncertain what the woman was requesting. Behind her, she could hear Jacob shuffling his feet and grumbling underneath his breath. Lydia was sighing heavily as she leaned against the wall. Thankfully, Susie and Sadie were waiting patiently, neither one fussing or adding to Leah's increasing blood pressure.

"The office should have given you papers to bring with you."

"Oh, *ja*, I have them," she mumbled as she began to shuffle through her gray bag. This whole process felt foreign to Leah: appointments, referrals, hurrying to arrive, only to wait. The last thing she wanted was to miss out on this important test because she had misplaced a piece of paper. "Is this what you are looking for?" Leah asked as she handed the paper through the opening in the window.

The woman nodded her head as she took the papers, her eyes briefly scanning them. Satisfied, she gestured toward the sitting area. "Just have a seat over there in the waiting area and we'll call each of you individually for the blood test."

Her siblings were already seated, Jacob leafing through a day old newspaper while Sadie and Susie chatted nervously about cleaning the house, later on that day. Lydia fidgeted in her seat before rising up, crossing the room, and getting a cup of water from the cooler in the corner. A few other patients were waiting and their eyes followed Lydia's movement. Leah tried to push back her irritation at their curious gaze. Didn't they realize that Amish people needed medical care, too?

"Jenny Yoder was kind enough to help arrange the food preparation for fellowship after worship on Sunday," Susie mentioned. "One less thing for me to worry about. She's a right *gut* woman, that Jenny."

Leah watched as Sadie flushed at the mention of her special friend's mother. Indeed, Leah thought, Jenny would be a good mother to Sadie, should she marry Manny Yoder.

"Miller?" A woman dressed in green scrubs yelled from the doorway. She glanced around the waiting room but immediately honed in on Leah. "Miller Family?" she asked again.

Getting to her feet, Leah held up her hand and walked toward the woman. "*Ja*, that's us," she said, a tremor in her voice. *Please God,* she prayed, *let one of us be a match for our Tobias.*

The woman glanced down at her clipboard and read something. "Come with me please."

"All of us?" Leah asked, looking at the lady and then glancing at her family and back to the lady again. Hadn't the other woman mentioned they would be called individually? She wondered if she should mention that but the woman did not appear to be concerned.

"All who are going to be tested," the woman replied dryly, turning and walking back down the hallway. Disappearing into a room, the woman did not seem to care whether or not anyone followed her.

Gathering their purses and hats, the Miller siblings quickly filed down the hallway trying to catch up with the lady in scrubs.

"Just lay your stuff over here." The lady said pointing to a particular area of the room. "I need to ask each of you some questions and fill out some forms. Since there are so many of you, we'll do this all at the same time." Gathering her clipboard and pen she began.

"I am going to assume you are Jacob since you are the only male here. The others names are...?" She looked pointedly at Sadie, a look of recognition in her eyes that Leah saw right away.

"This is Sadie," Leah jumped in protectively before Sadie could answer the question. She didn't like the way the nurse was studying her *schwester* nor did she care for the cold manner in which she was addressing all of them. "These two here are Lydia and Susie," she said before adding a quick, "And I am Leah."

"Everyone over the age of 18?"

"Ja," Leah answered for the group.

The woman checked something on her clipboard before moving onto the next question. "Do any of you have heart disease, cancer, hepatitis, AIDS or an autoimmune disorder? Any one pregnant?" she asked in an emotionless, robotic manner as if ticking off items from a list.

"*Nee*," Leah responded, taking on the role of family spokesperson. "We have none of those things." As the words slipped from her lips, she noticed Lydia start to speak but Susie elbowed her into silence. Sadie, however, paled and averted her eyes. Oh help, Leah thought, not liking the reckless thought that popped into her head.

"Who will be first?" the nurse asked looking at them all.

"I will," replied Jacob gruffly. "The sooner we're finished, the sooner I can get back to my chores."

"Come with me then," she asked, snapping her pen shut and slipping it into a pocket on her shirt.

It took less than an hour for everyone to have their turn getting their blood drawn. Jacob grumbled the entire time, pacing in the small private waiting room while his *schwesters* each had their turn.

Lydia, however, had fought with the nurse, begging to be excused until the results for the others had been analyzed. This had further irritated Jacob, causing him to snap at Lydia that he needed to get back to the farm. Just as Leah was about to step between the two, she noticed Jacob stiffen as a woman walked by. For a moment, the two seemed to recognize each other and he stopped complaining.

"Is there something wrong, Jacob?" Leah asked when Lydia had finally been convinced to leave the room with the nurse.

"*Nee*," he mumbled. "Just in a hurry to get home. Too much to do, is all"

"Shall we go see Tobias, then?" Leah asked when they finally left the testing center. "Michelle won't be here for another twenty minutes. She'll drop you off first, Jacob, before taking us to Susie's for cleaning." She added the last part to thwart any resistance on his behalf.

Reluctantly, Lydia and Jacob followed the rest of the group down the corridors of the hospital as Leah led them to the elevator. She felt a sense of relief that, despite the headaches of the day and the complaints of her two siblings, she had managed to get everyone tested. Surely one of them would be a match! She couldn't wait to tell Tobias the good news and certainly he would be excited to have the company, no matter how short a time for visiting they had!

Susie

"How thankful I am to have you all here to help me clean for Sunday church," Susie said. "With only a few days to go, I couldn't get it all done by myself, that's for sure and certain."

Leah responded with a light deflection of the praise by saying, "That's what family is for, ain't so?"

Susie couldn't help but wonder about another of her sisters: Jacob's Esther. With Lydia pulling her "woe is me" antics for the umpteenth time in recent days and Esther nowhere to be found, it was up to just the three sisters and Leah's two daughters to clean the house. It would have been right *gut* if Esther had come along to help. With *younger kinner*, Esther had volunteered to stay at home to watch Leah's younger ones, too, rather than come to help with the cleaning. While the offer was a kind one, her help at Susie's house would have been greatly appreciated.

"Where's Merv?" Leah asked, a hint of hesitancy in her voice.

Susie had dreaded that question. After her discovery of her husband passed out in their bed the other evening, the last thing she wanted was to deal with Merv and her sisters. *Please ask no questions,* she prayed as she quickly answered with a simple, "He's out somewhere working."

"A job, then?"

"*Ja, ja,*" Susie quickly agreed, hoping to change the subject. "Not as big as our job ahead of us, though," she added lightly, starting to move to the back closet where she kept her cleaning supplies. "I managed to move some of the smaller furniture out of the gathering room last night," she said. "Mayhaps Sadie could start in there while we move the rest, *ja*?"

When she emerged from the closet, her arms laden with cleaning supplies, Leah and Sadie laughed. Susie carried four buckets, filled with Murphy's Oil and vinegar. Under her arms, she had three new mops, which rattled as she walked. Setting the items down on the kitchen table, Susie took a deep breath. "Here are the cleaning supplies. I bought extra at the store the other day to make sure we'd had enough."

"Did you leave any cleaning supplies at the store for others, then, Susie?" Leah kept laughing, as she looked over the inventory of cleaning supplies on the table. "Let's start in the gathering room, Sadie." Leah spoke as she carried some of the supplies into the area of the house that would have the most visitors on Sunday.

Susie and Merv's house was a sparse one. As was true of most Amish farmhouses, the kitchen and gathering room were the largest rooms. In their district, simple blue curtains adorn their many windows. Windows are important in their homes for light and air. The floors were made of wide plank hardwood. The grey boxy church wagon, which held the benches and crates of songbooks, had been delivered the previous week. On Saturday evening, the church wagon would be pulled closer and the benches would be set up in the house in preparation for the church service. In the meantime, it was time to clean and that, in itself, would take several days.

Floors needed to be scrubbed and oiled. Walls would be washed down. Even the windows would be cleaned until they sparkled. If there was chipped paint on the floor molding, they would touch it up with white paint. Nothing was left to chance that someone…anyone…could point out that the room was dirty or ill-prepared for the church service.

Sadie began tackling the cobwebs, of which there were far too many for Susie to avoid flushing in embarrassment; meanwhile, Leah removed all the rugs and put them on the clothesline outside, to be beaten and cleaned later. Returning back to the house, Leah asked Susie: "Can you help me move this furniture to one side so I can wipe the walls down? Then we can wash the floors."

After moving the chairs and tables to one side, Susie and

Leah tackled the task of attempting to push the lone sofa out of the room. They'd have to store it, most likely in one of the outbuildings but they'd need Sadie's help for that task.

"*Gut* thing Lydia isn't here, ain't so? This sofa would be too heavy for us, *Ja*?" Mocking Lydia, Susie lifted her hand to place the back of her wrist on her forehead and flopped onto the sofa as she mockingly exclaimed, "Oh mercy, I feel faint. Everyone please, look: I am ill!"

Sadie looked up and laughed, the first time she had done so since Tobias had been admitted to the hospital. The soft sound of her laughing caused Susie to join her. Their laughter rang through the silence of the almost empty room. But, as always, Leah was quick to become somber and give a disapproving look at her sister.

"Susie. That's not nice!" exclaimed Leah, trying to look serious.

Susie sighed and dropped her hand so that her fingers brushed the linoleum floor. She was about to respond when she looked behind Leah, her eyes focusing on something at floor level. Out of the corner of her eye, she knew that Leah was frowning, probably wondering what had caused her to stop her gleeful impersonation of Lydia and suddenly become so distracted.

But Susie couldn't speak. She glanced over at Sadie and saw her youngest sister standing at the window, staring at the very spot Susie had just focused on. Only Sadie stood there with her hand over her mouth.

Susie flushed and jumped up from the sofa, hurrying over to the empty alcohol bottles that had been hidden under the sofa. They clicked and clanked in her arms, each noise sounding sharp in the silent room. She dropped one on the floor and it rolled in a wobbly line until it rested at Leah's foot.

Merv, Merv, Merv, Susie chanted angrily to herself, wishing that she could just disappear from the sight of her two sisters. The humiliation of her sisters having seen the empty bottles was almost more than she could bear.

"Susie," Leah asked as she bent down to pick up the bottle. For a few seconds, Leah seemed to stare at the bottle and try to make sense of it. Susie's eyes stayed trained on Leah's face, her arms still cradling the other bottles. "What are these?"

Susie averted her eyes, unable to meet her sister's gaze.

"Whose are these?" she asked again, flipping the bottle in her hand as she looked back at the label. While the answer to the first question was more than obvious, Susie didn't want to respond to the second question. With only two adults living in the house, there were only two answers to that question. "Susie," Leah said in a much stronger voice. "I asked you who these bottles belong to."

Feeling trapped, Susie glanced at both of her sisters, feeling the heat of their stare. It was too much and she couldn't hold it back any longer. Without warning, dropping the empty bottles on the sofa, she burst into tears, tears that, she now realized, had been building up for years. Her shoulders shook with each uncontrollable sob and she lifted her hands to cover her face, ashamed at such an out-pouring of emotion. Immediately, both Leah and Sadie had their arms around her.

Leah quickly moved Susie to a kitchen chair while Sadie went in search of tissues. "Susie, what's going on? Is it Merv?"

"*Ja*," Susie admitted, still sobbing. "I found him the other day spread out in our bed with an empty bottle next to him. When I tried to talk to him, later on that evening, he said he didn't have a problem but I know he does. I can *feel* it!" Her shoulders sagged as the tears streamed down her face. "Oh Leah, what am I going to do? What if the Bishop finds out? What if the rest of the family finds out? What if he gets worse? I…I just don't know what to do anymore!"

"It's going to be fine, Susie" Sadie spoke, her voice soothing and gentle as she handed Susie a tissue."

"Sweet Sadie, you always see the good side of every

situation," Susie retorted, an edge to her voice. "But you ain't living this life, my *schwester*. You don't know what it's like to live with a diseased person. It don't matter none if it's a disease of the body or disease of the mind. It's just plain awful, I tell you!"

"Why haven't you told me Susie? Why have you hidden it?" Leah asked, knowing in her heart why Susie had kept such a secret.

"How could I not hide it? It's against everything that is right! It's against our faith, our family ways and against God. I've prayed so hard for him to stop, but it just keeps getting worse and worse."

Sadie handed her *schwester* another tissue. "How long has this been going on?"

Susie waved her hand at Sadie but took the tissue anyway, dabbing at her eyes before blowing her nose. "The drinking? Mayhaps I had suspected in the past but I only just found out the other day. He's just been so ill tempered and angry all the time. When he comes home, he either ignores us completely or berates me in front of the *kinner*."

A gasp escaped Sadie's lips and Leah shot her an angry look.

"I guess I kept telling myself that he was tired from working so hard," Susie continued, a half-hearted laugh in her voice. "But that was a lie, too. He hardly works at all anyway. We're all but living on my earnings from Whoopie Pie Place."

"Susie, has Merv ever gotten out of control when he drinks? Leah asked gently. "Does he hit you, Susie? Or the *kinner*?"

"*Nee*," she replied firmly, shaking her head adamantly. "He's never laid a hand on us in violence. But words hurt. I try my best to keep the children from seeing him when he's in one of those moods. And Dora practically raises my *kinner* because he's just not reliable anymore. Just last week, he drank so much that he was passed out for two days!"

"That explains why you've been so tired recently," Leah said aloud, although she was mostly speaking to herself.

"I've had to do his chores as well as mine," Susie admitted.

A noise interrupted their conversation and all three women jumped, startled. They hadn't heard Merv walk through the door to the gathering room and into the kitchen. He seemed surprised to see anyone there, although his eyes were red and narrow. He glanced behind him at the empty room and frowned.

Immediately, Susie knew what he was looking for: the sofa. No one spoke as he stood there in the doorway, swaying slightly as he tried to catch his balance. But it was too late. He lost his footing and bumped against the doorframe, which caused him to stumble and fall, hitting his head against the floor.

The three sisters looked at each other for a moment before turning their attention to the inanimate form of Merv, passed out on the floor. With a deep breath, Susie was the first to stand and walk toward him. She bent down and grabbed one of his arms, starting to drag him across the floor toward the bedroom she shared with him. To her surprise, both of her sisters came to her side, Sadie pulling at his other arm and Leah lifting his legs. Together, they carried him out of the kitchen and through the bedroom door.

After laying him on top of the quilt, they retreated back to the kitchen, Leah pausing to shut the door behind them as they left the bedroom. In silence, they stood in the kitchen, at a complete loss for words. Finally, it was Leah who took the lead and motioned toward the kitchen chairs.

"I reckon we all should pray on this, *ja?*" she said and, without waiting for an answer, she pushed out a chair and dropped to her knees, folding her hands on the seat and lowering her forehead gently against them.

Sadie and Susie followed her example, the only noise in the kitchen the gentle ticking of the clock on the wall, a wedding present from Merv to Susie, and one that reminded all of them that it was time to address Merv's issue and help Susie free herself from a future that was heading down a dark path; one that was not filled with God and light but darkness and evil. Through prayer, they would find the strength to face the journey that lay ahead for both their *schwester* Susie and her husband Merv.

Lydia

Abe hadn't even asked how she was feeling. It infuriated her that he was so unconcerned about her health. If he had little compassion for the fact that she had not yet conceived a boppli, he had even less for her recurring aches and pains. Indeed, he had gone too far this time.

No sooner had she returned from the appointment at the hospital, her head spinning and eyes aching from the pain, Abe had harnessed the horse to the buggy and, without even a word, had left the house. She had heard the gentle humming of the wheels on the driveway as he had pulled away from the farm. In truth, she had been happy for the silence and the solitude. It gave her time to stretch out upon the bed, a cold cloth to her head, and take a short nap.

Only, the silence did not last long.

She guessed it must have been forty minutes later when she heard not one, but two buggies rolling in the driveway. Visitors? She had sat up in the bed, the cloth falling from her head and onto her lap. "What in the world?" she had said out loud as she swung her feet over the side of the mattress and hurried out of the room to peer through the kitchen window.

Now, as she stood at the window, the color draining from her face, she knew that Abe had finally done it. He was testing her limits, that was for sure and certain.

Quickly, Lydia hurried to wipe down the counter and put the dirty dishes in the sink. She glanced around and saw the blanket on the sofa, unfolded and messy. She didn't have time to fold it and store it in the closet. But she was able to push in the chairs around the kitchen table and pick up the napkin that was on the floor.

"Lydia," Abe's deep voice called as he entered the room.

She turned around, feigning surprise that he had a visitor with him. When she saw the bishop standing behind her husband, she forced a smile and welcomed him to her house. "*Wilkum*, Bishop," she said, trying to sound cheerful and inviting.

The bishop removed his hat and held it before him, his weathered face looking stern as he nodded his head in a return greeting.

"What brings you to our home today?" she managed to say.

Abe cleared his throat and averted his eyes.

She already knew but she wanted to hear it from one of them. Her heart was racing and she felt her palms begin to sweat as both men stared at her. If her head had hurt before, now it was throbbing.

"Lydia," the bishop began, stepping forward. "Abe has come to me with a most pressing concern."

And there it was, in all its glory. Her husband had gone to the bishop, complaining about her ailments. For sure and certain, she thought, the bishop would see that she was ill and reprimand Abe for being a non-caring husband. She felt a moment of satisfaction at the thought.

"And…?"

"*Ja, vell*," he continued, clearly uncomfortable with the conversation. "He has concerns about your health."

Ah ha! Finally, she thought. "It's about time," she said, sighing in relief. "I've been so ill and in such pain for so long. It's a wonder that I can barely get to work most days." She gestured toward the table, inviting the bishop to sit down. Without waiting for his response, she pulled out a chair and plopped down, placing her folded hands demurely upon her lap.

"I see," the bishop said, accepting her offer to sit at the table. Abe, however, remained motionless by the doorway.

"And I get absolutely no support from my family," she continued, casting a look in Abe's direction. "In fact, even today, my *schwester* Leah wanted me to help clean Susie's house for church on Sunday, even though I was feeling poorly after all those dreadful tests at the hospital!" Her fingers plucked at her apron. "Tobias is always so sick and seems to be all that anyone cares about these days."

The bishop squirmed in his seat, avoiding her eyes. "I understand Tobias is poorly again," he affirmed. "But we are here today to speak to you about *you*."

She smiled at the bishop. "That is most kind," she said softly.

"We are here to speak about you getting some help from a doctor for your…" The bishop paused. "*Ailments*."

There was something about the way that he said the word that alarmed Lydia. Her eyes shifted to Abe's once again but she noticed that he was staring at the floor. "I've been to doctors," she replied cautiously.

"When was the last time?" Abe asked quickly in response to her statement.

His contribution to the conversation threw her for a loop. "*Ja vell*," she said, stumbling over her thoughts. "Not that long ago, I reckon."

Abe took a step forward and placed his hand on the edge of the table, leaning toward her. "*Nee*, Lydia," he said. "Two years ago, and just because of the boppli." She flushed at the reminder and looked away. "And the doctor told you there was nothing wrong with you. It is a matter of marital duty that is required to conceive a boppli and that is why you have not!"

"Abe!"

The bishop held up his hand and silenced her. "Lydia, there is an Englische doctor that mayhaps might help you."

"A head doctor!" she shot out, her cheeks flushed red and tears getting ready to spring to her eyes. "That is what you are talking about, isn't it?"

The bishop shook his head. "He is a doctor that can help you with…" He hesitated over the word, glancing at his hands for a moment. "Depression."

Depression? Lydia caught her breath and leaned back in her chair. How on earth could they accuse her of being depressed? Because of headaches and pains? Every day she went to work and did her duty. She couldn't help it if she felt poorly. Depression?

Abe leaned down, taking her hands in his. "Lydia, you need to speak with someone and find out what is really wrong with you," he said with an unusually gentle tone in his voice that she had not heard for quite some time. He stared into her face, pleading with his eyes. "I need my Lydia back, the one that I married and the one that I want to have a family with."

"I…I'm not depressed," she whispered.

He shook his head. "Mayhaps not but let's have the doctor determine that." He squeezed her hands. "We cannot live the rest of our lives like this," he said. Then, after a brief pause, he stared into her eyes. "At least I cannot."

What was he saying? She felt a moment of panic. How could it have come to this? Was he so uncaring that he would threaten to leave her? It was impossible. Amish couples did not leave each other. At least not if they wanted to stay in the church.

She looked at the bishop and noticed that he stared at her, point blank, with no wavering of his eyes. There was no question about it. Abe was drawing the line in the sand. If she did not see this doctor, if she did not find the power to fight for herself and her marriage, Abe was willing to leave the church and her. She would be banned and no longer accepted within the community. Even her family could no longer share meals with her or permit her to visit their homes.

The wind was knocked out of her lungs and she realized that she had no choice. The tears began to fall from her eyes and she quickly covered her face with her hands. Her shoulders heaved as she sobbed. She wished that both men would leave her to her sorrow. But she knew that they would not. They had confronted her and she had no choice but to agree to do their bidding.

With a heavy heart, she wiped her eyes and looked up at her husband. He was watching her, a look of hope on his face. Her expression was solemn as she finally nodded her head. "I will see this doctor, Abe," she whispered. "For you."

Sadie

When his buggy pulled into the driveway, Sadie could hardly contain her smile. It seemed like weeks since she had last seen Manny. So much had happened, so much that she wanted to tell him. Yet, she knew that the timing wasn't right. Not yet.

"Hullo Sadie!" he called out from his buggy. He stopped by the barn and, after pressing down the brake, quickly jumped down and hitched his horse to the post. He hurried to greet her with a friendly wave.

"Why Manny!" she said, a smile on her face for the first time that day. "Whatever are you doing here?" She knew that it was time for the pre-supper afternoon chores at his house. She couldn't imagine why he had driven to visit her, especially during the middle of the week. On Sunday, they would attend the evening singing together. That was their usual time for visiting and, if it was dark enough, kissing in the solitude and privacy of his buggy.

She had been sweeping the front walkway, needing the time to clear her head after the long day that she had been through. They had only just returned from Susie's house, the long walk home taken in silence. Neither Leah nor Sadie had known what to say after the discovery of the empty alcohol bottles under Susie's sofa.

"Wanted to stop by and see my girl," he said, a happy grin on his face. "Been missing you, Sadie Miller."

The color flushed to her cheeks. When he talked like that, she felt her heart race and her pulse quicken. She knew that it was coming to the time when he was going to tell her that he intended to speak to the bishop about announcing their upcoming wedding. The timing was soon for an autumn wedding. Yet, he never did seem to actually state those words.

"Why Manny Yoder," she teased. "You know you'll see me at church, *ja*?"

He reached out and tugged on the string of her prayer kapp. "You know that's not what I mean," he teased back. Releasing the string, he shoved his hands into his front pockets. "Anyway, I wanted to see how today went. How your *bruder* is doing at the hospital."

Tobias. Yes, she should have known that everyone knew about Tobias. The Amish grapevine spread faster than poison ivy on an itchy arm. "Saw him earlier," she said. "They are running tests and giving him a lot of medicine to keep him feeling better."

"That's *gut*," he replied, nodding his head. "And the blood tests?"

Sadie caught her breath. How had he known? Certainly *that* had not yet circulated among the g'may. "*Vell*, we won't know for a few days, I reckon," she slowly admitted, omitting the fact that she had not been considered a donor from the very start. She had known it, from the moment that the doctor gave her results of the pathology report, but hadn't shared that information with the rest of her family. With all eyes focused on Tobias and his medical needs, she didn't feel it was necessary to share her own issue with the cancer in her breast.

Oh, she had managed to slip away and visit the breast surgeon's office while the family had been waiting to have their own blood tested. Dr. Conceicao had been good enough to see her, despite not having made an appointment. The visit had been short and to the point: She needed to have the cancer removed as soon as possible.

The time was soon coming for telling. Sadie knew that much was true but simply couldn't face it. There was too much going on within the family. No one was immune. It tugged at Sadie's heart that she would add to the issues and devastation that was already flooding through the lives of her *schwesters*.

And then, there was Manny. Would he still want to marry her if she did what the doctor said? Removing her breasts seemed so dramatic and unnecessary, especially for a small little lump. She was leaning more toward that lumpectomy, knowing that she would want to breast feed her future boppli. Still, she had to admit that she just didn't know enough about it.

Manny nodded his head and glanced up at the sky. The sun was starting to dip down, the warmth of the day having given way to a gentle breeze and the cool early evening air. "Reckon I best be returning to my *daed's*," he said; but he made no move to return to his buggy. For a long moment, he stood there, studying Sadie's face, a soft smile on his lips.

"Manny?"

He glanced around and, when he realized that no one was there, he took a step forward. Leaning down, he whispered into her ear, "Reckon it's time you and I had that talk, Sadie." His breath caressed her skin and she shivered. "Mayhaps we won't go to that singing but will spend some time alone…talking."

She knew what that meant. Her heart fluttered and she lifted her brown eyes to look at him. "Talking?"

He pulled away, just enough so that no one would suspect anything improper or intimate being said between them. "Planning for our future, Sadie," he said. "It's time we settled this and made it known, wouldn't you agree?"

Her eyes grew wide as she realized that there was no turning back.

"I want the *g'may* to know that you are Manny's Sadie," he said, the pride apparent in his voice. "And I want the bishop to announce our intentions after communion."

"Oh," she gasped. She had known it was coming but she had never suspected that it would be like this. So matter of fact. So determined. So….Manny. Yet, she couldn't agree to this. Not without him knowing the truth. A marriage started with secrets was not one that would be built on a firm foundation.

"That is…" he suddenly stammered, realizing that she had not responded with an affirmation of similar feelings. "If you feel the same."

She wasn't certain how to respond. She needed to tell him. If anything were to happen to her, if she were to find out the worst, she knew that it would be wrong to drag him into a marriage. But, as she stared at him, a look of desperation staring back at her, she knew that she loved him. It didn't matter if angels were knocking at her door.

"I…I do feel the same," she said quickly before adding, "It's just sudden, that's all."

A look of relief swept over his face. His sparkling blue eyes and ruby colored lips that hinted at a smile lit up his face. "It's not sudden, Sadie," he said lightly. "So I have your permission to speak to the bishop, *ja*?"

Short of denying him, Sadie had no choice. She nodded her head, knowing that any apprehension on her part would merely be seen as female shyness by him. His eyes twinkled and he gave her another grin. For a long moment, no words passed between them. There was nothing to say. She had just agreed to become his wife and, despite the mixed emotions that she was feeling, she knew that he was the only man for her.

"That makes me right happy," Manny said softly. He glanced around, making certain that no one was watching before he leaned down and planted a soft kiss upon her lips. "Right happy indeed."

Dear God, she prayed, enjoying the feeling of his arms pulling her close and holding her tight. She felt safe in his arms and knew it was where she belonged. *Please don't take me too soon. Angels might sing in heaven but I sure would miss this man.*

Part Three

For God has prepared for us
A joy which remains forever.
Therefore let us strive sincerely
Here on earth a short time,
That we attain the eternal crown
Which the Father would give us,
With Christ His Son.

Ausbund Song 120, verse 6

For I know the plans I have for you,' declares the Lord,
'plans to prosper you and not to harm you,
plans to give you hope and a future.'

Jeremiah 29:11

The Barn

Leah leaned against the barn's doorway, staring across the paddock with unseeing eyes. Her head was covered with a soft scarf instead of her usual prayer *kapp*. The hem of her dress was torn up the side and her black socks were covered in dirt. She wore plastic clogs on her feet, one with a ripped strap, and mud encased both shoes. Indeed, she had barely paid attention to her usually pristine and clean appearance.

It had been a long day and a traumatic one at that! Yesterday had been eventful enough but paled in comparison with today. Never in her life would she have imagined that so much could have taken place in just a single day! God had surely been busy watching over His flock, that was for sure and certain. For a moment, she felt a wave of emotion wash over her. Her knees felt weak and she could barely stand. The doorframe held her up but it was God who kept her standing.

"You all right, then, Leah?"

His voice startled her and she jumped as he placed his hand on her shoulder. Her nerves were rattled. That much was for sure and certain. Realizing that it was Thomas, she lifted her own hand to cover his. "I just can't believe it," she said. "All that power and strength!"

Thomas gave her shoulder a gentle squeeze but did not respond.

"I reckon it was right *gut* that the *kinner* were home then, *ja*? And Sadie and Michelle made it here just in time. A miracle!"

"We were lucky, I reckon."

Leah shook her head. "*Nee*," she corrected gently. "God protected us. I just pray that He protected others." Just as suddenly as relief had swept over her, a new thought jumped into Leah's head. She reached out and grabbed at Thomas' arm. "Oh Thomas!" she exclaimed. "What about Lydia and Susie? It went in that direction, didn't it?"

They both glanced toward the west where the path of destruction had torn through their fields, knocking through fences but not having touched their home. They couldn't see over the hill to find out what path the swirling winds had taken but it had clearly been along the fields before shifting toward the road at some point. Indeed, both of her *schwesters* lived in that direction and, depending upon which way the storm had traveled, either Susie or Lydia could have been impacted.

"Reckon I best go harness up the horse and check on the neighbors as well as your *schwesters*," her husband said. Then, with an encouraging smile, he reluctantly left her side. "Make certain those *kinner* stay close to the house, *fraa*" he warned. "Just in case another one comes by, *ja*?"

She couldn't find words to respond, so she merely nodded her head. The soft scarf slipped and fell to the ground. For a moment, she stood there, head uncovered, with her brown hair shining in the sunlight. She didn't have to look at Thomas, as he studied her, to know that he was noticing her wide part that exposed her scalp and the grey hair that was beginning to appear. The thought almost made her laugh.

"What's so funny?" he asked, but his voice sounded tired and weary.

She shook her head as she leaned down to pick up the scarf. Shaking the dirt from it, she replaced it on her head. "Reckon you were looking at my grey," she said with a faint smile. "Reckon I just earned a whole new collection to go along with it!"

Thomas forced a smile at her, one that spoke of understanding and tenderness. He reached out and rubbed her arm. "You go on inside now," he said. "I'm sure the *kinner* want to come up and see the outside. Just warn them to put on their shoes and to be careful where they walk. There's debris everywhere."

She nodded but made no move toward the house. Her feet were firmly planted on the ground. Instead, she watched as

Thomas walked away, his shoulders hunched over and his hands thrust into his pockets. He gave no mention to the tear in the side of his shirt where a flying piece of metal had cut into his side. It was almost ten minutes later when she heard the humming of the buggy wheels along with the clopping of horse hooves heading out of their driveway. She waited until the sound disappeared before she took a deep breath and walked toward the house, praying once again for God to give her strength and that Thomas would find everyone safe and well. Especially Susie and Lydia.

Earlier That Day

Whoopie Pie Place

After being closed the previous day, there was much catching up to do. Leah, not able to sleep, had gotten up early and had been in the bakery a couple of hours before the others. The sisters weren't their usual outspoken selves, each in their own world and not interacting unless necessary. A heavy veil seemed to shroud the bakery.

At the clanging of the bell, Leah knew that Sadie had unlocked the door and turned the sign to OPEN. Going to the front window, Leah recognized several people already walking up the front steps, women that were regulars at the store.

Reaching a hand up to smooth the back of her kapp, Leah greeted the first one with a cheerful, "*Gut mariye* Jenny! How are you this fine morning?"

"*Gut mariye,* Leah. I'm right as rain today, *danke!*" she replied, a bright smile upon her face. "Noticed you were closed yesterday, *ja*? Everything all right, then?" Jenny questioned, with a look of concern.

"We had some family matters to tend," Leah responded, not wishing to divulge more details. Normally, she would have gladly shared the reason for closing with Jenny, but there were other customers starting to enter the bakery. Besides, Leah wasn't ready to begin answering questions as of yet. Stepping aside to let Jenny through the door, she offered: "Would you like your usual whoopie pies this morning?"

"*Ja*, that will do me right nicely," Jenny responded, glancing over her shoulder at the three Englische women who were already lingering around the store, deciding what to buy. "Busy already," she pointed out to Leah. "Must be because you were closed, *ja*?"

Before Leah could respond, one of the other customers

spoke up.

"Why were you closed yesterday?" the other woman said as she walked up to the counter, her black handbag slung over the crook of her arm. She reached up and brushed her grey hair off her forehead. "You know, I really needed a pie for a women's meeting at church evening last!" With wide eyes, she stared at Leah, as if expecting an apology for the inconvenience. "I had to settle for one of those day-old pies from the local grocery store."

"Oh Layuna," her companion laughed. "I think you'd just about complain as well, even if everything was perfect!"

"Now, Julia, that's just not true!" Layuna fought back. Though a head shorter than Julia, Layuna was definitely a force to be reckoned with and Leah held back her smile at the exchange.

"Oh fiddle faddle," their third friend, Patti, scoffed teasingly. "You two would just about argue over the color of the sky! Is it blue or grey?"

These three Englische women had been regulars of the bakery for well over a year. While they didn't come in weekly, Leah knew that they visited at least twice, if not three times a month. It was their friend, Esta Mae, who had brought them along with her last fall to buy some whoopie pies for a book club meeting they were having. In fact, Esta Mae almost always accompanied them.

"Where's Esta Mae this morning?" Leah asked. "Sure is odd that she isn't with you. She ain't feeling poorly now, is she?"

"Oh, she just plain out ditched us today!" Julia said, waving her hand in the air. "Had some shopping to do with Richard."

Patti clucked her tongue disapprovingly. "Choosing shopping and Richard over whoopie pies and us! Who could possibly imagine?"

They spent a few moments wandering down the aisle, looking at the different pies and cookies that stocked the shelves. After handing Jenny her box of whoopie pies, Leah bid her a good day and then took a moment to retreat behind the counter and put on her apron. She had not done that prior to opening of the store.

"Have you ladies decided on what you want yet?" asked Leah, glancing up as she heard another car pull into the small parking lot in front of the bakery. It was early for so much traffic, she thought, and wondered if having been closed the day before had, indeed, anything to do with it.

"I want two of these glazed donuts." Julia said pointing at the freshly baked donuts that Sadie had brought from the kitchen and put in the display case. "One for each hip," she added with a wink.

Laughing, Sadie just about dropped the next batch of whoopie pies that she was carrying into the front of the store from the kitchen.

"I think she meant for our meeting!" Layuna pointed out. "Two donuts may serve your hips well but what about the other ladies? They have hips, too, you know!"

While Layuna and Julia laughed at the joke, Patti rolled her eyes and shook her head. "Never you mind them, Leah. Esta Mae told us to get one dozen whoopie pies, half chocolate and the other half pumpkin, if you have them."

After putting the last of the goodies in a box for the book club ladies and tying it shut with white string, Leah turned to the next customers, a man and a woman. With a pleasant smile, she enquired as to how she could help them.

"Are you Old Order?" asked the woman as she marched toward the counter.

"Kathy, you talk to much," said the man who appeared to be her husband.

"And you don't talk enough, Tim!" she retorted and turned back to Leah, her dark eyes waiting for an answer to her question.

"My family is Old Order, *ja,*" Leah reluctantly

acknowledged, suppressing the inward sigh that she wanted to exhale. "Speaking of orders, is there something in the display case that I might be able to get for you? A scrumptious ground cherry pie that we made with freshly picked ground cherries? Only available in the autumn and winter, you know. Or how about one of my sister Susie's scrumptious loaves of bread?"

While mulling over the delicious pastries, Tim spoke up: "Could you order already, Kathy? Weatherman says it's supposed to rain this evening and I'd like to get the grass cut before it starts."

"Well, I can only hope that Mother Nature changes her mind as the day goes on and that the storm heading our way goes around us. I've got a couple of silos that I need filled today. So, since everyone is standing around, mind if I order? My wife sent me for one of those ground cherry pies," replied one of the local farmers that had walked in unnoticed.

"Hey Bud, I didn't see your come in," Tim spoke reaching out to shake Bud's hand. "How is Kathleen doing today?" Tim said, moving to the side to let his friend approach the counter.

"She's good. Just getting ready to fix lunch for some Amish ladies that work for her. I tried to tell her I didn't have time for this. But you know how the *wives* get when an Amish woman is coming to visit!" Leah glanced up at his comment, curious to learn how, exactly, an Englische woman behaved in such a situation.

"Oh sure," Tim replied, gesturing toward his wife. "Mine's no different! She has to have the house spotless and the windows shinier than a new penny." Both men laughed while Leah suppressed a smile. "What'd you hear about that storm?" he asked, changing the subject. "I've got to get that field cleared and my silos filled before all this rain gets here. I hear tell it's going to be some dandy downpour!"

As Leah continued to wait on the customers that streamed through the bakery, she was glad when it slowed down for a moment. Walking into the office, she scanned over the contents of the paper she had filled out for the large order they had upcoming for the convention center, but she was having a hard time focusing on the words in front of her. She'd had a gnawing headache all morning and it seemed to be getting worse.

Looking at the clock on the wall, she realized she didn't have time to worry about it. She wanted to go visit with Tobias before she had to go see Dr. Bodine. Today was the day. He would have the results that she was so anxiously waiting for.

"Sadie, phone's for you." Susie yelled across the bakery. Leah was so into her own thoughts that she hadn't even heard the bakery phone ring.

Crash, Bang! "I swear Lydia. What is wrong with you today?" Leah cringed when she heard Susie cry out as she jumped when several metal pans fell from the counter onto the floor, causing quite the ruckus.

"Don't start on me Susie," Lydia cautioned back. "I'm not feeling well this morning."

Hearing the fussing, yet again, of these two sisters, only increased Leah's headache. She sat down and opened the right top drawer of her desk. Fumbling through its contents, she found what she was looking for: a bottle of aspirin. With some hesitation, she opened the bottle and dispensed not one, but two round tablets into the palm of her hand before snapping the top back on the bottle and shoving it into the drawer. Without waiting for water, she popped the two aspirins into her mouth and tilted her head back, forcing them down her throat.

Please let that help, she prayed silently.

Laying her head on the desk for a moment, Leah took the time to dream about her evening. Oh, she just couldn't wait to soak in a hot tub later on tonight. The thought of time alone, in hot water, just made her giddy with delight. It was exactly what she needed. Unfortunately, a knock sounded at the door and interrupted her daydream. She thought about ignoring it while knowing only too well that it wouldn't be possible.

"Who is it?" Leah asked, stress apparent in her voice

"It's Susie."

Looking up from the desk as the door opened, Leah replied, "I heard; and let me guess. Lydia's stormed out again?"

"*Ja.* That she did," Susie responded, shaking her head in disgust. "It's a daily act now, I reckon."

"Oh! For the love of peace! I'll handle it," Leah replied angrily, placing both hands on the edge of the desk as she pushed herself to her feet. She sighed and frowned as she brushed past Susie. "Well, for a moment I had quiet! Why do I have a feeling in my stomach that I won't have any more of it for the rest of the day?"

Walking out of the back door that Lydia had just stormed through, she spotted her sitting by the barn with her head in her hands. To her surprise, she saw Lydia sobbing, her cheeks stained with tears.

Despite all of the quarrels and arguments, her bickering and storming about, Lydia was not one to cry. In fact, none of the Miller sisters cried. Something must really be bothering her, Leah thought, but the last thing she needed today was to deal with Lydia. Would this sister ever get it together? Where was all this abundance of emotion and drama coming from?

"Lydia, what is it? What's wrong with you today?" asked Leah as she sat down beside her. Not getting a response, Leah tried a different approach. "Lydia, what can I do to help?"

"I just don't feel well and no one cares," Lydia managed to say in-between sobs.

Rolling her eyes, Leah reached over and rubbed Lydia's back. "That's not true Lydia. We all care. We do."

"We? *Nee*, you may care and Sadie may care but that mean ole Susie, she doesn't care about nobody but Susie."

Shaking her head in disbelief, Leah could hardly believe that her grown sister was acting yet again like a two-year-old. Leah responded: "Lydia, I need you today. Do you feel well enough to help me?"

"Help you with what?" Lydia sniffed as she lifted her head to look at Leah, her eyes red and her cheeks stained with tears.

"*Ja, vell*," Leah began, trying to sound calm and patient. "I've an appointment with the doctor this morning and Sadie is going to sit with Tobias for a spell. That leaves only you and Susie. After closing earlier this week, I sure would hate to disappoint our customers."

Lydia's face was softening.

"So, Lydia, you can see that I really need your help. I simply can't do it without you."

Another sniffle and she wiped at her nose with the back of her hand. "Really?"

Leah nodded her head. Inwardly, she wanted to scream. However, she had learned something important today. If Lydia was going to act like a two-year-old, the only way to deal with her was to treat her like one. "Can I count on you to help? It's important and I can't do it without you. Susie can't work both in the kitchen and the front waiting on customers. It's just not possible."

"She does well to work in the kitchen. Out in the shop, she'd just cause trouble for everyone," Lydia sassed in reply.

"Lydia, that wasn't nice," she scolded but with a gentle tone in her voice. "It would be helping *me*, Lydia. *I* need you." Knowing the only way to deal with Lydia right now was to plead on her sympathetic side, Leah traveled that path.

"Well, *ja*, I can help you, I reckon. Just you. I'm not raising one finger to help Susie."

"*Danke*," Leah said as she put one arm around Lydia's shoulders and squeezed. *Funny*, she thought. *Lydia sure doesn't seem that ill, all of a sudden.*

Tapping Lydia on the knee with the palm of her hand, Leah stood up. "I see Michelle pulling into the driveway. Let me go and fetch Sadie."

"Leah," Lydia spoke, her voice prompting Leah to turn back toward her just as she was walking away. "Why doesn't God like me? Why won't He give me a *boppli*?" Lydia asked in a sorrowful voice.

"What?" Leah asked turning full around and facing Lydia. *Not now,* she thought, hiding a grimace. *I don't have time for this.* Mustering up as much patience as she could find, Leah tried to sound calm. "What did you say?"

"A *boppli*. Why won't He give me one when He's giving one to Sadie?"

"Lydia!" She couldn't help but gasp at what her *schwester* had just said. "You're not making sense! Sadie isn't having a *boppli*. Why, our Sadie isn't even married! You're just spreading gossip and that's hateful bad!" Looking at Lydia, Leah knew in her heart that she was going to have to speak with Abe. Lydia was getting worse, not only making up her own illnesses, but now projecting them onto Sadie.

"Tobias told me she is ill most mornings now and I overheard her on the phone earlier, making a doctor's appointment! She didn't want anyone to hear, but I heard her talking to a doctor," Lydia replied bitterly. "I know what I heard." The tears were gone, replaced by anger as Lydia jumped up and stormed toward the bakery.

With a deep breath, Leah shook her head and turned back toward the store. Seeing a different side of Lydia, one that she hadn't seen in a while brought concern to Leah. Lydia was now inventing things in her head. *Or is she,* Leah wondered.

Sadie had been sick of late and had been acting funny. And, she did hear Susie tell Sadie that she had a phone call. With a hand to her mouth, Leah gasped. Oh, could it be? Not Sadie. Were the signs right in front of her and she was too preoccupied to see them? Oh Sadie and Manny, what have you done? No. It can't be. It mustn't be.

At that moment, a gust of wind brought Leah back to reality. "One thing at a time, sweet Jesus. Please, one thing at a time," she said out loud. "Lord, guide me. Wrap your arms around me and carry me through all of this. Help me be the rock that my family needs."

Sensing a smell of rain in the air, Leah looked across the sky for any sign that the rain would soon be there. It was said that living off the land made the farmers' senses keener with such things. Many of the Amish relied heavily on their instinct as well as their little aches and pains and their behavior of their animals to determine that there were changes brewing in the weather. Leah was no exception.

Yes, that's the reason for my headache...a storm, Leah thought. Then she laughed bitterly to herself: *Lord, please don't let my sisters be that storm and destroy our bakery while I'm gone.*

Leah

"I'm sorry Leah." His voice was somber and his eyes full of sorrow. While she didn't know what it meant, she knew it was not good news. He lifted his hands and shrugged, just slightly. "I'm afraid that there are no strong matches amongst your family members…the ones that you bought here, Leah."

No matches. The words seemed to reverberate in her head. How was this possible? How could none of her siblings be a genetic match to help Tobias?

Visibly shaken, Leah responded, "No one at all? Not even close?" She felt the tears brimming in her eyes. *Do not cry, do not cry,* she repeated to herself. Tears would not help solve the problem. She had known when he called and asked to see her that it was not good news. Good news could be shared over the phone. Bad news needed to be handled face to face. "How is that possible?"

The doctor gave a gentle shrug of his shoulders. "Genetics have a funny way of not always doing what we think it should," he explained softly. "There were close matches of the antigens but we are looking for six key antigens to match. Your one brother was the closest match but he shied short of the six." He paused and leveled his eyes at her. "Without an exact match, we cannot do the transplant."

"There are cousins and *kinner* and…"

He lifted his hand to stop her. "If a direct family member is not a match, it's just not likely that more distant relatives will be, either. Of course, you are welcome to test them." He gave her that look again. "But do you really think that other members of your church will do so?"

She knew he was right. It was hard enough to convince Jacob and Lydia to get tested. For most of the *g'may*, illness such as this was God's will and those affected should put their trust in God. She had often heard of Amish parents who watched as a young one died, rather than subject their *kinner* to Englische medicine. While it was the parents' choice whether or not they pursued expensive cures or treatments, no one frowned on such decisions.

With a heavy heart, Leah looked at the doctor and asked the burning question that was on her mind: "What do we do now?"

"Well," he began, switching back into professional mode, the sympathetic voice gone and replaced with one that was more focused on being matter of fact. "Being that there is no parent alive and all his siblings tested negative, we'll need to look for a donor elsewhere," the doctor said. However, there was a look on his face that told Leah another truth: Other donors would be hard to come by.

At that moment, Leah knew what she needed to do. The thought had been hiding in the deep recesses of her mind and she had fought to keep it there. Now, she knew that she had no choice but to confront it head on. "There might be one other person," she said softly. "I'll need a few days to sort it out, though."

The doctor raised an eyebrow but didn't pry. "The sooner the better," he replied, but left the matter alone.

One person. One person that could possibly hold the key to Tobias' future health and well being. Only Leah didn't know how to find her. Even if she did locate the woman, what a dreadful and hurtful task it would be. After so many years, she'd have to confront that woman, tell her the truth. Yet, as bad as that would be, Leah also knew that it could very well be Tobias' only hope. *Oh, God, please give me the wisdom and strength that I need right now,* she silently prayed as she left the doctor's office.

"You okay?" Michelle asked as Leah opened the door of the van, a dark expression shadowing her face. "I sense more bad news."

"There's no match for Tobias among our family," Leah said softly.

"Oh Leah," Michelle said, placing her hand on Leah's arm. "I'm so sorry."

The gesture was comforting to Leah. It reminded her of something that her *mamm* would have done. And in that moment, she could almost imagine her *mamm* whispering in her ear the very words that she needed to hear: *you can do this, Leah.*

"Would you mind taking me to the farm and coming back for Sadie?" Leah asked Michelle. "I need some time to think."

"Of course not," Michelle replied, a kind look in her eyes as she put the car into drive. "That's not a problem."

As soon as she returned to the farm, Leah paid Michelle. She had visited the bakery to tell Susie and Lydia that she would close up for the day. She hadn't had to tell either of them twice for they both barely said *danke* before they were hurrying out the door.

Today, Leah didn't mind. She needed time to think and plan what she would say. She went through the motion of cleaning up what she could while her mind ponder her options. By the time everything was cleaned and ready for the following day, Leah had no more excuses for delaying the inevitable. Like a bandage, she just needed to pull it off and address the underlying wound.

Her heart was heavy as she locked the door behind her and hurried toward the barn. She needed to talk to Thomas before she spoke to Jacob. She would need the support of her husband to do what needed to be done. She was sure that it would be a hard conversation and one that could surely do more damage than good. But she had no choice in the matter. Jacob was the only one that could help her find the single person who might still be able to help her Tobias.

He wasn't in the barn but in the backfield, the four mules pulling the hay baler for the season's last crop of hay. The sky was changing colors and she knew that he wanted to finish before the rain came. However, when he saw her approach, he pulled back on the reins and stopped the team. He watched her, his expression faltering for he surely knew that Leah was bringing with her more bad news.

"*Wie gehts?*"

She motioned for him to step down from the baler. The setting was not ideal to have this discussion, but she knew that she had no choice. "Need to speak with you a spell, Thomas," she said solemnly. "Family matter."

"Tobias?"

She nodded. "There was no match among us," she admitted as he jumped down and stood before her.

"Oh Leah," he said, removing his battered straw hat and wiping the sweat from his brow. "That's not *gut* news."

"*Nee,*" she admitted. "Sure ain't."

"What now?"

Leah inhaled, letting the air fill her lungs. She leveled her gaze at her husband and raised one eyebrow in a perfect arch. "It's time to have that discussion with Jacob," she said in an even tone. "And I'd like you there to help me."

"Jacob?"

She nodded her head, staring her husband directly in the eye. For a moment, neither spoke out loud for there was no need. Silent words passed between them and, when the look of disbelief had crossed her husband's face, she knew that he had finally understood what she was really implying. "It's time he knew the truth and it's time that he stepped up. He's the only one who will know where to find her and she's the only one who might be able to help Tobias."

The idea did not sit well with Thomas, that much was apparent. But she also knew that he would not deny her this request. Years ago, when she had first confided in Thomas, he had been understanding and supportive, even if just a tad shocked at the secret. The fact that no one else in the family knew the truth had been the most surprising aspect of the tale. Yet, they had never spoken about it again and, frankly, over the years, she often wondered if he had intentionally forgotten.

Clearly, that had been wishful thinking. He tugged at his beard and glanced toward the house. She could see his eyes glaze over as he digested what she had just said. Patiently, she waited for him to collect his thoughts. It took a few minutes, long minutes that seemed to drag on even longer, given the heat of the noon sun.

"Reckon this day had to come," Thomas finally said with a deep sigh. He planted his hat back upon his head and forced a smile of encouragement in Leah's direction. "I'll finish up here and meet you back in the yard. We can tell him together then, *ja?*"

"I'll go check on the *kinner*; perhaps Rebecca can watch them for a spell, and I'll meet you there," Leah replied before turning toward the house. Thomas was a *gut* man but she knew that he didn't fully understand the weight of the family that she carried on her shoulders. Nor did he understand that at times, being the strong one of the family didn't mean that she didn't need anyone. Quite the opposite. There were times that she yearned for someone to just hold her and tell her that everything would be okay. But that wouldn't be happening today.

Snapping back to reality, Leah walked across the dusty yard to the house. "Sure is humid today," Leah spoke aloud. At that moment, a gust of wind picked up dust particles as it swept across the yard, blowing them into Leah's eyes. Shielding her eyes for a moment till it passed, Leah continued on to the house. Finding all her *kinner* to be safe, Leah washed her hands in the kitchen sink and wiped her face, clearing any dust that might have stayed in her eyes. Placing the towel back on the peg hung by the sink, Leah placed a hand on each side of the sink and leaned forward lowering her head. "*Lord, be with Thomas and I, as we speak with Jacob, and please give Jacob a soft heart with which to receive the words he is about to hear.*" Taking a deep breath, Leah turned and walked out the door.

"I'm as ready as I'm going to be" Leah said with a sigh as Thomas approached.

"Let's find him and get to it, then" Thomas replied with a matching lack of enthusiasm. As they crossed the driveway toward the barn, Thomas lifted his head and looked at the sky. "Looks like the rain is moving in."

Leah stared at the dark sky. The clouds were rolling in quickly and the birds were chirping in rapid succession as if expressing warnings to each other. It did look like a storm but the air did not feel quite like rain. "I heard at the bakery this morning that it would be real bad this afternoon," she finally said. "Storms at the bakery, storms at the hospital, now a storm with Jacob. Let's hope whatever is blowing in this direction is a bit less dramatic, *ja*?"

As the winds picked up around them, they walked toward the barn.

Susie

She was sitting on the porch when Merv finally emerged from the house. His hair was disheveled and his shirt un-tucked from his pants. One of his suspenders hung by his hip and his feet wore dirty socks. He stood in the doorway, his red eyes squinting in the sun as he tried to adjust to the brightness of the sky.

It was blue. The clearest blue that Susie could remember having seen in months. Ohio skies had a personality, one that spoke of life and love and God's blessings. Today was no different, despite the weight that pressed upon her chest. With past experience though, Susie knew that blue skies could quickly turn grey. All morning long, people had talked about an upcoming storm and, sure enough, she could see dark clouds forming along the horizon. The wind was starting to blow harder than just a regular fall breeze, that was for sure and certain.

Here it comes, she thought as she took a deep breath and faced her husband, knowing full well that their own storm was brewing right there on the porch.

"Where's the *kinner*?" he asked gruffly, scratching at the untrimmed beard that covered his chin.

"Over at my *bruder* Jacob's," she responded. "Esther is watching them today."

If he thought to ask why, he never did.

"Leah and Sadie were here two days ago," she mentioned solemnly. Had it been that long already? Had he really been so incoherent during the two solid days that had passed? In truth, she hadn't even seen him. He had stayed in the barn until late and she had slipped from the bed before he even awoke. For the past two days, she had taken the *kinner* to Esther who watched them while she continued cleaning the house. While Sadie had volunteered to help, Susie had declined, knowing that it was best to handle this task on her own, especially given Merv's condition.

A condition that she had denied for years. A condition that was secret no more, she reckoned.

"So?" he replied, his voice scratchy and gruff.

"They helped me clean the house," she stated. She hated how flat her voice sounded but she knew that she had to be strong and devoid of emotion. "Church service is to be held here on Sunday. You remember that, right, Merv?"

He made a face but said nothing.

"You know they found your bottles, Merv," she said, forcing herself to sound stronger than she actually felt. "They found them and they now know the truth. They know you are drinking all that alcohol. You passed out, Merv. They helped me get you into the bed. Surely you do remember that much."

He waved his hand evasively at her and began to turn, attempting to retreat to the house. But Susie jumped up and, finding an inner strength that she didn't know she possessed, reached out to grab his arm. He swung back and glared at her. "What is it now?"

This was the moment. Susie took a deep breath as she leveled her eyes at him. For the past day, she had role played this moment, the moment when she would need to confront him. She had stared into the small mirror in the bathroom, practicing the speech she would deliver and the expression she would don. For hours, she had paced the floors, freshly waxed from her efforts to erase the sin from her house, as she replayed in her head what she wanted to say. *Ja,* she thought. *Now is that moment. It has come.*

"I understand, Merv," she started. "I understand now where your anger toward me is coming from. But I also understand that this is the time when you must face that demon and tell Satan to be gone! Rid yourself of this evil, Merv, and come back to me and to the *kinner.* Do you want to be like your *daed,* Merv? Is this the life you want us to live from now onwards? Because I sure don't."

"I don't know what you're talking about," he snapped, a harsh look on his face as he glared at her.

"The alcohol!" She clung to his arm. "It ruined your *daed*, Merv. Now it's ruining you and ruining our family. You hide it but not so well anymore. Now that people know…that family knows… it's time to face it and let it go."

He continued to scowl at her but said not a word.

"Your *mamm* told me about your *daed*, Merv. All of it. The way she felt. The way you felt. She told me how your *daed* would raise his voice and show his temper." She paused and, using her eyes, she pleaded with him silently. She could see that he wasn't going to respond but yet, she could also see that he was listening. "I felt for your *mamm* when she talked to me, Merv. I understood how she must have felt. You see, the angrier you get, the less I want to be here," she confessed.

It was true. It had taken her a long time to realize the reason behind both her desire…no, her *eagerness*…to abandon her home in exchange for working at Whoopie Pie Place. Despite the fighting and bickering, the long days and the headaches, it was better to be there, than to stay at home. Her kinner were safer at Dora's, that was for sure and certain. But the truth was that hiding was no life for anyone. And Dora had taught her that the truth had to be faced.

"Your *mamm* is practically raising our *kinner* and that's not fair to them or to her."

A shadow of darkness fell over the house. She glanced at the sky, suddenly aware of a huge dark cloud that was hiding the sun. A gust of wind began to blow through the air, the leaves of nearby trees rustling.

"We don't have a farm anymore and you are barely getting by, working with those Englische men," she continued. "They are dragging you down, Merv; this is destroying our family."

"You don't know what you're talking about," he snapped.

"I was there, Merv," she snapped back. "I saw the liquor bottles. In my heart, I've known it all along. It all makes sense now…the anger, the rages, the complaints." She refused to avert her eyes from his face. "It is unchristian and I won't be having it in my house." Lifting her chin, she dared him to defy her next statement: "And I'm telling you now that it needs to stop."

"I'm the husband," he said, his eyes narrowing as he studied her. "I run this house, not you!"

"Then do it, but do it with a clear head and not one full of demons!"

If he was surprised by her confrontation, he did not show it in his reaction. Yet, she thought she saw something shift in his confidence. In all of their years together, she had never stood up to him, never faced his wrath or fury with more than a dipped head, averted eyes and silent prayers.

"I pray for you, Merv," she continued when he did not speak. "I pray that you will make the right choice. We have *kinner* to raise and I want to do it in a house full of God and grace. I want a farm, a real farm, with a husband who rises early, praises God, and works the earth with his *kinner* and his *fraa* beside him. This life that we have been living has been too separate for too long." She paused and lifted her chin as if challenging him to defy her. "I won't live it any longer, Merv. And I reckon that, if you look deep within you, you don't want to live like this any longer, either. It sure must weigh heavy on your soul."

Silence.

He didn't respond. Not at first. He seemed to be thinking and she wasn't certain of what. Yet, the first sign of anything positive was the very fact that he had not responded. There was no anger in his eyes or harsh words upon his lips.

She took a deep breath and continued, this time with a softer voice. "We love you, Merv. Whatever problems you are facing, the problems that are causing you to hide in the sin of drinking, you don't have to face them alone." More silence. She took a deep breath. "It's time for you to put away that bottle and become the man that God wants you to be. The man that you are *capable* of being. The man that we *need* you to be."

Once again, Merv narrowed his eyes, the only reaction that he had during the last part of her confrontation. And then, just as quickly, his expression returned to being blank. For a hopeful moment, she thought he was going to open up to her, to talk and share his feelings. Instead, he turned on his heel and walked into the house.

As the door slammed shut behind him, she sank onto the bench and lowered her face into her hands. *God,* she prayed, *this burden is more than I can bear. I know that I should pray for stronger shoulders, not lighter burdens, but please, God, show me some mercy or, at least, guide me through these very murky waters.*

Her prayer was interrupted as the door reopened. To her surprise, Merv reappeared. He paused, just a brief hesitation, before he stepped back outside and onto the porch. In his hands, he had a brown bag that was folded over once at the top. He clasped it by the fold and stepped toward her.

"Here," he said, thrusting the bag into her hands. The sound of glass bottles could be heard. He lifted his chin and stared down at her. "Ain't making no promises," he mumbled. "But I reckon I can try. For you and for the *kinner*, at least."

Looking at the bag in her hand, Susie looked up in time to see Merv walk off the porch toward the barn. His shoulders were slumped over as though he had the weight of the world on them. With his hands shoved into his pockets and his head hanging down, he looked like a broken man, one that was lost.

She opened the bag and saw that there were three bottles of liquor inside. Satan, she thought, a shiver racing up her spine. Still, as she saw the bottles and then lifted her eyes to watch Merv disappear into the barn, she caught her breath. At that moment, she wondered if her prayers had finally been answered. If alcohol was at the root of Merv's problem and if he was willing to try to recover from this dreaded disease, then there must be hope for a better future! Surely this wouldn't be of the devil and one of his tricks. No, she was sure and certain that her sisters, upon finding the bottles, had set in motion their prayers for Merv. His gift to her, this bag filled with evil, was of God's will.

Lydia

She had ridden her bicycle back to the bakery, realizing that she had left her handbag behind the counter. Her headache pills were in her handbag and she needed them. Her mind was whirling as much as the wind around her. The sky had changed in almost no time at all. But she hadn't feared the storm. It would only take her but a short thirty minutes to make the trip and return. Besides, the time alone and out of the house did her good.

The conversation with Abe still lingered in her mind. How could he accuse her of faking her illnesses? How could her own husband bring the bishop to their home for a confrontation about Abe's desire for her to see a doctor? She had agreed, that much was true. But her feelings had changed overnight. If Abe didn't really believe that she was sick, why was he insisting that she go see a doctor anyway?

Setting her bicycle by the porch of the bakery, Lydia hurried to the door. Her hand touched the doorknob and turned it, surprised to feel resistance. Closed? Locked? Lydia peeked through the glass and tried to see if anyone was still inside. The sign said OPEN but the door was clearly not budging.

Standing on the porch, Lydia looked around the farm. Down toward the end of the driveway, she saw Leah and Thomas walking into the barn. That struck Lydia as odd. After all, only an hour earlier, Leah had come into the bakery and told both Susie and Lydia that she would close up. The store wasn't supposed to close this early, but it was obviously not open.

Hurrying down the driveway toward the barn, Lydia suspected that something had happened. *Most likely with Tobias,* she thought, a touch too bitterly as she realized that no one had brought the bishop to see *him* about his constant illnesses. As she rounded the corner and approached the doorway of the barn, she heard Jacob speaking with Leah and Thomas. For a moment, she paused, her ears stressing to listen to their private conversation, despite knowing that it was wrong.

"What do you mean I'm the only one that can help him?" Jacob said, an annoyed edge to his voice. "The doctors said my blood doesn't match!"

Lydia heard Leah clear her throat, hesitating before she replied. "Jacob," Leah said. "There's something you need to be knowing, *bruder*."

There was the noise of feet shuffling in the hay on the floor of the barn. The cows were still in the pasture, the evening milking time not quite upon them. "And what would that be?" Jacob asked.

A pause. A long pause. Lydia fought the urge to peek around the corner. Mesmerized, she just stood there listening, with her heart beating inside of her chest. Her hands pressed against the dry wood of the barn, her ear tilted toward the doorway.

"It's about Tobias and you," Leah finally said.

"What about Tobias now?" The impatience in Jacob's voice was more than apparent. Lydia knew that the two brothers had never really gotten along, although she suspected it was more on Jacob's part, than Tobias'. As the first and only son, Jacob had not reacted kindly to being supplanted by a new baby brother when he was eighteen.

"This might be hard for you to hear," Leah said softly and Lydia could imagine that her oldest *schwester* was placing her hand on Jacob's arm. "Do you remember that Englische woman from your *rumschpringe*?"

Silence.

Lydia caught her breath, remembering the turmoil that had happened in the house. Jacob had been sixteen when he began running around with those Englische boys. Two of his Amish friends had also joined him. *Rumschpringe* was a time of exploration before settling down with the church, after all. Yet, *Mamm* and *Daed* had been beside themselves.

And then there was that girl.

"Cheryl Weaver?"

Lydia heard Leah make a noise. It came deep within her throat. "*Ja*, that be the woman," Leah said. There was a strange edge to her voice and Lydia fought the urge to peek around the doorway. Cheryl Weaver? The name sounded familiar but Lydia just couldn't place the face.

"What about Cheryl Weaver then?"

There was a few seconds pause. Lydia could envision Leah glancing at her husband before she continued. "She came to *Mamm* after you had stopped seeing her."

Jacob's voice began to sound suspicious. "She moved away."

"*Ja*, she did that," Leah affirmed. "And eight months later, Tobias was born."

It took a moment for Lydia to understand what Leah was saying. When it hit her, she caught her breath and covered her mouth with her hand. Quickly, she searched her memory, trying to remember when Tobias had been born. Of all the children, he was the only one born in a hospital. Sadie had only been eight years old and Lydia had been but thirteen. *Mamm* and *Daed* simply went away one morning and came home the following day with a bundled baby in their arms.

"I…I don't understand what you are saying," Jacob stammered.

"We need to find his mother," Leah spoke up. "His *real* mother."

"Are you saying…?" He did not finish the sentence, the question left dangling in the air. "I cannot believe this," he mumbled. "It's not true."

"*Ja*, it is," Leah said. "And you must help us find her."

"You're saying that Tobias is *my* son?" The shock in his

voice was only equal to the shock that Lydia was feeling. How was this possible? How could Tobias not truly be her *bruder*?

"*Ja*, he is, Jacob."

In a rage of anger Jacob asked, "How do you know this?" There was denial in his voice. But as Lydia quickly digested what she was learning, she knew the truth. The blue eyes, the curly hair, even the way they walked. Tobias favored Jacob much more than he had ever favored either *Mamm* or *Daed*. And the hostility that Jacob had always felt toward Tobias? Lydia wondered if, deep down, Jacob had suspected that something was amiss. Perhaps, despite his denial, he had known after all.

Leah spoke softly, so softly that Lydia almost could not hear the word that slipped through her lips. ""*Mamm* and *Daed* felt it best to raise Tobias as their own. When the arrangement was made, the girl stayed home as the birth approached so that people wouldn't suspect anything."

Jacob made a noise, deep in his throat. Lydia couldn't tell if he was clearing his throat or scoffing at this wild statement that had crossed Leah's lips. "If this is true, why wasn't I told this from the beginning?"

They were in fear that if you found out you would leave the church," Leah explained, trying to carefully select her words. The last thing she wanted to do was to upset Jacob, for she knew her *bruder* well enough to know that he could shut down at any time. "That you'd refuse your kneeling vow and, mayhaps, pursue that woman."

Now it was Thomas who spoke. "Leah needs your help trying to contact her, Jacob. Tobias' life depends on it."

Stunned, Lydia had heard enough. Slowly, she moved away, hoping that she didn't make any noise as she did. It would do no good for Leah, Thomas or Jacob to know that she had overheard their conversation. *Eavesdropped,* she told herself, feeling a momentary stab of guilt. However, the damage was done and she could barely believe what she had just learned.

For several minutes, she stood behind the barn, far enough away from the other side so that no one would find her. Tobias was Jacob's son! How had this secret been kept from everyone for so long? Why had *Mamm* chosen to share it with Leah and not the rest of the family?

She shivered as dark clouds passed over the sun. They were rolling in rapidly and the air felt heavy. Lydia glanced up and, as she studied the sky, thought how appropriate it was that it looked so gloomy.

Keeping secrets was almost as bad as outright lying, she thought to herself, brushing a stray hair from her cheek. And she knew that there were far too many secrets going around these days. First, Tobias had told her about Sadie's morning sickness. Now, she had learned about Jacob having fathered a *boppli* when he was a himself a boy, a boppli that had been raised as their own sibling!

"No. I can't hear any more. This can't be so." Lydia whispered to herself. Moving as swiftly as the strong winds would let her, Lydia found her bicycle. Not hearing Leah who had came out of the barn yelling at her, Leah quickly hopped onto the bicycle and sped down the driveway and onto the road.

The sound of Leah's voice telling Jacob that he was Tobias' father began swirling in her head and the winds from the vehicle that had just barely missed her were dragging her bicycle from side to side putting fear into every part of Lydia's body. Fear that blinded her from the approaching vehicle that was out of control until the moment it was upon her.

Sadie

After sitting with Tobias for two hours, as she had promised Leah she would do, Sadie left him when he finally fell asleep; the medicine that had been slowly dripping through the IV was causing him to become drowsy in the afternoon. Dr. Conceicao had insisted upon seeing Sadie as soon as possible and instructed her that, as soon as she would end her visit with Tobias that day she should tell the nurse to page her as she needed to talk to her.

"Sadie, I have the results of your pathology tests," Dr. Conceicao said slowly, staring at Sadie as she stood before her in the small office. Taking a deep breath, she added: "I've gone over your file thoroughly and I've even consulted with some of my colleagues. I'm sorry Sadie. The news isn't good."

She was in shock as she left Dr. Conceicao's office. Disbelief. She couldn't comprehend the news that Dr. Conceicao had just given her. A mastectomy? A rare form of cancer? Rapidly spreading? It was all too much to take in at one time. Why hadn't she told Leah? Leah could have been here with her to receive this devastating news.

As she emerged from the hospital, she was both relieved and dismayed to see Michelle's van waiting by the entrance. She needed more time to digest what she had just learned. She hadn't expected Michelle to be so prompt. Or, rather, she had hoped for a few moments to herself to clear her head.

"You don't look so good, Sadie," Michelle said, a concerned look on her face as Sadie opened the door. "You okay?"

Shaking her head yes, Sadie said nothing further. She was still trying to digest the news and didn't want to speak further about the upsetting fact that, indeed, she had breast cancer. Yet, she knew that Michelle would never pry. Instead of asking more questions, Michelle shifted the van into drive and pulled away from the hospital.

About midway home, Sadie asked Michelle: "Michelle, do you believe that God does things for a reason?"

"Why, yes. As a matter of fact, I do, Sadie. I don't believe in fate or coincidence at all. I believe that God has our lives mapped out for us from the minute we are born," Michelle replied. "Remember Jeremiah 29:11? *'For I know the plans I have for you,' declares the LORD, 'plans to prosper you and not to harm you, plans to give you hope and a future.'* God knows everything about us and has plans for each and every one of us."

Sadie stared out the window, watching the farms pass by. Hope and future were not the two words that she was feeling very cheery about these days. Faith, however, was something that she understood could relate to. God had planned this for a reason. If only she knew what that reason was.

Her thoughts were interrupted when she heard Michelle break the silence. "Why did you ask me that question, Sadie?"

Turning in the seat, Sadie faced Michelle. "If this wasn't fate and this wasn't coincidence but a plan, that means God knew that I was going to get breast cancer before I was born, is that so?" she asked Michelle.

A grimace crossed Michelle's face. "Don't say that," she whispered. "Wait till all the tests are in."

"They are in," Sadie spoke quietly, yet loud enough for Michelle to hear.

"Are you sure?" asked Michelle empathetically.

"Yes, I'm sure," Sadie replied and then proceeded to tell Michelle what the doctor had said. "How am I possibly going to tell my family? Here they are, all so worried about Tobias passing. Now I have to burden them with my own health issues?"

"You have to tell them, Sadie," Michelle encouraged. "You can't put it off. You must have the surgery as soon as possible. And you need them by your side."

With a big sigh, Sadie frowned. "But Leah has so much going on right now. How will she ever be able to handle this?"

"Leah is a strong woman. God has given her the strength to carry such burdens on her shoulders. You need her Sadie. You need all of your family."

"I just can't do it Michelle. I just can't. Tobias is so sick and *he* needs her. And she has her *kinner* and Thomas to take care of. And Lord knows that at the bakery, Susie and Lydia keep her on her knees praying daily with all their antics. She just can't handle any more than that."

"Don't sell Leah short, Sadie. She's stronger than you think."

"*Ja, ja,*" Sadie admitted. "I just don't know how she'll feel to hear that angels are knocking at my door."

"Hush!" Michelle scolded. "I don't want to hear that kind of talk! And, as for Leah, you need to trust her to know what her limitations are. She would be so hurt if she knew that you didn't go to her. In fact, she'd think she had done something wrong if she found out that you didn't trust her enough to share the news of your illness with her."

Swerving on the road, Sadie quickly grabbed the handgrip above the door. "Oh help! Seen another turtle, Michelle?" Sadie forced a nervous laugh. "Or was that a jack rabbit jumping out in front of you, this time?"

Michelle squinted her eyes and stared into the sky. "Very funny, Sadie. Glad to see you still have your good sense of humor." The van shifted again and Sadie saw her grip the steering wheel. "The wind sure is picking up. It's blowing my van sideways."

"I suppose you are right, Michelle. I do need to tell Leah. I need her right now and she would be hurt if she thought I had purposely not told her. She should be home when I get there. I reckon I'll talk to her then."

At that moment, a loud screeching noise blasted from the radio in the dashboard of the van. The noise startled Sadie and she clapped her hands over her ears to dull it out. She had never heard such an intrusive sound and she glanced over at Michelle. "What is that?" asked Sadie.

"Ssh," Michelle said, reaching for the dial to turn up the volume.

A man's voice boomed over the radio and Sadie leaned forward as she tried to listen. A tornado. The man calmly explained that a tornado had been spotted just southeast of Millersburg. It was moving at a very rapid speed in a northwestern direction. She looked at Michelle and noticed the color drain from her face.

"We've got to get to your farm as quickly as possible!" Michelle said, her hands gripping the steering wheel tighter. She stared straight ahead, her eyes intent on the road before them.

"Can we make it in time?" Sadie asked softly.

"Just hang on," Michelle responded. "I'll get us there as quickly as I can."

"Is there really a tornado headed toward us? In September?" Sadie couldn't remember ever having experienced a tornado warning this late in the season. But the sky certainly looked like the man on the radio knew what he was talking about.

"Don't think about it," Michelle snapped. Then, as if instantly apologetic, she softened her voice and repeated her words. "Don't think about it, Sadie, but pray!"

For what seemed like an eternity, Michelle sped through the roads, the wind picking up and more branches flying through the air. The high-pitch noise returned and, immediately following it, the man's voice calmly urged people to seek shelter underground.

"Tobias!" exclaimed Sadie. "What about Tobias?"

As Michelle struggled to keep control of the van she explained to Sadie that, since Tobias was further north, he would be safe. Besides, the hospital has emergency plans for these types of emergencies, Michelle reassured her, not once taking her focused eyes off the road.

"But what about the farm?" Sadie implored, staring at her friend as the low hanging clouds, avocado in color, seemed to converge together. More debris seemed to swirl on the ground and, in the distance, Sadie saw it: the formation of the clouds, dark clouds, joining together into the telltale funnel of a tornado.

Sadie gasped as Michelle pressed the gas pedal down and the van lurched forward, moving even faster down the road. A plastic crate rolled across the road and Michelle quickly swerved the steering wheel to avoid it just as they passed a bicycle that was struggling to stay on the road. Another swerve and Sadie's head hit the side window.

"That looked like Lydia" Sadie exclaimed as she jumped to look out of the van's back window. "That person on the bicycle. Did you see her?"

Michelle didn't answer. Sadie could tell that Michelle was too concerned with driving the van. The wind was even more ferocious and keeping the vehicle on the road was clearly becoming a challenge for Michelle. Her concentration was fierce but Sadie knew what she had seen: her *schwester*.

"We should go back for her!"

"We can't!" Michelle hissed. "It's heading this way, Sadie! We have to try to get to your basement!"

"Oh help!" Sadie held onto the handle on the dashboard. She was staring into the sky watching the swirling clouds overhead. Branches and leaves were flying through the air and the noise sounded like a freight train. The funnel was still a good distance away but it was headed right for them. She shut her eyes and said a quick prayer, an image of Manny passing through her mind as she did so.

"We're here!"

The relief in Michelle's voice interrupted her prayer and Sadie immediately opened her eyes. As Michelle drove the van toward the entrance to the Miller's farm, they both saw a mailbox aimed for the van's windshield. Sadie screamed while Michelle slammed on the brakes, both women ducking as the mailbox slammed against the hood of the van then shot back into the air.

The van lurched forward and Sadie braced herself, pressing her one hand against the dashboard while her other hand clung to the strap of her seatbelt. She was too afraid to shut her eyes again, yet as afraid to keep them open. The funnel was moving across the fields of their neighbors' farms and the power was beyond anything Sadie had ever witnessed.

"Is it coming this way?"

Her question required no answer.

Once again, Michelle pressed the accelerator to the floor and spun the wheel, the van sliding and barreling down the driveway. Branches were falling from trees, a fence was knocked over and the wind was still picking up. But the driveway was clear and Michelle aimed directly for the house.

On Jacob's side of the dwelling was a basement storm shelter. The metal doors rattled in the wind but both women could clearly see that they were latched from the inside. Sadie felt a wave of relief as she realized that it meant the family was safe. And she knew that Susie's *kinner* had stayed over so, they too were safe from the treacherous tornado that was descending upon their farm.

As soon as Michelle slammed on the brakes and the van stopped, Sadie shoved open the door and raced to the shelter door, telling Michelle to follow her. The wind made it hard to see and she had to cover her eyes, glancing back just once to insure that Michelle was right behind her.

Banging on the shelter's doors, Sadie screamed as loud as she could. "Leah! Thomas! Where is everyone?" She was certain that her voice could not be heard above the noise from the storm. It was too loud. Looking over her shoulder, she saw the clothes line that extended from Esther's porch to the top of the barn, flapping in the wind, the few remaining clothes that were still pinned to it waving wildly. Just beyond the edge of the barn, she could see the swirling dark cloud begin to descend upon them, heading directly for the farm.

Michelle ran up to her, screaming in the wind, "We have to get inside, Sadie!"

Despite Michelle tugging at her arm, Sadie gave the cellar door one last desperate kick with her shoe, hoping that the noise would alert someone that they were outside. As if by miracle, the left side of the door moved and, within seconds, it flew open, the wind helping it, and a hand reached up.

Michelle pushed Sadie down the steps first and followed quickly behind as a large tree branch flew through the air and landed on the roof of the van. Without looking back, both women disappeared and the door slammed shut behind them, the latch quickly secured as the funnel from the tornado crept ever closer.

Book Three

Part One

But we have already been instructed
On which way we shall go,
And will not let ourselves be taught otherwise.
With God's help, nothing at all
Shall turn us from this way.

This causes the devil in his kingdom,
The pope and also others likewise,
To be angry above measure
With us the small flock of Christ.
Their plan is defeated.

They storm and rage continuously,
Each group at their place,
Wanting to crush the truth
Godliness has no place among them,
But must suffer and be suppressed.

Ausbund Song 63, Verse 12-14

Be strong and of a good courage, fear not, nor be afraid of them:
For the LORD thy God, he that doth go with thee;
He will not fail thee, nor forsake thee.

Deuteronomy 31:6 (KJV)

The Aftermath

Destruction. Devastation. Everywhere. Debris from barns and homes scattered across the lands. Buildings destroyed within just a few short minutes. Roofs ripped apart with pieces scattered in the corn fields. Roads covered with broke tree limbs and branches. Intersections blocked by uprooted trees, their unearthed stumps creating craters on the sidewalks and their roots turned up toward the skies as if imploring the Creator for a quick and painless death.

But what about human lives? Had everyone survived? Broken branches, glass and other debris littered the grounds creating further hazards to those who must walk among the destruction to first survey the damage and then begin building their lives back toward normalcy.

An eerie calm hovered over the area. The kind of calm that either precedes or follows a storm. No laughter from playing kinner. No soothing flapping of laundry on the clothes line. No gentle humming of buggy wheels rolling down the road just beyond the driveway.

Instead, the family spent the day picking through the sticks, wire, glass torn clothing, and other debris stuck in bushes, paddocks, and fields. The kinner donned large work boots to prevent stepping on sharp objects as they walked in a bulls-eye, starting close to the house with their trash bags to begin collecting the garbage. Slowly, throughout the day and into the evening, they began to move further and further from the house, their ring of collection becoming broader.

No one complained about the work, the endless hours of labor. Not once.

"You hanging in there?" Thomas asked as he joined Leah on the porch. He reached out and put his arm around her shoulder, a comforting gesture.

Resting her head on his shoulder, she sighed. "Ugly. That's

what today was. Just plain old ugly." She was thankful for the darkness for it hid her ashen face. Too much stress and emotion had robbed her of any joy.

Earlier, when they first emerged from the storm cellar, the damage did not seemed so great. Now, however, her heart pounded and the pain in her head throbbed at what she had learned throughout the day.

So much destruction, she thought. Just one storm.

"It will resolve itself," Thomas sighed. "It always does."

Leah disagreed, but she knew better than to contradict her husband. Instead, she merely stated the one fact that remained unspoken. "You reckon that the bishop will have to get involved now?"

For a split second, he did not respond. What words could he speak to comfort her? She knew the answer to that question: none.

Thomas shrugged his shoulders. "I reckon so. Seems like a bishop matter to me. But *mayhaps* that's not a bad thing."

A cheerless laugh escaped her lips and she shook her head. It wasn't funny, she knew that much. But she found humor in how easily Thomas offered that as a silver lining to the very dark cloud that hung over the family. "I fail to see why, Thomas," she said bitterly.

"*Vell*, if he does find out and feels it necessary, there will be confessions," he started, his hand gently massaging her tired shoulders. "Confessions are a good place to rebuild broken walls and foundations, don't you think?"

"You can't rebuild a city in one day." The mocking tone of her voice sounded out of character and she looked away, refusing to apologize for what she knew was the truth. Thomas spoke of foundations in need of repair. A confession or two was not enough to repair the damage from the storm that had struck her family.

Earlier That Day

Leah watched as Thomas's buggy navigated the debris in the driveway so that he could check on the neighbors and follow the path of the tornado to see if help was needed along the way. She stood there for a long time after the noise of the horse and buggy disappeared, her eyes following the trail of destruction through their fields. How close they had come to losing everything, she thought and said a quick silent prayer to God:

> *Our father, You are our comfort and strength*
> *in times of sudden disaster.*
> *Surround us now with Your grace and peace.*
> *Lift up those who have fallen,*
> *sustain those who work to rescue or rebuild,*
> *and fill us with hope through*
> *Jesus Christ, our rock and redeemer.*
> *We ask these things in Your precious Holy name.*
> *Amen*

"Mamm?"

Her concentration interrupted, Leah turned around when she heard young voices calling for her from the direction of the house. Three little faces peered at her from the storm cellar, each with wide eyes and pale cheeks. Taking a deep breath, she tried to force a smile. "You can come out now!" Her eyes quickly scanned the sky. "Just stay close to the house now. Just in case."

In case of what? She wasn't certain. Did tornados strike in pairs? She wasn't about to take any chances. Still, the thought struck her as she realized that Thomas was out there in a buggy. Should another tornado touch down, he would not have a chance to outrun it. A new wave of worry washed over her and she felt her heart racing.

Michelle and Sadie emerged next from the storm cellar.

God had surely been watching over those two sheep, Leah thought as she watched them. Michelle helped Sadie and held onto her arm as they walked toward Leah, stepping over branches and pieces of boards with protruding nails that had broken off from the damaged barn.

"Careful," she called out.

Michelle shook her head as she approached. A large tree branch lay across the van's crushed roof. Had they not escaped in time they would have been severely injured, if not killed. "So scary," she mumbled.

"You'll have to call for a ride," Leah pointed out. "You need to check on your own family."

"Mamm!"

At the sound of the high-pitched voice, the three women turned their heads in unison to stare at Sarah who stood on the porch with her older sister, Rebecca. "The back windows are all broken! There's glass everywhere!"

"Then stay away from it, please!" Leah tried to temper the tone in her voice, but her nerves were shot and she didn't need to be plucking glass shards out of the *kinner*'s feet. "Rebecca, keep those young ones out of the house for now! Go pick up sticks from the driveway!"

"Have you checked on the store, yet?"

Leah glanced at Sadie and frowned. No one had thought to check on Whoopie Pie Place. The building sat behind the barn and was harder to see from their vantage point. With a simple nod of her head, she walked up the slight incline toward the back of the barn, too aware that both Sadie and Michelle were following her.

"Oh Lord!"

She almost fell to her knees when she saw the store and a strangled cry escaped her throat.

Whoopie Pie Place was gone.

She envisioned what happened while they had all sought safety in the storm cellar. The winds from the tornado ripped the door from the hinges and it was gone. Vanished. Leah imagined that it was in the field somewhere, most likely in hundreds of pieces. The roof that covered the front porch hung over the side, pieces of it missing. From where she knelt, she could see inside the gaping hole where the window had been: the inside of the store was completely destroyed.

Reaching out her hand, she grasped Sadie's arm and whispered, "It's over." Swallowing her tears, she tried to get a hold of herself.

In her mind, she could still see it: the day the store was finished. In her memory, she saw her *mamm*, so pleased with the store when it first opened. She saw her *daed* standing behind her, his chest puffed forward with unusual pride as he watched his *fraa* admiring his handy work. Mamm slowly stepped onto the porch, her fingers tracing the carved sign that rested against the wall for *Daed* didn't want to hang it until told exactly where to put it. With a soft smile, Mamm turned around and looked at her husband, her eyes misting over as she simply said, "*Danke.*" It was enough. To say much more would be prideful. But they all had understood what she meant.

Leah clasped her younger *schwester's* hand and chocked back a sob. "The store is…" She couldn't complete the sentence as she blinked rapidly and fought the tears. It was too much for her to handle.

"Leah, we will rebuild it." Sadie's matter-of-fact tone did little to reassure Leah. "We have no choice, *Schwester.*"

Leah felt a hand on her shoulder and turned to look at Michelle. There were no words that she could say to express what she was feeling inside. Everything that their mamm had worked for and had left to the Miller sisters was ruined. A wasted shell of a building remained in its place. And that was exactly how Leah felt:

like a wasted shell of a person.

Whoopie Pie Place

They stepped over the broken glass, Leah glancing over her shoulder to make certain that the kinner remained outside. She warned them earlier to stay away from the building for she was uncertain how safe it truly was. She had waited almost an hour for Thomas to return. When he did not, she knew that it was up to her to assess what, if anything, could be salvaged.

Sadie stood there, her arms wrapped protectively around the two smallest kinner. Her face was pale and her eyes wide with fright. Despite trying to talk Leah into waiting for the men, Sadie had known that nothing would stop her *schwester* from going into that store.

"Now stay put," Leah warned one last time. The glass on the porch cracked under her boots and she pushed at a board that was hanging from the beams.

"Be careful!"

Leah shot a look over her shoulder at Sadie, but did not reply, before she disappeared inside the remains of the store.

The front room was a mess. She caught her breath and lifted her hand to her mouth, covering it to stop the gasp that threatened to escape. Shelves were ripped from the walls. The glass display case had shifted from its place and was shattered. The cash register lay on its side on the floor, covered in glass and papers.

The door to the kitchen hung from its hinges. Carefully, Leah slipped through the opening, a nail catching on her sleeve and ripping the fabric. Insult to injury, she thought as she freed herself.

She was not prepared to see the destruction to the kitchen. There was a hole in the back wall where the window had been. Glass lay scattered on the floor. But it was the work area that took her by surprise. Everything was broken, piled in a heap near the far wall. Bags of flour and sugar were everywhere, some torn, others damaged from the rain that had followed the twister. Timber from the ceiling crushed the ovens and she couldn't even make her way to the storage room that was off to the side.

"Leah?"

She glanced over her shoulder. "I told you to stay outside!" she shouted back.

It was too late. Sadie stood behind her and cried out when she saw the kitchen. "Oh Leah!"

A flash of anger flooded Leah. Her nerves were raw and the last thing she needed was just one more person leaning on her for support. When, she thought wryly, will I get to lean on someone? "Don't 'Oh Leah' me," she snapped. "There's not one thing I can do to make *this* any better."

Sadie took a step backward at Leah's harsh words.

"This just about does it!" Leah continued, waving her arm to knock a bowl that was resting atop a pile of debris. "This is the last straw!"

"Calm down, Leah," Sadie whispered.

"I will not calm down!" She spun around, broken glass crackling under her shoes. She felt out of control and, for once, didn't fight the feeling. "I am tired, Sadie! Tired of holding this family together! Tired of dealing with problems and issues, emotions and outbursts! The bickering between those two," she said, waving her finger in the air as she indicated Susie and Lydia, even though they were not there to defend themselves. "It's more than I can handle. I'm done. I'm finished. I quit!"

"Leah!"

She narrowed her eyes. "Leah what?"

"You don't know what you say," Sadie offered softly. "God will never give us more than we can handle."

"*Ja vell,* He did this time!" She gestured at the mess behind her. "This is way more than *I* can handle!"

Another voice called out from just beyond the door. "Leah?

Sadie? Are you all right in there?"

"We're fine, Esther," Sadie called back, knowing that it would do no one any good to see Leah in such a state. "Give us a minute. Just stay with the *kinner*."

For a long moment, Leah and Sadie stood there, no words necessary between them. The mess before them seemed daunting, as if there was no possible way to start cleaning it. While the frustration that Leah felt was great, she knew that there was something even greater: God's goodness.

She sighed, her shoulders falling as she accepted the defeat that she felt.

"Sadie, I'm ever so sorry," she said softly. "You're right. God does not give us burdens that we cannot handle. My shoulders are strong. The *kinner* are safe, our house is standing, and God is my light. We will overcome this, if that is His will." She looked over her shoulder and forced a smile at her *schwester.* Reaching out, she took Sadie's hand and squeezed it gently. Leave it to her, Leah thought, the peacemaker among the family. Always there to calm down the tempest in all of them.

"*Danke,* Sadie," she said. "Now, let's go back outside and figure out a plan of how to tackle this…" She glanced around at the remains of the store, a disgusted look on her face. "…This reminder that we are not in control."

Sadie smiled and reached out for Leah's hand. She squeezed it gently, giving her whatever little strength she had left. In response, Leah took a deep breath and nodded her head. As unfortunate as the situation appeared, she knew that worse things happened to others. No matter what she felt, God gave her broad shoulders for a reason. She could handle this, just as she had handled everything else in recent years. Tragedy and life could not be separated any more than joy and life could.

Together, they walked hand-in-hand through the front of the store and outside, trying to smile so that the others would not feel the weight of the world that lay on Leah's shoulders.

Leah

"Jacob, I don't really have time to talk about this right now."

She no longer tried to hide the frustration that she felt. After all, this was the third time she had said those very words to her brother. Her frustration grew from his inability to either comprehend or accept that she actually meant what she said. There was no time for his personal problems today. Instead, all hands needed to focus on the task at hand: recovering from the storm.

Jacob, however, felt otherwise. Clearly, his mind spun in circles, focusing not on the damage from the tornado. Instead, he focused on the storms of his past. While others helped with the cleanup, Jacob wandered around, restless and confused, occasionally seeking out Leah to mumble the same request as he wrung his hands and stared at the ground.

"For the last time, what you tell Esther is between you and your *fraa*," Leah said sharply. She didn't like using such a sharp tone with him but her nerves were shot. With so much cleanup in progress, Jacob had no right to burden her with his problems. "And what you decide to do in regard to finding the *mamm* of that boy is between you and God. I'd be more concerned about the one than the other." She frowned when he hesitated at her words. "And, to be clear, I'm not talking about fearing Esther!"

"This is all just too much," he mumbled, removing his battered straw hat and wiping his sweaty brow with the back of his arm.

A sigh escaped her lips. "*Nee, bruder*. What is too much is that we just survived a tornado and you are following me around, fretting like a washwoman instead of helping! Now I suggest you get those *kinner* to help you with the collapsed side of the barn while I tend to this mess in the house!" Before he had a chance to argue, she added, "We can attend to the *other* mess later!"

Her temper was shorter than usual; no doubt about that.

She'd pray to God for forgiveness later.

It seemed like hours passed since Thomas drove off to check on their neighbors and her sisters. The longer he was gone, the more she felt her stomach twist into a knot with worry. To keep her mind occupied, she focused on assigning tasks to everyone. Inside the house, Esther swept the broken shards of glass from blown out windows while the *kinner* picked up debris from the yard and road. While both houses suffered damage, Leah's side seemed the easiest to handle for the moment.

"What a disaster!" Sadie said when Leah approached her.

The kitchen table rested on its side, surrounded by glass from the windows. The torn green shades flapped in the gentle breeze that was blowing through the openings.

Esther stopped sweeping and rested her chin on her hands. "My side of the house is much worse," she sighed. Shutting her eyes, she shook her head and clicked her tongue.

"What are we to do with all of this?" Leah asked to herself looking around. The mess was overwhelming.

"I've started a pile. Over there," Sadie said, pointing toward the door.

The mound of garbage contained wood, fabric, paper, shards of glass, and other little things that Leah couldn't quite identify. A pile, Leah thought. That pile represented things in her life that, until an hour or so ago, seemed so important. Now, they were merely objects, garbage to be bundled up and thrown away. Her family's survival meant more than jagged shards of broken glass. God's gift to her was the safety of her *kinner* during one of the worst storms that passed their home in decades. What more could she expect?

"Sure do wish Thomas would get back," Leah said, more to herself than to Sadie. "Worried about the others."

They heard the sound of tires on the gravel and, simultaneously, looked toward the door. The barn blocked their view and Leah stepped over the pile of rubble and crossed the front yard, sidestepping some branches that had yet to be cleared.

To her surprise, she saw a police car pulling down the lane. It stopped in front of the remains of Whoopie Pie Place. After a brief delay, the door opened and an officer stepped out, whistling under his breath as he assessed the damage. When she rounded the corner of the barn and lifted her hand to wave, he greeted Leah with a sad smile. Besides being an officer of the law, he was also a familiar face at Whoopie Pie Place. Both Leah and Thomas considered him a friend.

"You folks made out all right?" he called out.

"*Ja*," she replied, nodding her head. "Nothing that can't be replaced, I reckon." Her eyes fell upon the damaged store and her heart dropped. No matter how many times she looked at it, she felt the same thing: shock. She forced herself to look away, the pain too great to keep looking at it. "Thomas is out checking on the others. Haven't heard back from him so I'm a bit anxious. You hear anything?"

The officer shook his head. "It traveled north and cut east. There are lots of uprooted trees down, roads blocked. But, judging from the direction it went, I sure don't suspect your sisters' had much damage, Leah."

That was good news. She breathed a sigh of relief. Still, she knew that the tornado must have destroyed other people's homes. "And the other communities? Lots of damage? Any injuries?"

He shrugged, removing his hat and running his hand across the brim. "Reports just coming in now. One community was damaged about three miles from here. An Englische neighborhood. Haven't heard of casualties yet." The look in his eye told her what his words didn't: casualties were expected, even if not reported yet.

"I'll pray for them," Leah whispered. God may have spared the Miller family, but she knew His protection to her loved ones did not mean protection for everyone. Whether they liked it or not,

God had His own plan for His people. Surely some had been called home. It wasn't her place to question His reasons, merely to accept the facts. "We all will."

He nodded his head and glanced at his watch. "Best get moving on to check on others. I'll spread the word about Whoopie Pie Place," he added, gesturing toward the ruined building. "I'm sure you don't need people descending upon you in the next few days, unless it's to offer a hand."

She watched as the officer backed the car out of the parking lot and turned left onto the road. She shut her eyes and prayed to God that He would comfort those in need. Surely there were other people who suffered greater losses than she had.

She glanced over her shoulder at Whoopie Pie Place. Destroyed or not, she'd have to rebuild it. It was the lifeblood of their family, the thread that kept her *schwesters* connected, whether they would admit it or not. Whatever happened next, Whoopie Pie Place needed to remain at the core of the family. Her mamm and *daed* had built it once. Their *dochders* would rebuild it again. Somehow, Leah would find the strength to make it happen.

Susie

Susie sat beside her husband in the buggy, a heavy silence hanging over them. There was not much to say. They both dealt with their inner feelings their own way. As the horse pulled the buggy along the road, Susie stared outside the window at the path of destruction that surrounded her. Trees were downed, fields were leveled, and there were buildings that lay in piles of rubble along the hills. She caught her breath when she saw a large tree limb that had crushed a barn and a buggy just parked at the entrance of a neighbor's farm.

"I sure do hope that everyone's all right at Leah's," she whispered.

For once, Merv was trying to take charge. When the storm had hit, Merv reacted by grabbing her arm and pulling her inside the house. He had dragged her as fast as he could to the storm cellar, using the inside staircase to descend into the darkness.

It had happened so fast. Too fast for Susie to comprehend that her *kinner* were at their *grossmammi's* house and she had no idea how they fared through the storm. The path of the tornado appeared to have come from a different direction and Susie prayed that God had placed His hands upon their heads, protecting them from the storm. Still, she didn't know what to expect and the not knowing pained her.

One thing that she did know was Merv had saved her. He had pulled her to safety. In the dark, she trembled in fright, listening to the howling winds as the tornado passed nearby. His arms protected her, the arguments of the past forgotten as she wept on his shoulder. His presence comforted her, his sobriety a blessing in more ways than one.

Now, he held the reins of the horse in one hand and reached out to clasp hers. His touch reassured her and she squeezed his hand in response.

"*Mein Gott!*"

Susie looked over at her husband and saw that he was staring ahead at the road. There was a large tree blocking the way, its massive roots having been lifted out of the ground and the trunk covering a ditch alongside the road. As they neared it, she could see what Merv had seen: a colored cloth that resembled the fabric of a dress. It was tangled within the branches and indicated that someone might have gotten caught up in the disaster after all.

"Whoa!" Merv pulled back on the reins and stopped the horse at a safe distance from the tree. The last thing that they needed was for the horse to spook. Already it pranced nervously, obviously jittery and skittish from the passing tornado.

"Stay here, Susie," he commanded as he handed her the reins and jumped down from the buggy.

She watched from the window, her heart pounding inside of her chest as he approached the tree. His feet moved slowly as he strained his neck to see what was wrapped within the tree.

"What is it?" she called out through the open window of the buggy, her hand resting on the front sill as she tried to see around him.

Merv didn't answer right away. Instead, he knelt down and reached over to push aside some of the brambles from the tree. Time seemed to hang in the air, endless and stale, as she waited. It was clear that he saw something but it was also clear that he had no idea what, exactly, he saw. She pressed her lips together and made a quick decision to jump out of the buggy. It would do no good to just sit there and wait, she rationalized.

"Don't come any closer!" His shout caused her to freeze at the halfway point between the buggy and the tree.

"You're scaring me, Merv," she heard herself say. The tremble in her own voice startled her and she took a slow step forward.

Merv stood up and turned to Susie, his face pale and his eyes wide. "Get back in that buggy and go to the closest farm! We need help! There's someone under this tree, Susie! I can't move it myself to get to her!"

"Oh dear Lord," she whispered and, without another word, she ran back to the buggy. Within seconds, she had turned the buggy around and slapped the reins on the horse's back, getting the mare to pick up speed along the road to the closest farm.

I can't move it myself to get to her. Merv's words rang in her ears. Without knowing the truth, she suspected that she knew exactly who was under that tree: Lydia. But, why would Lydia be out on this road during the storm? Nee, she told herself, it can't be Lydia. Yet, try as she might, her suspicions grew.

The Yoder farm was the first one along the road and Susie raced down the driveway, her heart in her throat and fear building within her head. She fought the urge to cry as she slowed the horse down and pulled the buggy to a stop by the house.

"*Wie gehts,* Susie?"

Elmer Yoder stood in the door, his *fraa,* Jenny, behind him. They must have heard the horse coming down the lane for Susie didn't need to get out of the buggy.

"There's a tree…" She gasped for air, feeling as if she ran the half-mile rather than rode in the buggy. "A person is caught under it! Merv can't budge it by himself." She paused and glanced at Jenny. "I don't know why, but I have a terrible feeling that it's Lydia!"

"Oh help!"

Elmer said something to his wife before hurrying out of the house and getting into the buggy with Susie. "Let's go! Jenny will get the boys to join us with tools."

She hadn't even been gone for five minutes. To her relief, she saw another buggy parked on the other side of the tree. Thomas stood beside Merv, both of them struggling as they tried to figure out the best way to move the tree branches to free the person beneath the trunk.

"It's Lydia, isn't it?" Susie whispered to Thomas as Elmer conferred with Merv. "I just know it is."

Thomas glanced at her. "She must be knocked unconscious. It appears she's stuck in the ditch but unharmed."

His words didn't register with her. How could Lydia be trapped under a massive tree and still be unharmed? How did he know? And why was Lydia here?

Susie stood behind the men, watching as the men removed a few of the smaller branches. "Lord, give them the strength they need to move that tree and keep safe the person under it." Susie whispered to herself and God.

In the distance, a horse and buggy approached, the rhythm of the horse's hooves fast and furious against the pavement. When she glanced up, she saw Manny in the driver side, slapping the reins against the horse's back as if the horse could possibly gallop faster.

Manny and two of his younger brothers emerged from the buggy and ran over to the tree. They carried handsaws and axes. Without being asked, they immediately hacked at the thicker branches while the other men grabbed and pulled. Slowly, an opening cleared and Susie saw the limp body that lay trapped underneath its massive branches: Lydia.

"I can't get this one to budge" Merv yelled, tugging at a branch.

Rushing to his aid, Thomas and Elmer grabbed pieces of it, pulling as Manny continued hacking at the base. Pieces of wood flew through the air. Susie ducked as one hit the side of her face, just missing her eye. She continued to pray, willing God to give the men the strength to save her *schwester.*

"That's working!" Thomas shouted. "Keep going! "

Susie clasped her hands to her chest, watching as the men worked relentlessly to free her *schwester.* They pulled at the branches, snapping them off while Manny used the ax on the larger ones. Together, they worked to clear a path to the tree trunk in order to free the limp form that was trapped beneath it. As they worked, Susie fought the urge to cry; knowing that whatever happened was God's Will. She only prayed that God Will chose to let Lydia live.

"That should do it!" Thomas called out. "I think I can get to her."

With the branches removed, the tree appeared less threatening. Susie clearly saw the ditch now and Lydia laying in it. By God's grace alone, she was alive. A split second later, Thomas pulled her from beneath the massive tree trunk, bringing her safely to rest on the grass.

"She's still unconscious," Thomas said as he tried to rouse her. Lightly, he tapped her cheeks and called her name. "Lydia? Lydia?" There was no response. "Did Jenny call the ambulance?" he asked, looking directly at Manny.

"*Ja, ja.*" Nodding his head, Manny's eyes never left the limp figure of Lydia. He looked frightened, his face pale as he swallowed. "She'll be all right, though?"

In the distance, a siren wailed. With each passing second, it grew louder. Susie glanced in the direction of the noise, silently willing it to come faster. Thomas hovered over his sister-in-law and continued tapping her on the face. "Come on Lydia. Wake up. Are you hurt? Lydia, wake up."

Susie thought she saw a fluttering of eyelids in response to Thomas calling to Lydia. She leaned over his shoulder and tried to get a better view. "Is she waking?"

"I think so."

Merv took a step back and stood beside Susie. He reached out a hand and touched her hand, a small gesture, but one that startled her. She realized that his touch felt foreign for months had passed, perhaps years, since his hand sought hers.

"You all right?" he asked, his dark eyes searching her face.

Compassion filled her and she nodded her head. Despite his shortcomings, the Merv she married so long ago still lived within this stranger before her. And he felt like a stranger to her. Yet, the way his eyes lingered on hers, she felt something akin to hope stir deep within her. Was it possible that their love might rekindle?

"*Ja*, I'm fine, I reckon," she replied softly.

The ambulance came to a stop behind the horses and buggies. Within seconds, a gurney appeared and three men dressed in white raced over to the grassy spot where the Amish men and woman stood, beside the crumpled form.

Susie watched as they carefully worked, checking her pulse and shining a light into her eyes before, as if she weighed no more than a feather, they lifted her into the air and gently placed her on the sheet-covered stretcher. Lydia's mouth moved, just slightly, and she groaned.

"Lydia!"

Susie ran over to the stretcher, the men hurrying after her. Grabbing Lydia's hand, Susie leaned over her. "We're here, Lydia. They're taking you to the hospital to make certain you're not hurt."

Blinking her eyes, she looked around at the faces staring at her. "What...?" Her eyes stopped on Manny and a dark shadow crossed her face as she recognized him. Anger replaced her confusion. "You! You made Sadie pregnant!"

Gasping, Susie released her hand and stepped away from the stretcher. The Amish men stood there, silent as the medics quickly released the wheels and lifted the stretcher into the back of the ambulance. No one spoke as one of the medics talked with Thomas about where they were taking Lydia.

Once the ambulance pulled away, Elmer turned to his son. "What she said, Manny," he managed to say, pain etched in his face. "That's not true, is it?"

Susie felt her heartbeat from her head to her toes. She stared at the young man, noticing that all of the color had vanished from his face. With wide eyes and a trembling lip, he shook his head, vehemently denying the accusation. "I have never…" But he couldn't even finish the words.

"She's talking crazy," Susie whispered. "She doesn't know what she's saying." Despite her words, Susie couldn't help but wonder. Sadie's recent sickness jumped to mind. Was it possible that…? She shook her head, the thought so horrid that she couldn't even finish thinking it. One look at Manny's face, however, convinced Susie. Clearly Lydia was speaking nonsense.

In the distance, another siren broke the silence, a reminder that they were amidst a disaster area that required their immediate attention.

"Reckon it's best if we get over to Abe's," Merv said softly, his hand on Susie's shoulder. "He'll be wanting to go to the hospital for sure, *ja*? And we need to get over to my *mamm*'s. Check on the kinner. They'll be worried, I'm sure."

Manny remained stunned, completely silent as he stared at the pavement, his eyes devoid of emotion. Elmer started walking back to their buggy but paused when he realized his son did not follow.

"Manny!"

Slowly, Manny turned, a dazed look on his face as he stared at his *daed*. Wordlessly, he nodded. Without looking at anyone, and with hunched shoulders, he walked to where his father stood.

Long after Elmer drove the buggy back toward their house, the remaining three adults stood there, silent and staring after it. Merv shuffled his feet, glancing toward the buggy. Susie knew that she wanted to leave, wanted to go to Lydia and Abe's but she couldn't move. The words from Lydia's mouth still echoed in her ear: *You made Sadie pregnant.*

Gently, he guided her toward the buggy and helped her climb inside the open door. She stared out the window, her eyes peeled on the road and her thoughts torn between worry for Lydia's safety and this unbelievable accusation about Sadie. If only it wasn't true, she thought. But only time would tell.

Lydia

Upon awakening, she tried to sit up, but the excruciating pain in her head stopped her. Lifting a hand to her temple, Lydia winced and sank back into the pillows. *What happened*, she wondered.

The surroundings looked vaguely familiar: pine furniture, a metal bed, machines, bright lights, even the framed print of the ocean that hung on the wall. Tobias? Was she with Tobias? She frowned, trying to make sense of where she was. Clearly, she was in the hospital, that much she realized. The only thing that confused her was why.

Shutting her eyes, she searched her memory.

First Leah's face flashed before her eyes and then Jacob's. They stood in the barn, talking to each other in hushed voices. Thomas was there, too.

Lydia tried to remember what they discussed. She couldn't hear the words clearly so she had leaned forward. Eavesdropping. What were they saying to each other?

"Well, well, well," someone said from the doorway. "Look who's back with us!"

Lydia snapped out of her memory and looked at the door, confused at first when she saw a young woman walk in, pushing a machine that rolled on wheels. "Who are you?"

With a big smile that exposed her perfectly straight white teeth, the woman stood beside Lydia's bed. "I'm your nurse. You're in the hospital, dear," she said as she patted Lydia's hand as if to comfort her. "You're lucky to be alive!"

She wore a multi-colored pastel shirt with a name badge over her breast: Cheryl Walsh. The name was unfamiliar but there was something about her face that made Lydia frown. The nurse mistook it for confusion and pulled the chair closer so she could sit for a minute.

"Do you remember coming here?"

"*Nee*, I don't," Lydia replied. "Where's my family? My *schwesters*? Abe?"

Cheryl gently squeezed Lydia's hand. "They'll be here soon, I'm sure. There was a tornado. Do you remember that?" Without waiting for Lydia's reply, the woman continued. "You were rather fortunate. A tree fell on you."

Another image flashed before Lydia. "I was riding my bike."

The nurse laughed. "That's a silly thing to be doing in a tornado!"

"I didn't know it was coming," Lydia said. "None of us did." And then, it hit her. The tornado had been coming from behind. That meant that it passed right over Whoopie Pie Place and the family farm. Leah, Sadie, Jonas, the *kinner*. "My family! Was anyone hurt? Is everyone else all right?"

"Don't panic," Cheryl said softly, glancing down at a buzzing cell phone that hung from a cord around her neck. "As far as I know, no one was injured from your family."

"And my younger *bruder*? Tobias Miller?"

Pushing the chair back, Cheryl stood up and turned around, reaching for the machine that she brought with her. "Let's check your vitals, shall we?" Without another word, she took Lydia's temperature and blood pressure then, with a quick smile, she hurried from the room to attend her next patient.

For what seemed like a long time, Lydia stared out the window at the blue sky and bright sun. A tornado? Lydia tried to remember what happened. She had ridden her bike home after returning to Whoopie Pie Place for her handbag. But there was something else, something before that. A fight.

Think, think, think, she scolded herself.

Abe's accusations about faking illnesses. His threat to go to the bishop. That was it.

Clenching her teeth, she fought the sudden wave of anger that welled up inside her chest. How could he have threatened her? What had he truly wanted to prove? Deep down, she knew his complaints were not about her constant ailments but the fact that she bore no children for him. He wanted a *boppli* and blamed her for not conceiving.

Her eyes opened wide and she caught her breath.

A *boppli*!

She remembered what she had discussed with Leah before the tornado: Sadie's pregnancy. What she couldn't remember was whether or not that was what Leah shared with Jacob and Thomas in the barn. They had been so serious and then Jacob was upset. Understandably so, Lydia reasoned. After all, Sadie's pregnancy reflected upon the entire family, not just her and Manny.

"Glad to see you're awake!"

Startled, Lydia jerked her head back toward the door. A man with a graying mustache and white jacket walked into the room, a broad smile on his face as he walked toward the bed. For a split second, Lydia stared at him, shocked that a man was in the room. She lifted her hand to her head and, to her relief, there was a handkerchief covering her hair.

"Dr. Shaw," he said, reaching out his hand to shake hers. "How's your head feeling, Lydia?"

She withdrew her hand from his and tucked it under the covers of the bed. "Hurts" was all she said.

"I imagine so!" He laughed and crossed his arms over his chest. "That's what happens when you get hit by a tree in a tornado. One lucky woman, you are!"

"Where's my family?" She hated the way her voice sounded, weak and timid. She didn't like being at this hospital, not as a visitor and certainly not as a patient. She felt out of her element and wanted nothing more than to go home.

He glanced at the clock. "I imagine they'll be arriving shortly. You've been here for almost four hours. But," he turned back to her and smiled. "I'm pleased to report that all of our scans came back and nothing is broken. You did, however, receive a knock on your head. Nothing serious but I imagine there will be a bit of pain and you may even experience some memory loss."

Memory loss? She frowned.

"We're going to keep you here overnight, Lydia," the doctor said.

"What!" She tried to sit up again but the pain in her head forced her to abandon that idea.

"Now calm down," he said softly. "Just one or two nights to observe you; make certain you're just fine."

Shutting her eyes, Lydia tried to block the words that continued to flow from his mouth.

"While I don't suspect there's any problem, I am concerned about the possibility of a concussion." He paused. "Any blow to the head is dangerous, but you were unconscious for a while. We need to rule out swelling of the brain. Just as a precaution."

"Swelling of the brain?" Lydia asked.

"I'm sure you are fine. Just a precaution to make sure. Now, can I have the nurse get you anything? Are you hungry? Thirsty?" Dr. Shaw asked as he moved toward the door.

"*Nee.* I'm fine," she mumbled. "I'd just like to see my family."

"I'll have the nurse bring them in as soon as they arrive. For now, you need to rest." And at that, Dr. Shaw left the room.

It was only ten minutes after the doctor left when Leah and Jacob walked through the door. Lydia glanced over their shoulders, expecting to see Abe behind them. When she noticed that they were alone, she realized that she felt a wave of disappointment.

Where was her husband?

"Lydia! You had us all worried half to death!" Leah said as she rushed toward the bed. "Are you feeling all right? How's your head?"

"Hurts," she mumbled in response. Her eyes searched behind them as if expecting someone else to walk through the door. When she realized that no one else accompanied Leah and Jacob, she returned her attention to her sister. "Where's Abe?"

Jacob stepped forward and touched her arm. "Tree fell on your house, Lydia. No one's injured, but there's a crew there, working on it."

None of this made sense to Lydia. "My house?"

"It's right *gut* you weren't at home," Leah said. "Smashed in the roof, apparently."

"Abe? Is he hurt?"

"*Nee, nee!*" Leah reassured her. "We're luckier than most. A little further north, an entire neighborhood of Englische lost everything. But, thank the good Lord, no one is reported missing."

Lydia shut her eyes and groaned. "How bad is the damage?" If Abe hadn't come to visit her, she knew it must have been extensive.

"Thomas went over," Leah answered. "Said there was a hole in the upstairs bedroom."

Lydia's eyes opened and she stared at her sister. A hole upstairs? That didn't sound like a lot of damage. She frowned, wondering why Abe would have chosen to stay home and tend to that instead of coming to ensure that she was all right.

And then she remembered. The fight. His words. The bishop. The threat. He wasn't there at the hospital, not because of a tree branch that fell on the house, but because he was angry. Angry with her. He didn't believe her complaints about fatigue and headaches. He thought she faked her illnesses. The irony was not lost on her. Here she was, laying in a hospital bed with doctors concerned that she suffered from a concussion, and her husband refused to visit her. Instead, he hid at home, tending to a 'hole' in the roof, using the tornado as an excuse.

"I'm sure he'll be here tomorrow," Leah said as a way to offer comfort to her sister.

Lydia lifted an eyebrow but didn't respond. Instead, she rolled her head on the pillow and looked out the window. She rested her eyes on the clouds, noticing the blueness of the sky. A few clouds drifted behind some trees. The green leaves shimmied in a soft breeze, reflecting the sunlight. The beauty of nature contrasted sharply with the ugliness from earlier that day. It was an ugliness that she still felt inside of her chest at the realization that Abe's lack of compassion for her injuries indicated his willingness to abandon her. Had she lost him for good?

Jacob cleared his throat and glanced at the clock on the wall. He seemed anxious, shifting his weight from one foot to another. "*Ach vell,*" he mumbled, glancing at Leah. They exchanged a look that Lydia could not interpret. "*Mayhaps* I might just go check in on Tobias while we're here."

Lydia watched as the muscles in Leah's jaw tightened. There was a tension between them, something that Lydia couldn't put her finger on. A secret, no doubt. Yet, deep inside, she suspected that it had nothing to do with Sadie. She also suspected that she should remember what caused the tension. Try as she might, she simply couldn't remember.

"We only have twenty minutes," Leah said tersely to Jacob. "Don't dawdle none!"

Once he had left the room, Lydia couldn't help herself but comment, "Don't understand why Jacob's here. Never been one to be all mushy over stuff like this." She tried to read Leah's reaction. "And he never did get on well with Tobias! Why, this is just downright strange!" No response. "Are you certain *he* didn't get hit by a tree?"

Once again, the muscles in Leah's jaw twitched. This time, however, she ignored what Lydia said. Instead, she turned her attention to Lydia, fussing over her by smoothing down the thin, white blanket and patting Lydia's hand. "Now, you rest up," Leah began. "I saw the doctor just before and they said you're going to be fine. They'll be keeping an eye on you overnight, just to make certain you didn't do more than just bonk your head." She smiled at Lydia. "Should I fetch you some water? I saw a small kitchen down the hallway."

Lydia shook her head. She wasn't thirsty. Instead, she reached out for Leah's hand. Her eyes studied Leah's face, looking for an indication of what was not being said. "How bad was that tornado?"

Leah paused, just for a split second. Lydia tried to read her sister's reaction, tried to see the truth in her eyes. But Leah had always been a good one at hiding her emotions. Only this time, she couldn't. The hesitation told Lydia all that she needed to know. Something was amiss. Unfortunately, Lydia knew that, while she wasn't one to sugarcoat the truth, Leah also wasn't one to cause needless worry in others. Lydia could tell that Leah weighed her words carefully, trying to determine how much information to share with her.

"It's not good, Lydia," she finally admitted. "Not good at all." She sighed and paced the floor, rubbing her hands together. "The store is demolished; our house and Jacob's are both in bad shape. Nothing we can't fix, peripheral damage for the most, but that storm sure left a mess. And there was damage to the far side of the barn. It got hit as the storm passed through before it damaged some of the crops."

Lifting her hand to cover her mouth, Lydia fought the urge to interrupt her.

"Now I didn't see your house," Leah said softly. "Merv and

Susie were the ones that went to tell Abe. And the only reason I know anything about the damage to your house at all is that Thomas went over to check on Abe when he could get through the back roads. That big tree that fell on you is still blocking the main road."

"Oh help! The store's gone?"

Leah nodded her head. "That's right."

She lifted her hand to rub her forehead. "I don't remember any of the storm."

"*Mayhaps* that's better," Leah said, smiling gently at her sister. "Although I sure would like to know what you were doing out in the storm anyway. Do you remember that?"

If only she did! Lydia tried, once again, to think back to that image of Leah standing with Thomas and Jacob. They looked distressed while they discussed something, something that made Jacob upset. Were they talking about Sadie or something else?

"I rode my bicycle back to fetch my handbag," Lydia said. Then, averting her eyes, she lied. She didn't want to admit that she had eavesdropped on their conversation, even if she couldn't recall what she heard. "Don't remember much else."

"We just need to say an extra prayer tonight. Thank the good Lord that He protected you," Leah said, glancing over her shoulder at the clock. Lydia could sense Leah's anxiety. It was as strong as Jacob's had been. "Now, I best go check on Tobias and get back home. An awful lot of cleanup to do. Besides, you need to rest now."

Long after Leah disappeared out the door, Lydia stared after her. Something was wrong, terribly wrong. If only she could remember that conversation from the barn, she thought. Then she would have the answers to Jacob's strange behavior and Leah's unusually tense mood.

Sadie

The sun set low over the horizon, the colors in the sky changing rapidly from oranges and reds to purples and blues. With no clouds overheard, the stars coming out twinkled like tiny fireflies in a vast field. The only other light came from the battery-operated lantern beside her. It cast a small orange glow on the porch, illuminating the pile of children's boots by the door.

Sadie sat on the edge of the porch, a glass of meadow tea in her hand. Her body felt weak, bone tired. Still, she knew it would be useless to try to sleep right now. Without the activity of the day, her mind raced back to the news that the doctor shared with her.

"You all right out here?" Leah asked as she pushed open the screen door that Thomas fixed while they visited the hospital earlier that evening.

Sadie nodded her head unconvincingly.

Sitting next to her, Leah took a deep breath and looked up at the sky. "Sure is ironic, ain't so? Such a beautiful night after such an ugly day!"

"Like God's rainbow to Noah's flood," Sadie whispered. "A promise, I reckon."

For a few minutes, they sat in silence, each absorbed in their own thoughts. Sadie wondered what Leah was thinking before she got lost in her own mind. Breast cancer. What lie ahead for her? The different options scared her: lumpectomy, partial mastectomy, bilateral? Would she have to subject her body to chemotherapy and radiation? Would her hair fall out? Would she live?

The thoughts rushed through her, a whirlwind of confusion. She hadn't the time to consider the news earlier. In a way, she knew that being busy kept her preoccupied. Then the news about Lydia sent everyone into a tailspin. There had been no time to think about her own problems. Now, with the still of night surrounding her, it was the only thing on her mind.

"Sadie," Leah said softly, interrupting her thoughts. "*Mayhaps* it's time we had a talk."

A talk? Sadie's heart jumped within her chest. She wanted to talk. Oh how much she wanted to talk! Earlier that day, she wished more than anything that she had confided in Leah. It would have done her a world of good to have Leah's strength beside her when the doctor had confirmed what Sadie suspected for weeks.

"*Ja*," Sadie whispered with a somber look on her face.

She heard Leah clear her throat and shift her weight. Clearly she was uncomfortable with whatever she had on her mind. Sadie just wished that the words "I have breast cancer" would pop out of her mouth, just blurt it to Leah and be done with the bad news.

Sharing the news would give her strength. Still, Sadie felt guilt in doing so. Leah's problems were broad and deep, encompassing everyone in the family, not just herself.

"Sadie," Leah began slowly, as if carefully selecting her words. "We've had quite a day, ain't so? One that I hope is never repeated. God was good to us. He spared our *schwester* and, for that, I can only thank Him over and over again."

Sadie remained silent, staring thoughtfully at her older sister.

"But Lydia shared something with me," Leah continued. "Something about you and your sickness."

For a split second, Sadie repeated Leah's words in her head. That had not been what she expected to hear. What direction was this conversation going? And then, it dawned on her. Her heart palpitated and her palms grew sweaty. Was it possible? "Lydia knows?"

Leah nodded her head slowly, a sorrowful look on her face.

"How? How does Lydia know?" Sadie asked.

"I don't know. She didn't share that with me," Leah said.

Sadie opened her mouth, ready to tell Leah everything: about the lump, about the doctors, about the dreadful decision that she had to make. But a loud noise interrupted them. Without the windows in the house, every noise carried outside, amplified by the still night air.

So when a pot clattered on the floor of Jacob and Esther's house followed by a loud scream, both Leah and Sadie jumped to their feet and raced toward their front door, not bothering to knock as they flung it open and hurried into the kitchen.

Esther stood with her back against the counter, her face covered with her hands. Her shoulders moved, ever so slightly, as she sobbed. Jacob knelt before her, his hand clinging to her apron with tears streaming down his face. The pathetic image of Jacob so desperate and Esther so upset startled Sadie.

"What's going on?" she whispered, her eyes darting from the distraught couple to Leah then back to her brother.

"You best be going to check on the *kinner*," Leah said. "I'll handle this."

And, for once, Sadie shook her head, defiant in her response. "No!" She shook off Leah's touch on her arm and stared at her. "I have a right to know. This is my family, too!"

Esther looked up and, through red, swollen eyes, stared at the two women standing before her. Her cheeks looked shallow and pale. In just minutes, she had aged. "You want to know?" she said, her voice shaking.

"Esther, don't…" Leah warned gently.

"You want to know?" This time, Esther screamed it. "Jacob is not my true husband! He knew another woman before me!"

The words didn't register with Sadie. She looked at Leah who merely stared ahead, stoic as ever in the face of family problems. "Is this true?" Sadie whispered, not believing what Esther had shouted but not comprehending the lack of response on anyone's part. Why wasn't Jacob telling her to stop lying? Why was Leah acting as if she had known?'

Esther grabbed her apron and yanked it free from Jacob's hands. "Don't touch me, you sinner! Don't touch me ever again!"

"Calm down, Esther." Leah spoke through clenched teeth, her voice, normally so calm and soothing, stern and direct. "This will not solve the problem."

Sadie shook her head. Nothing made sense. "I…I don't understand."

Esther jerked her head to look at Sadie, anger blazing behind her tired eyes. "Tobias isn't your *bruder*, Sadie," she snapped, the words harsh and spoken with contempt. "He's your nephew!" She turned her eyes to glare at her husband, a broken man on his knees at her feet. Still, she showed no mercy. "And Jacob is his *daed*!"

Part Two

Why does it come to pass
That the opposite befalls me?
When I want to live in joy,
Much distress enters in,
That I can never, wholeheartedly,
Anywhere in this time,
Observe a joyful feast,
I am hindered by sorrow.

Ausbund Song 105, Verse 3

When the wicked advance against me
to devour[a] me,
it is my enemies and my foes
who will stumble and fall.
Though an army besiege me,
my heart will not fear;
though war break out against me,
even then I will be confident.

Psalm 27:2-3 NIV

The Back Stab

Her hands shook and she clenched them into fists, burying them into the folds of her dress. Her jagged nails cut her palms, but she ignored the pain. It was nothing compared to the pain in her heart. She still couldn't shake the feeling of disbelief over everything that had happened.

It had been a long day. *Nee*, she thought as she stared at the fresh lumber piled on the driveway, the soft glow from the lantern casting shadows around it. A long week. Had it only been two days ago when the tornado had ripped through their community? God had been good to them, indeed. While plenty of people were injured and dozens of homes damaged, the only casualties were a few people with broken bones. No traumatic injuries. No one died and, for that, Leah gave thanks.

Still, not even the tornado had prepared her for what followed.

"There you are," Thomas said as he walked around the side of the barn. He handed her a steaming mug of coffee and reached down for the lantern. Lifting it over his head, he walked around the supplies that would soon be used to rebuild the store. "Elias was awful kind to get this for us so soon," he commented when he returned to her side. "Lots of people are in need of beams, boards, and nails."

Leah nodded, appreciative that Thomas' friend had managed to deliver the supplies, especially when so many others had suffered similar damage to their homes and outbuildings. Despite her gratitude, she remained silent. There were no words that she could say. Inside, she was still seething from the events of the day. Once again, life distracted her from the things that she needed to do: confront Sadie, deal with Esther, and talk to Jacob. Instead, Whoopie Pie Place consumed all of her time. If only she didn't need to rebuild it, she thought bitterly. If only they didn't need the income to survive.

"It's going to be all right," Thomas said softly, a concerned look on his face. He reached out and gently rubbed the side of her arm.

"You say that but you don't know it!" Instinctively, she brushed his hand away and regretted it as soon as she did. He was only trying to comfort her. Still, her foul mood dictated her actions. She'd apologize later.

Arching an eyebrow, Thomas tilted his head. "That's not *my* Leah," he commented slowly. In the glow from the lantern, Leah could see the sorrowful expression on his face. She looked away when he continued. "You know that God will provide. God will see us through this storm. And I'm not talking about the tornado."

Oh, she knew what he meant. In hindsight, the tornado had been the easy part. Dealing with what she had learned today, the betrayal from a friend and the fear from a community, had sent her into a tailspin: During her entire life, she never had to deal with deception. The human nature of the Amish community was no different than the Englische, that was for sure and certain. But deceit?

"Has Esther calmed down at all?" Leah asked, changing the subject to one that she could handle better.

He merely shrugged his shoulders.

"Sadie come down from her room yet?"

Another shrug.

Time, Leah thought. That was what they all needed. Time to heal the injuries of the past few days. After all, wounds were still open. It dawned on her that, despite the different circumstances, Esther felt the pain of deceit as deeply as she did. The only difference was that Jacob had not deceived his *fraa* on purpose. When he learned of the situation, he confessed to Esther.

As for Sadie, not another day could go by without the inevitable confrontation. Leah knew that much was true. The distractions from the previous days could no longer delay the inevitable for, unlike Jacob, Leah sensed that no confession was coming her way. Not this time.

Earlier That Day

"There's a match," Dr. Bodine exclaimed, a smile reaching from ear to ear on his face. "I can't believe it! A complete stranger stepped forward, was tested, and matched!"

Leah smiled but said nothing.

"A miracle!"

She nodded her head, too afraid to open her mouth and say what she really felt.

Oh, Jacob had told her what had happened the afternoon of the tornado when they visited Lydia in her hospital room. When he slipped away to visit Tobias, he had not taken the elevator to the other floor. Instead, he sought out his past.

"I saw her," Jacob confided in Leah just the previous day. "She's working at that hospital. I'm positive it was her."

"At the hospital?"

Jacob nodded, lowering his voice to a whisper. "The other day. Remember? I saw her walk by when we were all waiting to get our blood tests. I'm sure she recognized me."

The plan was easy. When Leah visited Lydia, Jacob would search out the woman. They both knew it would not be an easy conversation. Unfortunately, it was a matter of life or death: Tobias'.

Cheryl Weaver. Leah couldn't believe that God led them to this woman. It was a miracle that she worked at the hospital, the very hospital where Tobias awaited the bone marrow transplant. Only she wasn't Cheryl Weaver anymore. She had married a young man and had her own family now.

That had been two days ago. And only the previous night, Jacob shared his news with Leah in a hushed voice so that Esther would not overhear. His *fraa* was still reeling in shock, barely able to function. Ever since she heard Jacob's confession, she refused visitors, choosing to stay in bed, her blank eyes staring at the wall.

Reluctantly, Leah took over responsibility for the distraught woman's *kinner* during the day, one more burden that she did not need but was forced to accept.

"I heard she went to get tested yesterday," he whispered to Leah as they stood a safe distance from the house. "I reckon she got over the shock."

Leah didn't ask how he knew. She presumed that Jacob saw Cheryl earlier that day when they went to visit Tobias. Only Jacob had slipped away, refusing to see the sick boy. He simply wasn't ready to face the boy he had known as his brother for so many years and now knew was, indeed, his son.

Later that night, Leah had dropped to her knees, pressing her hands together and shutting her eyes. She prayed as hard as she could, begging God to protect Tobias and to let this woman be a match. Thomas had walked in on her and, seeing that she was praying, quickly backtracked out of the room, leaving her alone to share her innermost thoughts with God. She heard him close the door, appreciating his respect for the time she needed to be alone and unburden her cares and worries. Put them in a box and stick it in a closet, she used to tell the *kinner*. That's what she was doing now: letting God hear her needs. He would know what she needed and He would carry her through whatever troubles still remained unseen.

With the telephone lines still down, Leah had not received the doctor's message right away. Instead, Thomas found out when the neighbor ran down the lane with the message from the hospital on their voice mail, the secondary number Leah had left in case of emergency. Without delay, Leah arranged for Michelle to take her to the hospital.

After inquiring about Michelle's family and praising God when she learned that they had suffered no damage from the tornado, Leah fell quiet, deep in thought as her mind raced. Michelle respected her silence and focused on driving. They both knew whatever the doctor was going to share with Leah would change a lot of lives, whether for the better or worse.

The entire ride, a whole twenty minutes, felt as though it were an hour. The dragging of time didn't matter for Leah knew what the doctor was going to say. She smiled as she tapped her fingers against her knee, staring out the window, oblivious to the pockets of damage that still remained untended after the tornado. Yes, she knew all right. It was as if God spoke to her, placing His hand upon her head and telling her: *Be still and know that I am God*. She hurried to the doctor's office, knowing that her prayers had been answered long before he actually shared the news with her.

"What happens next?" Leah asked, leaning forward, anxious for the doctor to explain the next steps in the long-awaited treatment phase of Tobias' illness.

On her way home from the hospital, she shared the good news with Michelle, trying her hardest to perfect her story before being faced with the rest of the family. If anyone was going to tell others about Jacob's indiscretion so many years ago, it wasn't going to be her.

"They're starting treatment!" Leah gushed. "A donor was found!"

Michelle took her eyes off the road, just for a second, to glance at Leah in surprise. "How is that possible? I thought…"

Leah interrupted her. "Isn't it wonderful? Just right *gut* news! Why, he should be home in no time now!"

Nothing further was said about the donor, the focus of their discussion shifting to Tobias.

Whoopie Pie Place

Standing before Leah, Mattie looked about nervously as she waited for her reaction to the news. Leah knew what the older woman saw: the expression of a person who had just heard something horrible. For a moment, Leah thought Mattie was mistaken. Was it possible that one of the very people Leah thought was such a good friend, and not just to her but to the entire Miller family, had done something so outrageously horrible? Leah was left speechless.

She had returned from the hospital only two hours earlier. During that time, she focused on trying to figure out a way, any way possible, to still meet the deadlines for those two big orders. Now, more than ever, they would need the money. It was absolutely crucial. Without insurance, paying for the repairs to the store, or rebuilding it if necessary, would need to come out of pocket. And there was no money tree growing in the back paddock, that was for sure and certain.

Plus, there were the medical bills. Oh, she knew the community would chip in. They always did. But it would not cover all of the expenses. While she thanked God over and over again that Tobias' biological mother had not only been found and agreed to be tested but was also a match, that was the extent of her involvement with the boy. No one would rescue the Miller family from the debt that was headed their way.

And now this news. This dreadful, awful, unbelievable news that Mattie just shared with her.

Indeed, Leah was dumbstruck for one of the few times of her life.

"I'm so terribly sorry."

It was all that Leah could do to simply nod her head, knowing that Mattie meant those four words: the sorrowful expression on her tired face said more than her words. Certainly she felt as though she were between a rock and hard place.

"*Danke*, Mattie," Leah sighed, biting her tongue so that she didn't blurt out what she truly wanted to say. "I'm sure telling me was hard for you."

Her friend, an older woman from a stricter church district, shrugged her stooped shoulders. While Leah had grown up with Mattie and her family, Mattie's marriage to a former Swartzentruber Amish man had changed her life so that she had less time for socializing and more time to work toward being as Plain as possible. However, between her and her *dochders*, they made beautiful crafts that, in the past, Leah sold in Whoopie Pie Place to help Mattie and her husband support their family of eight children. Leah always welcomed the handmade items from the Amish women in the *g'may*. Selling their crafts on consignment helped increase the business at Whoopie Pie Place.

So it surprised Leah...and weighed heavily on her heart... to hear that Laverne who ran a fairly popular, if not overpriced, tour of the Amish country in Holmes County, a woman whom Leah considered to be a right *gut* friend, had approached Mattie behind Leah's back.

"What will you do then?" The question was spoken with a heavy sigh. Leah already knew the answer. After all, Mattie had eight children and one more on the way. Selling her crafts was of paramount importance to the survival of their family. Without Whoopie Pie Place, Leah knew that Mattie had but only one other option: selling to the tourists that Laverne bought to her home each week.

"I told her that you and I had an arrangement," Mattie admitted. Still, her eyes looked weary and the dark circles that shadowed them spoke of sleepless nights and long days. "But she told me that she has another farm to take the tours if she can't have an exclusive on my crafts." She lowered her eyes. "I need those tours, Leah. It's constant income and..."

Leah interrupted her by placing her hand on Mattie's arm.

She forced a smile and nodded her head. "I understand, Mattie." Steady income from the tours trumped items sold on consignment. Since she made more money with the tours, Mattie's back was against the wall. Leah sighed. "While I confess to being confused by Laverne's change of heart and the direction she wants to take her business, I do understand the difficult situation she has put you into. I'm just sorry that she put you in this position. Laverne should have come to me."

Mattie continued looking at the floor.

There was something else. Something left unspoken. Leah noticed that immediately from the way Mattie hesitated and refused to look her in the eyes. Putting her hands on her hips, Leah focused her gaze on the woman. "Mattie? What else aren't you telling me?"

Her question was greeted with silence.

"Mattie?"

"It's not just me!" Mattie blurted out the news, the pressure too much for her to bear. The expression of pain on the older woman's face hurt Leah for, without even being told, she knew. She suddenly knew why so few people had stopped in to see how they fared or to drop off their goods. She knew the truth and it hurt. Still, she needed to hear it for herself.

"What do you mean that it's not just you?"

Mattie shuffled her feet, the ripped black sneakers making a strange noise on the dirt of the Miller's unpaved driveway. "Laverne has talked to the other Amish women who promised to bake for you for that convention and the wedding. She said that you can't do it now, not without Whoopie Pie Place so she is going to deliver the goods to the convention and to the Glick farm for Mary's wedding."

"How does she think she can do that?" Leah exclaimed. "She doesn't have commercial equipment!"

Mattie shook her head, looking ashamed. "She's asked

several of the Amish women in our church district to help her. Or, should I say, to cook it all for her."

Leah's heart skipped a beat and the heat rushed to her brain. It took her a few seconds to comprehend exactly what Mattie was telling her. Of all the people in the community to betray her trust, to attempt to ruin her business, Laverne was the most shocking.

Or was she?

Leah took a deep breath and exhaled slowly. In her entire life, Leah had never heard of such a thing being done among the Amish. Of course, Laverne was not an Amish woman. In fact, she was anything but Amish. Her tours were well known but there were many places in Holmes County that banned Laverne from bringing her tours to their farms, homes, and stores. In fact, her lack of respect for the Amish customs, including posting photos of Swartzentruber children on the Internet, caused her to be completely shunned by one community.

It started during a tour. While the Englische tourists looked through the stacks of baskets made by the Troyer family, Laverne pointed her camera at the children, sneaking a photo of their dirty feet. The family had learned of this transgression, a photo of the children's feet that the mamm had told Laverne not to take. She hadn't listened but took it anyway. Word had it that David Troyer warned her to remove it from the Internet and never do such a sinful, deceitful thing again. However, when Laverne posted a photo of his *dochder* in the garden on an Internet group for Englischer people, the Amish grapevine learned of it from an Englische farmer who immediately informed David. Laverne's tour career among the Troyer family's farms ended after that second transgression.

Many people among the Amish questioned her unethical behavior, but Leah was always one to give the benefit of the doubt. Laverne never gave Leah any reason to suspect that she was anything less than a good person and true friend. Until now. From what Mattie was telling her, Laverne was trying to sabotage Whoopie Pie Place as well as steal those orders for the convention and wedding. Indeed, the Englische woman's attempts to blackmail the Amish women shocked Leah. No true Christian would do something so heartless and cruel, Leah told herself, trying to keep calm in front of Mattie. After all, Leah had never been anything but a good friend to Laverne. She even promoted the Englische woman's tour company when customers from out of state asked Leah for recommendations. In the world of the Amish, one hand washed the other. They took care of each other, sharing in friendship and success.

Apparently that was not a philosophy that Laverne understood.

"*Ja vell,*" Leah finally said, searching deep within herself to find the strength to hold back the bitterness that bubbled inside of her. Her disappointment and anger served no one, if misdirected. She'd deal with Laverne later. Forcing a smile, Leah straightened her shoulders and looked Mattie in the eyes. "I do thank you for letting me know, Mattie. Not certain what I'll be able to do about this, but I do know one thing…Whoopie Pie Place will reopen and be just as strong as it was before in the Amish community!"

"No doubt, Leah." But Mattie's eyes showed the concern that she was feeling.

Leah watched as Mattie Petersheim turned around and got into her buggy. Not once did Mattie look back, the shame too much to grant her that one friendly gesture that might calm Leah. Instead, the fact that Mattie drove away reinforced the anger that welled inside of Leah's chest.

"Stronger shoulders, Lord," she whispered as she turned to walk back toward the house. "Give me stronger shoulders, by all means!"

Leah

"And that's what Mattie told me," Leah said to Susie. She stood by her kitchen counter, her hands kneading the dough on the floured board. Roughly, she squished it between her fingers and pounded on it with a fist. Pretending to see Laverne's face in the rounded ball made it all the more easy to punch it.

Susie reached out and placed her hand on Leah. "Easy there, *Schwester*! You'll knock that dough and send it to Berlin!"

She exhaled sharply and shoved the dough away from her. Ever since Mattie had stopped by earlier that day, Leah thought of nothing else but Laverne. It hadn't helped when Martha Schrock stopped by an hour afterward, to drop off a basket of apples and, like Mattie, whispered that Laverne needn't know about her gift.

"I'd like to send that Laverne all the way to Berlin!" Leah snapped. "And I'm not talking Berlin, Ohio!"

Despite the seriousness of the situation, Susie found herself trying to suppress a giggle.

"It's not funny!" Leah said, glaring at her sister. "She's trying to destroy our business! No good Christian does that. At least no good Christian that I know!"

"*Nee*," Susie admitted somberly. "This is true."

"And what is that Sadie doing?" Marching to the bottom of the stairs, she leaned on the banister and yelled, "Sadie Miller! You get down here! I need some help and your dawdling isn't helping one bit!"

Within seconds, Sadie ran down the stairs, trying to adjust her prayer *kapp* on her head. Her bare feet pounded on the wooden steps and she greeted Susie with a sheepish smile. "Overslept."

"A blind person could see that!"

Susie rolled her eyes behind Leah's back, giving her head a soft shake to warn Sadie that a tiger lurked beneath the surface of their older sister's skin.

"I saw that, Susie!" She turned her attention to Sadie. Sleeping late. Again. They hadn't talked yet. It was high time for that discussion, Leah told herself. Except life kept getting in the way. For a long moment, Leah studied Sadie's face as if looking for some indication of guilt or sadness. There was none. "Make yourself useful, then! Pull those whoopie pies out of the oven," Leah snapped at her. "And put the other pans in."

"Oh help," Sadie whispered to Susie who responded with an 'I told you so' expression that didn't escape Leah's eye.

Hurrying to the oven, Sadie opened the door and pulled out two pans with fluffy whoopie pie cakes. The smell wafted through the room, comforting and familiar. Leah worked furiously, shaping the bread dough into small loaves. She could feel Sadie's eyes on her back, watching her. Ignoring both of her sisters, Leah plopped the shaped dough into the bread pans and shoved them down the countertop toward Sadie.

"Something bothering you, Leah?"

Whirling around, Leah glared at Sadie. "If you had awoken on time, Sadie, you'd have been here and heard what that nasty Laverne is doing to our business!"

A confused look crossed Sadie's face. "Laverne?" she asked, her eyes darting from Leah to Susie and back to Leah again. "I don't understand."

It was Susie who tried to explain. "Mattie Petersheim stopped by. Told Leah that Laverne is making her rounds to buy everyone's products to sell. Telling them that, if they do not sell to her exclusively, she won't bring her tours there. Martha stopped by, too. She dropped off some apples for us but mentioned that Laverne dare not know she was here."

Predictably, Sadie gasped. "What on earth…?"

Leah nodded her head, fury still etched in her expression. "She has them all running scared. And, even worse, she's trying to steal our big orders. While you were sleeping," she said, her voice dripping with sarcasm. "But don't fret none, Sadie. I used the neighbor's phone and left a voice message with the convention people, reassuring them that we'd have their whoopie pies and bread. And I sent Thomas over to Mary Glick's, to let the family know that we'd come through for them, too."

Susie sighed. "I just don't know how we can do it, Leah. I think we sure did bite off more than we can chew this time."

But Leah would hear none of that. She spun around and wagged her finger in Susie's face. "We did not bite off more than we can chew!" she shouted. "And we would have been fine had it not been for the storm. *Nee*, everything will be fine." She pounded her closed fist onto the counter. "I will not let that woman steal our business! We have to find a way. God sent us those two orders so He will find a way for us to make good on them." She took a deep breath. It wasn't easy to calm herself. Too much had happened in such a short period of time. Laverne's antics had pushed her over the edge. "I just hope those convention people call back with good news."

There was a moment of silence in the room. Sadie put the two other whoopie pie pans in the oven and shut the door, careful to set the timer before she turned back to her sisters.

"I think I know how we can do it," she said softly.

Leah stared at her, eyeing her younger sister with a skeptical look. She had yet to confront Sadie, something that weighed heavily on her mind. Too much had happened in the past few days and dealing with Sadie's issue…alleged issue, she reminded herself…just wasn't on the priority list at the current moment. If it was true, Leah reasoned with herself, it wasn't going away anytime soon. Plenty of time to deal with Sadie.

"Let's call a meeting of the women at the schoolhouse," Sadie offered. "We get everyone to help with the order and share the profit. With so much damage in the community, I bet everyone could use a little extra money, don't you think?"

The expression softened on Leah's face. Of course, she thought. The simplicity of the solution almost made her laugh. They had already arranged to use kitchens at two Mennonite churches. If the women of the g'may offered to help, it would be no hardship at all to fulfill the orders as promised. It was better to lose some of the profit than to let Laverne steal their business.

"Hmmph," Leah snorted, trying to hide her pleasure at Sadie's suggestion. "*Mayhaps* you better sleep late more often, I think!"

Sadie laughed and Susie joined her. Even Leah could not prevent a smile to sneak onto her face. The joy of sisterhood, she thought, reaching out to hug the two women. Joy indeed, as she let out a deep sigh of relief.

Susie

"I called you all together today to ask for your help."

She stood in the schoolhouse, standing before the rows of small desks that were occupied by the women of the *g'may*. Eighteen pairs of eyes stared back at her, curious and eager to hear why they were sitting there. Susie recognized many of the women in attendance. Half of them were, indeed, from her own *g'may*, but she also noticed just as many women that were from outside of the Miller's church district. Several women hadn't been able to attend, sending their regrets via Thomas and Leah's son, Aaron, when they visited each of the families in the *g'may* to inform them about the meeting. Those who accepted the invitation to attend the meeting must have spread the word to their own extended family who felt compelled to join as well.

Despite feeling uncomfortable speaking to such a large group, Susie knew only too well that it was now up to her to help Leah save their Whoopie Pie Place.

"You all know that our bakery was destroyed in the tornado. Even worse, Sister Lydia was injured and our *bruder*, Tobias, is in the hospital." She paused and stared out at the eyes watching her every move.

Leah had volunteered to stay home with the *kinner*. It was unusual for her not to be the take-charge person; but, as her nerves still rattled from what she learned earlier that day about Laverne, she expressed concern that she wouldn't be able to maintain her calm and composure at the schoolhouse meeting. That would certainly not bode well with the women and possibly trigger the opposite results the sisters were hoping for. Sadie offered to go with Susie to talk to the women, but it was Susie who volunteered to do the talking. She didn't know why but she felt the need to take a leadership role in recruiting the other women.

"Yet, we promised to help with Mary Glick's wedding as well as that convention coming up. We need your help to make our commitment which happens to be the only way we will be able to afford rebuilding Whoopie Pie Place." Susie paused and glanced at Sadie who stood by her side. "With our building in shambles, and most of our baking equipment, shelving and display cases destroyed, we just can't fulfill the order between the three of us."

There was a long moment of silence and then a soft mumbling accompanied by a nodding of some heads amongst the women.

"And I'm sure most of you know the other part of the story," Susie went on slowly, taking her time for more effect on the captive audience. She paced her words in a measured tone. "Someone is trying to steal our business so that we cannot open Whoopie Pie Place again. Money is more important to this person than friendship. I won't name anyone in particular but I'm sure it's no secret to many of you."

This time, the mumbling became an animated roar. Those who hadn't heard the news about Laverne's attempt to steal the Miller sisters' business leaned over to their neighbors, asking for details. Deliberately, Susie let the women talk amongst themselves, even if only for a few drawn out moments. If nothing else, Laverne deserved that much.

Finally, when the noise became too loud and the focus of the meeting had shifted away from the real dilemma, Susie silenced the women by lifting her hand. When the chatter died down and all eyes faced the front of the room once again, she continued.

"What we'd like to do is share the profits with anyone who can help us. Supplies come in tomorrow and we will separate them into boxes. Thomas and Merv agreed to drop them off at your houses. All we ask is that anyone who can help volunteers to bake the whoopie pies for Mary's wedding next week and then, two weeks later, help with the larger order of whoopie pies and bread for the convention. We'll split the profits with everyone who helps."

The plan was simple. Every woman seated in the schoolhouse knew how to make bread and most had whoopie pie pans. Those who didn't could bake them on cookie sheets. The hardest part was finding the time to make so many of them in one day. Also, Susie knew that some women preferred other chores to baking.

It was Jenny Yoder who finally stood up to speak. She looked directly at Susie and nodded her head. "I can only offer my own help, Susie. I can't speak on behalf of others. But my *kinner* and I will do whatever it takes to help you fulfill these two orders."

Slowly, other women stood up and offered the same service, each one commenting on how the community needed to support Whoopie Pie Place and how they would not want to see the business go to an Englischer, especially one who had so blatantly stolen the business from the Miller sisters.

"And furthermore," Jenny said, raising her voice so that she could be heard over the noise of the other women. "I want to donate my percentage to help you rebuild the store, even larger and better than before."

"Me, too!" another woman called out.

The room erupted into a general consensus: no profit needed to be split among the participants. Without Whoopie Pie Place, the neighborhood would feel empty. Whoopie Pie Place was an anchor store of sorts for the community. Besides, one of the women rationalized, tourists came from all over to visit the famous store, bringing business to food stands and other small shops and outlets throughout the entire community. Heads nodded in enthusiastic agreement.

"We cannot thank you enough," Susie managed to say, red in the face and fighting her own tears. While she should not have been surprised at their generosity, the overwhelming sense of relief that washed over her had a strong emotional affect that made it hard to keep her composure.

As the meeting adjourned, several women walked up to Susie and shook her hand, commending her on the initiative and expressing their joy at learning about Tobias' mystery donor. At first, she didn't notice that no one seemed to talk to Sadie. By the time Jenny Yoder approached her, however, she realized that something was amiss.

"Jenny," Sadie said as she stood beside Susie. She looked worried as she greeted Manny's mamm and her voice trembled. The desperation in her eyes pained Susie. "I…I haven't seen Manny since the storm. Is…is everything all right at home, then?"

The first thing Susie noticed was the cold look in Jenny's eyes. The older woman who had been so cheerful and pleasant during the meeting transformed before Susie's eyes. Jenny's body tensed and she refused to meet Sadie's eyes. "Right as rain," she said, her voice forced and emotionless. Without another word, Jenny turned and walked away, leaving Sadie staring after her and Susie staring at the floor.

Lydia's words. Elmer and Manny had overheard what Lydia said before the ambulance took her away. While Susie had chosen to believe that Lydia spoke out of delirium, clearly Manny and Elmer had not. They chose to believe Lydia's words and, from the looks of it, the Amish grapevine proved powerful once again.

Looking at Sadie, she wondered if her *schwester* had recognized the snub. As the color drained from Sadie's cheeks, Susie realized that she did. Now, the question remained whether or not she knew why Jenny avoided eye contact and that, apparently, the other women had learned of Lydia's words regarding Sadie's unfortunate predicament.

"You want to talk?" Susie asked softly.

"*Nee*," Sadie responded, shaking her head. "Nothing to talk about."

Without another word, Sadie turned away and began

collecting her things. Susie watched her, just for a minute, before she decided that she'd confide in Leah in the morning. Leah would know what to do, she reasoned. Leah always knew what to do when trouble fell upon the family. From the looks of it, Susie knew her younger sister was clearly in trouble.

Lydia

The cup of tea burned her hands and she quickly set it on the night table. "Ouch!" she muttered and looked up at Abe. "Did you have to make it so hot?"

He took a deep breath and exhaled, pacing himself before responding. "You asked for tea. I bought you tea. Tea is best served hot, ain't so?"

She tried to smile as she sat up in the bed, shoving a pillow behind her back so that it would support her properly. "I'm sorry, Abe. I didn't mean to criticize."

Two days ago, Abe had brought her home. She remembered all too well their fight and, during those two days, she tried with all of her might to behave better. The amnesia from the accident helped, especially when she pretended to not remember their argument and his threats to run to the bishop. Now, with a little help from a tornado and a lot of help from a big tree, she had slipped into a new persona, smiling at Abe and doing whatever she could to avoid that threatened confrontation with the bishop.

If he thought she didn't remember, she told herself at night while she listened to his gentle snoring in the darkness, he couldn't go to the bishop. No need to confess to what one does not remember, she rationalized.

"Now, tell me again," she began, sitting up straighter. "What happened to Whoopie Pie Place?"

He rolled his eyes and turned away from the bed. "I told you five times already, Lydia. The building's destroyed. Not much else to add."

Destroyed. Rubble. Needed to be rebuilt. She had loved hearing the story the first time and wished that he would tell it to her again. Finally she could stay home! No more working at the store. No more listening to Leah bossing her around. No more arguing with Susie. And Sadie…She clenched her jaw tightly. She wouldn't have to see Sadie as her belly grew large and round, carrying an unwanted baby that had been conceived in sin. A constant reminder of the one thing that she was unable to do: conceive a *boppli*.

"I just can't believe it," she said feigning sorrow in her voice. "Such a terrible disappointment. I'm sure Leah and Susie are just devastated!"

Abe looked in the small mirror hanging over the dresser, his eyes watching her. "You haven't asked much about Tobias," he said. "Aren't you even curious about your *bruder*?"

Inwardly, she cringed. Was his question a reprimand? Or was he merely testing her? "I presumed he was all right. Someone would have told me otherwise, *ja*?"

"They found a donor," Abe said. The tone of his voice cut through her. He stared at her, a serious look upon his face. "A one in a million chance! Right there in the hospital, too!"

This didn't make sense. Only family could be a donor. Hadn't Leah explained that to them? "That's impossible!"

"Apparently not."

He wasn't happy. That much was clear. Lydia just couldn't understand why. She was trying, wasn't she? Trying to be the wife that he wanted, despite wanting so much to complain about the throbbing in her head. Why, he hadn't even come to visit her in the hospital. Instead, he showed up an hour before her discharge. Didn't he care at all about her?

"Abe," she said, softening her voice. "I told you that I'd try, that I'd see that doctor you and the bishop wanted me to see."

He leveled his gaze at her but remained silent.

"I'm willing to try," she continued. "Just let me get better from this…" She gestured with her hand toward her head. "It hurts. Still hurts so much." She winced as she touched her forehead. "Can you do that Abe? Let me recover from this awful accident? Why, I could have been killed Abe."

His eyes narrowed and he shook his head.

"You don't believe me?" she asked incredulously. "Abe! I'm telling you the truth. Honest I am."

"*Nee*, Lydia," he said as he turned to walk out the door. "I fear that you don't know what the truth is anymore. And you certainly don't know how to be a godly woman or caring *fraa*."

Alone in the room, Lydia crossed her arms over her chest and scowled, fuming at his harsh tone with her. Accusing her of lying? How dare he? She remembered that she had promised to speak to the doctor, if only to appease the bishop. Still, Abe should show her mercy at such a time. Escaping death in the eye of a tornado should elicit some emotion on his part. Instead, her new injuries evoked even more anger from him.

Tossing the covers back, Lydia fought the pain that seared through her head and swung her legs over the edge of the mattress. Struggling, she managed to stand, the dizziness in her head forcing her to lean a hand against the nightstand to steady herself. Truth? She took a deep breath, fighting her rage. He wanted a caring *fraa*? She'd show him. She'd be a caring *fraa* by showing him just how wrong he was!

After changing from her nightgown into a dress, slipping the straight pin into the side to reinforce the seam, she forced herself to leave the sanctuary of her bedroom and, on bare feet, shuffled into the kitchen. Seated at the table, Abe looked up in surprise. He watched her, curious as to why she was out of bed, but did not speak.

"I know how to be a *fraa*," she snapped at him. "I won't be accused of that!"

She opened the refrigerator and began pulling food out, slamming it onto the counter. She glared over her shoulder at her husband. He appeared completely unaffected by her irrational behavior.

"Oh you think the bishop won't hear about this?" she

added. "You run to him with *your* complaints? *Ja, vell,* he'll hear about this, that's for sure and certain."

Abe shook his head and returned his attention to the newspaper that he had been reading. His silence further infuriated her.

"Forcing a sick woman to work! Showing her no sympathy!" She scoffed. "Oh the bishop will have something to say about that!"

"You used up all my sympathy, Lydia," he mumbled. "A lifetime of sympathy, in the past two years."

Hearing those words, she felt as though someone had flipped a switch inside Lydia's emotions chamber. Could this be true? Had Abe lost all of his caring and love for her? She panicked, her eyes wide and her pulse quickening.

She turned back to the food before her on the counter. Her hands shook and she took a deep breath, trying to calm her nerves as she wondered what Abe's words meant. Divorce was not a possibility among the Amish. But if Abe had given up on their marriage, given up on them as a couple, where would that leave her? What type of future did they have if Abe wasn't willing to give her time to change?

Sadie

The bishop stood on the porch, his hat in his hand as he waited for someone to answer the door. That someone was Sadie.

She caught her breath when she saw him and, with downcast eyes, she took a step back, holding the door open. Despite Esther's shock and silence, she must have confided in someone, sharing the heartbreaking news of Jacob's indiscretion and the subsequent years of lies that followed in regards to Tobias' genetic parents. She knew better than to be surprised. Once revealed, such secrets could not be contained.

"Reckon I know what this is about," she whispered, wishing that Leah hadn't gone for that walk with Thomas. She would need Leah's strength to speak to the bishop about what she knew regarding Jacob and Tobias.

"Might I speak with you for a spell?"

His voice sounded forced and conflicted. He, too, averted his eyes, having trouble looking at her. Sadie blushed, knowing all too well that the *g'may* would soon hear about this news that would forever stain the Miller family's good name.

Outside, the *kinner* giggled and played, the noise carrying on the wind through the open windows. She knew it was best that they'd remained outside. To them, Tobias would always be their *onkel*, regardless of what happened today.

"Sadie," the bishop began, clearing his throat and shifting his weight as he sat on the hard chair at the kitchen table. "Some accusations have been made and I fear it is time we discussed them."

Looking at the Bishop with tear-filled eyes, Sadie nodded her head. Oh Jacob, she thought. If only he had told us before now. "I understand. I just wish Leah was here."

"It's best that we talk alone, Sadie," he replied.

While she didn't understand that, she wasn't about to

disagree with him. Contradicting the bishop would not help the situation.

"There has been word spreading throughout the *g'may*, Sadie, about a pregnancy…an out-of-wedlock pregnancy," he said solemnly, forcing himself to stare at her. "This is a most disgraceful situation."

She nodded her head. "*Ja*, I agree," she whispered. "We were all rather surprised when we found out."

"I need not remind you that intimacy is reserved for husband and wife. As a baptized member of the church, you are well aware of that, Sadie. Such relations…" He paused, searching for the right words. "Such relations go against the *Ordnung* and, when the rules are broken, there are consequences."

She frowned. Was he speaking about the *Meidung*? The shunning? She had suspected that Jacob would have some consequences for his actions, but to shun him for something that happened so many years ago? Something that had also been kept from him? "That seems rather unforgiving," she said softly, surprised that she spoke up at all. But once said, she could not retract the words. Instead, she lifted her head and stared at the bishop, meeting his steely gaze. She'd deal with the consequences later. "It happened so long ago."

He seemed to ponder her words. "Was it a one-time thing, then?"

She laughed, a short laugh and one without mirth, but a laugh nonetheless. "I'm sure I don't know those details! You'd have to ask him. I only found out the other day. And I've asked no questions since."

While she might not have asked them, she certainly wondered about them. All she knew was that Jacob had confronted the mother and she had agreed to be tested to see if she was a viable donor. Sadie followed her own personal policy of asking no questions when information was not offered willingly. If someone had secrets, who was she to probe for answers?

Her answer displeased him. That much was clear. A shadow passed over his eyes and he gave her a stern look. "You should take this quite serious, Sadie. You face a consequence that would change your life. No contact with your friends and family. Raising the *boppli* alone."

His words stung and she blinked twice, repeating the one word that caught her off guard. "*Boppli?*"

"*Ja,*" he affirmed, his voice terse. "Your *boppli.*"

The color drained from her cheeks and she felt her heart pound. *What on earth was he talking about?* She hated to question him, but felt that she had no choice. "I'm sorry, Bishop, but I'm lost. I don't understand what you are saying."

He leaned forward, jabbing his fingers onto the tabletop, the noise echoing throughout the empty room. "Sadie Miller! Are you or are you not with child?"

Her mouth fell open. Suddenly she understood. Suddenly, as though a rush of wind had knocked her over, the odd behavior of so many people over the past few days made sense. Manny had not stopped by since the tornado. His mamm avoided her earlier that day at the schoolhouse. In fact, everyone seemed to avoid her when the meeting adjourned. And Leah had wanted to talk to her about something the night after the tornado. Sadie had thought it was about her health issues, but now she knew otherwise. Leah, too, thought she was pregnant.

"I'm speechless," she finally whispered. Her shoulders slumped and she leaned back in the chair. With misty eyes, she stared at the wall behind the bishop's head. She simply couldn't look him the eyes. "I don't understand how anyone could think such a thing."

The bishop frowned, his body relaxing just enough to indicate that he, too, was perplexed. "Are you saying it's not true, then?"

"Of course it's not true!" Sadie snapped. With all of her strength, she glared at the bishop. "And I'm insulted that anyone would suspect something like *that* from me! The sin of gossip runs rampant in your *g'may*, it seems!"

Her anger increased as she realized what had happened. Someone, somewhere had started this vicious rumor. Someone had thought so little of her that they sought to destroy her.

"I'm not certain what to say. Your sister Lydia…" The bishop stopped talking mid-sentence and lowered his own eyes. It was his turn to feel humbled in front of Sadie.

At the mention of her sister's name, Sadie snapped to attention. Lydia? What did Lydia have to do with this? Her blood boiled inside of her veins. After all that Sadie had done to maintain calm during the years, even when Lydia struggled to create waves in the most placid of water. Lydia's mouth had spoken these lies?

"If my *schwester* indicated that I was in a family way," she said in even, measured tones. "Then I suspect your discussion about the *Ordnung* and *Meidung* should be conducted with her, not me." Standing up, Sadie lifted her chin. "If there is nothing else, Bishop," she said defiantly. "I have chores to tend in order to prepare supper."

Without another word, she turned her back on the bishop, her hands trembling and her pulse throbbing at her temples. She stood at the counter, leaning against it for support as she shut her eyes, willing the bishop to leave the kitchen before she said something that she would regret later. The shaking in her hands trembled up her arms and she realized that tears were falling from her eyes.

Lydia. Of all people in the world to start such a terrible, humiliating lie! And to think that people believed it?

When she heard the door shut, she caught sight of the bishop walking down the stairs to the porch, his head hanging low as he headed for his buggy. She stopped pretending to work and let the tears fall freely down her cheeks.

Forget supper, she thought bitterly. She dropped the pan she held in her hands, letting it fall to the floor, the noise loud in the silence. Wiping at the tears, she turned and walked to the stairs, each step heavy and purposeful. It was time to stop thinking about others, she told herself. How could they think this of her? Had she not always been nothing but upright?

Running upstairs to her room, she quickly closed the door. Manny must hate her. If he thought she was in a family way then he must think that she had cheated on him for they had never done anything inappropriate and certainly nothing that would cause him to suspect she was an immoral woman.

And then it dawned on her.

Manny believed what he had heard! Suddenly, all the emotions of the last several days flowed from her body. The tears came rampantly and her body shook. For the next hour, Sadie felt nothing but the grief of what she had just learned. It wrecked havoc on her body and on her soul. Especially her soul. As she covered her face, quietly sobbing into her hands, all she could do was wonder why would God let any of this happen to her.

Part Three

Together before the Lord
Each expressed their faith,
The just and pure truth.
They spoke with understanding,
As much as was given to them,
According to God's good promises,
Enabled through His Spirit,
Through which one speaks.

Ausbund Song 28, Verse 6

I will lift up mine eyes unto the hills,
From whence cometh my help.
My help cometh from the Lord,
Which made heaven and earth

Psalms 121:1-2

The Recovery

It didn't matter that it was for only three nights. It felt like it was going to be longer; a lot longer. Leah stood on the porch, watching as the lights of the van gradually disappeared into the darkness.

Rebecca opened the door and poked out her head. "Little ones in bed, Mamm," she said, happy to have carried out her responsibilities

"That's right *gut*," Leah sighed and smiled at her oldest daughter.

Saying goodbye to Sadie had drained Leah's emotions. Now, watching the van drive her *schwester* away drained her energy. Despite knowing that she'd see her the following day, Leah felt a hollow emptiness inside of her. She feared she would never be able to deal with putting the little ones to bed. Their energy and endless demands for stories would only grate her nerves. Rebecca's offer to do it for her had been a timely gift of love.

"*Danke*," Leah said and reached out her hand. Rebecca smiled and took it, delighted with the invitation to join her mother.

Leah slipped her arm around Rebecca's shoulders, a rare embrace and display of emotion coming from an Amish mother to a daughter. But Leah needed to feel Rebecca next to her, even if only for a moment.

"She'll be all right, *ja*?"

Leah looked down at Rebecca, surprised by the question. At twelve, actually closer to thirteen, Rebecca was becoming a fine young woman. Next year would be her last at school. Then, she would stay home and help her mamm at the bakery. In another two years, little Anna would be old enough to start attending school. In the meantime, it was high time that Esther snapped out of her blue funk, faced reality, and began helping with the *kinner*. Everyone needed to pull their own weight, even in times of duress.

"*Ja,* Rebecca," Leah smiled softly. "*Mayhaps* she'll have some off days, but she'll be right as rain in no time."

"People die from cancer," Rebecca said. "She won't die?"

"Why Rebecca Mast! I'd no sooner try to guess God's plan than I would take His name in vain!" Despite the reprimand, Leah kept her arm around her daughter's shoulders and pulled her into another gentle embrace. "But I do know that the doctors will take right *gut* care of her. And God gave the medical people the knowledge of how to treat this cancer."

A small sigh of relief escaped from Rebecca. Leah hid her smile as she recognized that her *dochder* was a strong young woman with a large heart. All she needed was a little reassurance, Leah realized as she released Rebecca from her embrace.

"Now, we have a lot of work to do tomorrow," Leah said. "You best be going to bed now. And, with Sunday being a church day, we're going to need all the hours in the day, that's for sure and certain!"

Rebecca bade her goodnight and, reluctantly, retreated into the house. Leah knew that she had wanted to stay outside longer, to share those rare moments of mother-daughter time without interruption from others. But Leah was worn out, tired and in need of her own alone time. In fact, she thought as she lifted her eyes up to the heavens, she needed some Father-daughter time.

She shut her eyes and took a deep breath as she prayed: *Father, as we prepare for the physical and spiritual storms that arise on life's journey, we look to you for hope. Your spirit, our faith, prayer and the loving support of our community will sustain us as we endure the painful storms. We remain joyful in hope, patient in rebuilding, and faithful in prayer. We will not give up but continue to move forward. We ask that you keep us safe, secure, and ever hopeful as we rest in your loving hands. This we ask in Jesus' name. Amen*

The twinkling stars in the sky seemed to brighten and Leah

knew that God heard her prayer. With a satisfied heart, she turned toward the house, heeding the very advice she gave Rebecca just moments before. The following day would be long and hard. With her body aching and her emotions stretched to the limit, Leah knew that she, too, needed a good night sleep to prepare for whatever life would throw at her in the morning.

Earlier that Day

The darkness of the kitchen hid Leah as she sat at the kitchen table, her fingers drumming silently against the arm of her chair. She listened to the gentle tick tock of the clock, waiting patiently for the creak of a door and the familiar squeak of the third step on the staircase. Thomas had never fixed it, despite her numerous requests. This morning, in the darkness of dawn, Leah found herself thankful that Thomas had been too busy to address that squeaky step.

It was almost six o'clock when she heard it. When the door creaked, Leah sat up straight, her eyes peeled onto the staircase as she waited. Slowly, she counted. One, two, three…She glanced at the clock. Five minutes to six. Four, five, six…She heard a shuffle of bare feet on the floor above the staircase. Seven, eight, nine… Leah took a deep breath and placed her finger on the button of the battery-operated lantern that she had placed upon the table before her. Ten. The stair creaked and Leah stood up, carrying the lantern as she walked toward the staircase.

She pressed the button and light illuminated the room.

"Sadie Miller," she said, staring up at the startled face of her sister. "I do believe that we need to have that talk, *ja*?"

Sadie's hand hovered over the banister, her eyes wide as she stared at Leah, an expression of surprise on her face. Her mouth fell open, but she remained silent.

"I thought so," Leah said softly. She gestured toward the table. "Let's go, Sadie. Have a seat."

For a moment, Leah thought Sadie was going to ignore her. She hesitated, her eyes glancing at the door. Leah didn't know what she would do if Sadie merely walked out, ignoring her request to sit down. She said a quick prayer to God, asking Him to help her through this confrontation.

To her relief, Sadie finally walked to the table and settled on the bench where the *kinner* usually sat down for meals. She folded her hands and placed them on her lap, not looking at Leah as she waited. The silence in the room hung between them, for a long, drawn out minute.

With a deep breath, Leah found the courage to begin talking. From somewhere, deep within her heart, she found the words that she needed to say. "Been noticing some things, Sadie," Leah said slowly. "Sneaking out of the house, skirting your duties, ignoring your chores."

Sadie continued staring straight ahead, her eyes narrow and an angry expression becoming apparent on her face.

"And I noticed you been sick a lot," Leah added. "Something you want to tell me?"

Silence.

Leah sighed. "You can't hide this forever, Sadie," she said. "People are going to find out."

Sadie snapped her head so that she stared directly at Leah. "Find. Out. What?" Her words came out in a short, clipped tone, each word measured and terse.

"Lydia told me," Leah sighed, reaching out to touch her hand. "She told me about the *boppli*."

"Ah," Sadie said, leaning back and tapping her fingers against the tabletop. "*Boppli*. Do you mean Jacob's *boppli*? The one that you never told any of us about? The one conceived during his *rumschpringe* and concealed from all of us? Or do you mean the one that Lydia's telling everyone that I'm supposedly having? The insulting, disgusting lie that is being spread around the *g'may*? You mean *that boppli*?"

It was Leah's turn for her mouth to drop.

"That's right. A lie!" Despite Sadie's best intention, tears flooded her eyes. She wiped at them with the palm of her hand, hating the fact that she cried. The depth of hurt was too great to not cry. "And people believed it! That's the most painful part of it."

She laughed, a hollow noise filled with misery. "They believed that I would do something like that!"

"But…but the sickness and doctors…"

"You want to know the truth?" Sadie stood up, her hands resting on the edge of the table. "I'm not pregnant, Leah." She leaned forward, her face inches from the stunned Leah. "That's right. All that speculation, all that concern, all the looks from the people in the schoolhouse. Why? Because they believed gossip? They believed Lydia?" Standing up straight, she scoffed. "They think I am the sinner. How ironic! If they only knew the truth, they'd be the ones begging for forgiveness!"

The truth? Leah caught her breath. If Sadie wasn't pregnant, why was she always so tired and sick? Clearly there was more to this story and it was time that Leah heard it. "What is going on, Sadie? Tell me, *schwester*."

The softness of Leah's words and the worried look upon her face brought Sadie back to the present. "The truth, Leah, is that I have breast cancer." And with those words, she exhaled loudly, the fight leaving her. She felt as if a weight was lifted off her shoulders. "That's right. Cancer." The word tasted as awful as it sounded.

"Oh Sadie," Leah whispered.

Once again, she wiped at her eyes with the palm of her hand, trying to garner the strength to continue. Somehow she found it. "After all the good things that I do, the hard work and dedication, my faith in God and His word, people still believed something that Lydia said. Something so awful that the bishop came to visit me, to chastise me, and council me on the evils of my ways."

Leah averted her eyes, the shame of the moment apparent in her expression. "I had no idea."

"Of course you didn't," Sadie snapped, the anger returned. "Everyone focused on Tobias and then the tornado came. Finally, the revealing of the great secret about Jacob. No one had time to listen. And when you heard the lie…that awful, disgusting lie… from Lydia…of all people…you believed her." She shook her head, amazed at the unfolding of events.

"We were wrong," Leah offered as an explanation. "I never suspected…" She left the sentence unsaid.

"You believed her!" Sadie hissed from between clenched teeth. "Everyone believed her. Including Manny! Do you think I didn't notice that he has not stopped by once to see me since the tornado? And you weren't there at the schoolhouse meeting! Not one woman would look at me." A morbid laugh escaped her lips. "Oh they believed Lydia all right! Only this time, you all were wrong and I'm not certain whether or not the truth is any better than the lies!"

"I'm so terribly sorry."

This time, the tears flowed freely. Sadie sobbed and covered her face with her hands, ashamed of herself for crying. She let Leah stand and embrace her, holding her while she released the pent-up emotions of the past few weeks.

"We'll get through this," Leah said, holding Sadie and rubbing her back as if she were a child. "We'll get through this together, Sadie. I promise."

Whoopie Pie Place

Hanging up the phone receiver, Leah took a deep breath and closed her eyes. She exhaled and whispered a silent prayer to God, thanking Him for His everlasting love and support: *In everything give thanks: for this is the will of God in Jesus Christ concerning you.*

"Well?"

Leah opened her eyes and glanced over her shoulder. Susie had left the horse and buggy, despite Leah asking her to wait there. They had stopped at the neighbor's house to borrow the telephone one more time. Her first call was to the doctor's office. She demanded an appointment with Dr. Conceicao, knowing that too much time already slipped by with Sadie harboring her secret.

After that call, Leah looked through her pocket for the index card with the number to the convention center. She needed to talk to her contact there, to know that everything was all right and that the woman still wanted the order fulfilled by the Miller sisters and not Laverne. The answer to that question would determine whether or not Thomas would go to pick up the bulk supplies that she had ordered the previous week. If so, there was a lot of work ahead of them to organize the supplies for distribution throughout their *g'may.*

"You never did listen well," Leah quipped, the lightness of her tone answering any question that Susie might have. With a broad smile, Leah announced, "They aren't giving the business to Laverne. In fact, they sounded rather relieved to hear that we had a plan."

"Praise God!" Susie whispered.

"I just did."

Susie laughed. "Is that what you were doing?"

Leah sighed as she started walking back toward the barn, resting her arm across Susie's shoulders. "It just goes to show that the devil is not stronger than the Lord." She paused, her thoughts going back to Sadie. "This time," she added softly.

Leah knew that the time would come to discuss Sadie's medical problem with the entire family. Now, however, was not that time. Other more pressing issues needed to be addressed first, starting with a confrontation, one that had been a long time coming.

"Now, I have another problem to address and, I sure would like you with me, Susie," Leah said, her lips pursed together as she controlled her temper. "We need to take a ride over to Lydia's. I need a word with that girl."

When Leah stopped the horse in the driveway, the buggy coming to a rest at the hitching ring on the side of the barn, she was surprised to see another buggy already there. From the looks of the reflectors on the back of it, she immediately recognized who it belonged to: the bishop.

What was it Sadie had said earlier? The bishop had been to speak to her?

"Oh help," she muttered as she stepped on the break and, with her eyes on the house, slid open the buggy door and hurried toward the house. She didn't look back to see if Susie kept up. Her focus was on the house and what she feared was being said on the other side of the door.

Without knocking, Leah burst into the house. She stopped when she saw the bishop standing before Lydia, his hat in hand and his head bowed. Lydia sat on the sofa, her hands covering her face and her shoulders heaving as she cried. Both Abe and the bishop turned to look at her, surprised at her sudden appearance.

"What's going on here?" Leah insisted. Behind her, Susie was out of breath and staring, wide-eyed as she peered over Leah's shoulder.

Abe took a deep breath and gestured for her to join them. "You best be hearing this, Leah," he said. "Impacts the whole family now."

A chill spread throughout her body.

The bishop leveled steely eyes at Leah. He reached up and ran his hand over his long white beard before he spoke. "Lydia has sinned," he said in calculated tones. "She has spread gossip among the people, causing dissension among the *g'may* and harm to another's reputation."

"Bishop, I…"

He held up his hand, stopping her mid-sentence. "I feel for you, Leah. I know this will cause hardship for the family. But this is not the first time that I've spoken with your *schwester*. Unfortunately," he paused, returning this attention to Lydia. "It will be the last. I have spoken with the other leaders of the church and it has been decided. Lydia is under the *Meidung*."

"Shunned?" Leah blurted out the word, the shock too great to bear. She knew that Lydia was troubled, seeking attention through her illnesses, whether real or imaginary. But to be shunned? To be rejected by her own community to the point that nobody could acknowledge her any longer? For the Amish it meant being all but invisible to the people nearest and dearest to them.

Lydia lifted her head, staring at Leah through her tears. "Help me, *Schwester*! Tell him the truth! Sadie should be shunned, not me!"

Lydia's words tore through Leah. Always the victim, Leah thought bitterly. Straightening her shoulders, Leah returned her sister's cry for help with a cold look. The bishop spoke true: it would be a hardship on the family, in more ways than one. But she had brought it on herself. "I understand, Bishop," Leah heard herself say.

Shunned. Until Lydia repented and confessed before the *g'may*, before the *g'may* would decide about accepting her back, no one would talk to Lydia. She was to be avoided, non-existent to the family. She couldn't help with the baking for Whoopie Pie Place. She couldn't eat at the same table as them or join in fellowship. In all ways, Lydia was no longer part of the community and family.

"Leah!" Lydia cried out.

Lifting her chin, Leah ignored her distraught sister and kept her gaze focused on the bishop. "And I best be telling you that we'll be needing extra prayers for our family." She took a deep breath, knowing that the truth had to be told. "Sadie has the cancer, Bishop. She told me this morning."

Behind her, Leah heard Susie gasp. Leah reached out to take Susie's hand in hers.

"She's been sick, all right. But bearing the burden of this illness on her own," Leah added. Selfless Sadie, always the one to suffer in silence.

The bishop's face paled, but his expression did not change. He clenched his teeth, the muscles twitching in his face. Leah didn't need to be a mind reader to know what he thought and felt. Most likely, he felt the same way Leah did earlier that morning in the darkness when Sadie shared her secret: ashamed.

"I'll spread the word," the bishop finally said. "We'll be there to support her."

Leah nodded, understanding what he meant. Lydia's accusations must have traveled far and wide. Damage control was in order and the bishop knew that he was just the person to do it. *The truth shall set you free,* Leah thought bitterly, her eyes turning one last time to the defeated form of her sister, sitting on the sofa as she sobbed.

Leah

Neither Susie nor Leah spoke during the buggy ride back to the Miller's farm. Twice Leah glanced at Susie, knowing that she was shocked by the news of Sadie's health issue. It wasn't the way that Leah wanted Susie to learn about Sadie, but she knew that it was high time that word spread throughout the community. There were an awful lot of people who needed to beg forgiveness in prayer, including herself.

After Sadie shared the news with her that morning, Leah spent an hour alone, in the fading darkness of dawn with a pen and paper before her. She made a list of all the things that she needed to do that day. Already she could check off three items: confirm the order, confront Lydia, and send Thomas for the bulk supplies.

There was still a lot more to do and all of it in a short period of time. Getting the supplies to the women who offered their help was next on the list. Then, when the rest of her day was cleared, Leah needed to find out, exactly, what the treatment plan was for Sadie. That would entail a trip to the hospital and, most likely, a lot of waiting for doctors to have a spare minute.

By the time Thomas returned from the store with the supplies, it was almost eleven o'clock. She had been waiting for an hour, the boxes lined up on the floor and a handwritten list already prepared for each of the women who had volunteered to help. The only thing missing was Sadie.

"Have you seen Sadie out there?" she asked Jacob when he brought in the first forty-pound bag of flour and dropped it on the floor by the table. Leah wanted to tell her about their appointment at two o'clock.

"*Nee,*" he said, averting his eyes from Leah's.

His humbled demeanor became him, Leah thought. Gone was the haughty attitude. In its place was this new Jacob, a quiet and helpful one that seemed more reflective and less bossy. For the moment, it was a welcomed change, even if Leah knew that the root cause weighed heavily on his mind.

Tobias would be home soon and Jacob would have no choice but to face the boy. It was up to Esther, Leah realized, as to whether or not Tobias would be told the truth. And, if Tobias were informed, certainly the rest of the *g'may* would learn of Jacob's indiscretion fifteen years ago.

"Esther helping out or still in bed?" she asked, her tone sharp. There was no use trying to hide her irritation from her brother.

"Bed." The single word spoke of the tension residing in Jacob's house.

Leah sighed, frustrated. She needed Esther's help to sort through the supplies and organize everything into boxes. Susie had helped out already that morning, but had needed to return home to make dinner for Merv. Given the recent discovery of his drinking problem, regardless of his vow to stop sneaking alcohol, Leah suspected her sister wanted to keep an eye on her husband.

Without Lydia, Susie, and Sadie to lend a hand, Esther's assistance was more important than ever. "I've just about had it with your *fraa*," she said under her breath. "I'm heading over to have a word with her."

He looked skeptical and reached out to grab Leah's arm. "*Mayhaps* best to leave her be for now. Get Sadie to help out." When he said his youngest sister's name, he frowned as if realizing that she was missing. "Where is she, anyway? Haven't seen her in two days!"

Leah yanked her arm free and stared back at Jacob, a cold look in her eyes. "You leave Sadie be, now. She's resting and I told her she could. She's got a lot on her mind and has no business helping us out today."

When he lifted an eyebrow, Leah felt the urge to snap at him. She suspected what he thought. The irony of his scorn hit her like someone had thrown a rock at her. But she knew better than to let her temper get the best of her. Instead of retorting to his gesture, she merely scowled and stormed out of the room, headed toward Jacob's side of the house.

It was high time someone had a stern talk with that woman, Leah told herself. She needed to get herself out of bed and back into life. After all, Esther had her own *dochder* to take care of and the family needed her help. All of the family. It certainly wasn't as though Leah, Susie, and Sadie weren't facing their own problems. But life went on. Everyone had to pull their own weight and it was high time Esther started doing her share.

As she pushed through the front door of Jacob's house, she took a deep breath before heading toward his bedroom. With all of her suppressed emotions from the past few weeks, *this* was one conversation that Leah was actually looking forward to having.

Susie

When she returned from Leah's, she hadn't expected to see Merv's *mamm* at the house. After all, Dora was supposed to be watching the *kinner* at her own home while Susie helped at the Miller farm. That was the way that it usually worked. She sure hoped that something hadn't happened or that Dora wanted to drop the *kinner* home earlier than usual for Susie needed to return to the family farm after she checked on Merv.

A sense of dread fell over her as she stepped through the side door. After all that they had been through and the small advances toward healing, she didn't want to face the reality that Dora might be there because Merv relapsed. The last thing she wanted was to face the bishop with yet one more problem from the Miller family.

"Hello?" she called out as she set her handbag by the back door.

The smell of fresh cooked chicken greeted her. Slowly, she walked toward the kitchen door and peeked through the glass window. On the other side, the table was set and both little Gid and Sylvia were sitting on the bench, their legs swinging back and forth as they waited for their dinner. Little David sat in booster seat on a chair, playing with a carved wooden figure of a horse.

It was the picture of a perfect family.

"What's going on in here?" Susie asked as she opened the door between the mudroom and the kitchen.

Merv's mamm was at the stove, stirring something that looked like gravy. She looked over her shoulder and smiled when she saw Susie. "There she is!" Dora looked at the kinner. "I told you that your mamm would be home soon! And just in time!"

"Surprise!" Sylvia shouted with a lisp as she raised her arms over her head and grinned at Susie.

"Dora?" Susie questioned the older woman with a raised eyebrow.

"You sit down, now," Dora demanded in a light, cheerful tone. "Merv should be along shortly and we can enjoy some good, home-cooked food together! Won't that be nice for a change?" Pouring the gravy into a small metal bowl, Dora smiled at Susie. "Time for someone to wait on you a bit, I reckon."

There was something humbling about seeing Merv's mamm hustling about the kitchen, preparing a meal for the family. Obediently, or perhaps from the shock, pleasant for once, Susie sat down at her spot at the far end of the table. Her eyes roamed the room and, to her further surprise, everything was clean. Toys rested in the box by the corner, the floor shone from having been freshly washed, and the windows sparkled, letting the sun shine into the room.

Dora set down the mashed potatoes onto the table when Merv walked into the room. He glanced around and, when he saw Susie, he tried to hide his smile. But she saw it and knew: Merv had gone to his mamm and asked her to come help out at the house while Susie helped Leah with the big order. It was his way of making things right with his *fraa* and all of her hard work.

"*Ja vell,*" Susie said, looking over at the beaming faces of Gid and Sylvia. "This *is* a nice surprise!"

She tried to think of when the last time was that, during the day, everyone was seated around the table for what smelled like a right *gut* noon meal. With the kitchen cleaned and the *kinner* looking freshly washed, Susie felt as if she just walked into a dream. And the look on Merv's face, so contrite and sheepish. Did he think that she'd actually be angry with him for turning to his *mamm*?

Dora pulled out her chair, the wooden feet scraping against the floor. She sat down and waited for the signal from Merv. It took a moment for him to realize that he needed to bow his head, the signal for the family to say their silent prayer over the meal. Susie watched him, amazed as she realized that it had been so long since they sat as a family that he had forgotten!

Once the blessing was said and everyone began passing plates, Dora looked at Susie and asked, "How are things over at your family farm?"

She wasn't certain how to respond. After all, there was no reason to scare the *kinner*. They were far too young to understand such things as cancer and hospitals. And she definitely did not want to discuss Lydia's situation. While she knew that word would spread quickly enough, she wasn't quite ready to answer questions about her sister's awful behavior.

"Thomas was picking up the supplies for that big order," Susie said as she dished mashed potatoes onto Gid's plate. She motioned for him to hand her Sylvia's plate so that she could do the same for her *dochder*. "I need to get back there to help sort the goods for him to deliver everything to the women."

Dora shook her head and clucked her tongue. "What a story!" She glanced at Merv. "It did my heart good to hear how the women were coming to your aid. I'm just right glad that I can help out, too, by watching the little ones." With a big smile, Dora looked across the table at Sylvia. "Although with you starting school next year with your big *bruder*," she said. "Reckon I shouldn't be calling you little any more, *ja*?"

Sylvia grinned and nodded her head.

Merv cleared his throat and glanced from his *mamm* to his *fraa*. He seemed to have something on his mind. With an anxious look to his eyes, he stared at Susie until she set down her fork. She felt a moment of panic. All of this happiness had seemed too good to be true when she walked in; a vision of how life *should* have been if Merv didn't drink and she had more time to take care of the house.

"What is it, Merv? Something you not telling me?"

"*Ja*," he said slowly. "I mean, *nee*, nothing bad, Susie. Just an idea that I had."

From the way that his eyes sparkled, she knew that he was excited. Whatever this idea was, glimpses of the old Merv had returned: the Merv she thought she had married so long ago.

"Oh? Do tell," she coaxed.

"I drove past your family farm today," he said.

This was news indeed! "Why didn't you stop in, then? We sure could have used your help!" As soon as she said the words, she cringed. It sounded accusatory and that was the one thing Merv did not need now. He needed support and understanding. Surely things could not be easy for him, just dropping the bottle and trying to move on with his life. "I'm sorry, Merv," she whispered. "I didn't mean that to sound so harsh."

"It's the store I went to see," he explained. "Just to get a better understanding of the damage, *ja*? And…and I came up with something that I sketched on a piece of paper. An idea to rebuild it."

"Rebuild it? You mean Whoopie Pie Place?"

He nodded his head and reached into his back pocket. Carefully, he withdrew a folded piece of paper and, after one brief moment's hesitation, as if having a second thought, he reached across the table to hand it to her. "Rebuild it, *ja*. Open that paper and take a look. Tell me what you think."

Curious, Susie pushed back her chair to give herself some more room as she unfolded the paper and, with a tentative glance at him, she started to look at it.

And she caught her breath.

It wasn't just a drawing, something written hastily on a piece of paper. Instead, she found herself looking at a complete diagram with measurements and detailed plans of what needed to be done. Everything was meticulous, a rendering that appeared almost professional.

Even better, Susie liked what she saw.

"Why Merv!" she exclaimed. "I never knew you could draw plans like this!"

A look of pride crossed his face but, as soon as it was there, he quickly lowered his eyes and began to eat the food on his plate. "Nothing special," he mumbled. "Just an idea."

Susie knew that was not true. It was more than 'just an idea.' Indeed, she recognized it as the beginning of the healing process. After years of abusing the bottle, which had, in turn, abused his body and soul, he was healing. Without alcohol controlling his life, Merv was taking the reins and steering himself through recovery: physical, mental, and spiritual.

"I'm heading back to help Leah later," Susie said. "I don't think I should show this to her just yet. *Mayhaps* next week after this first order is fulfilled, *ja*? And," she paused. He had never gotten on well with her family. Instead of joining festivities, he often remained at home. In hindsight, Susie understood now why he avoided them. Would the new Merv do the same? "I think you should be the one to present the idea to her."

He paled and looked as if he was about to decline.

Hastily, she added, "You can answer any questions that she has better than I can, anyway."

To her relief, he did not decline. Instead, he nodded his head, agreeing to take a ride over to the family farm during the following week to talk with Leah.

For the rest of the meal, Susie could hardly contain herself. She watched as Gid and Sylvia giggled, one of them apparently poking the other under the table. When Merv gently scolded them, reminding them to have table manners, she tried to hide her smile. She felt a year's worth of anxiety lift from her shoulders as she realized that, quite possibly, things were finally taking a turn for the better in the Stutzman house.

Lydia

A warm breeze blew through the open door. Indian Summer, Lydia thought as she stood behind the screen and stared outside. The last warm days before winter kicked in.

In the distance, she could see Abe walking behind the Belgian mules as they pulled the cutter along the fields of grass. It would dry for a few days before being baled and stacked in the barn, good hay for feeding the animals over the upcoming winter months.

He hadn't spoken to her since the bishop had left the previous day. In fact, he seemed downright happy, as if he felt justified and vindicated by her shunning. The night before, at supper, he refused to sit at their table with her. In fact, despite her efforts at having set the table and placing nice, home-cooked food before his plate, he merely glanced at her before walking out the door. Moments later, she heard the buggy pulling out of the driveway, the horse's hooves click-clacking on the macadam as he drove away. She didn't know where he was going, but she suspected that he was going to enjoy the evening meal with another family.

Shutting her eyes, Lydia leaned her head against the doorframe.

She had heard of people being shunned. All of her life the threat dangled over the heads of the people in the congregation. As a child, she knew that, once one was baptized, the bishop's rules were meant to be followed. Furthermore, she had been told on numerous occasions that those who strayed would be shunned.

But it had never happened.

Until now.

Oh, she knew that she might have exaggerated some of her headaches in the past. *Mayhaps* some of her aches and pains weren't quite as bad as what she claimed. But to be shunned?

She shook her head and walked back to the kitchen. For a

long moment, she stood there, wondering what to do. She didn't have to cook, for Abe had made it clear that he wouldn't take food made by her hand. *That* was a little extreme, she told herself.

And he sure wasn't going to talk to her. His silence made that point quite clear.

All of this because of Sadie.

Maybe she did have the cancer, Lydia thought as she leaned against the counter and stared out the window. Just because of one little mistake, Lydia reasoned with herself, now she was shunned? Because she made a comment to Manny about Sadie being pregnant? How was *she* supposed to know that it was cancer and not pregnancy? After all, it was Tobias who had told her about Sadie's morning sickness.

That was the moment that she remembered.

The image of Jacob hearing the words from Leah's lips while Thomas listened: Jacob was Tobias' *daed!*

"Oh help!" she muttered, her eyes widening as the memory of the conversation came back to her.

Her baby *bruder*. After all of these years, the truth was that Tobias was not her *bruder* but her nephew, born out of wedlock, to her older *bruder*, Jacob! To make matters worse, it was Leah who kept that secret, tight to her bosom during the past years. It was Leah who deceived others by allowing everyone to think that Tobias was their *bruder* and Jacob was such a godly man.

He wasn't.

Lydia had always known that anyway. Now the entire *g'may* would know!

She stood up straight and found that her breath came in short, clipped waves. Her heart pounded and her blood raced. The bishop would surely lift the *Meidung* from her if she told him. She would redeem herself, Abe wouldn't ignore her any longer, and she would work extra hard to win him back. She certainly couldn't live the rest of her life like this, surrounded by silence!

When Abe returned from the fields, Lydia was seated at the kitchen table waiting for him. She lifted her eyes to meet his, doing her best to look remorseful. She knew what needed to be done. She knew that she would have to play by the bishop's rules, agree to confess to the *g'may*, and let Abe have his victory. But as soon as she had the bishop alone, she'd tell him what she overheard and Leah would see how far her superior, smug attitude would get her then!

Abe hung his hat on the peg in the mudroom, took off his boots, and walked straight to the stairs. Not once did he look at her.

"Abe," she said softly. "I…I can't go on like this."

He paused, his hand on the banister and one foot ahead of the other on the stairs.

"I'll apologize to Sadie," she said. "I'll confess to the *g'may*. Anything. Just don't desert me. Not now, Abe. Not when I've seen the error of my ways."

He remained motionless.

"It was the accident, I think." She stood up and walked toward him, her hand reaching out to cover his. "I didn't know what I was saying." When his eyes glanced at her, she tried to smile. "And when I awoke in the hospital, I knew I had been wrong. I knew that you and the bishop…you both were right. I need to speak to someone and I'm willing to do it. But I need this shunning to go away. I can't go on much longer without you, without my sisters…"

"You mean what you're saying?"

She nodded her head. "I do, Abe. I truly do!"

He withdrew his hand from under hers. "Let me pray on this, then," he said before continuing to climb the stairs and leaving Lydia alone in the kitchen.

She caught her breath, uncertain of whether or not he

would fetch the bishop to hear her confession. She heard the door to the empty bedroom shut, the bedroom where Abe had slept by himself for the past few nights since her return from the hospital.

The pain in her head hurt. The pressure of trying to convince Abe didn't help. Her nerves were eating at her stomach, too. Walking over to the sink, she poured some water into a small glass before she opened a cabinet in search of a seltzer tablet. That would help her headache and stomach.

Pray on it, indeed, she thought bitterly as she sat back down at the table.

Never had she felt more alone. Why was God punishing her? She wasn't perfect; no one was except Jesus. But she tried to be a good person. She tried to honor the Christian faith and follow Jesus' teaching. No matter what anyone thought, she *was* a godly woman. More so than her holier than thou *schwester*, Leah! That was something Lydia believed with all of her heart. And soon, she told herself, the rest of the *g'may* would believe it, too!

Sadie

She closed the suitcase, cringing as she clicked the latches shut. It sounded so final: packed, shut, locked. In all of her life, she had never slept away from the house and her family. Oh, there had been the occasional trips to Pennsylvania for a wedding of a second cousin. But, with her family traveling with her, it had not seemed as if she was away.

Now, she would be going away for at least two nights, maybe longer.

"You need to get this procedure done," Dr. Conceicao had told her before when Sadie and Leah had sat in her office earlier that afternoon. "I'm willing to do it tomorrow morning. When I heard you were coming, we managed to reserve the operating room for six o'clock."

"Six o'clock?" she exclaimed. "That's awful early!"

Leah's hand on her knee gave her the reassurance that she needed to calm down. "Then that's what we'll do," Leah told the doctor.

"She can arrive as early as five o'clock tomorrow morning to get into prep." The doctor leaned forward and stared directly into Sadie's eyes. "It may seem sudden, Sadie. But this is the best decision. Remove the breasts, go through chemo, and let's get you on Herceptin if we decide against radiation."

After the appointment with the doctor, they stopped in to visit Tobias. He was in better spirits, that was for certain. His doctor wanted Tobias to stay in the hospital for another few weeks, even though he had already started the chemotherapy to kill the existing bad bone marrow cells prior to receiving the transfusion.

Both Leah and Sadie felt it was better that he not learn about her cancer. For a fourteen -year-old boy, he had enough on his mind with his own medical problems. He didn't seem to notice how quiet Sadie was as she sat there, staring out the window and leaving the talking to Leah.

When they returned home, Sadie ignored Esther's frown and retreated upstairs. She needed to pack her suitcase. Michelle agreed to pick her up at nine o'clock to take her back to her own house. She had asked Sadie to stay over because It was closer to the hospital and Sadie needed that time away from all the activity at the farm. At first, Leah argued with Sadie, refusing to let her go alone. But Sadie won the argument, insisting that, this time, she needed to do this by herself.

Leaving the suitcase by the door, she slowly walked downstairs, knowing that Leah had just told the family about the cancer. The younger *kinner* didn't need to know. But Aaron and Rebecca were seated around the table, listening as Leah shared the news with Jacob and Esther.

"There's a black cloud hanging over this family!" Esther declared.

"Esther!" Leah snapped at her. "Don't say such things!"

Sadie stood on the stairs, watching without them knowing. Leave it to Esther, she thought.

"It's true! First this business with Tobias! Now Sadie? And forget the tornado! I'm at my wit's end!"

Sadie shook her head. Always the victim, she thought bitterly. Still, there was strong venom to Esther's voice, one that she hadn't heard before. Her comment about Tobias struck her as odd. There was nothing about Tobias' situation that impacted Esther. However, ever since the tornado, Sadie had noticed that Esther stayed to herself more and her *kinner* were often over playing with Leah's younger ones.

Thomas cleared his throat and glanced at the staircase. Almost in unison, three white prayer *kapps* turned around and the women looked in her direction while the men merely lowered their eyes. With a deep breath, Sadie continued her descent into the kitchen. She wondered whether Thomas and Jacob had heard the rumors about her 'pregnancy'. Undoubtedly so, she suspected, a bitter taste in her mouth. Thomas would have dismissed it. But Jacob? She could imagine him spreading the gossip with the same glee as Lydia.

"Sadie," Rebecca said. "I'll be praying for you."

"*Danke*, 'Becca," Sadie replied with a smile. "Prayers are right *gut*!" She wanted to sound positive and wanted to alleviate any fears, especially with Aaron and Rebecca. After praying about everything, she decided that a positive attitude was a gift from God. No one could take that away from her…not if she didn't let them.

"You're going to miss church on Sunday," Leah said evenly. She raised her eyebrows as she met Sadie's gaze. "There'll be an announcement after service, for sure and certain."

Sadie knew what that meant. After the worship service and before fellowship, the bishop would ask that all of the members remain seated while the unbaptized members and *kinner* left the room. If the weather were nice, they would go outside and enjoy the fresh air. If it was raining, however, they would retreat to the barn or basement, depending on where the service was being held.

The bishop would have several announcements. The first would be to alert the *g'may* about Sadie's surgery. If they hadn't already heard the news, there would be gasps of disbelief and stunned looks on their faces. Those who had believed the vicious rumor that Lydia had started would lower their eyes in shame. It would take a few minutes to calm down the congregation before they could vote on how to help the Miller family with the upcoming medical bills.

And then the bishop would announce the shunning of Lydia.

Sadie wasn't certain whether or not there would be gasps of disbelief and stunned faces at that news. Surely many of the members would feel that it was a long time in coming. Others might feel relief, vindicated for having believed the awful lie spoken from Lydia's lips about her youngest sister being pregnant.

Sadie nodded her head at Leah's statement.

"You want visitors at the hospital, then?" Leah asked her.

"*Nee!*" Sadie didn't mean to sound so forceful when she said the word. The thought of people coming to the hospital, visiting her while she recovered and dealt with the loss of her breasts, all the while knowing that they, too, had thought the worst of her, made her feel nauseous.

"I understand" was Leah's response.

"Reckon I'm going for a walk, then," Sadie said. "Need some time to think."

Rebecca offered to walk with her but Sadie shook her head, appreciative for the offer but wanting to be alone. After all, she thought as she stepped off the porch and began to walk toward the road, it sure did seem like the only person she could trust anymore was herself . Try as she might to swallow the bitterness and resentment that she felt, she knew that it would take some time to heal those open wounds.

Part Four

Just as I fell away from God through sin,
And came under His wrath,
Likewise He has regenerated me,
To be His child again,
In His Son, the Lord Jesus Christ
Who himself has become my mediator,
So that I would not be lost.

Ausbund Song 112 Verse 17

Therefore if any man [be in Christ,
He is A new creature:
Old things are passed away;
Behold, all things are become new.

2 Corinthians 5:17

The Rebirth

Leah didn't know if she could stand another woman stopping by the house to drop off the whoopie pies for Mary Glick's wedding. She was thankful that she had decided to pull Rebecca from school, needing her help at home to prepare for the delivery to the Glick's home. With her thirteenth birthday just around the corner, Rebecca could certainly run interference for her. She had enough to focus on with Sadie recovering upstairs and needing her drains tended to every four hours.

She should have known better.

The community's interest in Sadie's well-being started immediately following the worship service on Sunday. No sooner did the bishop announce Sadie's surgery the day before than all eyes turned to stare at Leah. She ignored them at first, but found it hard to do when, during the fellowship meal, so women approached her to inquire about Sadie.

"How is she, the dear girl?"

"When does sweet Sadie come home?"

"Do you know what stage it was at?"

The concern on their faces angered Leah. While she realized that they genuinely cared about Sadie, she also suspected that most of them had not hesitated to spread Lydia's claims of Sadie expecting a *boppli*. Of course, Leah knew how the gossip started. Elmer and Manny must have returned home, both still stunned with Lydia's accusation. Elmer certainly confided in Jenny, both of whom undoubtedly confronted Manny.

As the women crowded around her, asking her to send Sadie their regards, Leah looked over their heads and sought out the only pair of eyes that dared not approach her: Jenny Yoder.

Certainly Jenny knew what Leah thought about her for, without a doubt, it was from Jenny's lips that the story had started to spread.

Now, three days later, the outpouring of kindness from the women continued. News of Sadie's return from the hospital, delayed until Tuesday evening, seemed to spread throughout the *g'may* like wildfire. With Mary Glick's wedding the following day, most of the women who stopped by were dropping off their whoopie pies.

Leah shook her head as she heard Rebecca talking with another woman who didn't seem to get the hint that they were far too busy to stand around chit-chatting and listening to people pretend they had not spread gossip about the 'dear girl', sweet Sadie.

"Who is it now?" Sadie asked when Leah shut the bedroom door.

"Oh, no one important," Leah said, sitting down on the side of the bed. "How are you feeling?"

"Sore."

Leah nodded. "I bet."

On Saturday, Leah managed to get to the hospital by eight in the morning. The *kinner* were fed and given a list of chores to do. By the time Michelle pulled into her driveway, Susie already in the passenger seat, Leah felt anxious, her nerves raw and her temper short. She needed to get to that hospital and know that Sadie was all right.

The surgery took longer than anticipated. The tumor was larger than originally thought. Neither x-ray nor ultrasound measurements were very accurate due to the peculiar position of the tumor and the fact that it was, at times, contiguous with the chest wall, made it too close for a clean margin. When the doctor told Leah that news, she felt her knees buckle and she reached out to Susie for a steady hand to hold her upright.

"What does that mean?"

"Nothing right now," the doctor tried to explain. "Chemotherapy and radiation are a must, of course."

Of course, Leah thought wryly. She bit her tongue to keep it still.

"And we'll just have to watch it. There are new treatments. That's the good news. Preventative treatments. Once we test the tumor and lymph nodes, we'll have a better idea of what type of cancer it is."

None of that sounded promising to Leah at the time. But Michelle spent hours researching chest walls and breast cancer. She printed out dozens of articles from scientific and medical journals, websites and magazines. Only after spending hours trying to read them did Leah begin to breathe a sigh of relief: Cancer was not a death sentence.

"It'll quiet down here in a few days, I'm sure," Leah reassured Sadie.

She watched as Sadie rolled her head to the side. During the entire surgery and hospital stay, Sadie had been a brave soul. She never once complained, even when there was a minor complication with her white blood cell count that resulted in her extended stay at the hospital. Before she left on Tuesday, she managed to get dressed and visit with Tobias, pretending as if nothing had happened, despite the ache in her chest. If he noticed that she moved slowly or had a double mastectomy, he never said anything. Instead, he told her all about the miracle of God finding a donor to help save his life.

Sadie merely smiled in response, letting him chatter on, oblivious to her pain.

"I don't want to see anyone," Sadie said. Her voice was determined and her eyes narrowed as she spoke.

"I don't blame you." Leah patted her arm. It had been a long and hard day for Sadie. She understood how her younger *schwester* felt. "Now, let's see about those drains, *ja*?"

An hour later, Leah sat on the porch, peeling husks from some corn as she watched the cows in the field. Thanks to Rebecca's help, the whoopie pies delivered by the women were now safely at the Glick's residence. One thing to cross off her list, she thought with a satisfied smile. Next would be the order for the convention. But Leah knew that, based on the dry run for the Glick's wedding, the order would be fulfilled and then it would be time to concentrate on rebuilding the store.

She set down the ear of corn that she husked and stared into the distance. A horse and buggy trotted along the road half a mile or so away, the noise carrying in the early autumn breeze. Next door, she could hear the *kinner* laughing as they played in Esther's kitchen. The joyful noise warmed her heart.

Shutting her eyes, she felt the urge to pray: *Our precious Heavenly Father, with the darkness comes Your light. With Your presence, the day's burdens seem farther somehow. Watch over us, stay beside us and protect us as we renew ourselves both in body and spiritual growth. Fill our hearts with Your peace and restore us. Amen.*

Earlier that Day

"I've come to a decision," Esther said as she stood before Leah. The older *kinner* were at school, having left shortly after breakfast. Rebecca, however, was busy watching the little ones next door. Leah had sent her there when Esther appeared on the threshold of her kitchen, a fierce look upon her face and fire in her eyes.

Oh help, Leah thought. Not today!

"What now, Esther?" She didn't mean to sound exasperated but it was all that she could do to not want to shake Jacob's wife. While she did not agree with pre-marital relations, Leah knew better than to throw stones at another for past indiscretions. After all, what Jacob did was years ago and, frankly, before his baptism. Furthermore, he had been as surprised as Esther by the news about Tobias.

"You have no idea what I am going through!" Esther shouted back.

"Calm down, now," Leah said, glancing over Esther's shoulders to make certain no one could overhear. "Sit down and let me get you some coffee. No sense alerting the entire neighborhood."

Esther made no move toward the table. "I don't want to sit and I certainly don't want coffee."

Leah fought the urge to roll her eyes.

"What I do want," Esther continued. "Is the bishop to counsel us."

Leah fought the urge to groan. Not the bishop, she thought. Anything but the bishop. "Now hold on there, Esther," Leah began, choosing her words carefully. "You best be thinking this through." Gently, she placed her hand around Esther's shoulders and guided her to the table. "We have an awful lot on our plates right now and I fail to see how the bishop can help."

"I made up my mind," Esther snapped.

Leah wasn't so certain.

"And what will the bishop do, Esther? What, exactly, do you want him to do?"

"Why, he'll make Jacob confess!"

Leah nodded her head. "*Ja*, that's right and true. He'll be forced to confess. Confess that he only found out about Tobias last week. Confess that, during his running around years, he dated an *Englische* woman. He sure will have to confess that."

Esther watched Leah carefully, as if trying to figure out where she was going with her words.

"And then what will happen? Did you think that through, Esther?"

Leah's question caught her off-guard. "What…what do you mean?"

"I didn't think so," Leah said softly. "Why, people will surely talk, don't you think? Wondering why his *fraa* went to the bishop over something that happened fifteen years ago? Such an old transgression and it was well before he met you and even before he took his kneeling vow. Sure, he sinned. But wasn't it Jesus who said, 'Let he who is without sin cast the first stone'? It sure would look like you were casting stones just for the sake of hurting and embarrassing Jacob."

Esther was quick to deny what Leah said. "I'm not trying to embarrass him!"

"Oh, don't get me wrong! I'm sure many of the women wouldn't blame you. They might even sympathize with you, I reckon."

"I don't want sympathy."

"And Tobias will learn the truth," Leah continued. "He'll be wanting to move over to your side of the house." Pausing, Leah rubbed her chin with her thumb and finger as if considering something new. "Why, that might not be such a bad thing, I reckon. Will give Jacob and Tobias time to develop their new relationship and bond as father and son instead of *bruders*. And I sure wouldn't mind not having to do the extra wash or cook the extra food. He sure can eat a lot, that boy." She laughed. "And your little one won't mind. Might be nice to have a big *bruder* around the house."

A frown crossed Esther's face. "I see what you are doing, Leah Mast!"

Leah held up her hands and feigned innocence. "I'm just telling you the truth, Esther. And I won't be hearing you stating otherwise."

She shook her head and crossed her arms over her chest. "You think I can just forget about this? Move on as if nothing has happened, then?"

Something snapped inside of Leah. She felt as though the pressure of a thousand tons broke through the floodgate. Leaning forward, Leah pushed her face close to Esther's and lowered her voice. "It's called forgiveness, Esther," she said in measured tones. "Have you ever heard of it?"

Esther tried to look away.

"Jesus preaches about loving our enemies. It is not up to us to cast stones or seek revenge. What you are proposing sure does sound like vengeance to me." Moving away to give them both more personal space, Leah tilted her chin in the air as she stared at her sister-in-law. "And I don't think the bishop would like the sounds of that, now, would he?" Leah stood up and smoothed down the front of her black apron.

Esther glared at her.

Leah didn't care. Instead, she merely lifted an eyebrow and added, "Besides, I think one shunned member of the family is enough for now, ain't so?"

Esther stood up quickly, the chair falling over behind her. Despite the anger on her face, Esther also looked worried. Leah knew that her words struck a chord with the woman. If there was one thing she understood about Esther, it was the fact that she would not want to be the focus of gossip or speculation. And if that thought didn't shake her nerves, the thought of the bishop reprimanding her for not showing proper forgiveness, possibly even making her confess in front of the congregation before the next communion, certainly did.

Leah took a deep breath when she heard the door to the house slam shut behind Esther as the woman left. It might take some time, Leah told herself, but the waves of *that* storm were definitely weathered.

Whoopie Pie Place

Manny stood at the door of the house, a box in his arms and a shamed look upon his face. Leah hesitated, just long enough to let him know that she knew the truth and wasn't as forgiving as she ought to be. With her lips pressed together, she opened the screen door and let him walk into the house.

"Been a while since we've seen you, Manny," she said, her words dripping with sarcasm. "Sure hope everything is well over at your place."

"Mamm asked me to drop these off," he said as he set the box on the counter. "She also included some of her drop sugar cookies. Thought the *kinner* might like them." His eyes darted around the room as if he was looking for something. Or someone.

"*Danke*, Manny," Leah replied, trying as hard as she could to maintain a polite tone. What was it she had said to Esther earlier that very day? Forgiveness was a trait that Jesus preached about. It was not a destination to achieve but a starting point in the journey required for healing. "You be sure to thank her for us."

"And she said to let you know that she's ready for the convention order."

"So many things to share with us," Leah said. "It's a wonder that she didn't come herself." Immediately, she regretted her words, knowing that they didn't sound very forgiving at all. *Oh help*, she thought to herself. *I'll just ask the Lord to grace me with my own forgiveness later.*

Manny lowered his eyes and shuffled his feet. He looked nervous and tense. "Truth is that I wanted to see if Sadie was around," he admitted. "Heard about her condition..."

"You mean *her cancer*," Leah interrupted abruptly. She hated the way the word 'condition' had rolled of his tongue, knowing full well that the word was ambiguous as it had multiple connotations. As soon as he said it, Leah knew that it was a word used frequently in the past week to describe Sadie's situation.

Condition. A word he had grown used to hearing and even probably uttered on more than one occasion. Only, Leah knew, the definition of the word 'condition' had not meant 'cancer' at the time.

"Uh, *ja*, cancer." The color flooded his cheeks and he refused to meet her eyes. "Cancer, that's right."

"She's resting upstairs and in no shape for visitors."

Leah's words seemed to deflate him. Disappointment shadowed his face and his shoulder drooped. "I see," he mumbled. "*Ja, vell…*"

"You be sure to thank your mamm, now," Leah said, indicating that it was time for Manny to leave.

No sooner had he walked out the door than Susie walked in, Merv along with her. "What was that about?" she asked, looking over her shoulder as Manny's horse and buggy headed away from the house.

Leah waved her hand dismissively. "What does it say in Proverbs? *'Whoever goes about slandering reveals secrets, but he who is trustworthy in spirit keeps a thing covered.'* Manny's trustworthy spirit appears a bit broken these days, it seems." She noticed that Merv held a box in his arms. "What's this?"

"Dora made some whoopie pies," Susie replied, her eyes sparkling.

"She did, now, did she?"

For a moment, Leah watched the interaction between Susie and Merv as she directed him to put the box on the floor by the door. He didn't argue. He didn't appear stressed. Instead, he did as he was told without saying a word. This, Leah thought, is not the Merv from the previous week.

"Looks like things are going well," she said. "And you thank your mamm for me, Merv. That was right kind of her."

"Will do." He smiled and shoved his hands in his pockets.

Susie nudged him with her arm, as if encouraging him to say something else. He cleared his throat and glanced up to look at Leah. "I...I was talking with Susie and, *vell,* we looked over at the store before coming in here. I was thinking that I might be able to get started on some repairs to it."

Repairs? It would take a lot more than just repairs, Leah thought. Still, she knew that Merv was offering more than just help to repair Whoopie Pie Place.

"And I saw you already have all that lumber sitting there."

"What do you have in mind, then?"

He rubbed at his beard. "Round up a few fellows, knock down the inside and demolish that rear kitchen wall. Expand it a bit and give you women a bit more room in there."

Leah laughed. "That's a whole lot more than repairs, Merv."

"Show her your plans," Susie urged.

Withdrawing his hand from his pocket, he held a folded piece of paper. "*Ja vell,*" he mumbled as he unfolded it. "Look here, Leah. I drew this last night. Just a sketch, you see. If we can keep the front wall, it won't look any different from the road." He flattened the paper on the tabletop and leaned over, pointing to it with his finger. "But see here? Look how different this is."

Susie leaned against his shoulder. "And all that extra room! Why, we can certainly reopen and have even more product than before! We'll be bigger and better, showcasing even more goods from our neighbors and friends. Show Laverne that nobody messes with the Miller sisters!"

It was a lot of extra room, both in the front of the store and in the kitchen. What Merv outlined on that piece of paper gave her hope, an exciting glimmer of optimism that things just might turn out all right. "You merged the pantry into the kitchen, I see," she said, letting her finger rest on his drawing. "So really, you're just adding a new room on the back for supplies."

He nodded. "*Ja*, true. But we're also moving that inside wall back a ways. Gives you almost two hundred more square feet of space in the storefront."

It wasn't a bad idea. Leah stared at the drawing, trying to envision it in her mind. How long would it take? Would they be able to open for the autumn tourist season? "And you think you can do this, Merv? You up to this pressure?" From what Susie shared with her just the other day, Merv was trying. Really trying. The last thing Leah wanted to do was add unnecessary stress onto him.

"I sure can and I sure am," he said confidently. "What is it they say about idle hands?"

When he bent back down, explaining how much extra lumber he estimated they needed to buy, Leah looked over his head and met Susie's gaze. The glow in Susie's eyes spoke louder than words. And it warmed Leah's heart. She didn't know when the last time was when she had seen Susie so happy, a happiness that came from deep within her. It was a happiness that Leah wished that she, too, could feel.

Leah

The hospital floor was quiet. Leah wasn't used to visiting Tobias in the early afternoon. Typically she managed to visit in the early morning or early evening. Both of those times tended to be busier with parents, friends, or family stopping by to say hello on their way to or from work.

Today, however, with the Glick order being fulfilled and everything in place for completing the next order in two weeks, Leah found the time to come earlier to the hospital.

She *needed* to see Tobias.

It had never mattered to her whether Tobias was her *bruder* or her nephew. From the day that she found out about Tobias' parents, his biological parents, Leah never once thought about it again. At least, she reminded herself, until no one in the family was a match for the bone marrow transplant.

"You sleeping?" she asked as she peeked around the corner into the room. With the lights off and the blinds drawn, the room was dark. She heard the rustle of the sheet as she stepped through the door.

"So sleepy," he whispered.

Leah reached into the bathroom and clicked on the light switch, making certain to keep the door shut so that only a little bit of light disturbed the darkness. Then, stepping to the bed, she reached out a hand to touch his forehead. No fever. That was a good sign.

"*Ja vell*, the doctor said you might get sleepy after the chemotherapy, didn't he?"

She felt him nod his head under her hand. His eyes were shut and she could hear the steady noise of his breathing. In, out, in out. She smiled to herself, knowing that his sleep was more important than their visit.

With a happy heart, she sank to her knees and rested her

folded hands on the side of his bed. She shut her eyes and lifted her heart in prayer: *Heavenly Father, I come to you and humbly seek you. You alone are my only strength. Please watch over your Tobias and restore him to that perfect health which is yours alone to give. Watch over the Doctors and medical staff, giving them the skills and wisdom they need to take care of our precious boy. Give him good health and raise him up to a life of service to you Lord. We ask these things through Jesus Christ our Lord. Amen*

For the next hour, she sat in the chair by his bed, resting her cheek against her hand. She almost fell asleep, too, but forced herself to stay awake. Her body felt drained, completely exhausted. She couldn't remember what it was like to just sit for a moment and do nothing.

Over the past few weeks, so much happened that Leah took that time to pause and reflect. God had sheltered her family through the tornado, but He sure had thrown some other strong winds in their direction: Tobias' illness, Merv's addiction, Lydia's shunning, Jacob's past, and now Sadie's cancer. If only things would settle down now, she sighed to herself. She wasn't certain if she could handle much more.

"Oh, I'm sorry," a voice said from the doorway.

Leah squinted in the light realizing that she had dozed off. Sitting up straight, she recognized the woman as a nurse. "That's all right," she said. "You checking in on Tobias, then?"

The woman slipped through the door, making certain to shut it behind herself in such a way that the noise would not disturb the patient. She paused to open the bathroom door, just enough so that a sliver of light fell across the bed and she could see to whom she was speaking.

"I'm checking on him, yes," the woman said.

Leah squinted in the light, trying to place the woman. She recognized her, only Leah couldn't figure out from where. "Did you help my *schwester* the other day? Lydia Esh? The Amish woman injured in the tornado?"

The woman took a deep breath before answering. She seemed hesitant and that was all Leah needed to put the pieces together.

"Are you Cheryl Weaver, then?" Leah whispered.

"Walsh," the woman responded. "Cheryl Walsh. I'm married now."

With all of the chaos surrounding their lives, Leah had not considered that she might run into Tobias' mother at the hospital. Now, seeing the woman before her, Leah felt as if she should say something. Unfortunately, she found that words escaped her.

She was not necessarily tall but she was pretty. Her chestnut hair was pulled back into a fancy braid that hung between her shoulders. Even in her hospital uniform, Cheryl was fancy looking. For the first time in her life, Leah felt old and frumpy, her clothes too plain and her hair graying and wiry.

"I…I can't thank you enough," Leah finally said. "What you've done…"

Cheryl nodded her head. "I'm just glad that everything will work out for him." Her eyes traveled to the bed and she gazed down upon her son. "Tobias." She said the name as if trying to get used to the sound.

"We aren't going to tell him…" Leah stopped mid-sentence, not certain whether or not Tobias was able to hear them.

Cheryl smiled at her. "I understand. Probably for the better, anyway." She reached out her hand as if to brush the hair from his forehead, but, as if on second thought, she pulled her hand back and stepped away from the bed. "Well, I'll let you two visit a while. Have my own rounds to make." When Leah looked up at her, Cheryl shrugged her shoulders, a sheepish look on her face. "I'm on break. I like checking up on him when I have a few spare moments."

For some reason, her words touched Leah.

She watched as the nurse reached out and gently patted Tobias' leg before turning toward the door. She reached for the doorknob and paused. "I always wondered…" she whispered, her head dipped down and her back facing Leah. "I'm glad I know," she added before disappearing from the room.

Leah sat there, her eyes staring at the closed door long after Cheryl Weaver Walsh left the room. It took even longer for the image of the woman with the manicured fingernails patting Tobias' leg to leave her memory.

Susie

"That's the last bag of flour," Merv said as he set it down on the floor.

Susie smiled at him. "*Danke*, Merv."

He stood for a moment and assessed the supplies that were scattered throughout the kitchen. He had run errands that morning, picking up the different goods that were needed in order to help Susie sort and organize the supplies for next week's distribution to the women of the *g'may*. Susie had insisted that everything be distributed early so that the women could practice, just in case there were any problems.

"What kind of problems you think they might run into, anyway?" he asked, removing his hat and wiping at his forehead with the back of his arm.

Susie laughed. "Hopefully none!"

He frowned and looked at her, hiding his smile. But he couldn't. Instead, he reached out for her hand and, with a quick glance over her shoulder to make certain no one was in the kitchen and could see them, he pulled her into his arms.

"Oh!" she gasped.

"It's right *gut* to hear you laugh," he said.

Susie blushed.

He tilted her chin so that she was forced to look in his eyes. "I forgot how pretty your laugh sounds. I want to hear it more often, Susie."

She closed her eyes as he leaned forward to brush his lips against hers. *When was the last time he kissed her?* She looked away when he pulled back, his thumb brushing against her cheek. "I…I guess I just have more to laugh about these days."

He pressed his forehead against hers and sighed. "I need to apologize, Susie. I need to know that you forgive me for all of the years of disappointment."

She didn't know what to say or how to respond. She couldn't deny the truth: there had been disappointment. She also didn't want to believe that everything would be a smooth road. The destination was clear but the journey to get there was definitely not over.

"Life is full of disappointments, Merv," she managed to say. "But life is also full of fulfillment." She leaned her head so that it pressed against his hand. "Did you ever think that God gets us through the lows so that we can appreciate the highs?"

He seemed to ponder what she said, his brow wrinkled as he thought on her words. Then, in a moment of clarity, he brightened. "I reckon that's what the Bible means in Ecclesiastes when it says *'When life is good, enjoy it. But when life is hard, remember: God gives good time and hard times, and no one knows what tomorrow will bring.'*"

His words struck her as particularly poignant. After all, just a month ago, she never would have thought such a change in Merv was possible. She knew that she needed to remember the hard times, even though she wanted to forget them. His harsh words and constant criticism stung her heart whenever she remembered. *Nee,* she thought. *It's best to forget some hard times in order to move onto tomorrow.*

Looking up at Merv and his glowing face, she smiled. "Ja, that's exactly what the Bible means. But I must confess that I sure do like the good times better than the hard." Ignoring his laugh, she let him pull her into a gentle embrace once again. With a sigh, she rested her head upon his shoulder as she added in a soft whisper, "And I, for one, am looking forward to what tomorrow brings. Finally."

Lydia

By the time the bishop showed up, Lydia knew exactly what she was going to say. She had spent enough time thinking about it, especially since sleep eluded her the previous night. All night, she tossed and turned, kicking the sheet off and clutching at her pillow as she rehearsed telling the bishop without making it sound like gossip.

In the morning, Abe declined to eat the breakfast she made once again. His cold demeanor and refusal to eat with her frightened her. Immediately, she thought that her plight was hopeless. He had prayed on it, no doubt. But had he received an answer? until, on his way to the barn to tend to his chores, he paused and said, "I'll fetch the bishop later to hear your confession."

She knew what that meant: Abe was willing to give her another chance. Despite his bravado, he still cared enough to give her that much.

True to his word, she heard him leave about an hour later. The buggy disappeared down the road and Lydia hurried to clean the kitchen. She wanted everything to look spic and span for the bishop's visit. Not like the last time, she thought bitterly. She didn't like surprises and he had certainly caught her off-guard. Today would be different: She would be the one with the surprises.

"Lydia," the bishop said as he entered the room. He removed his hat and stood respectfully at the door, refusing to enter the room. "What is this that Abe has told me? You are ready to confess your sins already?"

"I am," she replied solemnly, her hands folded before her and her head bowed down. She saw the end of her prayer *kapp* ribbon hanging over her shoulder. It was perfectly ironed, not one wrinkle or crease in her *kapp* or dress.

"That is most unusual," he said, tugging at his beard.

She knew what he meant. The *Meidung* normally lasted

longer than just a few days. "I think the situation is most unusual," she said. "After all, I had suffered from an injury to my head. I didn't know what I was saying."

The bishop lifted his chin and narrowed his eyes. "That does not sound like remorse."

"I told Abe that I would see a doctor…talk to someone like you wanted. There are things that I need to discuss with someone," she said. "Secrets that have come to the surface and have triggered memories that haunt me." She glanced at him through her lowered eyelids. He crossed his arms over his chest as he stood there, watching her. Over his shoulder, Abe waited in the other room, listening to the conversation.

"Secrets, you say?"

She nodded her head, lowering her eyes once again. "I am having a hard time accepting the news about Tobias not being my *bruder* but, in truth, my nephew by Jacob." She paused, hoping that the hesitation gave the bishop time to digest the information. "It all happened so suddenly, learning this information. I…I think I'm still in shock."

The bishop took a sharp breath and straightened his shoulders. "I see."

She almost smiled, the relief like a weight off of her shoulders. But, just as quickly, she reminded herself to remain somber and penitent.

Clearing his throat, the bishop slid his hat back onto his head. He turned to Abe and simply said, "I'll be leaving now."

"What?" Lydia dropped the facade and looked up at the bishop. "You're leaving?"

The bishop looked at her, his eyes empty and devoid of any emotion. "There is nothing else I wish to hear from you," he said sharply.

"But what I just told you…!"

He held up his hand. "Enough!"

She blinked, stunned that he had just shouted at her.

"I've heard enough, Lydia. Your lies are more than enough. I can listen to no more!"

A lie? He thought she was lying? "But I'm telling you the truth!"

The bishop frowned, disgust written on his face. "I don't think you know the difference between truth and lies, Lydia. Your mind is gone."

"Ask Leah! She's the one I heard telling Jacob!"

"Then she is the one that should be telling me, not you! You tell me this to try to win favor. But, in fact, you have just done the opposite." As she watched, the bishop turned to Abe and shook his head. "I will pray for you, Abe," he said. "And I will pray that your *fraa* gets that help to understand the magnitude of her sins."

To her amazement, Abe followed the bishop outside, the two men walking shoulder-to-shoulder as they conversed, most likely about her.

A wave of disappointment washed over her. It infuriated her. Lydia clenched her teeth and squeezed her hands into fists. Was the bishop just going to walk away? Not believe her about Jacob being Tobias' biological *daed?* Clearly, he wasn't going to lift the *Meidung*. She was still shunned. And, based on the look that he had given her, the look of disbelief and disgust, the bishop didn't seem like he'd lift it anytime soon. He thought she was lying. The one time when she knew that she was telling the truth, no one would believe her, especially if the bishop didn't.

And then, she realized the truth: she was alone, truly alone in the world, until the bishop lifted the ban. If he didn't believe her now about Jacob and Tobias, she could never mention it again. And if she mentioned it to anyone else, she would be accused of gossiping.

She sank to her knees, fury from her disappointment suddenly giving way to despair as she realized that there was no one who would help her now.

Sadie

She heard the rock hit the pane of glass in her bedroom window. Not once but twice. Groaning, she tried to sit up in bed. At first, she thought it was a bird pecking at the window. Then, when the noise happened a third time, she knew exactly what it was. Or, rather, who it was.

Trying to ignore the shooting pain in her chest as she forced herself to sit up. She took her time to swing her legs over the side of the bed and, with a shaking hand, pulled herself to her feet. She shuffled across the floor and, when she reached the window, she leaned against the sill.

Another rap at the window pane and she knew that he was still outside.

She lifted the shade and peered out through the open window. "Manny?" she whispered as loud as she could.

"Sadie?" Manny called up to her. "Are you all right?"

"I'm fine, Manny," she replied, half hoping that Leah would hear and interrupt their conversation. Just seeing him standing down there, his face looking up with such desperation, made her feel weak. *He believed*, she reminded herself. She didn't want to remember but she knew better than to forget. *He believed!*

"When can I come see you? Leah says you aren't up for visitors."

She shut her eyes and leaned her head against the window. "*Nee,* I'm not. Besides," she found the strength to say. "I'm not so certain I'd want to visit with you, Manny."

Upon hearing her words, he looked crestfallen. "Sadie?"

"I thought you knew me, Manny," she said, not caring if Leah overheard. "But you made a choice that proved to me how wrong I was."

"I don't understand you."

Sadie sighed. "I know what you thought, Manny. I know

what Lydia did and I know why you never came to check on me after the storm. You believed her."

She thought she saw him swallow. He was as nervous as she was. With just cause, she thought, aware that she took no satisfaction with this knowledge.

"I…I…"

There was nothing he could say to make the situation right. Sadie fought the urge to have pity on him until she remembered that he had shown none to her. "The aftermath, Manny. There's always an aftermath to every storm. Don't you see that? You should have known me better than to believe something so awful. But you didn't."

He hung his head. "Your words are true Sadie. I can't say I'm sorry enough. I can only ask that you forgive me."

Sadie heard the bedroom door open. There was no need to look over her shoulder. She knew it was Leah. Ignoring her sister, Sadie kept her attention focused on Manny. "Forgive? Isn't that the ways of our culture? To forgive? If we don't, we will not receive God's blessings." She felt a hand on her shoulder. Leah's touch gave her strength to continue. "*Ja vell,* you can take comfort knowing that I forgave you days ago Manny."

He brightened at her words. "You did?"

"Ja, I did. But you need to know that, while I forgave you, I haven't forgotten. Those are two separate things."

He looked confused. "I…I don't understand. You haven't forgotten?"

"*Nee.* I haven't forgotten the hurt." The pain in her chest disappeared, even if only for the moment. She felt an inner strength that she never felt before. For once, she realized in a defining moment, she was standing up for herself. "You didn't have enough faith in me, Manny. You ran when I needed you most. I shall never forget that, Manny."

His mouth hung open and shame covered his face like a dark shadow.

Sadie found the strength to smile at him. "My heart tells me that I cannot marry someone who would ever think I'm capable of such an immoral act...capable of such deceit! I simply cannot spend my life wondering if it will happen again." Her hand lingered on the shade and she gave a slight shake of her head. "Goodbye, Manny."

The shade dropped from her hand and the room was cloaked in darkness once again. Leah's hands tightened on her shoulders and Sadie let her embrace her. Her sister's strong arms held her, comforting her as Sadie silently cried into her shoulder. She didn't know what hurt more: the pain of saying goodbye to Manny or the discomfort of knowing that she had just learned one of life's hardest lessons.

"Disappointment stings, Sadie," Leah whispered into her ear. "But it's the turning point for you, my sweet girl. It makes us stronger. It's a divine secret that no one ever thinks to tell you."

Sadie found a way to laugh through her tears. "A divine secret?"

Leah pressed her hands to Sadie's cheeks and stared into her face. "*Ja*, a divine secret all right. At least, a divine secret of the whoopie pie sisters!"

They both laughed as they hugged each other, knowing that, this, too, would pass. After everything they had survived, the storms of nature and the storms of life, they would survive as a family, one way or the other.

Epilogue

The outside wall wasn't yet painted and the men still needed to hang the sign over the porch. But Leah didn't care. She stood in the parking lot, staring at the building. A large planter with red mums, a gift from the Mennonite church on the other side of Main Street, stood on the porch. Overhead, pretty copper wind chimes hung from a hook, the metallic music ringing ever so slightly in the breeze.

Rebuilding Whoopie Pie Place hadn't taken that long. Merv's leadership certainly shone through when she gave him the go-ahead for the rebuilding of the store. By the weekend, he had a team of four men working on the demolition and, by the following weekend, twelve men came together to work on the restructuring. Leah was humbled by the generosity of the men in the *g'may*. She was especially grateful to see Abe join in.

The previous week, when Abe stopped by, he took Leah aside and told her the story about Lydia's confrontation with the bishop concerning Tobias. Leah managed to keep a straight face and shake her head, sharing in the wonder of Lydia's behavior, all the while seething inside. She remembered the day of the tornado, seeing Lydia leaving on the bicycle just before the storm hit. Of course, she thought. Lydia had overheard them talking in the barn. She had been eavesdropping and heard everything

When Abe told her about the bishop's reaction, she sighed a breath of relief. Whether he believed her or not, his concern was on the spreading of gossip, especially lies, and the evil that such disruptive behavior caused. Hopefully, Leah thought, Lydia would finally learned her lesson about lying. But it was a fleeting thought for she had too much on her plate to focus on Lydia and *her* problems. After all, she reasoned, Lydia had made her own bed and now it was time for her to lie in it.

Sadie stood beside her, her arms wrapped protectively around her chest. She was still healing, both physically and spiritually. Leah had noticed a change in her younger sister, a tendency toward isolation and withdrawal. It bothered Leah but she knew that Sadie would need the time to recover from all that had befallen her.

"It looks right *gut*, don't you think?" Susie said as she walked up behind them.

Leah glanced over her shoulder and gave Susie an approving smile. "Your husband did a right *gut* job, Susie. I wonder that he didn't do more carpentry work before now!"

The pride in Susie's face was apparent and Leah excused it this time. "He was a carpenter, remember? Back in Kentucky and over in Ronks." She paused. "Before he was fired, anyway."

"*Mayhaps* those days are over," Leah said optimistically. She looked over at Merv as he instructed his team of young men to finish cleaning up the scraps of wood and bent nails that were left at their work area. "Sure does seem like a brand new person," she observed.

They stood there, observing the store in silence, each sister lost in her own thoughts. In such a short period of time, they had come so far. Each sister had faced the secrets of their pasts, present, and even future. They had survived the storm of nature as well as storms of life, some of which left battle scars that only time would heal. But the one thing that they knew was that as long as they remained strong and united, sharing their faith and devotion to God, they could survive.

"I sure do wish Tobias was home to see this," Sadie said softly.

Leah nodded her head. "Me, too. Another two weeks and he'll be here. But," she smiled as she looked at both of her sisters. "What do you say we go into the store? Together, just the three of us, for the first time?"

They linked arms as they walked toward the porch of their new store. Leah paused at the door, fiddling in her pocket for the keys that Merv had handed to her earlier. Quickly, she unlocked the front door and pushed it open. She took a step back and gestured for Susie and Sadie to enter before her. Then, when she followed behind them, she shut the door and, with a broad smile on her face, she flipped the sign in the window: OPEN.

Whoopie Pie Place was officially back in business.

Recipes

My interest in recipe boxes began as a young girl. I knew there was "magic" inside those boxes that belonged to my mom and my grandmother Gladys. Because of my love for the contents of these recipe boxes, it was an honor for me to have the opportunity to create my Kitchen Collection to share with each of you. At present, there are five volumes. I am currently working on a couple more, which I am anxious to finish.

Both Sarah and I agreed that this story would not be complete if we didn't share with you some of the Miller Sister's favorite recipes, especially my personal favorite (and Leah's): the Chocolate Strawberry Shortcake Whoopie Pies.

For more recipes such as these, please join me at www.facebook.com/WhoopiePiePam and at https://www.facebook.com/groups/WPPKitchenCollection/.

Thank you for reading The Divine Secrets of The Whoopie Pie Sisters! We hope you have enjoyed it even more than we enjoyed writing it!

Chocolate Strawberry Shortcake Whoopie Pies

Ingredients

- 1 pkg. (2-layer size) chocolate cake mix
- 3/4 cup water
- 1/2 cup oil
- 3 eggs
- 1 pkg. (8 oz.) PHILADELPHIA Cream Cheese, softened
- 1 jar (7 oz.) JET-PUFFED Marshmallow Creme
- 1 tub (8 oz.) COOL WHIP Whipped Topping, thawed
- 3 cups fresh strawberries, sliced

Instructions

1. Heat oven to 350°F.
2. Beat first 4 ingredients with mixer until well blended. Drop 2 Tbsp. batter, 2 inches apart, into 32 mounds on baking sheets sprayed with cooking spray.
3. Bake 10 min. or until toothpick inserted in centers comes out almost clean. Cool on baking sheets 3 min. Remove to wire racks; cool completely.
4. Beat cream cheese and marshmallow creme in large bowl with mixer until well blended. Add COOL WHIP; beat on low speed just until blended.
5. Spread about 2 Tbsp. COOL WHIP mixture onto bottom side of each of 16 cookies. Top with strawberries and remaining cookies.

Shoo Fly Pie

Ingredients

- 1 cup shortening
- 1 ¾ cups brown sugar
- 2 eggs
- 2 cups flour
- ½ teaspoon salt
- 3 teaspoons baking powder
- ½ cup whole milk
- 2 cups corn flakes
- 1 teaspoon vanilla

Instructions:

1. Preheat oven to 375 degrees.
2. After creaming the shortening and sugar together, add the eggs and vanilla. Beat until mixture is light and fluffy.
3. In a separate bowl, mix the dry ingredients then sift.
4. Add corn flakes to the dry ingredients and mix by hand.
5. Add dry ingredients and milk to the cream mixture. Stir until smooth.
6. Use a soupspoon or melon ball maker to drop the mixture onto a greased baking sheet. Leave space between each, as they will spread when cooking.

   Bake for 10-12 minutes.

Amish Bread

Ingredients

- 2 cups warm water (110 degrees F/45 degrees C)
- 2/3 cup white sugar
- 1 1/2 tablespoons active dry yeast
- 1 1/2 teaspoons salt
- 1/4 cup vegetable oil
- 6 cups bread flour

Instructions

1. In a large bowl, dissolve the sugar in warm water, and then stir in yeast. Allow to proof until yeast resembles a creamy foam.
2. Mix salt and oil into the yeast. Mix in flour one cup at a time. Knead dough on a lightly floured surface until smooth. Place in a well oiled bowl, and turn dough to coat. Cover with a damp cloth. Allow to rise until doubled in bulk, about 1 hour.
3. Punch dough down. Knead for a few minutes, and divide in half. Shape into loaves, and place into two well oiled 9x5 inch loaf pans. Allow to rise for 30 minutes, or until dough has risen 1 inch above pans.
4. Bake at 350 degrees F for 30 minutes.

Meadow Tea

from Sarah Price as shared with her by her Amish friends in Lancaster County, Pennsylvania

Ingredients

- Fresh mint tea leaves
- Sugar
- Water

Instructions

1. Boil one gallon of water.
2. When bubbling, put in a healthy handful of mint tea leaves from garden (about two huge fistful of cuttings).
3. Take off of the heat and let sit for 7 minutes.
4. Remove mint tea leaves from water.
5. Add 1.5 cups of sugar (more or less to suit your taste).
6. Put pot of water in a sink of cold water (to cool down).
7. Refrigerate before serving.
8. Might need to be adjusted to accommodate your needs.

HINT: Growing mint tea plants in your garden is a wonderful adventure but be careful. Tea can take over your garden. You also need to cut the stalks BEFORE they flower. If they get spindly looking, cut them down and they will grow back. Most tea gardens can get 2-3 batches each season.

Amish Drop Sugar Cookies

from Whoopie Pie Pam's Kitchen Collection, Christmas Cookie Exchange

Ingredients

- 1 ½ cup sugar
- 1 cup butter
- 2 eggs
- 1 cup sour cream
- 3 ¾ cup flour
- 2 teaspoon baking powder
- 1 teaspoon baking soda
- 1 teaspoon vanilla

Instructions

1. Preheat oven to 375 degrees.
2. Mix the sugar and softened butter together until creamy.
3. Add the eggs and beat well.
4. Add remaining ingredients and mix together.
5. Using a teaspoon, drop onto a greased cookie sheet.
6. Bake for 8-10 minutes.

Lyrics to Songs

Written for
The Divine Secrets of the Whoopie Pie Sisters

Faithful
Written by Katie G. and Anthony Vitale

You're cold to the core
Don't know what I loved you for
I had faith in you
You never knew
My faith is still true
You can push me away
But I'm here to stay

I'm waiting for the day
My faith shows me the way

[Chorus]
Faithful
I'm faithful
Faithful
I'm faithful

I'm on my knees, begging please
Begging please
Faithful
I'm faithful
Faithful
I'm faithful

Life is rough, my faith is tough
My faith is tough

Go ahead push me down, right to the ground
Push and shove, it's enough, I'll still be around
You take, take, take,

You can take take take,
l'll stick around,
It's a piece of cake.
Do your worst, it will never work
My heart never breaks

[Chorus]

I'll pay any dues
And I'll pay any fees
Take my hand and you will see
I'll pay any dues
And I'll pay any fees
Take my hand and you will see

[Chorus]

Heaven

Written by <u>Katie G</u>. and Anthony Vitale
Available for purchase on iTunes and Amazon

If I went to heaven, I'll tell you what I'd miss,
Your sparkling blue eyes, your ruby red lips.
If I went to heaven, I'd have diamonds on the floor
But I wouldn't have you anymore.

If I went to heaven, someday by and by,
If I went to heaven, ooo someday I'll fly,
Fly up to heaven, heaven.

If I went to heaven, the angels would sing.
It wouldn't be the same as all the joy that you bring.
If I went to heaven, the sun would always shine.
To remind you, you'll always be mine.

If I went to heaven, someday by and by
If I went to heaven, ooo someday I'll fly
Fly up to heaven, heaven

Angels be knocking on my door.
Angels be knocking on my door.
Angels be knocking on my door.
Angels be knocking on my door.

If I went to heaven there'd be diamonds on the floor
But I wouldn't have you any more

If I went to heaven, someday by and by
If I went to heaven, ooo someday I'll fly
Fly up to heaven, heaven

If I went to Heaven, I'll tell you what I'll miss…

One More Thing...

If you enjoyed this book, I'd be very grateful if you'd post a short review on Amazon. Your support really does make a difference. Not only do I read all the reviews in order to see what you liked and how I can improve, but they are also a great source of motivation. When I hear from my readers and fans, it really makes me want to keep writing...just for you.

If you'd like to leave a review or see a list of my books on Amazon, simply click here. And don't forget to follow me on Facebook so that you can hear firsthand about new, upcoming releases.

With blessings,

Sarah Price

http://www.facebook.com/fansofsarahprice

Excerpt from Plain Fame

Sarah Price's Best-Selling Book

An Amazon Top 100 Book
(Book One of the Plain Fame Trilogy)
Available on amazon.com, BN.com, and kobo.com

Chapter One

New York City was as crowded as ever and traffic was backed-up for miles. Alejandro leaned his head back onto the plush headrest of his private limousine and shut his eyes for a few moments. After weeks of traveling, he was tired. Tired of living out of quickly packed suitcases, tired of hotels, tired of the lack of privacy. He missed the heart-warming sun, the long sandy beaches and the quiet of his own home in beautiful Miami. He made a mental note to remind his assistant to stop scheduling these trips for a while. He just needed some time to recuperate, to take a step back, to re-examine his life and to recharge his batteries.

"Ay mi madre," he said to himself. Then, leaning forward, he tapped on the glass that separated him from his driver. *"¿Qué está pasando? ¿Por qué hay tanto tráfico?"* He couldn't imagine why there was so much traffic at this hour. It wasn't even noon and well past morning rush hour. Yet, the streets were packed, bumper-to-bumper. Even more frustrating were the pedestrians, ignoring traffic signals and crossing when they shouldn't. That was adding to the traffic. Alejandro sighed. He was going to be late.

The driver glanced back and shrugged his shoulders in the

casual manner of a typical New Yorker. "Traffic, my man. It's just traffic."

"*Dios mio*," Alejandro complained under his breath. "We are going to make it in time, si?" His voice was deep and husky but thick with a Spanish accent. To the knowing linguist, he was Cuban. To the average American, he was just another Hispanic.

"Yeah, yeah, don't sweat it," the driver said.

Don't sweat it, Alejandro repeated to himself and shook his head. Spoken by a man who drives a limousine for a living, he thought. "If I'm late…" he said but chose not to complete the sentence. In reality, so what if he was late? It was only a meeting with Richard Gray, the largest music producer in America. But it was Richard Gray who had contacted him, Alejandro Diaz. It was Richard Gray who had requested the meeting, a lunch meeting, and that took all of the pressure off of Alejandro's shoulders. He was in control of this one. He was being sought after by the big man.

The stretch limousine lurched forward and the driver started to finally regain some speed. The traffic seemed to be breaking up somewhat, permitting the driver to make up some time and Alejandro began to relax. They'd get there on time. It was only twenty blocks from the hotel to the restaurant where the meeting was to take place. But they still had to pass through Times Square and 7th Avenue by Madison Square Garden.

"Don't these people work?" Alejandro grumbled as he began fiddling with his cell phone. Three texts from his manager and two from his agent. He was lucky. It was usually triple that amount. A slow day. *Must be a Tuesday*, he thought grimly. The only slow day of the week. And still, he had meetings and appointments and emails and text messages. When had life started to get so crazy, he asked himself.

He heard the crash before he actually recognized the jolt for what it was. The driver had slammed on his brakes, the car screeching to a halt, but not before the thud on the hood of the car made it apparent that something had been hit. Alejandro fell forward, despite the fact that the limo had not been driving over twenty miles an hour, if that. When he picked himself up from the floor and sat back on the black leather seat, he tried to assess what had happened.

"You alright back there?" the driver asked, his voice shaking and his face pale.

"*Sí, sí,*" Alejandro said, trying to calm himself. An accident. What were the odds of that? And why today of all days? He glanced around but didn't see another vehicle in front of the limousine. "What happened?"

"Hit someone. A jaywalker," the driver replied before picking up his cell phone and dialing 9-1-1.

The crowd was already gathering around the front of the car. People. There were always crowds of people around when he wanted them, but especially when he didn't. This was one of those moments. Alejandro exhaled loudly. Now he'd definitely be late. There was no way that he could get out of the limousine in this crowd without being recognized and that would be the kiss of death. He could see the headlines already: *Viper Strikes Pedestrian in Manhattan.*

He tried to do a quick calculation of how the next hour or two would pan out. The police would come and want to interview him. The crowd would gather, the traffic would be thick, and it would become a mob scene. He'd have no choice but to get out. Alejandro sighed, reaching into his suit pocket for his black sunglasses. If he had to get out and face the crowd, better to do it early on rather than look like he was avoiding it. And when the inevitable lawsuit happened, it would look better if he had seemed concerned. With that, the decision was made.

"What are you doing, sir?" The driver had turned around, just about to say something when he noticed Alejandro reaching for the door handle. There was panic in his voice. "You can't get out, sir. They'll notice you. There will be a mob!"

Alejandro nodded. "Exactly. But if I delay, that will be even worse than if I get out now." It would be a different headline then: *Viper Indifferent to Struck Pedestrian in Manhattan*. That would never do; so, ignoring the concern of his driver, he pulled at the door handle and flung the door back, careful to not hit anyone who was standing nearby.

It took a second, maybe two, for the beginning of the murmuring to trickle through the crowd. He heard it, the gentle hum of recognition. Whispers, looks, people pointing, and then the name: Viper. They were already talking about him. Alejandro ignored it and hurried to the front of the car. He pushed past several people, making certain to say "Excuse me" as he did so. Manners, his mother had always taught him. No matter what the situation, a man had to be civilized and mannerly. When he finally got to the front of the limousine, he noticed two men leaning over a woman.

"Is she alright?" he asked, pulling at his pants as he knelt down beside them.

"She's hurt bad," one man said, glancing over his shoulder at Alejandro. He frowned as if recognizing him but turned his attention back to the woman.

"But is she responding?" Alejandro asked. He reached out for the woman's hand. Holding it in his, he was glad to feel her fingers twitch and clutch at his hand. He looked at her quickly. Her face was rolled to the side and her eyes were closed. The color had drained from her cheeks and her brown hair, pulled back from her face, gave a sharp contrast to her pale skin. There was no blood and for that, he gave a quick prayer of gratitude to God. But, she was laying in a crumpled heap, one of her legs twisted in a crooked fashion from beneath her pale blue dress over which she wore a black apron. "My driver called for an ambulance. I wouldn't recommend moving her until they get here."

The driver was standing on the other side of the woman. "They said five minutes." He looked around at the traffic. It was even worse now since the limousine was blocking the intersection. "Like to see how they'll manage that."

As Alejandro continued to hold the woman's hand, he became well aware that people were beginning to take photographs. He frowned and motioned toward the driver. "Give me your jacket."

"What?"

"Your jacket! To cover her. They're starting to take photos," Alejandro snapped, trying to keep his voice down so that he was not overheard.

The driver quickly shook his black jacket off of his shoulders and handed it to Alejandro. Carefully, he laid it over the woman, hiding her face from the people who were taking pictures with their cell phones.

"Is she dressed in a costume?" the driver asked.

Alejandro looked up, caught off-guard by the question. "Costume?"

"She looks like Dorothy from the Wizard of Oz."

"She's Amish, you idiot," someone said from the crowd that was now forming on the sidewalk.

Alejandro wanted to ask what "Amish" was but didn't want to draw further attention to himself or to the situation than what was needed. Right now, all the media could say was that his driver hit the woman and he, Alejandro Diaz, had stayed by her side until the ambulance came. The police would soon arrive, question him, and then he'd be on his merry way to his meeting with Richard Gray. The worse thing that could happen is some minor damage to his bad-boy image.

The woman fluttered her eyes, trying to make sense of what was happening as she began to awaken. The color started to come back to her cheeks. Her chocolate brown eyes tried to make sense of all the people staring at her from above. "Where am I?" she asked.

"Oz, according to that guy!" someone from the crowd quipped.

Alejandro glared over his shoulder at the man who was laughing then looked back at the woman from behind his dark sunglasses. "You've been hit by a car," he said gently. "Don't try to move. Help is on the way, *princesa*."

But she didn't listen. When she tried to lift her head, she winced and fell back down to the street. "My leg," she whimpered, collapsing against Alejandro's body. He was still holding her hand and she clung to it, her head buried against his leg.

Alejandro lowered his voice. "You're going to be fine, but wait for the medical people. You can't move, *princesa*." He stared at her face, tanned with some freckles over the tops of her cheeks. She was fresh looking, like a country girl. The driver was right. She did resemble Dorothy with her blue dress and black apron. Except she had a white heart-shaped covering for her head that had been knocked off and laid in the middle of the street, a tourist stepping on one of the strings.

When she looked at him again, her dark eyes trying to make sense of what was happening to her, he felt a jolt. For as young and fresh as she was, she was also remarkably beautiful in a natural way that completely took him by surprise. Her tan skin glowed in the sun-rays that trickled through the skyscrapers. Her dark hair was pulled back from her face, a few loose strands curling down her neck. No make-up or fancy hair styles. Just a plain beauty that caught him off guard.

"My family," she whispered, moisture at the corner of her eyes.

"May I call someone for you?" His voice was soft, almost a whisper so that the people surrounding them couldn't hear, as he tightened his grasp on her hand. He was surprised when she clasped it, her grip strong, and he found himself staring into her face, once again amazed at how beautiful she looked.

Despite the clear pain that she was in, the young woman was still stoic and dignified, hiding her discomfort. Yet, when she tried to shake her head, a single tear trickled down her cheek. "We don't have a phone. They need to know," she said, her voice trailing off.

No phone? Not even a cell phone? He frowned but didn't inquire further. He could hear the sirens in the distance. He imagined the police would arrive first and, from that point on, he'd be questioned then able to leave. Another thirty minutes, he thought. Forty-five, tops.

"What is your name, *princesa*?"

"Amanda," she whispered. "Amanda Beiler."

Alejandro nodded, aware that she had a slight accent. He couldn't quite place it. It wasn't European and certainly it wasn't from South America. But it was different from the other American accents. "If you tell me your address, I'll make certain that a message gets to your family."

She clutched his hand and he leaned forward. "Creek Road in Lititz, Pennsylvania." She paused, shutting her eyes as tears started to well at the corners. "They think I'll be home tonight for my chores."

He laughed softly and caressed her hand with his thumb. "You won't be home for chores tonight, Amanda Beiler. But you'll be just fine." He paused before adding, "I'll make sure of it." She was the image of innocence and clearly a long way from home. While he knew nothing about Lititz, Pennsylvania, he suspected it was far from Philadelphia or Pittsburgh. And certainly not close to New York City. "I promise," he heard himself say.

He could hear the mumbling behind him. The crowd was beginning to liven up. If people hadn't recognized him before, he knew the word was now floating through the crowd. He could sense the energy as more people began to peer over the heads of others, trying to see him, trying to take a photograph of him. The cell phones were in the air snapping photos of Alejandro kneeling beside the Amish woman on the streets of Manhattan. *No*, he corrected himself. *Photos of Viper with the Amish woman.* Alejandro wondered which one would wind up on the entertainment channels and the tabloids later on this evening.

The police arrived moments later, their cars making their way through the crowded streets, avoiding the pedestrians who didn't seem to care that they were breaking the law by darting across the road. Once the police had parked their cars, ignoring the other drivers who began honking their horns at being blocked and delayed, two policemen began to push the crowd back, creating a buffer so that the ambulance would be able to get through when it arrived. Another police officer approached Alejandro, quickly assessing that he was a good person to start interviewing.

"What happened here, sir?"

Alejandro glanced up, peering at the officer from behind his dark sunglasses. He tried to pick his words carefully, knowing that too many people were probably recording the scene. What he said now would most likely be replayed over and over again, on television, on interviews, and in court when the young woman sued for having been hit by his driver.

"I'm not exactly certain," Alejandro said. "I just know that she was hit by the limousine."

The officer peered at him for a moment. It was the moment of recognition. "Aren't you..?"

And so it begins, he thought wistfully. Avoiding the question, Alejandro glanced at the woman. "No disrespect," he said. "But she's in a lot of pain, Officer. Do you have any idea when the ambulance will get here?"

To Alejandro's relief, the officer leaned his chin over to his shoulder, talking into his walkie-talkie. While the officer was trying to get a reading on the location of the ambulance, Alejandro turned his attention back to the young woman. "Amanda?" he asked softly. "Amanda? You hanging in there, *princesa*?"

She nodded slightly. Her face was pale and tears now fell freely down her cheeks. "I just wanted a pair of sunglasses," she said, her words barely audible.

"What?" He leaned down, trying to hear what she was saying. "What did you say?"

She reached for his hand again, holding it tightly in her own. "While I was waiting for my train," she whispered. "I was crossing the street for a pair of sunglasses."

He didn't have an opportunity to ask her about what she had said. The ambulance was pulling up behind them, the horn beeping for people to get out of the way. The officer in charge motioned for Alejandro to back away so that the paramedics could bring the gurney closer.

Respectfully, he moved back but stopped just a few feet from where she was stretched out on the road. He noticed the white cap laying on the ground a few feet away and stooped to pick it up. Clutching it into his hands, Alejandro watched as the paramedics worked, quickly taking her vital signs and asking a rapid barrage of questions. Within minutes, Amanda Beiler was gently lifted from the streets of Manhattan, placed on the crisp white sheet covering the gurney, and whisked away to a hospital.

Alejandro stared after it, too aware that his cell phone was vibrating in his pocket and the officer was asking him a question. But his mind was elsewhere. This young woman, dressed in such plain clothes and with such a pure, fresh look on her face, lingered in his memory and he found that he could think of nothing else. She was alone in Manhattan and clearly out of her element. He knew the feeling from his own days as an immigrant with his mother in Miami. And he also knew that he wasn't going to make that appointment with Richard Gray. Only this was now by his own choice, not because of being delayed by the accident.

About Sarah Price

The Preiss family emigrated from Europe in 1705, settling in Pennsylvania as the area's first wave of Mennonite families. Sarah Price has always respected and honored her ancestors through exploration and research about her family's history and their religion. At nineteen, she befriended an Amish family and lived on their farm throughout the years.

Twenty-five years later, Sarah Price splits her time between her home outside of New York City and an Amish farm in Lancaster County, PA where she retreats to reflect, write, and reconnect with her Amish friends and Mennonite family.

Find Sarah Price on Facebook and Goodreads!
Learn about upcoming books, sequels, series, and contests!

Contact the author at sarahprice.author@gmail.com.
Visit her weblog at http://sarahpriceauthor.wordpress.com or
on Facebook at www.facebook.com/fansofsarahprice.

About Whoopie Pie Pam Jarrell

Pamela Jarrell will tell you that she lives in a wacky, wonderful, blessed world where God is her ruler! It is her goal to love, laugh and face each moment with all the passion that she can find within. She and her husband Tom are blessed with five children, three son-in-laws, six wonderful, awesome, fantastic grandchildren and two dogs. A loving, dysfunctional family surrounds her. An active member of her church, she will not hesitate to tell you of her testimony in her relationship with God.

While battling Papillary Thyroid Carcinoma, Pam was inspired to create a Facebook group called the Whoopie Pie Book Club (WPBC). For years, she had called a group of ladies in her family, by that same name. Pam and those ladies would travel semi-annually to Amish country for a retreat of reading Amish fiction, seeing the Amish sights and eating plenty of Whoopie Pies. Inspired by the Amish for their simplicity in facing life and their love and honor for family, Pam continues to visit Amish country, all the while spending time with friends of the community that she has come to love. When not reading, writing or traveling, she spends a big portion of her time interacting with her cherished members of the WPBC.

Today, Pam is best known as "Whoopie Pie Pam".

Contact Pam at whoopiepieplace@yahoo.com

On Facebook at https://www.facebook.com/whoopiepiepam

Or Visit her Web Blog at http://whoopiepieplace.com

Made in the USA
Middletown, DE
29 November 2020